UNDER THE DRAGON'S SHADOW

ADAM ORION NORTH

Should A Dragon Fall

Calling Of The Dragon's Blood
Under The Dragon's Shadow
Chasing The Dragon's Tale

Under The Dragon's Shadow

EPUB ISBN 978-1-957324-18-0

Paperback ISBN 978-1-957324-20-3

Hardback ISBN 978-1-957324-19-7

Author's Note

'No One Kills A Dragon' was originally a five-book series. (And I apologize for all the cliffhangers.) I wanted to compile them all into a single volume, but due to publishing constraints, it was simply not possible without making the font so small that it would be difficult to read. Therefore, I decided to split the series in two, putting the first three novels in a new book titled 'Calling Of The Dragon's Blood,' and the final two novels in this book. These two books are now part of a series that I am calling 'Should A Dragon Fall.' A sixth novel, titled 'Chasing The Dragon's Tale,' will be the third installment in the series. It is a significantly larger novel and tells a full story. (It also doesn't end in a cliffhanger.)

PART ONE

Prologue

The wizard's coppery robes swished as he strode through the shadowed halls of the castle. He ran a hand through his rich auburn hair, anxious in the night. Celewis knew that time was short. The cult had been a mistake. It had left too many of them exposed. And now, their plans were beginning to come undone.

Lightning flashed outside, starkly illuminating the windowed hallway as thunder rolled through the castle walls. The storm outside was troubling. It was a thing unnatural in its intensity. Servants and nobles alike hid in their chambers, fearful of the storm's wrath. Celewis did not fear the storm. He feared the dark presence moving within it.

Marching past two metal clad guardsmen, Celewis shoved open the doors to the king's quarters. Lightning lit his way as he hurried through the parlor, moving past lavish furniture that was now nothing more than clutter. When he reached the king's bedroom, Celewis pushed on the door with enough force to rip its bolt from the hardwood frame. Stepping inside, the wizard flicked his wrist. Light flooded the chamber as the fireplace and every lamp in the room blazed to life at once.

"Arise, Agrum," Celewis commanded of the sleeping king.

Alone in a bed large enough for five, the king of Harbridge came awake.

Agrum sat up suddenly, his body responding to the wizard's volition. Confused eyes regarded the man who had interrupted his drug induced slumber.

Celewis had no time for the king to dawdle. "Get out of the bed. We must make haste." He quickly scanned the room.

Awareness rose behind Agrum's eyes. "Has it come for me?" His voice was strong despite the trying circumstance.

"We have no time, Agrum," Celewis insisted as he stepped over to a nearby armchair and grabbed the royal blue cloak draped over it. "Get out of the bed."

Agrum threw off his sheer bedsheet and rolled over to the edge of the bed. He then swung his legs over the side and stood. When the wizard held out the cloak, Agrum protested, "I will not flee in my bed clothes."

"Then you will die garbed in finery," Celewis countered impatiently. He threw the velvety cloak at the king and then walked to the other side of the room.

The hem of Agrum's cloak fanned out as he donned it around his shoulders. "What of my family?"

"They will follow once you are safe," Celewis explained. "But you must leave this place now. I cannot stop what comes for you."

The satin cloth of the wizard's sleeve fell back as he reached his arm up and placed his hand on the side of the fireplace. The panel to the left swung out from the wall, revealing a darksome passage.

"What?!" Agrum exclaimed. "How long has that been there?"

"Since before you were born," Celewis replied as he swung the secret door open wider.

Agrum's voice became angry. "I should have been told."

Celewis ignored the king's complaint. He pushed out into the air with his left hand, manifesting a gust of wind that surged into the passage, clearing away the cobwebs. With his right hand, the wizard reached up and gripped the air as if wrapping his fingers around an invisible knob. A ball of pure white light appeared above his hand, banishing the darkness lurking in the passage.

The ball of light hovered above Celewis's shoulder faithfully, moving with him as he stepped into the secret passage. "Pull the door closed behind you."

Agrum pulled the secret door closed as he followed the wizard into the passage. "Where does this lead?"

Celewis began walking away briskly, sure of his path. "This passage is part of a maze that encompasses the castle," he replied without looking back. He knew that the king would follow the light. "Presently, we will use it to leave unnoticed."

Agrum did indeed follow the wizard's light. "There is a passage that leads from my bed chamber to outside the castle?!" the king demanded furiously.

Celewis turned right at an intersection. "The passages lead beyond the city walls."

Agrum's anger echoed in the passage. "How was I not told of this?! I could have been murdered in my sleep! My children could have been murdered!"

Celewis allowed the king to fume and then he calmly explained, "Anything with the ability to use these passages would not need them to slay you or your family." He turned left and began to descend a spiral staircase. "It is your proximity that endangers your family."

Agrum followed silently as he considered the wizard's words. Celewis allowed the king his silence, knowing that Agrum had reason to be angry. Though the king was a true believer, it had been difficult for him to trust the wizard. Celewis worried that the king might yet come to regret that decision. After twists and turns and long corridors, the two men came to a dead end.

Agrum gestured angrily to the wall ahead, "Are we lost, or have you betrayed me?"

Celewis offered no answer, instead placing a hand on the smooth stone wall before him. The wall became transparent, revealing a tunnel that bore through solid rock. Then the wizard stepped through the wall and continued walking down the tunnel.

Agrum moved forward and attempted to touch the wall, but his hand passed through it as if it were not there. "More magic," he mused to himself as he stepped into the tunnel.

Lightning flashed in the darkness ahead as Celewis hurried through the stretching tunnel. He waved his left hand in the air above himself as he stepped out into the night. Rain fell in a deluge around him, but the wizard remained dry. He waited until the king exited the tunnel, and then Celewis held his hand out to the translucent stone. Agrum stumbled away as the tunnel became solid rock once more.

Celewis gestured away from the rockface and raised his voice above the storm. "This will take you the rest of the way." In flashes of lightning, a four-horse carriage was shone to be waiting.

Already drenched by the rain, Agrum glanced at the carriage. "Are you not coming with me?" he asked, shouting to be heard.

Celewis shook his head firmly. "I have other tasks before me."

Agrum nodded his acceptance. "Thank you, Celewis. May The Deep be with you." Then he ran barefoot to the carriage.

Celewis watched as the king boarded the carriage. "Maybe there is hope yet," he dared say to the night.

The carriage exploded as fire engulfed it. Celewis summoned his defenses as burning wood was thrown into the air. Broken horses screamed in pain as the flames consumed them. A weight of darkness pushed back the storm like a herald of death.

Celewis reached for his ball of light, knowing that it must be dispelled lest it make him a target. As his hand wrapped around the light, fire burned through his defenses. Twisting in the inferno, the wizard's mind desperately searched for a way to stop something not bound by the arcane. He died never knowing the answer.

One

Belac kicked at the hinges of his primitive cage. Though the heels of his boots landed squarely, the vines that held the woven branches might as well have been steel. *I hate prison!*

A man spoke with the voice of melancholy. "I have tried that, Belac."

Belac turned to his right and glared up at the cage hanging from a gnarled tree. "You have tried kicking my cage open?" he asked irritably.

Sitting with his feet pulled up into his wooden cage with him, the man stared back without giving any indication that he was offended by the elf's tone. Despite his filthy, ill-fitting clothes and rough beard, the disheveled man appeared to be in much better condition than he had been when he and Belac had last parted ways.

"Obviously, not," Ecard replied tiredly. "However, great effort was exerted in attempting to escape my own."

Though the man's cage had been hoisted into the air, Belac's cage still rested on the mossy forest floor. Surrounded by tall evergreens and a naturally hilly terrain, the two cages were isolated from the other parts of the encampment. Four silent figures stood watching the cages and the captives inside.

Shaped to resemble men, the guards were made of dry sticks held together by thorny vines. In the center of their brushwood chests, a deep, garnet red glow pulsed like a heartbeat.

Ignoring the voiceless sentinels, Belac addressed the man in the cage. "If you want to give up again, then that is on you." He turned back to the door of his cage. "I am getting out of here." He resumed kicking at the hinges.

There was a trace of indignation in Ecard's response. "I am not proposing we surrender. I am merely suggesting that your efforts might be better directed elsewhere."

Belac stopped kicking. "Do you see something I don't?" He gestured wildly to the bars of his cage. "Because I see a cage!"

"That..." Ecard began, but then stopped himself. "What I mean, is that we should conserve our strength until a worthier opportunity presents itself."

Belac narrowed his eyes at the man. "That sounds a lot like giving up."

"I..." Ecard frowned. "Giving up,' as you would put it, implies the loss of hope. I will not lose hope again."

He thinks we are going to be rescued. Belac shook his head. "We can't just sit around and wait, Ecard. We have to try everything we can think of to escape. And if none of that works, then we have to spend all of our time thinking up more things to try." Belac pointed at the man forcefully. "Stop trying to find reasons to wait patiently, and start thinking about how you are going to help us get out of here."

Belac resumed kicking the door of his cage. After a moment, he stopped and looked back to the man. "And why did you get to keep your shirt?!"

Ecard gazed down at the bare-chested elf. "A grievous oversight, I am sure," he answered dryly.

Belac did not really care about his missing clothes. What troubled him was the loss of his starmetal sword. He would have happily accepted any weapon at that moment, but the starmetal sword was more than just a weapon. It was an icon of legend and a tool forged for the salvation of the world.

There is no way Serath is going to trust me with another sword if he finds out that I lost this one. Belac kicked his cage door in frustration.

Ecard's attention shifted away from the elf. "Belac," he hissed insistently, "they are here."

Belac looked to his left. An elven woman emerged from around a rise in the terrain. Her simple trousers and sleeveless tunic were of a heather gray fabric that reminded Belac of a patch of sunlight in shadows. He took in the sight of her delicate features, finding the woman beautiful despite the oxblood tattoo of thorned vines that covered the right side of her face and shaved scalp. *Why would an elf do that to itself?* Belac ran a hand through his long, black hair just to reassure himself that it was still there.

The two horrific things that followed behind the woman were enough to end Belac's admiration. Half again as tall as the elven woman, the towering things were an amalgamation of nature and pure hatred. Large sections of bare wood held together by thick roots comprised bodies that were harsh and masculine. In stark contrast, hauntingly feminine faces had been carved into their wooden skulls. Pointed roots grew above their heads like a malefic crown, and nightmarish red light shown forth from their eye sockets.

The elven woman's lithe form moved through the early evening shadows and then halted next to the cages. Speaking in Elven, she asked, "What are you doing, Belac?" Her silvery voice was not amused.

She has to know what I was doing. Belac met the woman's pale amethyst eyes. "I was trying to escape," he admitted plainly in Dwarven.

Ecard began to make choking sounds of disbelief.

The elven woman laughed, her voice as musical as birdsong dancing on a river. "There is no escape, Belac," she explained in Elven. "The briar men would hunt you down, and then the spriggans would tear off your arms and legs."

Belac swiped the air with his hand dismissively. "Nah." He continued speaking Dwarven with a friendly tone. "Your sister likes me too much."

"Kaelem is my brother!" she replied vehemently in Elven.

"Wait." Belac furrowed his brow in mock confusion. "Are you the girl?"

The woman's face hardened, her countenance becoming more threatening than those of the spriggans behind her. "Before you die, I am going to cut your tongue out of your mouth and then nail it to your forehead." Elven made her words sound no kinder.

Belac knew the woman was not allowed to harm him. *Kaelem needs me for something.* He smiled like he had just been handed a gift. "Does that mean, I am immortal?"

"What?" the woman voiced her confusion in Elven. "No." She glared at the caged elf. "You are not making any sense."

"Sure, I am," Belac argued. "I still have my tongue." He stuck his tongue out and wiggled it. "That must mean, I can't die yet."

"You are not funny, Belac." Her Elven words were stated coldly.

"Thank you," Belac replied as if he had been paid a complement. "It would feel awful to not be taken seriously." He leaned forward in his cage. "How do you cope with it, Talia?"

The woman stared silently at Belac. As time stretched on, he began to wonder if she would actually try to hurt him. He smiled at her brightly. *Come on… Just take one more step closer…* It took all of Belac's self-control to not glance at one of the single, wire wrapped daggers strapped to each of the woman's thighs. *Come on… You know you want to strangle me…*

Talia took a step back and then gestured to the cage. One of the spriggans walked past her, its red eyes directed balefully at Belac. *Not good.* Belac scooted to the rear of his cramped cage. *I need a new plan.* The spriggan reached out with one of its oversized wooden hands. Belac's eyes widened as the massive, hooked claws on the tips of the wooden fingers moved closer.

The spriggan's hand touched the side of the cage and then paused. The vines holding the door shut began to unravel from the cage as if suddenly alive. Slithering across the spriggan's monstrous hand, the vines wound themselves around its wooden forearm before going still once more.

The spriggan opened the cage door and reached inside. Belac kicked at the thing's hand, but it took hold of his ankle and dragged him out of the cage.

Ecard found his courage. "Let him go!"

Talia chastised the man in Elven. "Shut your mouth, Human."

The spriggan gripped Belac's upper arm and then released his leg. Held by the spriggan's unyielding grip, Belac was yanked to his feet. The spriggan turned, jerking Belac forward to stand in front of the elven woman.

Belac nodded toward the man in the hanging cage. "You know that he can't understand what you are saying, right?"

Talia's pale amethyst eyes bore into the elf. "I do not care if that human understands me or not," she declared in Elven.

Belac furrowed his brow again. "If you don't care if he can understand you or not, why would you bother speaking to him?" He pointed at the woman with his free hand. "Do you know how speech works?" he asked as if he were genuinely concerned.

Two

"Why will you not speak properly?" Talia asked peevishly in Elven.

"I don't know what you are talking about," Belac lied in Dwarven. He had never heard the woman speak Dwarven. Though he did not know why she objected to the language as strongly as she did, Belac enjoyed vexing her.

"That!" Talia gestured angrily as she admonished the other elf in Elven. "That language is vulgar, Belac."

Belac looked up at the face of the spriggan that was ushering him down the shadowy forest path. "What is she talking about?" he asked the spriggan.

The spriggan offered no response.

"You know what I am talking about!" Talia declared forcefully in Elven. "You are an Elven Lord. You should speak Elven!"

I am not an Elven Lord. Continuing to speak in Dwarven, Belac replied, "I am speaking Elven."

"You. Are. Not!" Talia said indignantly in Elven.

Belac felt himself jerked backward as the spriggan holding his arm halted.

Talia wheeled on the captive elf and bore into him with her pale amethyst eyes. "You are a mockery!" she proclaimed in Elven.

Belac nodded agreeably.

Talia bared her teeth and then shouted wordlessly.

Belac grinned mischievously while affecting a disapproving tone. "Now, that is not very dignified, Talia."

The Elven woman clenched her jaw so tightly that Belac thought she might break a tooth. *Please. Please, break a tooth.* A short, silent laugh escaped him. *That would be amazing. It might almost be worth getting captured just to see that.*

Talia pointed at Belac, but she was too upset to speak. Belac found his eyes tracing the oxblood tattoo of thorny vines that covered her right arm and shoulder. He wondered at what other hidden places the twisting pattern might touch.

Talia turned away and resumed walking down the forest path. Belac was jostled into motion as the spriggan holding his arm began following the elven woman.

Belac poked at a wooden finger wrapped around his bicep. "Hey. Not so rough."

Though the spriggan said nothing, Belac could feel it hating him. He looked to the other spriggan that walked beside Talia. *What hold does she have on them?* To Belac, the spriggan seemed like the embodiment of mindless hate. He did not understand how anyone could command them.

Belac attempted to survey the encampment to his left, but was unable to make out much beyond the trees and thick underbrush. Muted green cloth flittered in and out of view, hinting at large, camouflaged tents. He sniffed at the air, but could detect nothing burning. *No campfires…* Ecard and he had been given hard biscuits and water, but Belac did not believe that his captors would be content with such meager provisions. *I guess Talia is not taking me to dinner.*

Belac looked to his right and wondered what Ecard was doing on the other side of the rise. *He is probably just sitting in his cage and waiting to be rescued.* Belac shook his head. *I don't know how Enevic maintained its borders with generals like Ecard.*

The forest path bent left and then opened up into a rectangular clearing filled with two rows of long, wooden cages. Six cages in total, five of the spacious prisons were empty. Over two dozen haggard men stood naked in the final cage. *I guess Ecard and I each got a private room.* Dirty and ill-cared-for, the men shifted uneasily at Talia's approach. There was not so much as a murmur from the prisoners.

At every corner, and on each long side of the occupied cage, a briar man stood a pace away. Staring toward the prisoners facelessly, the briar men seemed less reserved than the ones that guarded Ecard and the smaller cages. Blood decorated the large cages in several places. None of the prisoners were willing to move within arm's reach of the bars.

Talia stopped next to a door on one of the long sides of the cage. She gestured to the men cowering inside. "Pick one," she ordered in Elven.

Confused, Belac turned toward the cage. Sorrow washed over him as he took in the pitiful people inside. *Why would they do this?*

"Pick one, Belac," Talia ordered again in Elven.

Belac looked away from the cage and the suffering inside. "I am not going to pick one, Talia." He met the woman's pale amethyst eyes. "These people are not chattel."

"That is exactly what they are," Talia disagreed in Elven. "Now, pick one." She gestured to the cage. "Or I will pick one." With unwavering focus, she returned the other elf's stare. "I will have it dragged out. I will carve it in front of you. I will make you watch. I will make you listen." She leaned in aggressively. "And then. Once it's dead. We can try this again."

This woman needs to die. She was too far away for Belac to reach her, and he knew he could not get free from the spriggan even if he broke his own arm. *I will find a way.*

A man with unruly hair and a graying beard stepped forward from the group of prisoners. "Choose me." His voice sounded so dry that it must have pained him to speak.

Talia smiled brightly in anticipation.

Belac did not know why Talia wanted him to choose one of the humans, but he knew that if he did not select the man who had stepped forward, Talia would. *She would butcher him while the spriggans held me in place.* Belac shook his head, closed his eyes, and then nodded.

Talia was not satisfied. "Say it," she ordered in Elven.

Belac opened his eyes and glared at the woman. "I choose him; the man who volunteered." *Maybe he understands what is going on here.*

Talia nodded with pleasure before stepping away from the cage. The spriggan that had been standing beside her moved to the cage door. A wooden hand touched the bars and then vines began to unwind themselves from the cage. The vines slithered up and around the spriggan's arm like a pet returning to its favored place at its master's side.

When the spriggan opened the door, one of the men inside rushed forward and darted out of the cage. The spriggan reached out and caught the man's head as he attempted to run past. A hooked claw dug into the underside of the man's chin, pulling his head back as his legs continued forward. The man lifted into the air horizontally, and then the spriggan threw him to the ground.

The spriggan raised a foot made out of tangled roots, and slammed it down on the man's abdomen. The man let out a wretched sound under the crushing weight of the spriggan. With one swipe of its massive claws, the spriggan struck the side of the man's head. Bloody chunks of gore tore free and splattered the leg of Talia's heather gray trousers. The elven woman had not stopped smiling.

The spriggan removed its foot from the mangled corpse and then reached down with one of its monstrous wooden hands. Hooked claws sunk into the sides of the corpse's ribs. Blood seeped from the body like a saturated rag as the spriggan lifted it off the ground. Then the spriggan tossed the dead man into the cage contemptuously.

The men inside shied away from the corpse, but continued to keep their distance from the bars of the cage. Huddled together, the men looked like lost children. The spriggan's red eyes stared at the men with burning hate. *That thing wants one of them to try another escape.*

The volunteer stepped between the spriggan and the other men. "Are you going to let me out?" he asked, almost in challenge.

Some of the other prisoners stood taller at witnessing the man's bravery. Belac found himself experiencing an odd sense of pride. *Even now, they are not completely broken.*

Belac looked up at the feminine face of the spriggan holding his arm. He reached up with his free hand and rapped his knuckles against the spriggan's wooden cheek like he was knocking on a door. The spriggan turned its crowned head and glared down at Belac with its glowing red eyes.

Staring up at the thing that obviously wanted to kill him, Belac pointed his free hand at the other spriggan. "Are you going to just let your partner eat my prisoner?" He did not wait for an answer. "That's just disrespectful. Why would you let yourself be treated that way?" He shook his head. "Your partner is making all of you tree people look bad." He nudged the spriggan's arm. "You should do something about that."

Though the spriggan's face was unmoving, Belac could sense the hate within it. Tension built in the air as the spriggan silently wrestled with the unseen forces that controlled it.

"Don't look at me like that," Belac scolded the spriggan. "It's not my fault that your partner over there has absolutely no respect for you." He shrugged as best he could. "Maybe if you stood up for yourself, the other tree people wouldn't treat you like that."

"Enough, Belac," Talia stated threateningly in Elven.

"What?" Belac asked as he made an exaggerated show of looking around the spriggan that held his arm. "How is it my fault that your spriggans can't get along?"

Three

Belac could not have explained why he refused to stop talking. "Maybe what they need is just a holiday." He looked up at the spriggan holding his arm as it led him through the forest. "You do get holidays, right?"

Talia had become no more tolerant. "Belac…"

Belac turned his head toward the elven woman walking alone in front of him. "What? You don't give them holidays?" He glanced at the spriggan escorting the naked man behind him. "You tree people need a guild or something."

Talia led the others off the forest path and onto a heavily tracked dirt road. Turning right, she continued on toward the expansive stone ruins that waited ahead. Belac took in the time worn slabs of dull gray rock that jutted from the ground amidst toppled blocks of matching stone. *What is that…* Belac guessed at what the ruins may have once been. *… A temple, maybe?* There was not enough of the structure still standing for Belac to be sure of anything other than that it was ancient. *This place might be older than humanity.*

As they entered the ruins, signs of recent excavation became apparent. They followed a roped off walkway between staked sections of seemingly abandoned dig sites. *I wonder if they found what they were looking for.*

"It looks like you have been busy," Belac said, attempting to sound casual.

Talia ignored the comment.

Six cages and five of them empty... Belac thought back to the bloody cages and considered the state of the surviving prisoners. *How many men did Talia and Kaelem work to death?*

Not far into the ruins, an elven male lounged in a wooden armchair next to a portable folding table. Dressed in the same loose fitting, heather gray cloth as Talia, he mirrored the elven woman's style. Scalp shaved to expose the oxblood vines tattooed onto his right side, the elf could have easily been mistaken for his sister at a distance. Sipping white wine from a long-stemmed glass, he waited patiently for Talia to bring the prisoners closer. Behind the enigmatic elven man, two spriggans glared at the world with eyes of glowing red hate.

Belac licked his lips at seeing the wine.

Talia gestured angrily behind herself while addressing the seated elf. "Here he is," she announced in Elven. "But I still do not understand why we don't just kill him!"

Belac raised his free arm and waved his hand like a happy child. "Kaelem!" He called the elf's name in greeting.

Kaelem set his glass of wine down next to the open bottle and stood from his chair. He smiled, showing off his chiseled chin and high cheekbones. "Belac!" He held his hands out to his side welcomingly.

"You should kill him," Talia insisted in Elven as she moved to stand next to her brother. "Or let me kill him." She glared at the captive elf. "Please. Let me kill him."

Belac jerked to a stop as the spriggan holding his arm halted. A leg in mid step lifted out in front of him and then swung back down into place. *Rude.*

Kaelem stepped over to his sister and embraced her. With their left cheeks pressed against each other, the two elves' matching tattoos made them appear bound together in a tangle of thorny vines. *I wonder if they share each other's clothes.*

After their embrace, Kaelem stepped away from his sister. "Tell me what has you so upset, Talia," he said in refined Elven.

Belac switched to speaking Elven. "She does not like the way I speak," he answered for the woman.

"He refuses to speak properly!" Talia said immediately after him in Elven.

Belac held his free hand out as if to say, 'See what I mean?'

Kaelem's pale amethyst eyes looked from his sister, to the captive elf, and then back. "He has lived apart from the Elves for a rather long time, Talia," Kaelem reasoned in Elven. "It is not overly surprising that he would develop a slight accent."

Talia began to correct her brother in Elven. "No. That is not…"

"That is what I keep telling her," Belac lied, continuing to speak Elven. "I try to be nice to her, but she just won't have it. No matter what I do, she just wants to kill me."

Talia glared at Belac. She wanted to kill him.

Belac held out his hand again and then gestured to Talia as evidence.

Kaelem raised both eyebrows and regarded his sister curiously.

Belac decided to change the subject. "Is that wine?" he asked in Elven. *And can I have some?*

Kaelem turned away from his sister. "Ah, the wine," he acknowledged in Elven. "It was offered as tribute by those who understand that the forests belong to the Elves."

Belac shook his head ruefully. "We don't own 'all' the forests," he argued in Elven. *Greedy elf.*

"We do if we say we do," Kaelem replied resolutely in Elven.

Talia seconded her brother in Elven. "Our responsibility to the world does not end where it is convenient, Belac."

Though Belac did not appreciate that she made his name sound like an insult, he had to admit that what Talia said rang true. Then he realized that the noble sentiment would only be used to justify villainy. *Even ideas are not safe from the corrupt.* Belac found the direction of his thoughts uncomfortable.

Kaelem gestured deeper into the ruins. "Come with me, Belac," he prompted in Elven. "I have something that I would very much like to show you." He turned and began walking away.

Belac clapped his free hand down twice on the wooden fingers of the spriggan holding his arm. "Let's go," he chided in Elven as if spurring a horse. Then he stuck out his foot and leaned against the spriggan's grip.

The spriggan proceeded to follow Kaelem.

Belac smiled. Though he did not believe anything he said or did could command the spriggans, Belac knew that the childish game would irritate Talia. He winked at the elven woman as the spriggan escorted him past her. Belac turned his head slightly and angled one of his pointed ears behind him. *I really want to hear it if she cracks a tooth.*

The two spriggans that had stood silent at Belac's arrival remained with Talia, while the two spriggans with prisoners followed after Kaelem. Belac made a mental note of the exchange. *Talia and Kaelem don't each have their own spriggans.* He considered the implications. *That must mean that either of them can command any of the spriggans. Could there be more of those monsters?* He wondered how much autonomy the spriggans possessed.

Once they had left the elven woman behind, the human took the opportunity to speak. "I can make no sense of you, Elf," he stated accusingly.

"Ha!" Belac barked the laugh. "That is the secret to my success!"

The human was not amused by the levity. "This does not seem like success to me."

Belac nodded and then spoke over his shoulder. "Exactly."

Only a short distance ahead, Kaelem stopped and turned toward his captives. "I believe that you will find this most enlightening," he predicted in Elven. There was a friendliness to his tone that sounded sincere.

Belac's smile was exceedingly insincere. *I don't think he is still going to want to be friends once he realizes that I am not going to help him with whatever it is that he needs me for.* Belac only pretended to like Kaelem because he knew it drove Talia crazy. *Still... Kaelem is the one who doesn't want me dead. It is probably a good idea to be nice to him anyway.* Belac's smile dropped when he saw what Kaelem was standing next to.

A wide, reinforced, stone rampway tunneled down into the ground. Though more than three times the size of the entrance to the hobgoblin lair in Cavasca, Belac recognized the architecture. *There is nothing down there that I want to see.* Beyond what would be a short stint of darkness, firelight danced with shadow.

Belac cleared his throat. "Uhm... Is there any chance we could have the enlightenment brought to us up here?" he asked in Elven.

Kaelem smiled in good humor as he turned and began descending into the underground domain.

Belac was pulled by the arm as he unintentionally resisted moving toward the rampway. "Hey... Ah," He had to remind himself to speak in Elven. "I have an idea." Belac strove to think of an idea.

"All will be well, Belac," Kaelem assured him in Elven.

The words did not comfort Belac. *The last time someone told me that, they trapped me in a box and tried to drown me.*

Four

The rampway led to a stone platform afore a seemingly endless abyss. Only a short, knee high railing of stone divided the security of the platform from a plummeting fall into darkness. On the other side of a cylindrical chasm, a spiraling ramp connected additional platforms that descended into the black at regular intervals. The flames of free-standing braziers lit the first three of the distant platforms. After which, the spiraling ramp that connected them faded into the darkness below.

At least I got away from all that green up there in the forest. Dull and gray, the stone of the underground domain was seamless. Though rough and lifeless, the precision of its angles was perfect. To Belac, such a place seemed beyond the skill of man.

Belac gazed over the ledge as he was led down the spiraling ramp. "I wonder who made this," he mused aloud.

Kaelem sounded pleased to answer. "Vaquians."

The human provided an alternative answer. "Demons."

Ignoring the human, Kaelem expounded in Elven, "Long ago, they abandoned this world." He gestured into the darkness. "This, is but a remnant."

"So… Uhm…" Belac switched to speaking Elven. "I guess you are not showing me to the wine cellar?"

Kaelem chuckled deeply. "I will enjoy having you with us, Belac," he professed in Elven. "I love my sister dearly, but she can be..." he searched for an appropriate descriptor.

"Crazy?" Belac supplied in Elven.

Kaelem glanced back and smiled at the captive elf. "Severe," he moderated in Elven.

Severely crazy. Belac wondered if Kaelem comprehended how bad of a person Talia was. *How could he not know? The woman is awful. I would not be surprised if I found out that she eats babies.*

As they stepped onto the second platform, Belac noted that it was much like the first on the other side of the spiraled void. Half recessed into the wall, half suspended into the open air, the platforms were uniform enough to be disorienting. Inside the recess to Belac's left, a draping, green canvas covered another wide opening. *I doubt that is another ramp to the surface.* In both of the recessed corners, a briar man stood sentry. Light from the burning braziers flickered on their faceless heads, while a garnet glow pulsed in each of their chests.

Speaking in Elven, Belac asked, "What is in the super secret hidden room?"

"All in good time," Kaelem replied in Elven as he led them onto the ramp on the other side of the platform. "Once I know that you are with us, I will explain everything."

Belac frowned. *I would really rather have you do that in the opposite order.* "What exactly do you mean by 'with' you?" he probed in Elven.

They walked down the shadowy ramp in silence for a moment before Kaelem answered in Elven, "I want you to marry my sister."

"What?!" Belac almost forgot to speak in Elven. "Do you have another one other than Talia?!"

Kaelem voiced his wishful thinking in Elven. "I am certain that she will come to be more affectionate in time."

"Not if she is married to me!" Belac argued in Elven. "That woman would not let me survive the wedding night!" *And if I did, she would probably eat me in the morning!*

"She will understand," Kaelem disagreed in Elven. "You are of a noble house. A union of Rhynvek and Melavar would strengthen our claim over the southern lands. In time, we may even be able to petition for reconciliation."

The Elves threw them out… Belac nodded to himself. *Talia and Kaelem are exiles. That is why they are this far south.*

"I see that you understand already," Kaelem said approvingly in Elven.

What?! Belac shook his head before arguing quickly in Elven, "No. No, I don't."

Kaelem's optimism was unthwarted. "When the storm heralded your coming, and then I found you stranded on the shore, I knew that destiny had brought you to me," he proclaimed in Elven. "You need not worry. I am certain that I can convince Talia," he added as if the captive elf had already agreed to the engagement.

"That is not going to happen," Belac insisted in Elven. *If I don't find some way out of this, that crazy woman is going to take out one of her knives and cut off all of my favorite parts!*

Kaelem glanced back at the captive elf and smiled again. "I could threaten to make her marry the other noble we captured if she protests too much," he joked in Elven.

"Ecard?!" Belac almost tripped over his own feet. *The man would be better off if we had let him hang himself in prison.*

Kaelem waved his hand dismissively as he stepped onto the third platform. "I jest," he confessed in Elven. "I would not do that to my sister."

Kaelem veered left and led them toward a green canvas covered opening guarded by two briar men. Though two free standing braziers flickered brightly, their light felt small in the darkness of the underground domain. Belac noted absently that they were now underneath the entrance. With platforms on both sides of the descent, it would only become more difficult to keep his bearings if they continued deeper.

Kaelem had settled into his good cheer. "Talia will agree," he insisted in Elven. "You and I will be brothers."

There is no way that I am marrying into your crazy family of Elven exiles. A frightening thought occurred to Belac. "Wait! Are you going to try to make me shave my head?" he asked in Elven.

Kaelem laughed without answering.

Tattoos are next! I know it! First, they are going to make me shave my head, and then they are going to tattoo those red vine things on me! Belac could feel his skin itch at the thought. *I have to find some way out of this!*

Kaelem pulled back the curtain and allowed the spriggans to usher the prisoners through the opening. Belac walked into the chamber beyond, a bit surprised. Where he had expected the corridors of a sprawling complex, there was only a single chamber. A stone altar lay afore two larger stone tables. In the back of the chamber, mist rose from a well of sinister red light. Though spacious, the chamber's dull stone and ominous lighting created a confining atmosphere. Despite the well's illumination, Belac felt as if he had just walked deeper into the dark.

The spriggan holding Belac's arm halted in front of the altar while the other followed Kaelem to the table on Belac's left. The human prisoner began to kick and punch the spriggan as he was dragged to the table.

"This place is evil!" the naked man yelled. "You will not trade my soul to demons!"

The spriggan ignored the man's violent protest and wrapped its other monstrous hand around the man's leg. The spriggan swooped the man up and then slammed his back onto the stone table. The man's head bounced off the tabletop, the concussion ending his fight.

Kaelem took hold of the man's right arm and wrenched it toward the corner of the table. He grabbed a leather strap that was fixed to the table and slipped it around the man's wrist. After cinching the arm down over the man's head, Kaelem walked to the other side of the table and took hold of the man's right leg.

While Kaelem proceeded to strap down the disoriented prisoner, Belac searched his surroundings for some means of escape. *There are two tables.* Belac did not want to be next. Amidst the strange paraphernalia laid out on the stone altar in front of him, he spotted a small, guardless dagger. Belac looked from the dagger to the spriggan holding his arm. He could not reach the dagger with one of his arms locked in the spriggan's grip.

Belac considered reaching out with his foot and attempting to drag the dagger across the altar under his boot, but he did not think that the spriggan would allow it. *Even if I got the dagger, my arm would still be trapped by the spriggan.* He reappraised the dagger. *That thing is too tiny to do any real damage to the spriggan. Though... I guess maybe I could carve a smiley face on it.* He imagined what one of the spriggans would look like with a smiling aspect. In his mind, he saw smiling hate illuminated by smoldering red eyes in darkness.

Belac looked up at the spriggan holding his arm and pointed a finger at its wooden face. "No smiling for you!"

Five

The spriggan stepped away from the stone table as Kaelem cinched down the last of the prisoner's restraints. Without being given a verbal command, the spriggan turned and began walking toward Belac. The wooden monstrosity's eyes glowed balefully bright despite the chamber's homogeneous lighting.

They are going to feed me to demons! Belac grabbed one of the wooden fingers wrapped around his arm and began tugging on it frantically. The spriggan's finger would not budge. Belac looked at the other spriggan in rising panic.

The approaching spriggan strode past Belac and continued on toward the canvas covered exit. The spriggan pushed the muted green curtain aside and then left the chamber. Belac looked away from the opening as the curtain fell back into place. Kaelem was standing on the other side of the stone altar, rearranging his strange implements.

Kaelem opened a hinged box and removed a handful of dried herbs. He picked up a piece of twine and tied it to the base of the bunched stems. Then he began to wind the loose end of the twine around the herbs, tying small knots as he went.

...Is he not going to feed me to a demon? Belac let go of the spriggan's finger. *I guess he can't feed me to a demon if he wants me to marry his sister.* He thought about Talia. *Though, now that I think about it, there does not seem to be much difference one way or the other.*

Kaelem slammed the lid on the box closed, drawing Belac's attention back to the altar. Kaelem dropped the bundled herbs onto a silvery tray and then picked up a small, jagged rock and a steel striker. He struck the steel against the flint, throwing sparks toward the looser end of the bound herbs. After striking twice more, he set down the flint and steel. Taking the herbs by the tighter end, he brought them up to his mouth and blew softly.

Once the herbs began to burn, Kaelem waved the bundle, and the flames were replaced with a light gray smoke. The smoke had a harsh vetiver smell that Belac did not care for. Breathing through his mouth, he attempted to blow the smoke away from his nose. Remembering that he still had one arm free, he began to wave the smoke away from himself.

Kaelem stepped away from the stone altar and began to circle the chamber. He waved the herbs into the empty spaces as if he were painting them with the effluvium. Gray smoke swirled and hung in the unnerving red light of the stone chamber.

Belac complained in Elven, "That is not making this place smell better."

Kaelem smiled as he continued to fumigate the chamber. "You will become accustomed to it," he assured in Elven. "Just try to breathe naturally. The smoke will not harm you."

Kaelem returned to the stone altar and dropped the remainder of the bundled herbs onto the silvery tray. Smoke continued to rise from the dried herbs, but Kaelem seemed content to let them burn. He removed the lid from a wooden bowl, revealing the waxy yellow substance inside. First setting the wooden lid aside, he picked up a tiny metal spoon and began to scrape the contents into a small ball no larger than the tip of his finger. Balancing the waxy ball on the scoop of the spoon, Kaelem stepped away from the stone altar and walked over to the restrained prisoner. Carefully, Kaelem placed the waxy ball on the center of the man's chest and then pressed the ball down with the back of the spoon.

The man's head lulled side to side, and he began to groan. After a moment, the man began to breathe forcefully as if attempting to expel the fumes he had inhaled.

Unconcerned with the man's distress, Kaelem returned to the altar. He set the metal spoon down and then placed the lid back on the wooden bowl. "The spriggan will be here shortly," he informed in Elven.

"What are you doing?" Belac asked in Elven. *This is not how elves should behave.*

Kaelem smiled. "I am changing the way you see the world, Belac." He replied in Elven.

Belac turned his head as the curtain moved behind him. A spriggan entered the chamber carrying a lifeless collection of sticks and brush shaped to resemble a man. The curtain fell back into place as the spriggan stepped away. Cradling its burden as if holding a child, the spriggan walked to the stone table on Belac's right.

The spriggan laid the lifeless briar man down on its back, spreading it out across the stone table. *It's dead…* Broken twigs jutted from a gaping cavity in the brushwood torso. *It looks like something tore a hole in its chest.* The spriggan stepped back, its glowing gaze remaining on the lifeless form.

Kaelem palmed a wooden chalice with his right hand and picked up the guardless dagger with his left. He walked over to the lifeless briar man and set the chalice down next to its head. Kaelem's fingers traced the imagined cheek of the faceless wood. Leaving the chalice behind, he walked across the room to the other stone table and looked down at the prisoner stretched out atop it.

Faint smoke swirled in the red light above the naked man as he struggled to breathe. Arms strapped down tightly above his head, the prisoner could barely move. Kaelem reached down and took hold of a circular protrusion on the side of the stone table. He slid the circular piece along a recessed track in the stone until it was positioned directly under the small of the prisoner's back. Then Kaelem pressed the protrusion into the side of the table.

The stone table growled with the voice of rock and began to change shape. All four corners sank downward as the stone morphed into a rounded surface that arched the bound man's back cruelly. Head upside down, the man's eyes were now wide and alert. Confusion and disorientation fed the man's animalistic terror.

Kaelem plunged his dagger into the man's abdomen and then pulled, creating a horizontal gash slightly below the man's ribcage. The man made sick, choking sounds as he attempted to scream. Kaelem slid his right hand into the cut he had made, reaching into the man's chest cavity. The man thrashed his head violently, unable to resist, unable to scream. Kaelem jerked his arm back and the man lost consciousness.

Kaelem pulled a fistful of gore out of the prisoner's chest and then cut it free with his dagger. He held up his bloody hand and inspected the human heart. Dripping thick blood, the heart continued to contract and expand as it beat against the elf's fingers.

Kaelem walked to the other stone table and placed the heart in the lifeless briar man's broken chest. He palmed the wooden chalice he had left on the table and brought it up to his mouth. After taking a drink, the elf grimaced in disgust and shook his head. Then he poured the remainder of the chalice's contents into the briar man's chest. Whatever the liquid may have been, it gleamed crimson in the chamber's smoky red lighting.

The sharp snaping sounds of breaking sticks filled the chamber as the briar man's chest repaired itself. A deep garnet glow pulsed through the twigs as they knitted themselves back together. Then the briar man sat up.

Belac tried his best to pretend that he was not there. He did not want to be involved. What he witnessed in that chamber was worse than demonic. *This is not how elves should behave.*

Life pulsing in its chest, the briar man climbed off the stone table. *Each one of those things is a dead human.*

The briar man stood in front of the spriggan motionlessly as if awaiting orders. The spriggan turned, its glowing eyes no less malevolent in the presence of the newly arisen briar man. Striding toward the exit, the spriggan led the briar man out of the chamber.

Kaelem set his wooden chalice down on the stone altar. "Do you now understand?" he asked in Elven.

Belac shook his head. "Is this a threat?" he replied in Elven. "Is this what you are going to do to me if I don't marry Talia? Are you going to cut out my heart?"

"No," Kaelem answered in Elven. "I do not want to cut out your heart, Belac." He reached through the cloud of smoke hovering above the altar and set his dagger down on the other side. "I want you to wield the blade."

Belac instinctually moved his hands away from the guardless dagger. With his left arm restrained by the spriggan, he was only able to raise his right. "You want me to cut out my own heart?!" he asked in Elven.

Kaelem chuckled and shook his head. "The ceremonies will continue," he elucidated in Elven. "I want you to help us with the work. I meant what I said about you becoming family."

I am not joining your crazy family! Belac looked at the dead man splayed over the torturous stone table. "These are people, Kaelem," he lamented in Elven.

Kaelem scowled as he voiced his disapproval in Elven. "They are humans." He looked at the corpse with disdain. "Pathetic creatures that live for nothing but their own base pleasure. Every thought they have is a lie they tell themselves." He gestured to the man that he had murdered. "That human would be dead soon anyway." He returned his attention to the captive elf. "Turtles live longer than these things you would call people."

Belac shifted uncomfortably under the other elf's gaze. *He is not completely wrong.*

Kaelem shook his head. "They are worthless, Belac," he concluded in Elven.

Belac's eyes pierced through the haze. "If the humans are so worthless, then why do your plans depend on them?" he asked in Elven. "If they are so pathetic, then why do you need all of this to defeat them?" He raised his hand, indicating to the atrocity surrounding him.

Kaelem's face hardened. Cast in red shadow, his own darkness showed through. "You disappoint me, Belac," he articulated in Elven with cold command.

Six

Kaelem said nothing more as he led Belac out of the smoky, stone chamber. Pulled along by the spriggan, Belac did not protest. *The sooner we get out of this place, the better.* Kaelem's demeanor was no longer friendly. There was a stiffness to his movements that spoke to a wavering restraint.

Belac walked up the ramp carefully, not wanting to draw any more of the brooding elf's ire. Though the air outside the chamber was not particularly fresh, it tasted clean compared to what he had left behind. He looked into the open darkness of the underground domain. *How far does this place go down?* The unknowable depth worried him less than what horrors might be waiting below.

I bet that if I asked him how deep it is, Kaelem would say something like, "As deep as it needs to be," or some other nonsense. Belac shook his head. *I hate answers like that. They are just a pretentious way to avoid saying, "I don't know."* He scowled at the other elf. *I don't know all kinds of stuff. No one sees me running around spouting nonsense like some kind of discount wizard.*

Belac wondered what Serath would think of the Vaquian stronghold. He debated whether the wizard would succumb to the alure of ancient magic, or if he would see the evil place for what it was.

The last time I found a place like this, Serath dropped a volcano on it. Belac nodded to himself. *Serath has his own magic. He does not need a place like this.*

Belac thought back on every time he had seen Serath work magic. Never once had anything Serath done felt evil to Belac. He could think of no time that the wizard's magic had ever left the world feeling wrong. Then Belac was struck with a vision of something that had. In his mind, he saw a dwarf standing over a dying giant, illuminated by tendrils of red light. *Is what Rolan did the same kind of magic that Kaelem used?* Belac could easily imagine Rolan sacrificing one enemy for the power to defeat another.

Shortly after Belac stepped onto the subsequent platform, the canvas covering the opening on that level was pushed aside from within. As Kaelem's second spriggan moved through the opening, Belac was given a glimpse of what lay beyond. Garnet lights pulsed in darkness, revealing a countless collection of briar men in the previously concealed chamber.

When the curtain fell, Belac looked to the other elf. "You made an army of them," he accused in Elven.

Kaelem did not attempt to defend his actions. 'We will need an army," he stated in Elven.

He still thinks there is a 'we.' Belac decided not to argue. *I should just let the crazy elf believe whatever he wants to for now.* "How did you get so many humans?" he inquired in Elven as the second spriggan joined them.

With the spriggan at his side, Kaelem continued up the ramp. "The first, we harvested were the members of the excavation team that we brought with us," he explained in Elven. "After that, we began to accept some as tribute. Lately, we have simply been capturing any of them that wonder too far into the forest from a nearby logging community." He waved a hand. "Depraved humans that feed on the forest."

"You are just snatching people?" Belac asked in Elven.

Kaelem shook his head. "Not the ones that are sensible enough to offer tribute," he qualified in Elven. "Right now, it is preferable to spare those that recognize our sovereignty." He glanced back at the captive elf. "The forests belong to the Elves."

This crazy elf is going to start a war. Belac began to understand the severity of the situation. *Humans might not be the smartest creatures in the world, but they know how to wage war.*

"You will see," Kaelem insisted in Elven. "You simply need more time to consider." He laughed. "Maybe I should convince Talia first." He glanced back again, this time smiling. "It could be that she might offer a more compelling persuasion."

Oh, please no. Belac did not think Talia would employ the same tactics that Kaelem was suggesting. *That woman is going to flay me!* He thought about the slender blades strapped to her thighs. Then he tried not to think about the shape of her thighs.

Due to the inherent politeness of the Elven language, Belac was able to parse his response. "I think it would be better if you waited for me to ask her." *Not that I am ever going to do that.*

"Excellent!" Kaelem exclaimed in Elven. "I will need some time to prepare, but we can begin making arrangements in the morrow."

I think Kaelem might not comprehend the concept of waiting. "Don't you think that is a little soon?" Belac complained in Elven. "I think it might be a better idea if we wait until she actually says, 'yes,' to my proposal." *Which will never happen, because I am never going to ask her!*

Kaelem dismissed the captive elf's concern in Elven. "Nonsense. She will agree." He turned around and walked backward up the last of the ramp while he spoke. "I am telling you, this will be perfect, Belac. After I bind you to us, you can marry Talia. You and I will be brothers. And our family will be positioned to reclaim these lands that the humans have infested." He spun around happily as he stepped onto the top platform. "You will see!"

Skimming past the whole evil plan thing, I can't help but notice that he said, bind and then marry. Belac did not know if the binding could be worse for him than being forced to marry Talia, but it worried him none the less. *Even if Talia refuses the marriage, I would still be trapped.* Belac assumed that magic would be involved; something dark and vile. As he walked across the platform and into the shadowy exit, he did not feel like he was heading toward freedom.

The ascent from the underground domain was difficult for Belac. That the world above was filled with green, did not improve his experience. Though the fallen ruins held back the worst of the offending color, the evening sun cut through the trees with a golden edged jade glow. As he was led away from the rampway, he thought that with his luck, zombies might rise from the dirt and try to eat him next.

Talia had waited for them to return. *Just as bad.* Sitting on top of the folding table, she had her feet in Kaelem's chair. Leaning back, she supported her weight on her right hand while she drank from a bottle of wine in her left. *Something tells me that she is not going to be a nice drunk.*

Talia leaned forward. "So, how do you feel about your choice?" she asked in Elven.

I thought that she didn't know about the marriage… Belac frowned, not attempting to hide his confusion.

Talia continued to gloat in Elven. "Do you think the brave human will make a good briar man?" She smiled prettily. "I bet you chose the best one."

Kaelem laughed. Apparently, he did not understand that his sister was attempting to hurt Belac. Talia joined her brother in laughter. However, her pale amethyst eyes remained fixed on the captive elf.

Belac felt sick. *Naked and alone, that human was worth more than both of you.* He listened as the other two elves laughed at their own cruelty, and he said nothing.

Kaelem offered acclaim in Elven. "He did indeed choose well."

Talia smiled her revenge. "Then, I think we should have him choose another one," she suggested in Elven.

I am going to kill that bald… Witch. I am calling her a witch.

Kaelem turned to face the captive elf. "Do you see, Belac?" he asked in Elven. "She welcomes you already." He turned back to his sister. "Talia, would you please show Belac back to his accommodations?" He obviously thought that he was being clever. "The two of you can use the walk to discuss our bright future together."

"Of course, Brother," Talia agreed in Elven before chugging the rest of her wine. She slammed the empty bottle down on the table. "I would love to talk about Belac's future."

Kaelem seemed oblivious to his sister's irony. "Excellent!" he said approvingly in Elven.

Talia hopped off the table spryly, only to lose her balance and stumble into her brother.

Kaelem caught the elven woman in his arms. "Careful, dear sister," he counseled in Elven. "We cannot have you injuring yourself." He put his hands under her elbows to support her and then he took a step back. "Do you want me to have one of the spriggans carry you?" he asked teasingly.

Talia swatted her brother's hands away, though there was no passion in it. "I am fine," she insisted in Elven and then stumbled a step backward.

Please, fall and break your neck. Please, fall and break your neck.

Kaelem chuckled. "Are you sure you can manage?" he asked in Elven.

Talia slung her arm in the general direction of the captured elf. "I can manage him!" she asserted belligerently in Elven.

Kaelem grinned slyly. "Well, that is certainly good to know," he replied in Elven, still sounding like someone who believed they were clever.

Talia waved for the spriggans to follow her. "Let's go," she ordered in Elven as she began walking away.

Belac was jerked forward when the spriggan holding his arm marched off after the elven woman. The spriggan that had been standing next to Kaelem walked away with Talia, leaving the other two spriggans to remain. Kaelem smiled and nodded at Belac as the captive elf was escorted past.

As Belac was pulled toward the fading light of day, he wondered if he would survive the night. *If survival means that I have to marry Talia, I don't know that I want to survive.*

Seven

Though Belac was fairly certain that there was a shorter path to his cage, Talia led him back to the misery of the human prisoners. Naked and frightened, the humans cowered in the center of their shared cage. *Even livestock would be treated better than this.* As far as Belac was concerned, there was no excuse for such conditions.

Talia swept both of her hands out toward the prisoners. "Which one will be next?" she asked in Elven.

Belac said nothing.

Talia spun around and smiled at the captive elf as she walked backward. "You know that is what they are asking themselves," she asserted in Elven. She tripped, but then caught herself on her spriggan's arm. "But it doesn't matter," she said as she got her feet back under herself. "We are going to use them all." After regaining her balance, she turned back around and proceeded walking forward.

Belac said nothing. *This is not the time to provoke her.*

Walking past the cage, Talia continued in Elven, "We are going to make you watch, Belac." She giggled. "Every one of them." She nodded aggressively. "We are going to make you watch, and then I am going to cut you open myself."

Belac said nothing.

Talia filled the silence with Elven venom. "You are going to watch, and you are going to know that there is nothing you can do about it. You are going to know that you are next, and that there is nothing you can do about it. You are going to die, knowing that there is nothing you can do about it."

Belac said nothing. However, he was beginning to worry that his silence was only making things worse.

Walking through the darkening shadows of the forest path, Talia began to laugh maliciously. She struggled to repress her laughter and then she expressed her thoughts in Elven. "I am going to tie ribbons on the one that is you." She laughed again. "I am going to make the briar man that has your heart follow me around, and I am going to use it as a footrest."

Belac was repulsed by the beauty of her laughter. Still, he said nothing.

"That's your future, Belac," Talia explained in Elven. "A mindless eternity with your heart beating under my foot!" She no longer attempted to control her laughter.

Belac bit his tongue to keep himself from saying something stupid. He really wanted to say something stupid.

Talia was still laughing when they rounded the rise in the terrain that sequestered the two smaller cages. Ecard looked on with perplexion as Belac returned with the jubilant elven woman. *Don't say anything, Ecard. Just keep your mouth shut.*

The spriggan walking beside Talia stepped away and then halted. It turned and glared with glowing red hate at the human in the hanging cage. While maintaining its reserved role as Talia's protector, the spriggan obviously wanted to kill the man.

Talia swung out the door to the empty cage and held it open. "Are you scared now, Belac?" she asked in Elven. Her glazed amethyst eyes were dark in the failing light. "Do you wish you had been a better elf?"

The spriggan holding Belac's arm released him and then stepped past the open cage. Now, Belac had a dilemma; he was unsure how he should get into the cage.

Talia voiced her impatience in Elven. "Get in."

Keeping his back as straight as he could, Belac lowered himself down onto his knees in a manner that suggested hopeless submission. *I don't really have much choice.* He then hobbled into the cage on his knees.

Talia laughed brightly. "That's right," she crowed in Elven, "get used to being on your knees."

The door to the cage closed behind Belac, trapping him in his defeated posture. He leaned his head forward slightly and looked back over his shoulder. *Don't tell her you like her sister better. Don't tell her you like her sister better.* The spriggan reached down and took hold of Belac's cage. The vine that was wrapped around its arm unwound itself and slithered onto the wooden bars. Twisting around the edge of the door, the vine secured itself in place.

Talia came into view as the spriggan stepped away. "You know what?" she asked sweetly in Elven. "Kaelem was right. I did enjoy talking about your future." She all but danced as she backed away from the cage. She twirled on one toe, stumbled, regained her balance, and then laughed as she led the spriggans out of the small clearing.

Once the elven woman and her spriggans were gone, Ecard said, "So… That seemed rather cordial." His tone was halfway between teasing and accusation.

"Shut up, Ecard," Belac replied irritably. "It was not like that."

Ecard sided with teasing. "Will I be invited to the wedding?"

"How do you know about the wedding?!" Belac demanded as he reached into the back of his trousers.

Ecard coughed as if he were having a fit. "You cannot be serious!"

Carefully, Belac pulled the ceremonial dagger out of his trousers. Then he sat back on his heels, exhausted.

"Is that a knife?" Ecard shifted in his cage to get a better view. "Did you have that in your…"

"No!" Belac refuted. "Why would you ask that?!"

Sounding uncomfortable, Ecard muttered, "There would be no shame in it."

Belac frowned at the man. "It was just down my trousers." He rolled around in the cage to face the door. "It made walking all the way back here a chore, but it will be worth it if I can get this door open."

Ecard gesture to one of the four briar men guards. "Are you not concerned that they can see what you are doing?"

"They don't have eyes," Belac said dismissively as he considered the door.

Ecard's tone became disapproving. "I hardly think that matters when magic is involved."

Belac shrugged. "I don't think they can do much on their own. I think they need someone else to tell them what to do." He glanced at the pulsing garnet chest of the briar man closest to his cage. "They might just be there to scare us." He thought of the blood on the larger cages. "Though, uhm… Maybe tell me if one of them moves."

Ecard was not mollified. "What if someone told them that they are to kill us if we escape from our cages?"

Belac shrugged angrily. "Then, it is extra important that you tell me if one of them moves!"

Trusting Ecard to warn him if the briar men showed any signs of hostility, Belac returned his attention to the door. He considered trying to cut off the vine that served as a lock on the left side, but he worried that the vine might come back to life and bite him. *Maybe it tries to kill me, maybe it raises an alarm, maybe it does nothing…* He tapped the blade of the dagger against the thinner vines hinging the door on the right. *I should go through this side.*

Ecard interrupted the elf's thoughts. "Where did you get that?"

Belac assumed that the man was referring to the dagger. "I stole it while Kaelem was busy telling me how stupid humans are."

Belac appraised the guardless dagger in his hand. Its short, narrow blade felt sturdy, but its edge was less than razor sharp. *It would take too long for me to use this to saw through the vines.*

Though thinner than the supernatural vine holding the door shut, the vines that made up the hinges were tightly wrapped. *I doubt the blade would keep its edge if I tried.* He thought about stabbing at the hinges, but was concerned that he would end up damaging the dagger's tip. *I can't afford any mistakes. If I don't get out of here, I am going to have to either marry Talia or watch her cut out my heart.*

Belac transferred the dagger to his left hand as he shifted his body into a more comfortable position. Aligning the flat of the blade toward the door, he slid the tip of the dagger under the bottom of the top hinge. With his right palm, he hammered the dagger upward, wedging it farther under the wrapped vines.

Ecard cleared his throat. "So… About that wedding…"

"There is not going to be a wedding," Belac said shortly as he pressed the back of his shoulder into the corner of the cage to the right of the door.

"And is your intended aware of your decision?" Faint amusement colored Ecard's words.

Belac glanced back over his left shoulder. "Kaelem says that you have to marry her if I don't."

Ecard did not find that amusing. "We must escape with all haste."

"Are you sure?" Belac asked. He wrenched the dagger's hilt away from himself, causing its edge to bite into the vines of the hinge. "You could stay… shave your head, get some tattoos. I am sure Talia would not cut too many pieces off of you."

Ecard was quiet for a moment. "She is rather fetching," he mused.

Belac frowned. *Stupid human.* He turned his head to the side, but spoke without focusing on the man. "They are killing people, Ecard. They are chopping people up and using them for parts."

Ecard was appalled into silence.

Belac returned his attention to the door. He repositioned the ceremonial dagger and then hammered it upward with his palm again. The process would not be quick, but he was convinced that he would be able to cut through the hinges.

Belac pushed against the handle of the dagger. "Don't worry." He repositioned the blade. "Like I said. There is not going to be a wedding."

Eight

Working in moonlight obscured by the trees, Belac finished cutting through the hinges of his cage. He rolled to his side and kicked the door open though the force was unnecessary. The vine that served as a lock acted like a hinge, and the door swung out into the night. The excess force caused the door to bounce off the edge of the cage and then swing back inside. The swinging bars slammed into Belac's forehead as he rolled toward the exit.

Belac put his left hand to his head as the door shuttered away from him. *It's a conspiracy!* He pointed at the vine that was keeping the door attached. "Don't do that again!"

Worried that the door might try to close shut on him like a toothless wooden jaw, the elf shot out of his cage. As soon as he was free, he turned around and pointed at the vine. *You're just lucky that I can't turn into a gorilla-wolf-monster!* He briefly considered dragging the cage along with him as he escaped so that he could set it on fire later.

"Belac!" Ecard warned sharply.

Belac turned toward the man in the cage. As his gaze swept past the cages, Belac saw three pulsing garnet lights moving in his direction. *The one on the left is the closest.*

A fourth briar man grabbed Belac from the rear. As wooden, misshapen fingers tightened on the elf's left arm, the other three briar men continued to race closer.

Belac raised his captured arm as he pivoted to his left. Instinctually, he plunged the ceremonial dagger into the center of the briar man's glowing chest. Though the blade was short, it proved long enough to reach the human heart inside. The garnet light died immediately, and the briar man collapsed. Belac fell to the ground with the lifeless bundle of sticks.

Four! Belac thought angrily to himself. *I know that I know how to count to four!* He let go of the dagger and used his right hand to break off the wooden thumb wrapped around his left forearm. Grabbing the dagger again in an underhanded grip, he ripped the blade free. *Now, there are three more.*

Belac got his feet under himself and turned just in time to see a briar man reaching for him. Its splintery arms glowed red in the night as its stolen heart pulsed in its brushwood chest. The elf sprung into the outstretched arms, leading with the tip of his dagger. The blade slid through sticks and twigs and then darkened the glowing heart.

Belac's attack carried him forward, lifting the briar man up into the air. He slung the dead thing to his right, throwing it away from himself. The dead briar man slammed against the bars of Ecard's cage and then fell to the ground below. *Two more.*

Belac stumbled to his left as his momentum drove him toward an advancing briar man. Turning into the stumble, Belac slapped the briar man's arms away. As he stepped past the briar man, he grabbed its faceless head and pulled it to his bare chest. Continuing backward, he jerked the briar man off balance as he dragged it with him. Belac's dagger rose and then arced forward as he plunged the blade into the briar man's glowing heart. *One.*

Belac dropped the lifeless briar man and faced the last of the glowing garnet lights. Though moving at less than a run, the briar man closed quickly. When the wooden arms reached out for him, Belac grabbed the briar man's right wrist with his free hand. He stepped to his left while turning right, intending to pull the briar man off balance.

His feet tripped on the dead briar man hidden by shadow, and he fell backward. Maintaining his grip on the attacking briar man, Belac succeeded in pulling it off balance. As they fell over the mound of dead brushwood, their combined movements slung the briar man over the elf and then headfirst onto the ground. The briar man's head snapped off with the sound of breaking sticks.

Belac let go of the briar man's wrist and moved his arm under himself. Pressing the knuckles of his right hand into the dirt, he pushed himself up and onto his knees. *And now…* Garnet light still pulsed in the headless briar man's chest. Belac groaned. *Now there is still one.*

The briar man lurched to its feet. Headless, the thing no longer resembled a man. A twisted horror of vines and sticks, the briar man clawed at the air as it moved toward Belac. The elf turned right while rolling onto his left hip. His right foot shot out and the heel of his boot stomped against the briar man's knee. The force of the kick spun the briar man around as its feet flew out from under it. The briar man's back crashed onto the ground, but it immediately began to right itself. Belac rolled forward onto his knees and grabbed hold of a wooden arm. He pulled the briar man toward him and then slammed his dagger into the glowing chest.

The night was shadows, moon, and stars. Faint firelight edged over the rise in the terrain, but no garnet hearts still pulsed. Belac jerked his dagger free and then listened for sounds of approach. *Nothing.* If any alarm had been raised, he could not hear it over the sounds of chirping crickets.

Belac stood. He pointed at the briar man's headless remains. "See? I know how to count!"

Ecard spoke from behind the elf. "That was spectacular."

Belac turned toward the hanging cage. "Not really." He thought back on the fight and how the first briar man had grabbed his arm. Then he recalled the blood that had stained the prisoners' cages. "I don't think they are allowed to hurt us."

"From where I was sitting, it appeared as though they were attempting to do exactly that," Ecard argued.

Walking around the dead briar men, Belac made his way to the hanging cage. "I think they were just trying to stop me from getting away." He held up the ceremonial dagger. "If I had not had this, they would have been able to just hold me down until Talia returned." He halted next to the bottom hinge of the cage's door. "Not being allowed to kill us is going to make it a lot harder for them to do their job." *If I am right...*

"Be that as it may," Ecard glanced at the slain briar men outside his cage, "the way you delt with those things was truly spectacular."

Belac shrugged the complement away. *Dead is dead. Who cares if it's fancy?* That much of what he had done had been unintentional did little for his pride. He wedged the dagger into the top of the henge, sliding the blade between the vines and the bars.

Ecard spoke softly in shame. "I should not have doubted you, Belac."

Belac hammered the dagger in deeper with his palm. "Let's just focus on getting out of here."

Ecard ignored the redirection. "I will not doubt you again."

Belac grinned. "That would make you the wisest human in the world," he said jokingly. Then he pulled back on the dagger's hilt and lowered his weight onto it. The blade cut through the vines with less effort now that his leverage was improved.

Ecard's words became almost reverent. "You would do that for me?" There was something fragile in his voice. "You would show me the way to wisdom?"

Belac laughed. "Right now, let's just worry about finding the way to freedom."

As Belac worked on cutting through the vines, he considered what it would be like to have a disciple. In his mind, he saw Ecard following him around, attempting to decipher some hidden meaning in every mundane thing he did. *If I stubbed my toe, he would probably think it was a demonstration on how pain is an essential element of life.* He imagined his followers growing in number. *The Order of the Stubbed Toe.*

Belac laughed to himself as he toyed with the idea of making them all dress in silly outfits. *I could have Ecard wear a big leather hat shaped like a giant shoe.* The dagger cut through the last of the lower vines, and Belac fell onto his backside. The shock to his tailbone ended his amusement. *Stupid human. Distracting me with his crazy hat...*

Ecard leaned toward the bars. "Are you alright?"

Belac nodded and stood. He gripped the side of the cage and hopped up onto it, placing his feet on the lower bars. The motion caused the cage to swing gently back and forth. Standing on the side of the cage, he stabbed the dagger into the top of the upper hinge.

The swaying of the cage seemed to make Ecard uneasy. "Are you sure that is safe?"

Holding on to the cage with his left hand, Belac hammered the palm of his right hand down on the hilt of the dagger. "Do you want to stay in there?" He grabbed the dagger's hilt and then began tugging it toward himself and down. "Because, I can leave you in there if you want."

Ecard was quick to shake his head. "No. That is quite all right." He nodded to the hinge. "Please proceed."

"Are you sure?" Belac asked as he cut into the vines. "If you stay, you can marry the pretty elf girl that likes to play with knives."

"I dare say, I will pass on that," Ecard said, sounding ready to be out of his cage.

Nine

Belac waved to be followed. "Let's go." Though the quarter moon shone through the tree leaves, the elf's gesture could barely be seen.

"We cannot go that way," Ecard voiced in discontent. "We should flee into the woods."

Belac shook his head. "We still have more people to set free."

"If we escape into the woods, we may be able to find safety before our disappearance is discovered," Ecard reasoned. "We could then gather aid and return."

Belac shook his head again. "We can't just leave those people to be butchered." *Besides, every one of those humans that dies is one more briar man that we will have to fight later.*

Ecard's cowardness showed on his face despite the shadows of the night. "But, we could escape…"

Belac wondered if the fallen lord would ever stop disappointing him. "Go." He nodded to the forest behind the man. "You might escape, but you will never feel free."

Ecard looked at the elf through tears of indecision.

Belac stood taller. "You said you would not doubt me."

Ecard closed his eyes and then nodded. When he opened them, his choice had been made. "I am with you."

Belac grinned. *Maybe there is hope for the man yet.* "Then, let's go be heroes." He began to turn around, but stopped halfway and looked back. "Quietly," he added with a nod.

Ecard nodded his agreement. "Forgive my reticence, Belac. I would not have forsaken you." He took a deep breath and then began to confess, "It is simply that I do not want to…"

"Get married?" Belac supplied, saving the man what little remained of his pride. "Don't worry. I don't want to get married either. We are still going to escape. We just need to take some people with us."

Belac led Ecard around the rise in the terrain and onto the forest path on the other side. Light flickered from the tents ahead to their left, drawing the elf's attention. Cautiously, he moved into the trees to get a better view as he approached. *If Talia and Kaelem are at the tents, they can't be at the other cages.* He searched for movement as he crept closer.

Beyond four large tents, an open fire burned on the far side of the camp. Yellowy light danced on the drab green canvas and through the center of the camp. Closer to Belac, on the side of the camp opposite the fire, a matching pavilion stood with its walls rolled up. Next to boxes covered with tan cloth, a solitary glass lamp sat on a small desk. The soft light of the lamp shone on a pair of scabbarded swords wrapped in black leather straps.

Belac halted in his tracks. *My swords!* He could not leave the swords. Reclaiming the starmetal sword was almost as important to him as escape. *They are just sitting there!* It was an opportunity he could not pass up. *All I need to do is sneak over there and take them.*

Belac turned around and spoke in a hushed voice. "New plan." He proceeded to explain and formulate the plan in unison. "You stay here. I am going to sneak over there and grab something."

"You cannot be serious!" Ecard hissed back.

Belac held up a hand to forestall further argument. "It can't be helped." He glanced over his shoulder toward the camp and then looked back to the frightened man. "If I can get in and out without being seen, I will."

Ecard attempted to argue. "But…"

Belac spoke over the man. "If someone sees me, I will make some noise and then try to draw them away." He nodded as his plan began to come together. "With any luck, they will send the briar men after me. If that happens," he gestured to the path behind the man, "follow that trail until you get to some giant cages. They should still have all the humans in one cage. It will be easy to find." He held out the ceremonial dagger hilt first. "Get those people out."

Ecard accepted the dagger, but balked at the plan. "Will there not be guards?"

Belac nodded. *I should have mentioned that.* "Six. They're briar men. When I was there, they were all staring at the cage." *As much as something can stare without eyes.* "If they don't chase after me, you should not have any problem sneaking up on them. Depending on what their orders are, you might be able to kill them all without any of them fighting back." *I really would not expect that though.* "If you do have to fight them, try to stay close to the cage. The people inside might help you if they can."

The terseness of the information triggered Ecard's military bearing. His face hardened and he gave a single nod.

Belac tapped the man in the chest. "Make sure you stab them here."

Not wanting to give Ecard a chance to lose his nerve, Belac turned away and began moving closer to the camp. *Sneak in. Get the swords. Sneak out.* As he crept through the trees, he caught himself fixating on the swords. *I need to study the trap, not the bait.* He forced himself to look away from the pavilion and scan the tents instead.

Belac paused in the shadows of the tree line. *Maybe they went to sleep…* He shook his head. *They would not leave a lamp lit and a campfire burning if they were in bed.* Intuition told him that the spriggans did not sleep. *I can't just wait here forever.* He crouched low and stepped away from the trees.

Don't see me. Don't see me. Don't see me. Belac attempted to balance speed and stealth as he hurried toward his swords. He felt safer as soon as he stepped under the canopy of the pavilion, despite knowing that the light would make him more likely to be seen. *Almost there...*

As Belac neared the lamplit desk, he saw that the two swords had been lain on top of an open book next to an ink well. *What are they doing to my swords?* The book appeared to be some kind of journal or log. He thought that the flowing script might be Elven. Then something moved in the camp.

Belac turned away from the desk to find Talia standing outside the far right tent. She was staring at him like she did not believe that he was really there. She tilted her head as if confused by his surprising apparition.

Belac lurched into action. He turned back to the desk, grabbed his swords with his left hand, and then the handle of the lamp with his right. He spun around to face the camp with his arms held out to his sides. "I'm immortal!" he shouted and then turned again, throwing the glass lamp into the pavilion.

The lamp shattered against the desk, setting it on fire and splashing oil onto the nearby boxes. Flames spread across the oil with eager intensity.

Talia shrieked in unintelligible fury.

Belac ran.

I'm a master of distraction! Belac rushed into the trees and proceeded to lead any pursuit away from the human prisoners. His left foot snagged on the shadowed undergrowth, and he pitched forward. He tried to catch himself with his right foot, but the maneuver turned into a hop that sent him flying headfirst through the forest. Reaching out with his right hand, he palmed a tree trunk in a desperate attempt to halt his fall. Instead of stopping, the elf was spun to his left. He clutched his swords to his bare chest just before his left shoulder slammed into the ground. His momentum carried him into a clumsy half roll, and then he was back on his feet.

Acutely aware that he was running for his life, Belac continued to flee at a hazardous speed. *I just have to make it to the road.* Somehow, the road had come to represent freedom to him; a path to escape. That he would be more exposed on a road had yet to occur to him. *Where is the road?!*

A river of moonlight shown through the trees ahead. *I knew I would find the road!* Belac burst from the tree line and onto the road. His right foot tripped in a depression, and he spilled onto the hard packed dirt. *Stupid road!* He got his feet under himself and then stood. Pain lanced through his ankle where he had twisted it in the fall.

Belac turned away from the direction that he thought would lead back to the ruins. *I need to keep moving.* He limped for a couple of paces and then forced himself to jog. Belac heard Talia's voice in his mind as he recalled her telling him that the briar men would hunt him down and then the spriggans would tear off his arms and legs. *I just hope she sends the briar men that are guarding the humans.*

Belac reconsidered. *I guess that is not the only thing I hope for. I also hope that the briar men don't catch me. And that the spriggans don't tear off my arms and legs. And I hope that Talia doesn't cut out my heart.* He thought for a moment. *Maybe I should hope that two beams of light shoot down from the sky and set Talia and Kaelem on fire.* He nodded to himself. *There are all kinds of things that I can hope for.*

Belac continued to catalog his hopes as he ran. Only most of them were completely selfish.

Ten

Rent dirt scattered noisily across the surface of the road behind him. Stumbling as he ran, Belac looked over his shoulder. Glowing red hate stared back. Belac grit his teeth and ran faster. He remembered rapping his knuckles on a spriggan's face. *I really hope that this is not the same one.*

Running through moonlight, Belac raced toward freedom. Behind him, dirt was torn from the road as the spriggan gave chase. Belac could feel the horrific construct of wood and malice moving closer to him despite his frantic pace. Though he could endure the pain in his ankle, Belac knew that he would not be able to outrun the savagery of the spriggan.

Belac glanced over his shoulder again and called out, "You were always my favorite!"

The fury in the abhorrent red stair convinced Belac that the spriggan was the same one that had ushered him to and from the ruins. *I need a new plan.* He scanned the tree line on either side of the road. *The forest would slow me more than it would the tree monster.* The road curved gently into the distance ahead. Regardless of what might be hidden behind forest and perspective, the spriggan would catch him long before he ever learned what was there.

Absent the prospect of sanctuary, Belac saw only one alternative. He stopped running. The steel blade of his dwarf-sword slid free from its scabbard as he turned to face the spriggan. "I am not food," he intoned in Elven. Though the broad blade had never been meant to chop wood, Belac was determined.

The spriggan charged at Belac without slowing. Red light shown on the elf's naked skin. Basked in glowing hate, Belac's hardened visage was as unyielding as the spriggan's. *Let's find out if you bleed.*

The monstrous claws of the spriggan's right hand raked at Belac's head. The elf ducked down and pivoted on his left foot toward the charging horror. Hooked claws swept past his head as he dodged out of the spriggan's path. Continuing the turn, Belac swung his sword at where he expected the spriggan to be behind him. Shock shot through the elf's arm as steel hacked into solid wood. A small chunk of the spriggan's thigh flew into the air as Belac's sword reverberated in his hand. Dirt ground under the spriggan's misshapen feet as it slid to a stop. Turning to its left as it changed direction, the spriggan clawed backward with its lead arm.

Pain flashed in Belac's right ankle as he stepped left and under the spriggan's attack. With his weight on his left foot, Belac whipped his sword up in an angled backhanded slash. The blade scored across the spriggan's wooden chest, but did nothing to stall the monster's advance. Stepping forward, the spriggan reached for Belac with the massive claws of its right hand. As Belac pivoted away on his right foot, he swung his sword down and to his left. The blade struck the spriggan's arm, but his ankle gave out under him. Twisting as he fell, Belac rolled away from the spriggan before coming to his knuckles and knees.

The spriggan continued to bear down on the elf, its red hate illuminating their fight. Belac rolled away and onto his feet. He turned his left side toward the spriggan and pointed his sword in the opposite direction.

Silently, Belac attempted to gauge which foot the spriggan would be stepping with when it came into range. *Left.*

As the spriggan's foot stepped down, it raked at Belac with its left hand. Belac pivoted forward while stepping to the side with his right foot. Leaning away from the path of the claws, he swung his sword left as a counterbalance. Grimacing against the pain in his right ankle, he stepped back with his left leg as he swept the sword up over his head. Transferring his weight to his left foot, Belac brought the blade down in an arc as the spriggan raked back out with the claws of its left hand.

Though aimed at the thick roots that composed the spriggan's elbow, the sword hacked into its forearm slightly below the joint. The blade sunk deeply into the hard wood, lodging itself into the spriggan's arm. Pushed and then pulled by his grip on the hilt of the sword, Belac was lifted from his feet as the spriggan slung him backward. While being whipped through the air, he lost his grip on the sword and was flung down the center of the road.

Belac landed awkwardly, but was able to turn his fall into a sprawling roll. As he came to his feet, the spriggan turned around, Belac's sword still imbedded in its arm. Hate poured from the spriggan's eyes as it glared at the indomitable elf.

Belac looked from the dwarf-sword trapped in the spriggan's arm to the scabbarded starmetal sword he carried in his own left hand. Red light gleamed on the sword's blood drop pommel and the stylized claws that formed its cross-guard. *I am not supposed to use this.* The sword was a specialized tool, forged for a particular purpose. *Serath said that it's not even ready.* The sword was meant to slay dragons. *What if I break it?*

Belac reached over with his free hand and thumbed the snap that secured the starmetal sword's narrow cross-guard. *The sword does not matter if I'm dead.* He pulled the milky white blade from its scabbard. *Only I can use the sword.* Alone, bare chested in the night, Belac locked stares with madness and hate.

The elf dropped his empty scabbards onto the hard packed road and then ran at the spriggan. Pain hammered into his ankle, but he pushed himself onward. The spriggan stepped forward and reached for Belac with the claws of its right hand. Belac grabbed the spriggan's wrist with his left hand and then stepped onto the spriggan's thigh. Turning away to his right, the elf released his grip as his back rolled across the outside of the spriggan's outstretched arm. The forest spun around Belac as he twirled through the air behind the spriggan. Roaring as he turned, Belac swung his sword in a horizontal arc that slashed through the side of the spriggans neck.

Belac landed on the road facing away from the spriggan. He stumbled forward three full paces as the spriggan fell to the ground behind him. He turned around and looked down at the spriggan's severed head. Red light still shown from the hate filled eyes. He glanced at the sword in his hand. *Wow, this thing is sharp!*

Belac pointed his sword at the spriggan's head. "You should have taken that holiday." He could feel the thing hating him.

Belac limped over to the severed head and kicked dirt into its eyes. Dust hung in the red light above the road. He then limped around the spriggan's inanimate body, careful not to get too close. He remembered how the headless briar man had risen to its feet.

Belac retrieved his empty scabbards and then sheathed the starmetal sword. After snapping the cross-guard's securing strap closed, he unwrapped the baldrics from their scabbards. He dropped the dwarf-sword's scabbard back onto the ground, and then slipped the starmetal sword's baldric over his head.

Belac looked at the decapitated spriggan. *...I chopped off the glowing part...* The spriggans did not strike Belac as creatures of cunning. *I don't think it can get up.* He knew that more fighting was to come, and he did not want to rely solely on the starmetal sword.

As he moved over to where the dwarf-sword was stuck in the spriggan's arm, Belac noted a growing numbness in his ankle. It was almost as if the pain itself was getting tired. He tried to put the injury out of his mind. *I need to get my sword back.* He took hold of the dwarf-sword's hilt with both hands, groaning as he braced his left foot against the spriggans arm.

Wood squeaked as Belac worked the sword's blade back and forth. Pushing and pulling, he wrestled with the steel until it came free. With the sudden release, he was forced to shuffle back on his left foot to keep his balance. *I am taking too long.* He glanced in the direction of the encampment. *I need to get out of here before something else comes to kill me.* He stepped over to the dwarf-sword's scabbard.

Belac bent and picked up the discarded scabbard. *I bet Talia did not expect me to survive the spriggan.* He tapped the scabbard against his thigh to knock loose any debris that might be inside. *She also has to deal with the fire.* He shook out the scabbard and then sheathed his sword. *I don't know what was under all those leather tarps, but they wouldn't have covered it up unless it was important.* The glow of the burning pavilion could still be seen above the trees.

Again, Belac heard Talia's voice in his mind telling him that it would be the briar men that tracked him down. *If I keep following the road, they won't even need to track me.* He shook his head. *There is no way I can outrun them with my foot messed up.* He looked toward the tree line. *My only chance is the forest.* Then he recalled how he had almost broken his neck running through the shadows. *The trees block too much of the moon's light.*

Belac smiled. He slung his dwarf-sword onto his back and limped over to the spriggan's severed head. He picked the head up by its crown of pointed roots and turned the wooden face toward him. Red eyes glared balefully at the elf.

Belac's smile broadened. "You work for me now."

Belac spun the head around and aimed the glowing eyes away from himself. His first impulse was to flee into the forest on the side of the road opposite the encampment. He wanted to be as far away from the ruins and the crazy elves as he could get. *That is probably what they would expect me to do.* He turned back toward the encampment. *But they wouldn't expect me to double back.*

Belac began limping toward the tree line. *And this way, I can make sure that the humans escaped.*

Eleven

Using the spriggan's severed head to light his way, Belac limped through the forest. His plan had been to circle around the encampment and approach from the rear. However, as he had stumbled through the shadowed trees, he had lost his sense of where the encampment was. The fires of the burning pavilion no longer glowed in the night, and without that distant beacon, his sense of direction had become less and less sure. Though the moon still shone, the silvery beams that cut through the trees did little to help Belac find his way. Without the glowing red light of the spriggan's eyes, he may have admitted that he was lost.

"I'm not lost," Belac lied to the spriggan's head.

Belac continued to limp in the direction that he thought of as forward. He narrowed his eyes at the back of the severed head. He could feel it being smug at him.

Belac shook the head. "You think that's funny?" he asked threateningly.

Belac spun the spriggan's head around to face him. A forever disapproving, feminine countenance stared back at him with hate in its eyes. Belac and the spriggan glared at each other in the red light.

Belac let go of the head. "Oops," he said unconvincingly.

The spriggan's head fell to the ground and then rolled face first into the dirt, its crown of roots landing on the tips of the elf's boots. Careful with his injured ankle, Belac stood on his left foot and shoved the head away with his right. The severed head rolled through the shadows, throwing flashes of red light into the forest until it collided with the base of a tree. The evergreen's trunk shown red as the spriggan stared up along the side.

Belac limped over to the glowing tree and pointed down at the severed head. "Now, behave," he admonished. "Or I am going to carve you into a chamber pot."

Belac bent down and grabbed one of the roots that made up the spriggan's crown. Standing, he aimed its eyes away from himself. *Uhm… Which way was I going?* He guessed at a direction and began limping onward. While it may have been his imagination, he thought that the spriggan's red light had grown brighter.

Eventually, the elf came to the edge of a river that flowed freely to his left. Moonlight glistened off the water and illuminated the far bank. Though Belac thought that he could have swam to the other side, he did not want to make the attempt with his injured ankle. The gentle sound of the water's course betrayed a perilous depth hidden beneath the glittering surface. Despite the possible hazards, the elf saw opportunity.

"I knew I would find a way!" Belac tossed the spriggan's head up into the air and then caught it with its glowing red eyes facing him. With his right hand, he pinched its wooden nose and shook the head side to side. "Who's a good spriggan?" he asked as if speaking to a favored hound. Then he dropped the head on the ground beside him.

Belac looked out over the river and listened to the sounds of the night as he considered his situation. After a calm moment of relative peace, the elf nodded to himself. *I think Talia lied to me.* It was the only explanation that made sense to him. *I don't think the briar men can track me.* He thought that the briar men's limited autonomy would be insufficient for a task as complex as tracking. *It's the spriggans that I need to worry about.*

Belac turned away from the river and looked down at the spriggan's severed head. "You can track me."

Belac knew that there were at least three more spriggans. He did not think Talia or Kaelem would leave themselves without a guardian, but that would still leave at least one spriggan that could be hunting on its own. *The spriggans move fast.* Belac scanned the shadows of the forest. *If I see a red light, it might already be too late to get away.* He decided that he needed to keep moving.

Belac reconsidered the severed head. He did not know how the spriggans communicated, but it was obviously magical in nature. *Anyone that wants to track me, has to follow a trail.* He frowned at the spriggan's head. *But they don't need to track me, if this thing is telling them where I am.* His concern began to grow. *Even if they only have three more spriggans, Talia and Kaelem might want me enough to come after me themselves.* He did not think he would survive if they caught him. *They might even be able to use some kind of magic to locate the spriggans.*

Belac bent down and picked up the spriggan's severed head. *This thing could be leading them straight to me.* He gripped the head by one of its roots and pointed a finger at its face. "I have a new job for you."

Belac turned and threw the head as hard as he could. It soared out over the river and then splashed into the silvery water. Red light flashed above the flowing surface as the head bobbed up and down. Carried by the steady current, the head continued to bob in the water as it drifted away.

Belac gave a mock salute to his improvised decoy. "You are still my favorite!" he called out after it.

Once the wooden head had floated out of sight, Belac began to climb down into the river. *This way, if the spriggan has been telling them where I am, they won't know where I've gone.* He grimaced at the unpleasantly crisp water as he lowered himself from the bank. *If they have to track me like normal people, my trail should make it obvious that I'm hurt.* His left boot sank down into a muddy river bottom. *Most any injured person is going to want to use the flow of the current to help them escape.*

Standing chest high in the water, Belac turned to face upriver. *Whether they follow my trail, or just follow the spriggan's head, they should be led downstream.* Using the side of the bank on his right for support, he began the arduous process of pushing himself upstream.

The cool of the water seemed to seep into Belac's injured ankle as he traversed along the bank. Before long, the numbness bled away and the pain returned. What began as icy needles, soon became cold fire. Though he tried to avoid using his right foot, he could not keep himself from kicking in the water. He wiped clammy sweat from his brow and continued to struggle against the current.

The river bent and the moon moved in the sky, leaving half the river black. As the shadows slowly stretched across the water, Belac felt like it was despair itself reaching for him. *I can't just keep crawling through the water. I am moving too slow. If they catch me like this…* He thought of blood dripping from hooked, wooden claws. *I need a new plan.*

Belac's eyes began searching the tree line for a path that would lead him away. While he did not expect to find a paved road, he thought a deer trail would be easy enough for him to spot. He continued to search as he moved up the river, but only found himself becoming frustrated. *Really?!* He glared at the forest. *There are no animals that need to drink from the river?*

An owl hooted in the night.

Belac narrowed his eyes. *Owls can fly.* "Cheater."

The absent owl seemed unoffended.

"You just wait," Belac grumbled to himself as he trod through the water. "Once all this is over, I am coming back here. I am going to build a cabin, and I am going to breed owls." He nodded to himself. "A whole herd of them!" He swept his arm out in front of himself.

The owl offered no response.

Belac began pointing with his finger as if talking to someone who was not there. "And then, I am going to pluck out all their feathers!" His grumblings had taken on volume. "And I am going to take those feathers, and I am going to use them to make a bunch of giant feather pillows." He continued to point aggressively at no one. "And then, I am going to sit on those pillows and watch my herd of owls march back and forth to the river," he began to shout, "and make me a trail!"

Fuming, Belac saw that the bank ahead steadily rose high above the water line. His sight would be blocked by a wall of dirt. He could not help but feel like the ground had been shaped purely to vex him. *It's a conspiracy!* He pressed onward, hoping that he would be able to find a path farther up the river.

As the bank rose and the forest was blocked from view, Belac considered what the perspective would be like from above. *However they go about tracking me, they are not going to do it from the water.* He was sure that if his pursuers searched for him upriver, they would do so from the dry side of the bank. It would not only allow them to travel faster, it would make it easier for them to spot any signs of where he may have exited the water.

An old, gnarled tree caught Belac's attention. Hanging off the edge of the raised bank, the tree had long fed from the river below. Undercut by erosion, thick roots protruded from the dirt above and then stretched down into the water. *The river must have washed out so much of the dirt underneath the tree, that some of the dirt from above the undercut fell down.* The muddy space behind the roots created a watery cage that reminded the elf of the prison he had only recently escaped.

Belac searched for movement behind the roots as he approached. *No one would see me in there.* He thought that as long as nothing else already occupied the hidden shelter, he could rest there until sunrise. *Maybe when the sun comes up, I will be able to see where I am going in the woods.* Moonlight showed him nothing but mud behind the hanging roots.

Belac climbed up the side of the bank and crawled into the undercut. Once inside, he wriggled into a sitting position with his back against the dirt wall and his boots in the water. In his mind, he heard Rolan's voice telling him that he needed to let his boots air out at night. *Bossy dwarf.* Though there was little room to maneuver in the muddy cave, Belac turned to the side and repositioned his feet so that they were out of the water and resting on the comparatively dry ledge. He took a deep breath, exhausted. *I really just want to go to sleep.*

Rolan's voice spoke in his mind again. *"Your feet are going to rot."*

Lifting his left knee up to his chest, Belac removed his boot. *I swear... If that owl steals my boots...* After relaxing his leg, he poured the water out of his boot and set it next to the dirt wall. Raising his right knee was simple enough, but removing the boot hurt so much that he almost decided to just leave it on. He poured the water out of the boot and then tossed it next to the other.

Though his ankle was swollen, it did not look as bad as he had feared. *The cold water probably helped a little with the swelling.* He probed at the ankle gently. *I think it will be fine.* He laid his leg out gingerly and then closed his eyes. *But I refuse to considerer any of this 'lucky.'*

Twelve

The elf awoke with his scabbarded swords pressed uncomfortably into his back. Despite the discomfort, he was immediately reassured by their presence. While he had come to respect both swords as weapons, the starmetal sword was invaluable. More than merely utility, the starmetal sword was a responsibility that he had committed himself to. Stiffness had set into his entire body, but the early morning air was cool enough to encourage him to get moving. When his azure blue eyes opened to the gray of the morning, the first thing he saw was his own bare feet.

"Thieving owls," Belac mumbled disparagingly.

Dried mud cracked on his skin as Belac prepared to chase after the feathery menace. His left hand landed on one of the boots beside him. *Oh. Right.* He shook his head and then relaxed. *I probably would not have been able to catch the owls barefooted anyway.*

He yawned, knowing that he needed to get up. A tiny, long legged bug flew into his mouth and got stuck on the back of his tongue. His yawning turned into a hacking fit as he attempted to spit out the diminutive intruder. He reached into his mouth with dirty fingers and ran them across the back of his tongue. The taste of mud almost made him gag.

"Gauh!" Belac spat into the river. He was fairly certain that he had swallowed the bug.

Belac pointed angrily at his stomach. "Serves you right! Now you are going to die in a pit of acid!"

Belac spat again and then began to twist and scootch until he had his feet in the river. The chill of the water reminded him that his ankle was still injured. He leaned forward and began rubbing his feet, cleaning them in the river as best he could without soap or a brush. The swelling in his right ankle had gone down as he slept. He rotated his foot, testing its range of movement. Though still sore, he thought that he could walk on it without harming himself further.

The elf reached back and grabbed one of his boots. Worried that something may have crawled inside while he slept, Belac shook the boot out over the river. In his mind, he imagined an irate crab poking its head out and then snapping at him with oversized pinchers.

"I don't care what's in there." Belac slapped the heel of the boot for good measure. "It's my boot."

Belac slipped his left foot into the boot and then tucked it under his right thigh. *Why does everything want to steal my boots?* After ensuring the vacancy of his other boot, he carefully pressed his right foot into it. The injured ankle silently protested, but its mild swelling did not prevent it from fitting into the boot.

Grumbling inarticulately, the elf rolled onto his hands and knees. He crawled backward over crusted mud until he slid down into the river. The fresh chill of the flowing water stole what was left of his morning grogginess. His left foot sank into watery mud and then he pushed himself away from the wall of roots.

Belac dropped below the surface of the water and let the current carry him downstream. While both relaxing and invigorating, he soon remembered that he needed to go the other way. *But do I?* His head popped up out of the water as he set his uninjured foot in the mud. He leaned back against the steady flow of the river and reconsidered his options.

He did not know where he was or what all was in the area. He did not know if Ecard had freed the human prisoners or even if the fallen lord were still alive. *It's not like the man is overly reliable.* What Belac did know, was that the elves at the encampment would need to be delt with regardless. *Running away does not make any sense unless I am running to something also.* Belac did not think it was likely that they would search for him upriver. However, if he fled in that direction, he would have no idea where he was headed. *If they did try to track me upstream, they would probably find me. And if they found me, they would probably catch me.*

He attempted to predict where his pursuers would be now that the night had passed, but there was simply too much that he did not know. His best guess was that they would either be following his trail through the forest, or they would already be looking for him farther down the river. *Either way, I should have a window.* He nodded to himself. *I can float downstream for a while, then I can crawl out and search for the ruins. If I can't find the ruins, maybe I can find a road or something.*

Belac untied his hair and then dunked his head under the water again. He scrubbed at his scalp and ran his fingers through the thick strands of his long, black hair. After coming up for air and resubmerging himself twice, he resurfaced feeling like he had removed the worst of the tangles. Next, he unslung his dwarf-sword and rubbed the mud off of it with a quick, perfunctory manner. Then he drew the blade and swished it through the water. *Seems like the scabbard did a good job of keeping the mud off the blade.* He sheathed the sword and returned it to his back. *I can worry about rust later.*

Belac considered taking the time to clean his starmetal sword and to bathe himself more thoroughly, but he decided that it was more important that he get moving. *The river should wash off most of the mud for me.* He raised his foot and let the water carry him downstream. As the wall of dirt to his left declined, the light of the morning sun began to glow brighter. When the eastern forest came into view, terror gripped the elf's heart.

Sunrise shown over the tops of the trees like fire. Standing, eyes wide, Belac stared at the dark green of the looming forest, but in his mind, he saw fire in the night. He could feel the heat of the flames and hear the screams of his friends. He closed his eyes to shut out all the green, but the memory did not relent.

He had never met humans before. He had known that they were not supposed to be in that part of the forest, but they had been kind to Belac in a way he had never experienced. They had not seen a lady's bastard son; to them, he had been an alien creature of beauty and grace. Belac had been educated on how stupid and destructive humans were, but no one had ever told him how friendly they could be. The females had been especially attentive.

Belac had danced, and drank, and listened to incredible stories of faraway lands. In exchange, he had told them of himself and what his home had been like. He had felt more than accepted, he had felt welcomed. It was one of the happiest times of his life.

Then the fires had come. Belac had been struck on the head in the chaos, but he could still remember the screams as he had crawled away disoriented. He remembered the feel of the humans' fear as it fed on death and confusion. He remembered the smell of ash and burning blood. And he remembered flames so bright that they had looked green among the leaves.

He had awoken hidden under a low, rocky outcrop. The world around him had been blackened. The trees had been burned to ash, and whatever remained of the humans had been scattered in the air. He had been alone in a quiet wasteland of scorched soil. Humans were not supposed to be in that part of the forest.

I still wonder if it could have been a dragon. Belac shook his head, dispelling the images. *It could have been anything.* He opened his eyes. *And it's not here now.*

As Belac turned away from the sunrise, his hair got caught on one of his swords. "Aieow!"

Belac reached back and freed his hair from the cross-guard of his dwarf-sword. *Stupid, traitor sword!* He gathered the rest of his hair and tied it in a knot behind his head. While an Elven knot was more difficult to tie with wet hair, he did not want his hair to get pulled again. He wished for a ribbon that he could use to tie his hair back, but then he pictured a briar man decorated with pink and yellow ribbons. *I think Talia may have ruined ribbons for me.*

Thirteen

Angled forward in the water, arms outstretched for balance, Belac glided with the current of the river. Keeping his right leg bent backward, the toe of his left boot sank down into the river's muddy shelf as he propelled himself onward. Even with the aid of the water's flow, the elf was beginning to tire. His left hip ached from overuse and his fingertips felt bled dry. However, if his plan were to have any chance of success, he needed to hurry.

As he raced downstream, Belac realized that there was a problem with his plan. *I don't know how far I need to follow the river.* He did not allow the complication to slow his progress as he considered it. *It is not like there is going to be a road sign showing me where to go.* He imagined a wooden signpost with an arrow on it that read, 'This way, Stupid.'

I would not be able to call it a 'road sign,' anyway. He wondered what such a sign might be referred to as. *A river sign?* He shrugged mentally. *Whatever people want to call them, they sure would be useful.* In his mind, he saw mischievous owls flying down the river and altering the signs before he could get there. *Stupid owls think they're funny.*

Once again, the banks on either side of the river began to incline away from the water. Though the river narrowed noticeably, Belac kept to the muddy shelf on the eastern side.

The speed of the water's flow increased, but not to such a degree that it troubled the elf. What concerned him was the magical bridge that he was fast approaching. Seemingly grown in place, the bridge spanned the river on the trunks of trees that had risen from the water. Draped in vibrant greenery, the bridge appeared to be alive. To the elf, the bark encased pillars of the bridge looked like fangs.

Water echoed around Belac as he glid between the high walls of dirt and vegetation, the current pulling him toward the magical bridge. *The forest is trying to eat me!* He closed his eyes as he passed under the bridge, its magical nature only making him more sure that it was a trap. *I don't want to be food!* After escaping the wonderous bridge unscathed, Belac glanced left and right to see if anyone had witnessed his cringe.

Belac turned in the water and gazed back to the bridge. *That thing has to lead to the ruins. I must be getting close.* He immediately doubted his own assessment. *The river is kind of loud here. I don't remember hearing the sound of a river while I was a captive.* His speed began to worry him. *If the river takes me too far away from the ruins, I may not be able to find them again.* Belac attempted to guess at where the encampment might be located. He could not be certain, but he no longer felt like the river was taking him where he wanted to go. He glanced up and to his left, debating whether or not he should climb out of the water. Every moment of indecision carried him farther down the river.

The river bent east, revealing a small lake that opened to the south. The early sun shown down on the lake's surface and scattered across its gentle waves. As the far side of the bank grew farther and farther away from him, Belac slowed in the water. The wall of dirt that lined the north side gradually moved away from the lake's edge, leaving behind a grassy shore. Standing on the tranquil shore with their heads stretched low, two does and a fawn drank from the shining waters. *I wonder if I could ride a deer…*

Belac waved in greeting as he waded closer to the deer. "Hello." *Please, don't run away.*

All three deer darted away from the elf at the same time. The fawn ran the wrong way and splashed into the lake. It kicked and bleated wildly as it tried to get back on the shore. *Poor thing. Maybe I should...* Something pulled the fawn down below the surface of the water.

Belac rushed to the shore. *The sneaky-lake-monster is going to eat me!* He pulled himself up and then crawled over the grass and moist soil on his hands and knees. He crawled quickly.

Once the elf was clear of the water's edge, he climbed to his feet and hobbled backward away from the lake. His right hand gripped the hilt of the dwarf-sword while his left held the scabbard in preparation to remove it from his back. There was no evidence of the fawn or what had taken it. The water looked as peaceful and inviting as it had only a moment before.

Belac halted his retreat, but kept his hands on his sword. "I'll make you a deal," he called out to the lake. "You stay in the water. And I will stay out."

The lake did not answer.

Belac nodded. "I am going to take that as a 'yes." He began to back away slowly. "I think you have made a really smart decision here," Belac assured the lake as he continued his withdraw.

Belac backed away until the sharp rise in terrain prevented him from going further without having to turn around and climb. He glanced over his shoulder. *It would be really nice to have this hill between me and the sneaky-lake-monster.* He returned his focus to the lake and watched for the sneaky-lake-monster as he proceeded along the base of the rise.

Belac was attempting to conceive of a way to blame the owls for his situation, when he happened upon a pass. He would have liked to believe that he would have noticed the narrow path leading from the lake to the pass, but he could not be sure. *I was being distracted by the owls.* He followed the path through the pass and away from the lake.

Once again surrounded by the green of the forest, Belac studied the cart tracks in the path he traveled. *This could be how they get water to the ruins.* He wondered how Talia and Kaelem delt with the danger of the lake. *They probably just make the spriggans and the briar men get the water. I bet the sneaky-lake-monster doesn't eat wood.* Thoughts of the spriggans reminded Belac that there were monsters other than the one in the lake.

Though he still favored his left leg, Belac was able to walk with less discomfort than he had expected. As he continued to follow the path, he began to notice the green around him more and more. *I feel like I am walking into a trap.* He was suddenly worried that the path would lead him to a clearing with Talia and Kaelem waiting for him patiently. Belac could almost feel the spriggans' wooden fingers digging into his arms. He shuddered. *I need to find a way to kill those things.* He considered the last spriggan he had fought. *I don't think that the rest of the spriggans are going to politely stand in a line and let me chop their heads off one at a time.*

Belac wondered what would happen if he simply killed Talia and Kaelem. *Would their army of tree monsters just die? Or would they be set free to kill everything around them in blind rage?* Belac remembered the feel of the spriggans restrained hate. *What restrains them?* He frowned. *I should probably just plan on having to kill all of them.*

A scent in the air caught the elf's attention. *Is that…* Ash and wet char, the fain traces drifted past him and toward the lake that he had left behind. Belac smiled. *I bet that is not just a doused campfire.* He remembered the blaze of the pavilion. *I hope I burned up all their booze.*

Stepping off the path, Belac moved toward the smell. He crept into the woods, climbing the sloping rise on his left. He did not know what was worse; not being able to see where he was going at night, or having to look at all the vibrant green in the light of day.

Why are all the forests green anyway? Why doesn't someone make one that is a different color? Why not blue? I like blue. It could have blue trees and blue grass... He attempted to picture what such a forest would look like. *I guess all the blue would blend in with the sky too much.*

Belac stopped. Beyond the trees ahead, the sun shone down on the wooden bars of a long cage. *I found them.* Though the cage appeared empty, he knew that there would be more cages to check. *There is no doubt that I'm in the right place now.* He crept forward, pausing periodically to listen for movement.

As he had expected, Belac found five more cages arranged next to the first. Dirty, malnourished men huddled in the center of the cage farthest away from where the elf had approached. Among the unclothed prisoners, one man stood full dressed. *At least I don't have to go searching for Ecard.* A briar man stood facing the prisoners at each corner of the cage and on both of the longer sides. Belac tested his ankle. *I can probably handle six of them.*

The elf removed his dwarf-sword, drew the blade, and then returned its scabbard to his back. He tongued one of his teeth as he reconsidered the cages. *I think I might be making a mistake.* He did not know where Talia and Kaelem were. *This could be a trap.* Belac bent at the knees slightly and looked up, half expecting to see a humongous cage poised to fall down and cover the entire clearing.

Though there was no visible trap, Belac decided that he should investigate more of the encampment. *It does not do any good to free the prisoners if they are just going to get slaughtered by crazy tree monsters.* Moving through the shadows of the forest, Belac stalked the edge of the clearing until he came to the path that would lead back to the two smaller cages. He halted at the tree line and considered the exposed path. *Should I go slowly? Or just dart across?*

After a moment of indecision, Belac decided to move cautiously. *Quick movement is more likely to get me noticed.* He stepped away from the concealment of the trees and crossed the path at a hurried walk. *Don't see me. Don't see me. Don't see me.*

Fourteen

With every step Belac took into the trees, he expected to find a pair of glowing red eyes hidden behind the trunk of an evergreen. *If I were on Team Evil Elf, I would leave behind at least one of the spriggans. Not only to guard the camp, but so that there would be something to control the briar men.* The elf's delicate fingers tightened on the hilt of his dwarf-sword. *This won't be much use against a spriggan.*

Though he could not have explained why, Belac did not want to use the starmetal sword more than he absolutely needed to. There were obvious reasons for his reluctance. The sword was created for the incredible purpose of slaying a dragon. The sword was incomplete. The sword was a tangible responsibility. And the sword was a symbol of trust. However, it was not these obvious reasons that kept the starmetal blade in its scabbard. Something inside the elf warned against the sword's use.

Belac wrestled briefly with his thoughts about the starmetal sword before finally deciding that if he saw a spriggan, he was going to throw his dwarf-sword at it and then draw the sharper blade. *I have a lot of things to worry about right now, but if I'm dead, none of the rest of it matters.* He crept to the edge of the camp and halted in the tree line.

Drab green tents blocked Belac's view of the pavilion, but he could still smell its burnt remains. The camp felt empty to him. *I don't think that they would hide a spriggan in one of the tents.* He stepped away from the trees and began walking toward the nearest of the tents. *I still need to check and see what's in them.* He stopped at the side of the tent and listened for movement inside. *Even if all the spriggans are gone, Talia or Kaelem might still be here.*

Once he was certain that he could hear nothing inside, Belac crept to the front of the tent and peeked around the corner. The flaps of all four tents were closed. Beyond the tents, soggy lumps of char were all that remained of the pavilion and whatever had been stored under it. *It's a shame the fire did not spread more.* He thought of the prisoners trapped in the nearby cage and then changed his mind. *Maybe I should just be glad that I didn't burn the humans to death.*

Belac rounded the corner of the tent and moved to the closed flap. Not wanting to touch the green canvas with his hands, he pushed the flap open with the blade of his sword. Though there was room inside for two iron bound trunks and a small stool, the majority of the interior was taken up by an oversized, four posted bed. In order to fit the bed under the tent, someone had sawn the thick posts short at uneven levels. The lack of care invested in the alterations imparted a disregard for the bed's lavishness.

Belac frowned at the bed. *And they made me sleep in a cage.* He let the canvas flap fall back into place and then he moved on to the next tent. Once again, he used his sword to push aside the drab green canvas flap. Despite housing a smaller bed, the interior of the second tent was arranged much the same as the first. A tidy pile of heather gray cloth lay in the back corner, but even that detail was not enough for Belac to determine which of the elven siblings owned the tent. He turned away and walked across the camp to the next tent.

I am going to be really upset if I find another bed in here. Belac opened the flap with the blade of his sword. *Who tries to recruit someone by making them sleep in a cage anyway?*

Unlike the other two tents, the third was set up as a dining room. A table sized for a small family had been pushed to the side on the right. *Only two chairs.* Until that moment, Belac had not even considered that Talia and Kaelem might be part of a larger group.

Belac glanced past a lidless box filled with tableware, and looked at the four open barrels of water lining the left wall. *Those men in the cage are going to be thirsty.* Belac had yet to formulate a workable plan, but he knew that he was not going back to the lake. *Me and the sneaky-lake-monster have a deal.* He dropped the canvas flap. *Once I free the humans, I can let them raid the camp while I figure out what to do next.* He nodded to himself as he hurried to the last tent. *Maybe I can find some food for them too.* The thought of food made his stomach grumble.

The final tent was fairly disappointing. Behind the drab canvas flap, a copper bathtub waited with another six barrels of water. Belac's sword slipped away from the flap. *No food.* He turned and gazed at the charred remains of what had once been a pavilion and leather covered stores. The elf found himself conflicted. *I'm glad that I burned up all the food for Team Evil Elf... But, I'm hungry.*

Belac turned to the dead campfire. *I wonder where they went.* He glanced over his shoulder and considered going to investigate the ruins. *No. I need to free the humans while I have a chance.* He walked past the shallow firepit and into the tree line.

No longer worried about hidden spriggans, Belac moved quickly through the woods. *If there were a spriggan here, it would have already tried to tear off my arms.* He stopped at the edge of the clearing and studied the prisoners' cage. None of the briar men had moved. Aside from the garnet glow pulsing faintly in each of their chests, the brushwood guards gave no indication that they were alive. *I wonder if those things are going to try to kill me this time.* Belac shrugged. *It is not like I am going to let them live if they don't try to kill me.*

Ecard appeared unharmed. *He looks less miserable than he did in the hanging cage.* Belac could not be sure, but it looked like the man was passing whispers with the other prisoners.

Maybe it's a human thing. He followed the thought as he appraised the huddled men. *Maybe they need to be with other humans so much that they are willing to suffer for it.* He considered the social drives of the other races. *Maybe it is just a people thing.*

Belac shook his head to clear his thoughts. *I need to focus on the task at hand.* He stepped away from the trees and began slowly walking up behind the briar man at the closest corner of the cage. He pulled his right hand back, preparing to thrust with his sword. He looked past the briar man and to the prisoners inside the cage. Disbelieving eyes gazed back.

Belac crossed his lips with the slender index finger of his left hand. *Blood on the cages. I don't know what the briar men will do once they realize I am here.* He positioned himself behind the briar man and then thrust the tip of his dwarf-sword into the center of its back. The blade ran through to the hilt, piercing out of the briar man's chest and sliding between the wooden bars of the cage. Belac pinned the dead briar man against the cage with his left forearm as he pulled his sword free. The movement became a spin to his right that brought him to face the briar man on the back corner of the cage. The briar man's featureless head turned toward Belac and then its body followed. *Yeah. That thing is going to try to kill me.*

Belac's ankle twinged as he darted forward and drove his sword into the briar man's pulsing chest. The blade of the dwarf-sword punctured the briar man's stolen heart, ending its pulsing glow. Belac bulled over the dead briar man and then ripped his sword free. Spinning, pain shot through Belac's ankle as he changed direction. The two briar men on the back side of the cage were already charging toward him, their wooden hands reaching out.

With little time to react, Belac swept his sword up in an angled back cut that slipped under the outstretched arms of the closer briar man. Sticks cracked as the blade hacked upward into the briar man's chest. Though the briar man's glowing heart stopped pulsing, Belac's sword was now lodged in its brushwood chest. And the other briar man was still coming.

Crouching down as he stepped closer with his left foot, Belac took the hilt of his sword in both hands and wrenched its blade inside the dead briar man. Pushing forward, he shoved the blade through the dead briar man. The sharpened steel protruded from the back of the corps and impaled the briar man that was rushing toward the elf. The combined weight of the dead briar men pulled Belac's sword down. His right leg buckled, and he collapsed onto the ground.

"Belac! Behind you!" Ecard called out in warning.

With a quick glance over his left shoulder, Belac confirmed the threat. A briar man, moving with their strange juddering speed, ran past the back corner of the cage. Belac brought his left foot up to the tangle of dead briar men and kicked himself away. His sword pulled free and then he rolled backward. Coming to his knees, he led with his right shoulder and swept his sword out in a back handed slash. The blade cut through the thorny vines that made up the briar man's right knee and then pulled Belac around and off balance.

Belac's left palm slammed onto the ground as the maimed briar man fell behind him. Scrambling away, Belac rose to his feet with the use of his left leg. He turned to his right and looked back as he continued to retreat. The last briar man had rounded the corner of the cage and was closing fast. Belac planted his left foot, arresting his movement as he turned right and raised his sword horizontally with its tip pointed at the oncoming briar man. With a lunge that pained his right ankle, he pierced the monster's pulsing heart. The now lifeless collection of sticks and thorned vines continued forward, sliding down the sword's blade. Rotating the sword as he turned to his left, Belac directed the dead briar man's fall to the ground.

Belac ripped his sword free as a crawling briar man reached for his leg. Frantically, he yanked his foot back and hopped away at the same time. In his haste, he lost his footing and spilled backward onto the ground. The briar man clawed its way after him as if swimming across the surface of the dirt. *No, no, no, no, no!* Azure eyes locked on the briar man, Belac began to scootch away. *It's too fast!*

Twisting onto his left hip, Belac pulled his feet back. With the weight of his upper body supported on his free hand, he thrust the dwarf-sword into the top of the briar man's left shoulder. Belac collapsed onto his chest as his blade slid into the briar man's torso. A clawing hand of bent sticks stopped a heartbeat away from the elf's face.

Was that six? Belac forced himself to look away from the wooden fingers. *I lost count!* He jerked his sword free and scanned for movement. All was still. Not even the humans in their cage moved more than to breathe. Belac counted his kills. *Yeah, okay. That was six.* Grimacing against the renewed discomfort in his ankle, Belac rose to his feet and faced the prisoners.

Ecard stood afore the others. His unkempt beard could not hide the broadness of his smile. "I told them you would come."

Fifteen

Cutting through vines proved easier with a sword than a ritual dagger. However, unlike the small dagger, the blade of Belac's dwarf-sword was too broad to fit between the wooden bars of the cage and the vines that made up the hinges of the door. So, he resorted to hacking at the vines. The whispering of the men inside the cage grew louder as he worked.

"…Free…"

"Not yet."

"Will be…"

"… Said he would come."

"… Another of them elfs."

"Not one of them."

"Looks like an elf to me."

"No… He's a prisoner too."

"The lord said he would come."

"He is getting us free."

Ecard spoke above the others. "Lord Belac is the wisest and bravest man I have ever met."

"But he's an elf," one of the other men protested.

Belac opened the door of the cage.

Ecard gestured grandly to the open door. "Yet even still, it was he who set us free."

Uninspired by the humans' behavior, Belac said, "You people can argue about me later. Right now, we need to get moving." He pointed his left hand at the tree line. "There is an empty camp on the other side of that hill. The two tents on the right have water. You can take whatever you want, but be quick about it. We need to be gone before they return with the spriggans."

The unclothed humans looked from Belac to Ecard.

Belac glared impatiently. "Or stay here and die." He turned away and began limping toward the hidden camp.

Dozens of bare feet tramped on hard dirt as the humans hurried from the cage.

The first of the men to pass by the elf pointed to the trees and asked, "That way?"

Belac nodded and continued to limp onward.

As a stream of freed prisoners moved past the elf, Ecard matched his pace. "I knew you would come."

Belac glanced at the Enevician lord. "How did you get caught again?"

Ecard gazed down at his boots. "I could not kill even one of them."

"The briar men?" Belac guessed. *I did not really expect you to try.*

Ecard nodded. "I stabbed one in the back, but the blade missed its heart."

In his mind, Belac attempted to recreate what had happened. "They did not try to kill you back?"

Ecard shook his head. "Two of them wrapped their arms and legs around me and held me on the ground until Kaelem had me thrown into the cage with the other prisoners. Little was hurt other than my pride."

Belac frowned. "Did the other humans not try to help you?"

Ecard shook his head again and then looked up. "The briar men would reach in and tear apart anyone that got too close to the bars of the cage."

Belac remembered the blood on the cages and how the men had cowered inside. *He should have used the blade to sharpen a stake and then thrown the dagger into the cage. That way, the humans could have worked on escaping while Ecard distracted the briar men.* Belac considered Ecard's ragged state. *But that is not what he needs to hear right now.*

Belac clapped the lord on the back. "It was brave of you to try."

Ecard's ensuing smile was as open as a child's. He said nothing for a moment, and then spoke in an amused tone. "Kaelem did seem rather displeased at discovering that his own dagger had been used in our escape."

Belac laughed. "I doubt he was any more happy that I set all his food on fire and then killed one of his spriggans."

"You slew one of those monsters?" Ecard asked in disbelief.

"Uhm…" Belac did not know if what he had done actually counted as a slaying. "Sort of." He shrugged. "I cut off its head and then threw it in a river." Then he added, "But I think the head part was still alive."

Ecard shook his head slowly. "Your plan worked perfectly."

I would not say it worked 'perfectly.' Belac was barely willing to call it a plan. "We still haven't escaped yet. We need to find a way out of this forest."

As he entered the campsite's clearing, Belac saw that the tents were no longer there. The mob of humans had pulled down the structures and were in the process of tearing apart the canvas. *Are they using their teeth?* For reasons he did not fully understand, Belac was troubled by the speed at which the humans were able to demolish the campsite. He stopped beside the unlit firepit and watched the men pillage.

Unconcerned by the display, Ecard continued the conversation. "As to that. The men think it would be best if we were to travel east. Once we are free of the forest, we can make our way south to Gofell. There, we could find the safety of numbers."

Belac agreed with the proposal. However, safety was not his primary objective. "They have to be stopped, Ecard."

"The Elves?" Ecard asked.

Belac nodded gravely. *This is not how elves should behave.* "What is happening here is not something we can ignore. We need to get these men to safety, but then we have to rally support."

"Support for what?" Ecard inquired, confused.

Belac met the man's eyes. "War."

Ecard took a step away. "You want to start a war?"

Belac shook his head. "No." He could predict what would happen if the exiled elves were left unchecked. "But there will be one."

Ecard offered no response.

Belac motioned to the right. "Come on. We need to get something to drink." *Even if it is just water.* "Then we need to get moving."

As Ecard followed the elf to the nearest of the water barrels, he asked, "Will we be going east?"

Belac nodded. "Yeah. But first, we need to go north past the road. That way, we can avoid the ruins." *We still don't know what could be waiting there.*

Clad in scraps of green canvas, three men drank from the barrels. One of the men handed Belac a wooden cup and then bowed his head slightly in deference. Belac nodded his thanks before scooping water out of a barrel and drinking his fill.

Ecard accepted a cup from one of the other men. "Why not south?"

Belac shook his head. "I came from the south. We need to go north." *And away from the sneaky-lake-monster.*

When another of the men walked up to the barrels, Belac handed his cup off and stepped away. *I am not sure how long I should give the men to get a drink.* He limped to the burnt remains of the pavilion and then turned around. The humans seemed more interested in looting than water.

Belac raised his voice. "If you want water, get it now. The monsters are coming back, and we do not want to be here." *I don't anyway. At least, not until I have some men in better shape. As soon as I can trade these people out for some fighting men, I am coming back here and killing everything.*

Sixteen

Despite the rough condition of the escaped prisoners, six of the men chose to bring three of the iron bound trunks with them. Working in teams of two, they carried the heavy trunks between them with a taxed determination. Belac had almost ordered them to leave the trunks behind, but then decided that he should let them struggle until they were ready to drop the unnecessary burdens. *I told them they could take whatever they wanted.* He grinned. *And this way, Talia and Kaelem might lose more of their stuff.*

As per the plan, Belac and his band of escaped prisoners had traveled north past the road that led from the ruins. While the elf had not spared any time to search for the decapitated spriggan's body, he had silently noted its absence. Many of the men had grumbled about being asked to go north, when their destination was to the south. *These humans act like I want to walk farther than I have to.* Belac had to stop himself from grumbling. Not only did his ankle hurt, he was becoming increasingly concerned that he had damaged it permanently. It was not the intensity of the pain, so much as the depth of it that caused his worry.

Leading from the front, Belac did his best to pretend that he knew where he was going. *I don't have time to stand around and listen to a bunch of humans argue about which way east is.* He shifted his shoulders, readjusting the scabbarded swords strapped to his back. *I need to get these people away from Talia and Kaelem. That army of briar men is too big already.* He saw a vision of countless garnet lights pulsing in darkness.

Belac looked in the direction of the ruins. "This should be far enough." He turned right and began limping east.

Turning with the elf, Ecard asked, "Are these ruins really so dangerous?" He sounded more curious than doubtful.

Belac nodded. "Think about those bloody cages, Ecard." He paused for effect. "Those cages were filled with people. People, that are now briar men." He looked toward the ruins. "There is a darkness in that place. It is a bottomless hole that only gets more evil the farther down you go." He nodded again. "Yes. They're dangerous."

The men following behind began speaking in hushed voices. They spoke of demons, corruption, and death. Though no one said the word 'Vaquians,' Belac could fault the men not at all. *This whole forest needs a volcano dropped on it.*

As they passed by the foreboding Vaquian ruins, Belac thought that he could feel the evil of the place. He felt like he could have pointed directly at them. To him, they were a dark spot on the world; a stain on the fabric of reality itself. He worried that no matter how far away from the ruins he got, he would always be able to feel them.

A man wearing a drab green canvas skirt walked up beside the elf. "You have two swords." The man's voice had the harshness of age.

Belac looked at the man sideways. "I do."

"You should let one of us borrow one of them," the man asserted.

Belac shook his head dismissively. "No."

The man was not satisfied with the simple answer. He gestured to the elf's other side. "You can let Lord Ecard carry it, if you don't trust any of us."

Belac did not bother looking in the lord's direction. "No."

The man was obviously becoming frustrated. "Why not?" He gestured to the men behind him. "We would all be safer if both of you were armed."

Belac tried to think of a reason to refuse sharing his swords that did not involve revealing that one of the blades was worth more than a castle. "One of them is cursed."

The man took a step away from the elf, stumbling as he continued to maintain his pace. "Those swords?"

Belac nodded. "One of them."

"Cursed?" the man asked uncertainly.

Belac wanted to laugh. Instead, he kept his face blank and nodded somberly. "Any man that touches it, will have their soul burned and their luck sapped away."

"Then…" the man stammered, "Then, why would you keep it?"

Belac answered without thinking. "I need it to kill a dragon."

"No one kills a dragon!" the man responded immediately.

Many of the other men voiced their agreement.

Belac no longer felt like laughing. "I will," he stated calmly. The conviction in his words quieted the chattering men. He turned his head and looked at the lord walking beside him. "I will avenge Enevic."

Ecard nodded his acceptance. "I will help you in any way in which I am able." His words sounded a vow.

One of the men following spoke from the crowd. "It was The Danorin that burned Enevic." When no one disagreed, he asked, "You want to kill The Danorin?"

Belac did not think that the question was a particularly useful one. "Everyone wants to kill The Danorin." *What was it that Rolan said?* "If all it took was a vote, the dragon would already be dead."

The announcement sparked speculation and debate among the men.

"…Can't kill a dragon."

"Not The Danorin."

"Not any dragon!"

"Why not?"

"Because it's a dragon!"

"There has to be some way to kill one."

"Sure. You leave it alone, and let it get old and die."

"Dragons live forever."

"How would you know?"

"...Best to just let it have Enevic."

"After what it did to all those people?"

"It killed everyone!"

"I had a brother that lived there."

"Well, there is no one left for it to kill now."

"And, leastwise, we know where the monster is."

"Still rather have it be dead."

"Do you really think it is just going to stay there?"

"Why would it leave?"

"Why does a dragon do anything?!"

"What about when it gets hungry?"

"That's right. There is no one left in Enevic for it to eat."

"I told you, I had a brother there..."

Belac let the men continue to prater on as he led them farther away from the ruins. *They can say whatever they want. I am still going to kill that dragon.*

As the day dwindled, dark clouds gathered in the sky. The shadows of the forest grew darker, and the men spoke less and less. It took little time before the gloomy atmosphere brought the men back to hushed voices. Belac gazed up past the scales of the conifers and into the overcast sky. While the temperature was warm enough that exposure to the rain should not harm the escapees, he worried how the shroud of clouds would interfere with his ability to navigate.

Belac leaned toward the lord walking at his side, and spoke softly. "I think we are still headed east. But if you start to feel like we are off course, then let me know."

Ecard nodded without speaking. He too seemed troubled by the darkening sky.

Footfalls, heavy breathing, and the shifting of cloth became the only sounds their party made as they continued in the direction that Belac thought was east. *We can't go on much longer.* The world was darkening faster. Soon, the sun would set. *We can't travel through the woods in the dark.* The elf's injured ankle was a persisting reminder of the hazards of the night. *But the spriggan's will not have that problem.*

Belac sighed and then held a hand up high to signal a halt. He turned around and waved the men toward him. "On me."

The scattered collection of ragged men began to gather around the elf. Quiet in the ominous lighting, the men had reverted to the mindset of prisoners. Though bars no longer held them, the palpable sense of looming danger pinned them in.

Belac waited while some of the men moved around trees to get a better view. "We can't wonder through the woods blind. We have to stop for the night." He scanned the faces around him, but found no signs of derision. "We will get some rest tonight, and then maybe tomorrow we can move a little faster." He pointed a thumb at the lord standing next to him. "Lord Ecard is going to organize a watch." He pointed his hand toward two men at random. "You two are going to come help me with something."

After a nod to Ecard, Belac stepped away. He gestured to the two men he had selected, indicating that they should follow him as he limped through the trees.

Ecard began issuing orders. "All right, listen up! We are going to have at least three men awake at all times. If any one of you catches someone sleeping on duty, you slap the snot out of that man. If anyone has a problem with getting slapped, feel free to come have a discussion with me about dereliction."

The man actually sounds like a general. Belac continued to limp away from the men until he found what he was searching for. Then he turned and addressed his two helpers. "How many men do we have?" *It has to be over twenty.*

The man on the right readjusted the drab green canvas tied over one of his shoulders. "I never thought to count."

Belac looked to the other man. "What about you?"

The other man, dressed in a green skirt tied around his waist with a strip of heather gray cloth, shrugged his shoulders and shook his head.

Belac frowned. "What are your names?"

The man on the right gave his name first. "I'm Ben."

"Simon," the other man answered with a surprisingly deep voice.

Belac nodded and then pointed to the man on the right. "Ben. Go talk to Ecard. Find out how many men we have. Including him, and including you."

"Including you too?" Ben asked.

Belac almost said, 'no.' "Yes." *I need the humans to think of me as one of them. And I know how to subtract by one.*

Ben nodded and then readjusted his clothing again before hurrying away.

Belac looked at the other man. "You and I are going to make spears." He turned and wrapped his left hand around the trunk of a tall sapling. "I need you to look around and find me more of these." He let go of the young tree and proceeded to ready his dwarf-sword.

"That is not the best wood for a spear," Simon argued.

Belac did not disagree. "It will work well enough." *Even if we could fire harden the tips, the spears would not be much use against the spriggans.* "We just need something pointy that is long enough to punch through the briar men's chest." He tapped the center of his own chest. "Just make sure you stab them here."

"What about the elves?" Simon asked with a stone face.

Belac missed the undertones of the question. "You can stab them anywhere you want."

Seventeen

Belac was awakened by screams of terror and pain. He shot up, the pads of his bare feet grinding into the gritty forest floor. Pain shot through his ankle, further adding to his confusion. *Not going to eat me!* He had his dwarf-sword drawn before he even knew what was happening. His mind, slowed by sleep, raced to catch up with him. The shouts of men surrounded him in the dim light of the obfuscated moon. He spun around, trying to make sense of things.

Belac's eyes locked on something that at first, he thought was an enormous bear. The hulking beast's maw was buried in a silent man's chest. Even bent over, the beast was almost as tall as Belac. *Are those feathers?* Its green and brown patterns looked dark gray and black in the moonlight. Terrified men ran past Belac as they fled from the beast.

That thing can run faster than we can. While most of his party might have been able to get away, Belac knew that with his ankle injured, he was not likely to be one of them. "I am not food," he resolved in Elven.

The beast's head rose from its mangled prey and turned toward the elf. Dark blood dripped from a short snout that protruded from the beast's feathered face. Eyes, black as death itself, stared at the elf remorselessly. *That thing thinks I'm food.*

The beast's body turned to follow its gaze. Muscle and feathers rose as the monstrous thing reared up onto its hind legs. Dark feathers of its underbelly exposed, the beast stood taller than a giant. It let out a deep, shuddering roar. Blood and spittle flew from its fanged jaws as its rage reached out into the night. Then the beast dropped back down on all fours, its black eyes intent on the elf that had dared to challenge it.

I should have run. Belac did not move. He looked into black eyes and tried not to ruminate on the mistakes of his life. Golden hair flashed in his mind. *I need to focus…*

The beast charged, its clawed paws digging into the ground as it surged toward the elf. Massive jaws opened, and fangs glistened in the dire light. Belac threw his scabbard as he darted to his right. The empty scabbard clacked into the beast's feathered face as the elf dodged away. Despite the beast's size, it was able to stop and redirect its charge at a frightening speed. However, it was not as nimble as the elf.

Belac's sword slashed across the beast's face. Steel scraped against bone, and flesh tore open. *I told you!* He turned with the swing and ran away from the beast. *I am not food!* The beast roared behind him.

Belac ran to the nearest tree. Though its tall trunk was scarcely wider than he was, he turned and put the tree between himself and the wounded beast. He leaned to the right side of the trunk and pointed his sword at the beast. "That's a bad bear!"

The beast roared in answer.

Belac shouted back, "It's not my fault that someone covered you in feathers!"

The beast charged toward the tree. Belac waited until the beast was almost to him before he dodged back behind the tree. Spinning to his right as he danced around the tree, fear and adrenaline made the pain in his ankle a distant complaint. He brought the inside of his right wrist up to his chest, and then thrust the tip of his sword into the beast's backside as it stopped to turn.

Belac hopped backward, careful to keep the tree between himself and the beast. "I will make you a deal," he said in negotiation. "You want to eat an elf?" He gestured away dramatically with his entire left arm. "Well, there are two of them over there!" He repositioned himself as the beast circled the tree. "How about, I let you eat both of them?"

The beast did not answer.

"What if I throw in an owl?" Belac asked speculatively.

The beast roared angrily.

Belac held his free hand up in placation, "Okay, okay! No owls."

The beast rushed forward, attempting to catch the elf before he could dodge behind the tree. Though Belac was quick enough to evade, the beast gave him no time to bargain further. Savage claws raked through the air as the beast followed him around the tree. Enraged, the beast locked its jaws on the side of the tree's trunk. Bark and wood ripped free as the beast jerked its head away. With a roar, the beast spit the splinters from its mouth.

The ferocity of the shuddering roar caused Belac to question how long a simple tree would hold back the beast. The bloody laceration on the side of the beast's face only added to the primal nature of its hostile temper. Belac stared at the blood, feathers, and fangs. *I should have run.*

A man in a drab canvas skirt shot in from Belac's peripheral. Wooden spear held tight, the man rammed the sharpened tip deep into the beast's side. *That's the man that wanted my sword…* The beast backhanded the man, throwing him off his feet. Rounding on the fallen man, the beast grabbed his shoulder, its taloned claws digging into the man's chest and back. The beast lifted the man up and slammed him down onto the ground twice, the savagery breaking bones and forcing them to puncture the man's own flesh. Fanged jaws clamped down on the man's head and then tore off the top of his skull.

A thrown spear stabbed into the beast's thigh, only to fall free from its own weight. As the beast let out one of its shuddering roars, another spear struck its left arm. More men with spears moved in and began to surround the beast. Even in the muted light, Belac could see the fear in their eyes.

I could run. The beast's back was to Belac. *I could get away while they fight this thing.* The elf's eyes darted to each of the men who had chosen bravery. *If they die here, they can't be turned into briar men.* His eyes stopped on the back of the beast. *I could run. But even if I escaped, I would never feel free.*

Belac tossed his sword up and then caught the hilt in a reversed grip. He heard Vairug's voice in his mind. *"What if the world needs a hero?"* Belac surged forward, flying past the tree as he dashed toward the beast. He leapt into the air, slapped his left hand onto the beast hindquarters, and then vaulted up above it. As he fell, his sword plunged down into the beast's back, the tip piercing feathers and flesh. The blade of the sword slid between massive ribs, sinking down until stopped by the cross-guard.

Belac landed on the beast's back with his knees bent and his legs spread apart. The beast began to thrash beneath him. *I missed its heart.* Belac clung to the hilt of his sword with both hands as the beast attempted to dislodge him. Violent roars sprayed blood from the beast's mouth, but its rage only seemed to grow. *I need a new plan.*

As Belac was slung side to side, the blade of his sword wrenched inside the beast's chest. Then, suddenly, the beast fell forward onto the ground with a lifeless thud. The elf did not let go of his sword. All was silent around him. If not for the hammering of his own heart, and the harshness of his own breath, he would have thought himself deaf.

Belac looked to the men around him. "Somebody stab this thing in the eye!"

"You killed it..." one of the men said in a voice that was equal parts relief and disbelief.

Belac glared at the man. "Then, it should be easy," he paused before shouting, "To stab this thing in the eye!"

One of the other men moved forward tentatively. He slowly placed the tip of his wooden spear against the beast's open right eye. Then he shoved the spear into the beat's eye socket. Everyone was quiet as they waited for the dead beast to respond. The man looked up to Belac and held out his hands questioningly.

Belac nodded. "Good man." He began to wiggle his sword back and forth as he pulled it from the beast's back.

Ecard spoke with pride. "Brave men, one and all."

Once Belac's sword was free, he slid off the beast's back. Then he thrust the sword into the feathered mass again just to be certain that it was dead. He narrowed his eyes at the beast. "Who puts feathers on a bear anyway?"

A deep voice spoke from behind the elf. "It is a kuma."

Belac turned around. "The angry-feather-bear?"

Simon nodded. "It is called a 'kuma." His attention shifted to the dead beast. "It should not be this far east."

Belac turned and looked at the kuma. "This thing should not be anywhere." *I wonder if the owls sent it after me…*

"Something must have driven it here," Simon asserted.

Belac reappraised the feathery beast. Despite its size and obvious power, there was a thinness to the kuma that he had not noticed when confronted with its rage. "My guess would be hunger." He gestured to the darksome forest around him. "And I don't see any goats."

Eighteen

"You cannot eat a kuma," Simon insisted.

Belac reconsidered the dead beast. He could easily appreciate the beauty of its feathers now that the thing was not trying to kill him. "Are they sacred?"

"No," Simon replied as if responding to a joke. "They are poison."

Belac frowned. One of the problems he had with humans was that he could not always determine if they knew what they were talking about, or if they were merely being superstitious. "That does not seem fair. It was totally going to eat us."

Ecard spoke with a tired voice that feigned amusement. "I doubt that a sense of fair play was high on its list of virtues."

Belac turned toward the lord. *He needs sleep.* "If we stay here until morning, would you be able to get any rest?"

Ecard shook his head tiredly. "No."

Belac nodded. The lord's response was what he had expected. *No one is going to want to sleep next to their dead friends or the kuma.* He looked up through the underside of the evergreen branches that canopied the forest. Though the moon was present, it lit little more than the thick clouds above.

"You want to go back to sleep?" one of the men asked disapprovingly.

Belac frowned at the man. "No. But it is going to be dangerous to travel in this dim light."

Simon's deep voice offered reassurance. "We are foresters. We know the forest as well as the Elves do."

Belac barked a laugh. "You probably know them better than I do." *A forest is nothing but misery and green.*

Ecard asked, "What would you have us do?"

Belac assumed that the lord was speaking to him. "We travel east as best we can for as long as the moonlight lasts. Then we can take another break until dawn." *Hopefully, nothing will try to kill us next time.*

"The moon won't be up much longer," noted another one of the men.

Belac glanced at the man. *I don't know his name.* The elf's azure eyes scanned the gloom. *I don't know most of their names…* While he felt like the men deserved to be known, Belac did not think that he would be able to remember twenty-two new names if he tried to learn them all at once.

Belac nodded, acknowledging the man who had spoken. "We can still put some distance between us and the dead." *And it will let the men burn off some of their nervousness.*

"We should bury them," said yet another man with a name unknown to the elf.

Belac shook his head. "No tools. No time." *No point.* The rotting kuma would attract carrion-eaters regardless of the two dead humans left behind. Belac raised his voice. "Gather whatever you have. We need to get moving." Then he added, "It is probably a good idea to leave the heavy boxes." *I am kind of surprised that they brought them this far.*

Following his own instructions, Belac limped over to his boots and sat down. *This is going to be unpleasant.* He picked up one of his boots and then stuffed his right foot inside, grimacing as he forced his injured ankle into the boot. *At least it hasn't swollen so much that I can't get the boot on.* The second boot went on far easier than the first.

Ecard walked over and stopped next to the elf. He gazed out into the shadows as he asked, "How did you find the courage to stay and face the kuma?"

That is really not how it happened. Belac looked up at the melancholy lord. "Courage, was you and those men coming back."

Ecard closed his eyes. "We all ran…"

Belac nodded. "Fear made you run. Courage made you come back." He climbed to his feet. "Courage is not good for much if you are not scared."

Ecard offered no reply. Catastrophe had taken everything the man had loved; his family, his friends, and his country. Then, in captivity, torture had begun to destroy who he was.

Belac put a hand on the man's shoulder. "You can come back."

Ecard nodded and then stepped away. He turned and shouted at the other men. "Grab your spears and prepare to move out!" Once more, he sounded a general.

With an exhausted sigh, Belac attempted to face himself toward the east. Though he expected his orientation to be off, he did not think that it was overly important. At the moment, he thought that simply moving was more consequential than moving in the correct direction. *I can get a better sense of east when the sun comes up.*

Once Ecard was done glaring at the other humans, Belac led the way. While slower than he would have liked, Belac's measured limp ensured that no one living was left behind. The evergreens' scaly leaves shut out most of the little light above, and a quicker pace could have risked small clusters of the group wandering off in the dark. Belac found a queer comfort in the idea that his pain might serve a greater purpose.

As they continued on, the thick cloud cover began to slowly dissipate. However, when they lost the light of the moon, the clouds still masked the stars. His forehead glazed in a clammy sweat, Belac was glad for the excuse to stop. He chose a tree and sat down next to it.

Belac leaned back and rested his head against the bark of the tree. "Can you see to the watch?"

"Of course," Ecard assured the elf.

Belac's hair made the bark crackle behind him as he nodded. "Thanks." He closed his eyes.

The annoying song of a distant bird pulled at Belac's attention. He opened his eyes to a gray morning that had yet to be graced by sunrise. He opened his parched mouth and flexed his jaw. *It does not feel like I slept at all.* A quick glance showed him men being roused by their fellows. His focus then settled on his injured ankle. *I forgot to take off my boots.* He rotated his ankle. It hurt.

Ecard spoke from the elf's side. "The men will be ready to move soon."

Sitting up away from the tree, Belac nodded. His body was stiff, but he knew that more rest was not an option. He untied his hair and began to comb his fingers through it. A bloody feather fell away. He stared at the feather, and for a moment, nothing felt real to him.

"Belac?" Ecard asked, concerned.

Belac shook his head. "I'm fine." He began to tie his hair back in place. "Do we have any new problems?"

"Certainly," Ecard said with a smirk.

Belac climbed to his feet and looked at the man. "Okay, what are they?"

Ecard shrugged. "I do not know. That is one of the problems."

Belac grinned ruefully. "Yeah, alright."

Once their few tasks of the morning were completed, the cohort of escaped prisoners began their march toward the rising sun. Belac's ankle complained even more than it had the day before. *It will just have to hurt. We need to get out of this forest before something else tries to eat us.* Though the dawn's light made traveling easier, Belac was not entirely convinced that it was worth having to suffer all the verdant green.

When he finally found the edge of the forest and stepped away from the shaded trees, Belac growled. The late morning sun shown down on a sea of faded green grass that flowed over rolling hills. *It's a conspiracy.* He narrowed his eyes at the grass. *Not only do I have to walk around on a broken ankle, I have to wade through all that green?!* He rolled his shoulders. *Maybe my sword does sap luck.*

The men fanned out into the open grassland. They seemed unconcerned by the grass that brushed against their shins. Tears welled in many of the men's eyes as they were overcome with a sudden sense of freedom. The forest had become a dark place to them, and they had just stepped into the light.

Stupid humans. Belac narrowed his eyes at the grass again. *I guarantee that there is something hidden in all that green that wants to eat us.* A northern breeze stirred the grass. "I'm watching you," Belac muttered threateningly to the grass.

Ecard's voice drew the elf away from the menacing green. "Belac." He pointed to the south. "Smoke."

Belac stared out into the distance. "That looks really far away."

Ecard's words were grim. "And that means that the fire must be substantial."

Gofell.

Nineteen

Once the men had realized that their homes could be burning down, Belac had been unable to prevent them from rushing ahead. Had they stopped long enough to listen, he may have convinced them to be more prudent. However, worry for their family and friends carried them away. Ecard remained at Belac's side, a stoic companion as the elf limped onward.

Belac grumbled angrily, "Even if it's not a trap, those men can't run the whole way there."

Ecard chose his words carefully. "That may be true. Still, they must make the attempt."

Belac scowled. "They are going to be exhausted when they get there. If it's a trap, they won't be able to put up a fight. If it's not, then they are going to be too tired to be of any real help." He gestured to the dark smoke rising from Gofell. "Anyone still in that fire will already be dead."

A brief time passed before Ecard replied. When he did, his voice sounded hollow. "No matter what has happened in Gofell, it will be tragedy. Every moment that those men delay, will be one more thing that they blame themselves for later." He took a deep breath to steady his emotions. "Even if Gofell were nothing but ash, I would wish those men all speed."

He understands their loss more than I do. Belac sighed. "It's just…" He shook his head. "I did not save those men so that they could just run off and get themselves killed."

Ecard smiled. "You are worried about them."

Am not. Belac remembered how the humans had returned to face the kuma; half naked men with pointed sticks standing against fangs and insurmountable rage. *Yeah, okay. Maybe I am worried about them.* He glanced at the lord walking beside him. "You're worried about them too," he insisted accusingly.

Ecard nodded. "That I am."

Belac continued to limp forward at a steady pace, but it was well past midday before they reached the smoldering remains of Gofell. A harsh veil of drifting smoke lingered in the air despite the light, persistent breeze. Everything not made of stone was embers, ash, and despair. Precious few of the buildings had been made of stone.

Hazy smoke stung the elf's eyes as he gazed upon the village. *This is my fault.* He remembered Serath's words. *"Everything you do."* Belac took in the desolation that was Gofell. *This is Talia and Kaelem's response to me burning down their pavilion and stealing their sacrifices.* His face hardened as he saw the two elves in the darkness of his mind. *I should have found a way to kill them there in the ruins.*

"There are no corpses," Ecard noted professionally.

Belac's neck was tight as he nodded. "They took the people with them." *They need new sacrifices for their army.*

On the south-east edge of the village, the largest of the stone buildings still stood. Though its wooden annexes had burned, the structure had endured the fires that took them. Ragged men in bedsheets and torn canvas labored in ashy mud as they moved charred lumber away from the building's entrance.

Belac limped past one of several discarded buckets as he approached the men. "Do we know if anyone is inside?"

One of the men, his green canvas smeared with soot, stepped away from the others to answer, "It's the gathering hall." He gestured behind himself. "Anyone here is like to be in the cellar."

I hope it's a big cellar… Belac turned and scanned the smoky remains of the village. *Is it worse to die in a fire, or have your heart cut out and used to make a monster?* He returned his attention to the man. "Has anyone called out for help?"

The man shook his head. "No. We hollered, but no one answered." He gestured to the burned village. "But you got to figure that they are scared."

Belac nodded. *Even if no one is in there, we still have to check.* The man took the nod as a dismissal and returned to the rescue effort. Belac wanted to help as well, but it was painful for him to simply stand. He knew that he should rest his ankle, but he was not willing to sit comfortably while the men dug their families out of burned rubble. So, he stood by, watching as he tried to think of something that he could do to help.

Though Ecard stood at the elf's side, his voice sounded far away. "I am going to scout the outskirts of the village."

Belac nodded without saying anything. He did not expect Ecard to find anything useful. Nor did he think that the lord expected to. *This must be hard for him also.* Dragon's breath had taken Enevic. And while Ecard had yet to see it, he must have realized that his home would now look much like Gofell.

Belac was suddenly reminded of another village that he himself had seen burn. He remembered a hidden village filled with monsters and children. And he remembered the warring flames that he had brought down on them. *I know what I did. It was awful. But I would do it again.* He pushed his shame away and focused on the lives that might still be saved.

A man with a red bedsheet tied over one shoulder walked up to Belac and offered him a tin bucket half filled with water. Belac raised an eyebrow at the man.

The man continued to hold the bucket out. "I thought you might be thirsty."

Belac took the bucket. *I don't know his name. I need to just start asking. The longer I wait the more awkward it is going to get.* "What's your name?"

The man smiled amiably, showing off a missing eye tooth. "Name's Craig."

Belac nodded, fixing the name to the man's face. "Thanks, Craig."

Belac brought the metal bucket up and sniffed at it. All he could smell was smoke. *I guess it does not really matter what it smells like.* It was a testament to his thirst that he then drank the well water straight from the bucket. Despite the taste of ash in his mouth, Belac found the water refreshing. *I did not realize how thirsty I was.*

Belac handed the bucket back to the man in the red bedsheet. "I needed that."

Craig nodded and backed away. "Happy to help, Lord Belac." He turned and went to offer water to the other men.

Belac frowned. *I'm not a lord.*

Once the men cleared away enough of the charred lumber to access the entrance of the gathering hall, a new problem presented itself. Large doors, completely bound in iron, sealed the entry and prevented the men from reaching anyone who might be inside. *I'm glad the doors held back the fire, but now, they are kind of in our way. How are we going to get those things open?* Four of the men picked up a burned timber and began to batter it against the doors.

Belac could only imagine how frightening the hammering must have been to anyone trapped inside. He limped forward and held up a hand. "Stop."

The men halted and looked at the elf, confused.

Belac limped past the men and then moved his ear close to the iron bound doors. He took a deep breath and shouted, "Hello?"

There was no answer.

Belac could hear no movement inside. "You can come out now. The monsters are gone." *At least, I hope the monsters are gone...* He frowned to himself. *I should probably have made sure that the humans checked.*

There was still no answer.

Belac took a step back and studied the entry. Whatever wood was protected under the iron sheeting, going through the doors would be a chore. There was a visible gap where the doors met, but it was too narrow for even his slender fingers to fit through. "Are all the windows barred?" he asked the men nearest him.

"Every one of them," one of the men answered.

The other men nodded their agreement.

I am going to look really stupid if I just have them go ahead and break the door down now. Belac moved closer to the doors, closed an eye, and tried to peak through the gap. He looked over a dark shadow in the center of the gap and into the room beyond. The sunlight shown through the bars of the windows, creating beams of light in the haze of smoke and dust. Empty of life, the space was filled with rows of wooden pews that faced a wide podium in the back of the room. *Someone had to bar this door.* To both the left and right of the podium, stout doors closed off the ways to the rest of the building. *The cellar must be through one of those.*

Belac took a step back. *One door at a time.* He removed his dwarf-sword, unsheathed it, and then handed the scabbard to the man closest to him. The man took the scabbard without saying anything, though there was a question on his face. Belac slid the blade of his sword into the gap between the doors, pushing it in until its cross-guard rested against the doors' iron sheathing. Keeping the sword as horizontal as he could, he lifted the blade up under the thick timber securing the doors on the other side.

Belac quickly realized that he was not going to be able to move the bar by himself. He nodded to the doors and said, "Somebody give me a hand with this."

It was Simon who stepped forward. "I will help."

Belac did not think that it was necessary to explain what he was attempting to do. He repositioned his left hand to under his right, making space for Simon to grip the end of the hilt. Together, they tried to lift the bar, but were barely able to make it rattle in its supports. *We are just fighting each other as we try to keep the blade straight.*

Belac stopped struggling with the sword. *I need a new plan.* He motioned for Simon to step away and then he lowered himself onto his knees. Belac moved the hilt of his sword to the ground with the blade angled upward into the gap. He placed the tip of the blade against the underside of the heavy timber, and then pressed the steel into the wood.

Belac nodded to the hilt of his sword. "Grab the back of the cross-guard and pull upward."

Steel scraped against iron as the sword blade slid upward in the gap. Then, suddenly, the tip of the sword swung forward as the bar fell free from its supports. An echo boomed inside the gathering hall. *Ha! Take that, you stupid doors!*

Simon pushed on one of the doors, but the dislodged bar prevented it from opening freely. When the man pushed harder, Belac's sword bucked in his hands.

"Hey!" Belac snapped.

Simon stopped pushing, but it was clear that he wanted inside the building. Belac wiggled his sword until the tip pulled out of the wooden bar. Once the elf's sword was free, Simon threw his shoulder into the door on the right. The iron bound door shoved the heavy bar out of the way as it swung into the hall. Simon rushed into the building, trailed by the four men that had wanted to batter down the doors. *They think that they have family inside.*

Belac climbed to his feet and followed the men inside. *That short one ran off with my scabbard!* He hustled forward and took back his empty scabbard. *Scabbard thief.*

"Marjorie!" one of the men called out as they moved toward the door on the left side of the podium.

Belac sheathed his sword and returned it to his back. Then he limped after the men, following them through the door and into a smaller room. Pulleys and ropes hung above a long wooden door set into the floor. *Someone else can figure out how to open this one.*

One of the men stomped a cloth wrapped foot down on the door. "Leeson!" he shouted. "Are you in there? Open the door!"

A muffled voice called up from below. "Denis?" There was a pause. "How do I know that you are not one of those monsters?"

The man presumably named Denis replied, "Did one of those monsters sleep with your sister before she ran off with that wool headed trader?"

A bolt slid free on the other side of the door. Belac looked from the complicated workings of the door to the man who had so easily ordered it opened. *Cheater.*

Twenty

The cellar under the gathering hall turned out to be a spacious sublevel that was larger than the building above it. Within the underground shelter, the women and children of Gofell had been hidden away from the horrors that had visited their homes. Crowded in among stockpiled supplies, the survivors of Gofell showed no desire to brave the world above. Mothers hushed frightened children while clutching them to their breasts protectively. Lit by scattered candles, the cellar was more shadows than light.

Fewer than half of the escaped prisoners had family hiding in the refuge of the cellar. As the men rushed past Belac, his heart ached for the wives that would have no reunion. *This is going to be awful for the women that have to watch other families reunited, only to realize that theirs would not be one of them.* It would not be long before the survivors learned that every man who had remained above was now gone. *And the children...* Soon, the sons and daughters of Gofell would discover that their fathers had been taken by monsters.

In addition to Leeson, there were eight men who had sheltered with the women and children. Though five of the men were advanced in age, the other three appeared fully hale. *Soft men that believe they should be protected.*

Well dressed, the soft men sat in the shadows, seemingly no braver than the children clinging to their mothers.

A baby began to cry, its voice a shrill representative of Gofell. Before its mother could quiet the babe, two more babies joined in its unhappy song. While Belac found the sound immensely unpleasant, he could not argue with the sentiment.

Leeson ran a hand through his short, brown hair and then leaned down toward the elf. "I think it would be best if we spoke in my office."

Belac kept his voice low as he answered the tall man. "There is not much of the village left."

Leeson's surprise was evident despite the poor lighting. "But why..." He shook his head as he set the thought aside. "My office is just upstairs. We should talk there." He straightened and began walking toward the stairs with the expectation that he would be followed.

Belac's eyes drifted over the families of Gofell. *Where will these people go when they finally return to the surface?* He took a deep breath. *Nowhere will be safe if Talia and Kaelem are not stopped.* Belac watched as Simon kissed the forehead of a pregnant woman with disheveled, sandy blond hair. Simon whispered something to her, and then he stepped away. Her hand reached out in longing, but the woman let him go.

Simon walked over to the elf and gestured toward the stairs. "We need to let Leeson know about the elves."

Belac nodded. *Bad as it is, the burned village is not the worst of it.* "I am on my way to his office now. Do you want to come with me?" *It would probably help to have a human with me when I explain.*

Simon glanced back at the sandy haired woman that he was leaving behind. With a nod, he said, "We should have Lord Ecard with us also."

Belac began limping up the stairs. "We would have to send someone to find him. That, or wait for him to get back from his scouting mission." He shrugged. "It's a delay either way."

"What does he expect to find?" Simon asked as he followed the elf up the stairs.

Belac waited until they had both climbed the stairs before answering, "Nothing good."

Simon frowned, but nodded.

The men who had not gone below were waiting in the gathering hall above. Sitting together in the pews, the men passed two silver chalices to each other. Upon seeing Belac limp into the hall, Craig bent over and dunked one of the chalices into a tarnished metal bucket. He then stood and brought the filled chalice over to Belac.

Craig held out the chalice. "Thirsty?"

Belac nodded and took the chalice. "Thank you."

Craig gave a nod that verged on a bow. "Least I can do, Lord Belac."

I am not a lord. Belac drank from the chalice and then offered it to Simon. Simon downed the remainder of the water and then handed it back to Craig.

Belac pointed to the men still sitting in the pews. "Craig, can you and the other men go look for Ecard? He should be somewhere around the edge of the village."

Craig rubbed the silver chalice on his red bedsheet robe nervously. "Are you sure that the monsters are gone?"

No. Belac almost lied to the man. "No." He shook his head. "But that is something we need to know. Be careful while you are out there. Take your spears, and make sure that no one goes off alone." *I should not have let Ecard run off on his own.*

Craig nodded like he wanted to bow but did not know how to. "We'll find Lord Ecard for you." He turned and headed toward the men in the pews.

Simon asked, "Are we going to wait for Lord Ecard?"

Belac shook his head. "No. These people need to know how bad their problems really are. We can't wait. Ecard can vouch for us when he shows up."

Simon frowned. "Lord Ecard is known in Gofell?"

Belac nodded. "He was here looking for people to help him rebuild Enevic."

"After you kill the dragon?" Simon asked dryly.

Belac narrowed his eyes at the man. "Yes. After I kill the dragon."

Simon's words took on a thoughtful tone. "That does not explain how he came to be captured."

Belac saw no reason to keep the story a secret. "He was here. He heard that there were elves in the forest. He sought them out."

Which is... kind of my fault. Belac heard Ecard's voice in his mind. *"The Elves are wise."*

"He sought them out?" Simon asked incredulously.

Belac held his arms out to his sides. "He did not know that they were crazy-evil-exiles-that-want-to-take-over-the-world."

Simon seemed unconvinced.

Belac put his hands on his hips akimbo. "Did you know that the elves were crazy-evil-exiles-that-want-to-take-over-the-world?"

Simon scratched his beard.

"That's what I thought," Belac concluded. He waved the man to follow. "Let's go talk to Leeson."

Belac limped to the now open doorway on the opposite side of the podium. He was reasonably certain that he would find Leeson's office inside, as the doorway was the only unexplored option in the gathering hall. The room beyond was of a modest size, with three chairs arranged around a single desk. The office was one of the most tidy that Belac had ever seen. Though the waist high cabinets behind the desk must have held documents and ledgers, not a single piece of paper lay on the desktop.

Belac entered the office without preamble. Despite his intention to speak with Leeson, Belac's attention moved past the man sitting behind the desk, and up to the painted map hanging above the cabinets. *Well, that looks useful.*

Leeson set a glass of something amber down on his desk. "Tell me what you know."

Belac ignored the man, and limped around the desk. He looked up at the map, glad for the sunlight shining through the barred windows. *I wonder how accurate this is.* His eyes traced the edge of the blue depicting the ocean until he located Gofell.

I am west of Harbridge... While he had already acquired a general idea of where he was, Belac appreciated the visual aid.

Belac reached up and tapped a white star in a forest of green. "Is this map accurate?"

Turned in his chair, Leeson answered with displeasure. "It would not be very valuable if it were not."

Belac nodded as he committed three white stars to memory. Then he turned around and limped back to the other side of the desk. "You people have a problem."

Simon interjected dryly, "I think he knows that, Belac."

Belac pointed over his shoulder with his thumb. "Your village being burned is only the beginning."

Leeson studied the half-naked elf for a moment before asking, "The beginning of what?"

"War," Belac answered grimly.

Leeson held up his hands and shook his head. "I do not want anything to do with a war!"

Belac pointed his entire hand toward the open door. "Did that stop your village from burning? Did it stop your men from being taken?"

Leeson stood up and walked around his desk. He held a hand up between the elf and himself as he moved toward the door. "I do not need to listen to this."

Belac followed the man out into the gathering hall. "Not wanting to fight won't stop a spriggan from tearing off your head!"

Leeson turned around and threw his hands out to his sides. "And what would you have me do?!"

Belac answered calmly, "We have to stop them." He ignored the dismay in the man's eyes. "We need to send word to Harbridge, asking for help. We need to get the women and children somewhere safe. And we need to rescue the men that were taken."

One of the escaped prisoners, a soiled blue bedsheet wrapped around his waist like a skirt, stood from where he had been sitting in the pews. "Leeson," he said as he approached.

Leeson turned toward the man who had spoken his name. "What?!"

The man in blue plunged a dagger into Leeson's chest. He then followed Leeson down onto the floor, continuing to stab him in the chest repeatedly. Simon grabbed the attacker and struggled to pull him off of Leeson. The attacker made no attempt to cut Simon as he was pulled away. Instead, he dropped the dagger and screamed wordlessly at where Leeson lay bloody on the floor.

A single glance was all it took for Belac to know that Leeson was dead. *That is a lot of stab wounds…* He looked at the incensed attacker. *That guy is reeeeealy angry.*

"Have you lost your mind?!" Simon shouted as he locked the man's arms. "Why, Charles?"

Weeping, Charles shouted, "He gave me to them!"

Belac pursed his lips. *Ooh…* He bent down and picked up the bloody dagger. *Yeah. I probably would have stabbed him too.*

Twenty-One

Escaped prisoners poured into the gathering hall with their wooden spears held ready to fight. Ecard entered with them, his back straight and his shoulders wide. Belac thought that the men looked oddly heroic despite their shabby apparel. *I hope that they feel heroic. They're the only men I have.* He could not help but compare the bravery of the escaped prisoners to the cowardness of the soft men still hiding in the cellar below.

Ecard planted the butt of his spear. "What happened?"

Belac pointed with the bloody dagger in his hand. "It seems Leeson has been giving people to those crazy exiles in the forest." He rotated his wrist, pointing the dagger away from the dead man on the floor. "So, Charles stabbed him to death."

"Charles?" one of the men asked.

Though Charles's arms were pinned behind his back, the hold appeared to have become more supportive than restraining. "He gave us to them," Charles wept. "Me, Terry, and Raz." He looked to the other men helplessly. "He's the reason my brothers are dead."

Belac did not doubt the man's story. *Kaelem told me that some of the humans were offering up their own.* He considered the bloody corpse on the floor. *It also explains some of Leeson's behavior.* Belac frowned. *Now, I kind of want to stab him too…*

Simon shook his head sadly. "Why didn't you tell us?"

There was anger in Charles's reply. "How was I to know?" He glared at the man he had murdered. "He did not tell us that he was the king of Gofell!"

"He's not the king," one of the men offered as correction. When some of the other men gave him irritated glances, he continued defensively, "He's not. Gofell doesn't have a king. Leeson is just the headman."

Charles must not be from Gofell. Belac realized that the man must have been a captive for longer than the others. *He survived while the other people around him were dragged away to be slaughtered.* The cruelty of the man's imprisonment was something that would follow him forever.

Belac spoke with authority. "Let him go."

Simon gave the elf a confused look, but then released his hold on the other man's arms. Charles's posture appeared no less defeated. He remained where he was, staring down at the man he had stabbed to death. Belac limped closer, his azure eyes boring into the man.

"You're a murderer," Belac pronounced coldly.

Charles looked up, his eyes meeting the elf's judgment. A tear fell from the man's cheek.

Belac held the bloody dagger out to the man. "There are more things that need to be murdered."

Charles's arm shook as he reached for the dagger. When his hand wrapped around the hilt of the dagger, the blood on them both matched perfectly. "You want me to go back."

Though Belac let go of the dagger, his eyes held the man firm. "I want to kill the people that did this."

Simon's deep voice spoke with guarded emotion. "You would die for revenge?"

I would kill for it.

Belac turned, his gaze sweeping across the men he had saved. "This is not the end." He held his hands up and out to his sides as he raised his voice. "This is not where it ends." He gestured forcefully toward the hall's entrance and the forest that waited beyond the burned village. "They will not stop here! The evil growing in that forest will spread out into the lands of man. First it will be the villages, then it will be the cities. By the time the other nations realize the danger, this country will be covered in fire and blood."

The gathering hall was silent as Belac's prognostication sank in. He continued, knowing that so too would the war. "We can fight them now and win, or you can fight them later and lose." He did not mention the greater threat. He did not explain that once the armies of man were marshaled, they would not stop with the death of two elves. *The humans don't understand what would happen if they attacked the Elven Lands.* Belac knew the raw devastation that the Elves could rain down on the human kingdoms. *They would never be allowed to build cities again.*

One of the men asked, "How are we supposed to fight those things?"

'How.' Belac smiled. Despite the argumentative tone, the word made him optimistic. "By letting them think that we're the ones that are crazy."

"You are crazy," someone muttered.

Secret to my success. Belac pointed at the crowd. "See? The plan is working already."

Ecard was not amused. "Belac. What you are asking these men to do…" he left the rest unsaid.

Belac shook his head. "I am not asking." He met the fallen lord's eyes. "I am offering." He looked to the other men. "I am offering to help you. This is your village. These are your people." He gestured again toward the forest. "And those are your men that were taken." There was a moment of silence. "I say we take them back."

Simon asked the question again. "How?" There was no argument in the word when he said it.

Belac nodded. "Okay. The first thing we need to do is…" He trailed off as more men entered the hall from the door that led to the cellar.

An escaped prisoner with a name the elf did not know spoke into the pause. "I hope this plan includes us."

Belac noted that two clean shaven men had come into the hall with the escapees. One wore a red doublet decorated with yellow squares, while the other was dressed in plainer garments of navy blue cloth. Both of the men appeared healthy enough to have fought in defense of their village. *Those soft men are only here so that they can pretend like they're in charge.*

Belac had not realized that he had been speaking loudly enough to be heard all the way down in the cellar. "How much did you hear?"

One of the newcomers answered, "We heard enough to know that you're right."

Another added, "Everyone heard."

Belac did not like the idea of frightening the women and children below. However, he suspected that there was little he could say that could frighten them more than they already were. "My plans include everyone," he announced. *Or, at least they will once I get through making them.*

The man in the red doublet affected an air of superiority. "That seems rather presumptuous."

Belac nodded agreeably. "Thank you," he replied as if the man had paid him a complement. He turned to his left, angling the soft man out of his view. "Ecard," he said, addressing the man directly. "I need you to search Leeson's office. Try to find something that you can use to draft a letter to Harbridge. I doubt that they will send aid in time to help, but they need to know what is happening here."

The task clearly made Ecard uncomfortable. "The missive cannot come from me, Belac."

Belac nodded. "You're right." *Harbridge wants to kill him.* He pointed. "Simon, you're king of Gofell now. Go help Ecard with the letter."

The man in the red doublet objected. "Gofell has no king."

Belac waved a hand dismissively. "Headman. Whatever." He continued before the man could argue further. "The rest of us need to take an inventory. I know that no one wants to go into the center of the village, but we need to find where all the fighting took place. If we look around, we might be able to find some weapons that were left behind." He gestured toward the main entrance. "There are also a couple of other stone buildings out there that did not burn up with the rest of the village. We need to find out what's inside them and if we can repurpose the buildings."

The man dressed in navy blue stepped forward and needlessly brushed nonexistent dirt off the chest of his tunic. "One of those buildings is most certainly my factorage." He held up a finger. "I will not have my property stolen."

While Belac was not averse to the concept of private property, he thought that it was a little absurd that the man would assert his claim while the world burned around them and monsters prepared for war. He opened his mouth to speak, but then closed it. Changing tact, Belac smiled and said, "Of course. We will happily deduct the value of what we take from your bill."

The merchant leaned back away from the elf. "My bill?!"

Belac nodded. "These men dug you out of a burning building." He gestured to the congregation of escaped prisoners. "And every one of them is about to risk their lives trying to save the men who stood and fought while you hid in the dark." His face hardened as his eyes met the merchant's. "There is a cost for that."

Twenty-Two

As the men filed out of the gathering hall, Belac raised his voice again. "Not you, Charles." Then he added, "Ben, you stay too."

Charles halted, his posture similar to that of a child who had been caught misbehaving. He turned slightly, head down and eyes to the side.

Belac pointed his hand at the dead body on the floor. "You still have to clean up this mess."

Charles moved in close and spoke as to not be overheard. "Do you want me to bury him?"

Belac shook his head. "I don't think that's necessary." He held out a hand, indicating to the corpse. "But we can't just leave this here. Eventually, the women and children down below are going to want to come out of the cellar. They should not have to look at this."

Charles nodded his agreement.

Ben remained silent, seemingly uncomfortable with being included.

Belac continued, "Strip him down. His clothes should fit Ben well enough. Don't bother with his tunic. All the blood and knife holes would just remind people of what happened, and we need to put this behind us."

Ben, his brow raised, asked, "You want me to wear a dead man's clothes?!"

Belac nodded. "That's right." He gestured to the man's canvas attire. "You can keep wearing that green tent if you want, but we have some hard work ahead of us. Boots and trousers might save your life."

Ben squirmed where he stood, but he did not argue.

Belac pointed his hand at the corpse. "Once you have him stripped down, drag the body out of the village and dump it in the forest somewhere. Try to find someplace that looks out of the way."

Ben did not seem to like this part of the plan much better. "Wouldn't it be better if we buried him?"

Belac shrugged. "If you want to try to dig a grave using nothing but a water bucket, go right ahead." He pointed to the other man. "But I don't think Charles is going to want to help you."

Charles glowered at the body of the man he had murdered. "Let him rot."

Ben did not argue, though it was obvious that he wanted to.

Belac turned to leave, but then stopped. He looked back over his shoulder. "Charles." He waited for the man to look at him. "Be careful around Denis. I think he was friends with Leeson. Grief can make a person stupid," he shifted his eyes to the corpse, "even violent."

Neither of the humans had anything to say. To Belac, they seemed lost in thoughts that were incompatible with each other. He left the two men to their task, hoping that their deep thoughts would not distract them from the dangers they all still faced. As he limped toward Leeson's office, Belac remembered the glass of amber liquid that the man had set on his desk. *I think I should investigate what is in that.* He nodded to himself. *It's the only responsible thing to do.*

When he entered the office, Belac saw that the glass was now empty. He narrowed his eyes at the empty glass. *Greedy humans.*

Ecard had taken the seat behind the desk, while Simon sat in one of the two chairs opposite him. The lord's hand dipped a short quill into an inkwell and then scrawled dark lines across the surface of a brownish sheet of paper.

Simon looked away from the discolored page and turned toward the elf. "I don't know my letters, Belac."

Belac shrugged. "It's fine," he said as he limped past the desk. "Ecard can write the message and then you can just scribble something that looks like a signature on the bottom."

Belac reached down and opened the first cabinet on the right. Fortunately, he found what he was searching for. He grabbed a wide decanter of amber liquid and carried it with him back to the other side of the desk. With his free hand, he picked up the empty glass and then set it down in front of the third chair. Groaning, he eased himself down into the seat.

Sounding worried that he might be doing something unethical, Simon asked, "How will I know what it says?"

Belac removed the glass stopper from the decanter and set it on the desk. "Ecard can read it to you before you sign." He filled the empty glass half full and then set the decanter down next to the stopper.

Simon seemed unassured.

Belac raised an eyebrow at the forester. "If you are really that concerned, I can make the squiggly line." He picked up the glass. "But if I sign, you don't get to be king of Gofell."

Simon frowned.

Belac took a drink of the amber liquid. "Ugh!" He almost spat it back out. "This is foul." *Why would anyone drink this stuff?* He took another drink, hoping that the liquor would dull some of the pain in his ankle.

Simon exhaled audibly. "I will sign."

Belac relaxed into his chair, not caring that his swords pressed into his back. "That's great," he said dismissively before taking another drink. He then pointed across the desk with the hand still holding his glass. "I am going to need to send a second letter."

Ecard looked up from his writing. "To whom?"

"The Lucky Duck," Belac said and then took another drink.

Ecard tilted his head. "I do not know who that is."

Belac shook his head. "It's not a person. It's a place in Harbridge. My friends might look for me there."

Ecard nodded. "You are referring to Lord Vairdoe."

Belac took a small drink. "It will probably not be him." *I hope Vairug is okay.* "I don't think that he would be very comfortable waiting in Harbridge." *Seeing as that Harbridge wants to kill him.*

Ecard was careful with his response. "While I am unfamiliar with that particular establishment, I do understand your meaning."

Simon asked, "Who is going to carry the news to Harbridge?"

Belac knew that the forester was not going to like his answer. "We are going to need to send some of the women."

Simon turned in his seat. "You would send women alone on the road?!"

Belac raised an eyebrow at the forester. "No." He gestured up and away with his glass. "I would send them in a group."

Anger crept into Simon's voice. "You know what I mean!"

Belac nodded, acknowledging the forester's point. "We can't spare any of the men. We are already outnumbered, and we need every man that can fight."

Simon gestured angrily toward the floor. "Then, send the men that won't fight!"

"That's…" Belac considered the three men hiding in the cellar below. *That's actually a good idea.* "Do you think we can trust them?"

Simon shrugged, mollified. "They might be cowards, but I don't think they have any reason to betray us."

Belac nodded. *And that would get them out of the way.* He pointed at the forester. "I knew it was a good idea to make you king."

Simon smiled. "You cannot make me king."

Belac held his left hand up in casual acceptance. "Headman. Whatever."

Ecard tapped a finger on his draft, drawing the elf's attention. "Is there anything you would prefer that I not mention?"

Belac took a moment to review the situation in his mind. "No. Tell them anything that you think they need to know."

Ecard nodded and then went back to writing.

Belac leaned forward and set his unfinished drink on the desk. "I need something to eat." He thought about the state of the men who followed him. "We all do."

Belac stood from his chair, immediately feeling lightheaded. *That's what happens when you drink on an empty stomach.* He picked up the glass stopper and put it back in the decanter. Then he slid the unfinished glass of liquor toward Simon.

Simon took the drink and downed it. "There is food in the cellar." He set the empty glass on the desk. "I can show you where it is."

Belac waved the forester to stay. "I can find it. You stay here and help Ecard."

Simon relaxed back into his seat. "Ask Josey for help." He grinned. "I don't think she has ever met an elf."

I guess the delegations can't go everywhere. Belac asked, "Is Josey the pregnant woman?"

Simon nodded. "She is." He smiled broadly. "I am going to be a father."

Belac clapped the forester on the shoulder. "I will be sure to save some food for the kid."

As Belac limped from the office, he silently vowed to ensure that the child would be born into a safer world.

Twenty-Three

Candlelight flickered, casting dim illumination into the sub-level under the gathering hall. Even with the faint lighting, it was easy to see that the women and children hiding in the cellar were growing restless. Children strayed into dark corners as their mothers whispered in speculation. Though they knew that their men had been abducted, so too did they know that the immediate threat had retreated into the forest. *Monsters become less frightening with distance.*

Josey, her swelled belly pushing out her brown dress, gestured to the rows of shelved supplies. "Most of what we have down here needs to be cooked." She tapped one of the wooden bins on the shelving unit next to her. "But we have some sweetened deer jerky in these," she turned and pointed to another shelving unit, "and some tack biscuits over there."

Biscuits! Belac pointed to the shelving unit. "You have biscuits?" He nodded. "I would like a biscuit, please."

Despite the shadowy space, Josey's smile was bright. "Elves like biscuits?" she asked.

Belac nodded. "The yummy ones," he replied, remembering the biscuits that Rolan had given him.

Josey's face twisted into a strange caricature. "I don't know that I would call these 'yummy." She opened a bin and took out a small, dense puck of dry flour. "But they will make you full enough that you won't ask for a second one."

Belac accepted the hardtack dubiously. "Maybe I should try the jerky also."

Josey moved to the other shelving unit. "It's hard to chew, but it tastes better." She opened a bin and took out a strip of dried meat. "You are going to want to drink water with them either way."

Belac thought the strip of dead animal looked no more appealing than the biscuit. *This thing is harder than boot leather.* He bit into the jerky. *Wow!* The meat was both salty and sweet. He worked his head side to side as he tore the bite free. "This is good!" he said as he chewed.

Josey leaned forward, her pregnancy making the movement pronounced. "Then, I don't think that you will like the biscuits very much." She smiled as she leaned back.

She has a pretty smile. Belac swallowed the softened jerky. "Would you do me a favor?" He pointed the gnawed strip of dried meat toward the stairs. "Would you go ask those fancy men over there to carry a box of each of these upstairs?"

Josey placed a hand on her chest. "Me?"

Belac nodded. "You are prettier than I am." He gestured to her swollen belly. "And you're pregnant. They have to do whatever you ask."

Josey's smile split her face. "I don't think that is how it works."

Belac shrugged. "Maybe." He pointed with his jerky. "But we don't have to tell them that."

Continuing to smile, Josey rolled her eyes. "Okay. I'll go ask them."

Belac sniffed at his biscuit as Josey went to enlist aid. *If those men won't help a pregnant woman carry a box, then we can't trust them to carry our messages all the way to Harbridge for us.* His eyes drifted over the women sitting together in huddled groups. He saw that many of them were staring at him.

Most of these people have probably never seen an elf before. He waved with his jerky. *I am glad that they met me instead of those crazy ones in the forest.*

Belac turned and took in the shelves of neatly organized supplies. *I wonder if Leeson was responsible for all this.* The thought of the man made Belac angry all over again. *Did he think of it as sorting supplies when he gave his people to monsters?* Belac found himself lamenting that Leeson had not been forced to wait in a cage before he was killed.

Two open crates in the back corner caught Belac's eye. *I wonder what's in those.* He took a bite of his jerky as he limped to the crates. *Maybe Leeson kept more booze down here.* He looked down into the open crates and considered the piles of crumpled brown cloth he found there. …*Are the booze hidden under the rags?*

Belac took another bite of jerky and then set his food on a nearby shelf. Reaching into the first of the crates, he proceeded to dig down in search of treasure. *It's just old clothes…* He narrowed his eyes at the clothes. *That is kind of a mean trick.*

Josey spoke from behind the elf. "I should have thought of that." She put a hand on his shoulder to stabilize herself. "You and the other men should take whatever you need."

I do need a new blouse. Belac began to dig around in the clothes, searching for something other than brown.

"No, not that one," Josey said, stepping away from the elf.

Belac turned his head; at first, thinking that the woman had been speaking to him. He watched as Josey issued orders to a pair of well dressed men. *Maybe we can trust them to deliver the messages.* Belac smiled to himself. *Though, we might need to send a woman with them to make sure it gets done.*

Belac went back to rummaging through the clothing. *Why is everything brown?* Eventually, he found a pale brown sleeve among the assortment of various other browns. He pulled on the sleeve, stretching out a worn blouse as it slid from the pile of clothes. *At least it doesn't look like what those crazy exiles wear.* He shook out the blouse and then draped it on top of the pile of clothes that he had been searching.

"That will work," Belac said aloud.

Though brown, the blouse was so pale that it could have almost been called gray. Something dark had stained a wide blotch onto the front of the blouse, but it seemed to have been cleaned as well as it could be. Belac removed both of his scabbarded swords and set them on the other crate. Then he picked up the blouse and pulled it over his head. *It's kind of soft.* The blouse was a little tight in the shoulders, but the fabric was flexible enough to be comfortable.

Belac considered the crates of old clothes. *There might be enough clothes here to outfit all the men, but they are still going to need something for their feet.* He turned and studied the other neatly organized supplies. *I need someone to tell me what all we have down here.* He grabbed the edge of a large box sitting to the left of the clothes. He lifted the lid and peered inside, finding a collection of old belts. Belac grinned. *It looks like someone is trying to start their own evil empire of belts.*

Simon approached from behind the elf. "Lord Ecard wants you to come read the message and tell him what you think."

Belac dropped the box's lid and then turned around. "I'll go look at it, but I am sure it's fine."

Simon tried to hide a smile behind his beard. He pointed at the elf's new garment. "That is a woman's blouse," he said, chuckling.

Belac narrowed his eyes at the forester. "You're wearing a tent."

Simon flexed his shoulders. "It's a manly tent."

Belac could not help but laugh at the forester's machismo. He pointed behind himself with a slender thumb. "You should still probably get some real clothes."

Simon pointed to the crate that the elf's swords were resting on. "Sure. But I think that I will pick some from that box."

Belac shrugged. "Alright. But…"

A man's voice shouted above, "Lord Belac!"

Belac grabbed his starmetal sword and slung it onto his back. Then he took the dwarf-sword in hand and began limping toward the stairs. "It sounds like they found something."

"Lord Belac!" the voice called again.

"I'm on my way." Belac shouted back.

Simon followed behind the elf. "Do you think the monsters have returned?"

Belac shook his head. "They would not come back this soon." *They need time to cut out their new prisoners' hearts.*

Belac hurried past the woman and children. Frightened anew, they had moved back away from the stairs. Grimacing, Belac limped up into the building above. *Should I have them close the hatch behind us?* He shook his head. *I will send someone back to close it if it comes to that.*

A man in green canvas met the elf at the door to the gathering hall. "Lord Belac! We found a monster!"

Belac gestured for the man to lead. "Name?" he asked as he followed the man through the empty gathering hall.

The man looked back. "The monster's?"

Belac frowned. "No. Yours." *I don't think the monsters have names.*

"Oh," the man said, realizing his mistake. "I'm Jeffrey." He glanced back at the elf. "But everyone calls me Jeff."

Belac nodded for the man to hurry. "Okay, Jeff. Where are we going?"

"It's just out here," Jeffery said as he hustled out of the gathering hall.

Then, why is there not more of an alarm? Belac followed the man outside. "What kind of monster is it?"

"I don't know." Jeffrey looked back at the elf while pointing ahead toward the road that led into the village. "But it's an evil looking thing."

Belac gazed off in the direction that the man was pointing. The half-naked escaped prisoners had surrounded something, their spears pointed inward. *Whatever they found, it's not a tree person.* As Belac got closer, he began to smile.

Twenty-Four

Belac pushed his way between the men with spears. Without hesitation, he threw his arms around the hulking, gray monster that the men had surrounded. A gray arm that ended in a gleaming metal hand wrapped around the elf and returned the hug awkwardly. *They're not dead!* Belac stepped back and appraised his friend. Though dressed like a buccaneer, Vairug was obviously an orc.

Vairug clapped the elf on the shoulder with his gray skinned hand. "I am glad that you're not dead."

A rich voice spoke from the elf's right. "There was a growing concern that the mermaids may have decided to keep you."

Belac turned toward the thin man dressed in immaculate black. "Mermaids?" he asked the wizard. Lithe beings of translucent grace flashed into his mind. *Why would mermaids save me?* The image turned to fangs.

Serath's smile twisted the perfectly trimmed beard around his mouth. "It seems as though you have escaped once again."

Belac took in the man's handsome features. "I hate your face," he said, and then wrapped his arms around the skinny wizard.

Rolan offered no greeting, instead saying, "Alright, Vairug. You win."

There was pride in Vairug's reply. "I told you so."

Belac let go of the wizard and stepped back. "You told him what?" he asked, looking to the orc.

Vairug smiled around his tusks. "Rolan thought that you would lose the sword."

Belac did not need to be told which sword they were referring to. He looked down at the dwarf. "You thought I would lose the sword?"

Rolan shrugged. "You lose stuff."

Belac narrowed his eyes at the dwarf. "Hey, Rolan." He did not wait for a response. "Where is your backpack?"

Though the dwarf still had leather pouches and sheathed blades strapped over his splotchy gray uniform, Rolan had lost his rucksack before the crash. With it, he had lost both his springer and the tools necessary to rebuild the wonderous device.

Rolan's stubbled cheek pulled back into a grin. "Die in a fire."

Belac hugged the dwarf. Rolan hugged back, popping the bones in Belac's spine. Belac muttered, "Stupid dwarf," just as Rolan muttered, "Stupid elf."

When the hug had ended, Belac stepped away, stumbling in the process.

Rolan sniffed at the air. "Are you drunk?"

Belac shook his head. "I hurt my ankle."

Rolan frowned, seemingly more disapproving of the injury than of the prospect of the elf being inebriated. "And you are just walking around on it?"

Belac gestured to the wizard. "Serath hasn't made me that flying carpet yet."

"You are not getting a flying carpet," Serath stated sternly, though his green eyes were bright with mirth.

Simon's deep voice interrupted. "Belac. Are these the friends you were talking about?"

Belac nodded as he turned. "They are." He gestured to the dwarf. "The grumpy dwarf here, is Rolan, master craftsman, master trader, master..." *murderer?* "...negotiator." He glanced at the dwarf.

Rolan shrugged and gave a nod.

Belac turned and gestured to the man in immaculate black. "The disgustingly handsome man is the wizard Serath, advisor to kings, and champion of the people."

Serath raised an eyebrow.

Belac limped closer to the orc and put a hand on his shoulder. "And this. This is Lord Vairdoe of Enevic, a man brave enough to face the dragon Danorin. In that tragic conflict, he lost a hand and gained a curse. Until he slays the monster that took his hand, Lord Vairdoe will be forced to walk the lands of man as an orc."

Vairug tilted his chin slightly upward.

Simon's response was one of surprise. "That's Lord Vairdoe?"

Vairug looked at the elf questioningly.

Belac shrugged. "Ecard is here." *Hey... I wonder why Ecard didn't follow me out here.*

Belac scanned the escaped prisoners, attempting to measure their belief. They had all seen the effects of magic far worse. Some of the men had lowered their spears; many of them had not. The men's beards made it difficult for Belac to make a confident determination. *I am just going to assume that they believe me.*

Belac made a lowering motion with his hands. "You can put the spears down. We are all friends here."

Craig planted the butt of his spear on the ground. "You heard Lord Belac!"

The other men followed suit, the tips of their spears rising up and away. Belac suddenly felt like he was inside a cage made of spears. The men were quiet, unsure of what they should do next. *This is not much better.*

Belac pointed with his entire hand. "I've had food brought up into the gathering hall." He scanned the bearded faces around him. "I am sure you are all hungry. Go ahead and get something to eat, and then you can finish searching the village."

As the men began to disperse, Rolan inquired cheekily, "Lord' Belac?"

Belac waved his hand dismissively. "It's an honorific. I rescued them from some crazy-evil-exiles-that-want-to-take-over-the-world, and I'm friends with Ecard."

Serath smiled and said in an amused tone, "It seems as though you have had a rather eventful time."

Belac nodded and then met the wizard's eyes. "And we need to talk about that. A couple of Elven exiles, a brother and sister, have moved into the forest. They dug up some kind of old temple and are using it to create monsters." He glanced at the burned village. "They are chopping people up and using their hearts in a magic ritual. They are turning people into these crazy looking things that are like a person made out of sticks, vines, and chunks of old wood. The exiles called them 'briar men' but the name does not do them justice. These things are strong enough to tear people apart, and I don't think that they can feel fear. I don't know how long the exiles have been taking people, but they have made a whole army of the things."

Serath's face was impassive. Belac glanced to his left, wondering if Vairug would offer more of a reaction. The orc appeared concerned. Belac then turned to Rolan. The dwarf looked like someone who did not understand a joke that had just been told.

Belac returned his attention to the wizard. "They are telling people that they represent the Elves." He shook his head determinedly. "We have to stop them."

Serath's demeanor became reflective. After considering the elf's words, he summarized, "So, two elves have uncovered an ancient temple. With it, they are amassing dark forces that they intend to dispatch into the lands of man."

Belac ignored the dramatic tone. "That about sums it up."

Serath continued, "And you have chosen to oppose them. You would stand with Humanity as a champion against the Elves?"

Belac did not like the wizard's phrasing. "I would stand with people against monsters."

Serath shook his head ruefully. "Belac. I had planned none of this for you." He placed a gloved hand on the elf's shoulder. "Still, I believe it is worthy of you."

Despite the color of the man's green eyes, Belac could understand why even kings trusted the wizard.

Serath removed his hand and then clapped the elf on the shoulder. "I will see to it that you have the time you need." He nodded his commitment. "I will also see to it that word of this reaches Harbridge. It will require that I revise my designs, but I can only account for the importance of such an event."

What? Belac wondered if the wizard was trying to confuse him. "What are you talking about?"

Serath stepped back. "I need to go." He gestured with both hands, one directed to either side of the elf. "Rolan and Vairug will remain with you. When you are finished here, set a course for Harbridge."

Belac did not like any part of the wizard's plan. "But Harbridge wants to kill me!"

Serath shook his head. "Things have changed in Harbridge. From what I understand, the crown has moved to another royal family. I doubt your capture is a priority for them at the present." He smiled at the elf. "Though I leave, my hopes remain with you." He nodded to both the dwarf and the orc. "Take care of each other." Then he turned and began walking away from the sun.

Belac watched as the wizard strode away, confounded by the abruptness of the man's departure. He raised his voice and called after the wizard, "You know?! This would be a lot easier if I had a wizard's help!"

Serath raised a gloved hand, waving his goodbye without slowing. "And you shall have it!"

Belac narrowed his eyes at the wizard's back. *I bet that they make wizards human just to make them more annoying.*

Rolan did not seem to share the elf's frustration. "Let him go. The man knows what he is about."

Belac directed his glare at the dwarf. "Do you know how to deal with magical problems?"

Rolan shrugged. "The same way that I deal with most of my problems."

Belac's glare broke into a grin. *People are going to die, and something is going to get set on fire.*

Vairug nudged the elf. "You mentioned something about food."

Belac nodded. "It's just dry rations right now." He turned his grin on the orc. "But the biscuits are probably bad enough that you might like them." He laughed at his own joke. "Who would have thought that dwarves were the only people that know how to make biscuits right?"

Rolan shook his head. "I didn't make the ones that you got from me."

Belac frowned. "That kind of messes up my joke." *But I guess that makes sense. If dwarves made travel rations, the biscuits would probably get people drunk.*

Rolan shrugged. "You can always make jokes about elves if you want to."

Belac narrowed his eyes at the dwarf.

"Hey Belac," Rolan said, failing to hide a smile. "Why did none of those men have shoes?"

A grin forced its way onto Belac's face. "Die in a fire."

Vairug complained, "I do not understand the joke."

Belac shook his head. "It's a stupid human story."

"About shoes?"

"Yes, about shoes."

"And how is that funny?"

"It's not."

"Obviously."

Twenty-Five

"I still do not understand," Vairug said as the three made their way toward the gathering hall. "Why were the elves making shoes in the first place?"

Belac pinched the bridge of his nose.

Rolan was still trying to explain. "I don't think that is the point of the story."

"I do not think the story has a point." Vairug sounded offended.

"I didn't write it," Rolan said defensively.

Vairug seemed not to hear the dwarf. "I am supposed to believe that a pack of elves were simply walking through human cities in search of shoes that needed to be finished?" He swept his gray hand through the air. "That's absurd!"

"That's…" Rolan began but was cut off.

Vairug glared at the elf limping along beside him. "And why were they naked?!" he asked accusingly.

Belac arched an eyebrow at the orc. "Orcs ate their clothes," he lied.

Vairug's dark eyes went wide. "They would not!"

Rolan tried to hold back a laugh but failed. The wheezing noise he made sounded almost painful.

Vairug crossed his arms. "Humans are bad at telling stories," he stated with authority.

Rolan gestured to the soot blackened stones of the gathering hall. "Be careful. You are supposed to be a human."

Vairug growled.

Rolan glanced at the orc. "That's not helping."

Vairug smiled angrily.

Rolan chuckled. "Maybe you should just growl."

Vairug looked away from the dwarf. "If I were human, I would not have survived the mermaids."

The comment troubled Belac. "Mermaids kill humans?" *Then what happened to all the humans on the ship?*

"Not on purpose," Rolan answered. "The mermaids feed on the vitality of the people they find. Most humans can't survive it."

I thought I had just been weak from drowning. "Wait!" Belac lowered his voice. "Does that mean that I am sterile now?"

Rolan shook his head. "That's virility. Vitality is sort of like your life essence. You'll be fine." He took a deep breath and then let it out. "But we haven't found any of the ship's crew alive."

Belac frowned. *They were all cowards, liars and thieves, but I kind of liked them.*

Vairug added, "We really were worried that the mermaids had kept you."

Belac's head turned toward the orc. "Then, how did you find me?"

Vairug gestured to the burned village. "We followed the smoke."

Belac glanced at the dwarf and then looked back to the orc. "So, you saw something on fire, and just assumed that it was my fault?!"

Rolan replied calmly, "Was it your fault?"

Belac did not know how to answer that. "Well..."

"Right," Rolan said with a nod.

As Belac limped into the gathering hall, he noticed that silence entered with him. The men, speaking casually as they ate, grew quiet and reserved. Belac found himself disappointed with the humans' behavior. *Maybe I am expecting too much from them. At least no one is trying to poke Vairug with a stick.* He continued limping until he reached the podium, and then he turned around. The room of silent men gazed back at him.

Belac spoke into the silence. "Alright, I get it. He is big and gray," he gestured to the orc, "but that is a person. He is my friend, and you people are lucky to have his help." Belac wanted to say more, but he did not know how to convince the humans.

Simon added his voice. "He looks like he can swing an axe to me." It was high praise from a forester.

Other men began to speak as well.

"He is so big, he looks like he could swing you!"

"Going to have a tough time chopping a tree down like that."

"Maybe he should use someone with a harder head."

"Are you volunteering?"

"I would rather have a hard head than have a soft one like yours."

The quality of the conversation devolved as more men joined in. Belac grinned. *I guess sometimes humans just need a little encouragement.* He motioned for his friends to follow him as he limped to Leeson's office.

Inside the modest office, Ecard still sat behind the desk. The lord's head lay face down on the desktop, with his arms sprawled out to the sides. Belac limped into the room, absently checking the open area to the left of the door. *I don't see any assassins.* His eyes ran over Ecard and the desk. *No blood.*

Belac stopped in the middle of the office. "Are you dead?"

Ecard did not answer.

Belac could see the lord breathing. "Ecard!" he shouted, trying to wake the man.

Ecard's head shot up, a sheet of paper stuck to his face. He pulled the page away and looked at it. "Death of all," he cursed. Dark ink had stained his right cheek and the side of his nose.

Belac grinned at the lord. "Don't worry about it. I have already sent word to Harbridge."

Rolan stepped around the elf and grabbed the back of the chair on the left. The back legs of the chair groaned loudly as he dragged it into the corner.

Ecard set his ruined missive on the desk and looked up. "How?" Startled, his back straightened at the sight of the orc standing in the office. He then breathed out, relaxing as comprehension found him.

Belac's grin crept farther up his face. "I have a wizard on his way there now."

Ecard rubbed sleep out of the corners of his eyes. "If anyone else had told me that..." He shook his head as he brought himself more awake. "Greetings, Lord Vairdoe. Rolan. It is good to see you both."

"Greeting's, Lord Ecard," Vairug replied formally.

Rolan nodded hello to the lord and then pointed his hand at the chair in the corner. "Belac. Sit here."

Belac did not care for the dwarf's tone, but he limped over to the chair all the same. *He probably wants to look at my ankle.* After removing his scabbarded swords, he set them in the corner behind the chair and then sat down.

Vairug nudged the dwarf. "I am going to get something to eat. Would you like me to bring you something back?"

Rolan shook his head. "I will find something later."

Belac did not think it was a good idea for the orc to explore too much on his own just yet. "There should still be some dry rations left in those boxes next to the podium out there."

"Where can I find water?" Vairug asked.

Belac did not know where the well was located. "The men have some buckets of water lying around in the gathering hall." He remembered the unique properties of the orc's saliva. *I can't have him drink from the same cups as the humans.* "Take that glass on the desk." He pointed to the empty glass that he had used earlier.

Vairug walked to the desk, picked up the glass, and then left the room. As the orc moved through the office, Belac noticed that while Vairug still had his crimson sash, the orc's cogged mace was absent from his hip. *He must have lost his mace in the wreck.* Though Belac knew that the orc was formidable even without a weapon, he made a mental note to find Vairug a replacement.

"Take off your boot," Rolan ordered gruffly.

Removing his boot caused Belac no small amount of discomfort. "I hope you can fix this."

Rolan knelt down and put a callused hand behind the elf's calf. "Let me look at it," he grumbled.

Rolan then proceeded to poke and prod at the elf's foot and ankle. No part of the experience did Belac find enjoyable. *I think he is just making it worse.*

After the examination, Rolan lowered the elf's foot. "You need to take better care of your feet." He gestured to the injured ankle. "If you had rested this, it probably would have healed on its own." He shook his head. "Now, it's a real problem."

Belac frowned at the dwarf. "It's not like I had a lot of choice in the matter. Evil tree people were trying to kill me, and they were not going to just wait patiently for me to heal."

Rolan nodded, showing that he accepted the argument as valid. "I don't have my kit with me, but I can try something that might work." He stood and pointed his hand at the elf. "Stay there," he ordered and then walked out of the office.

Belac narrowed his eyes at the empty doorway. *Bossy dwarf.*

Ecard spoke from the other side of the room. "Would it be safe to assume that your friends will be assisting in our efforts?"

Belac shrugged. "I don't know if it is safe or not, but that is what I am assuming."

Ecard smiled tiredly.

Belac regretted waking the man up. "Why don't you go get some rest?"

Ecard shook his head, his exhaustion clearly demonstrated in the motion. "There is still too much that remains to be done. You were right to send the men scouting, but we still need to organize patrols. We should also post guards on whatever food we have. It would be better to avoid… misunderstandings."

Belac recognized the wisdom. *If I don't have a wizard to help me, at least I have a general.* "Would you do me a favor before you take care of all that?"

Ecard nodded. "Of course."

Belac pointed his thumb at the door. "I need you to go downstairs and explain Lord Vairdoe's condition. Those people are scared enough as it is. If one of them sees him and starts screaming, there is no telling what the others will do."

Not arguing, Ecard asked, "Are you certain that I am the best person for this task?"

Belac nodded. "You're a human and they know that you're a lord, even if you are a foreign one. They will listen to you."

Ecard stood. "I will see to it now." As he walked around the desk, he added, "This is a subject that would be better addressed sooner rather than later."

Belac agreed. *Preferably before someone tries to stab my friend.* "Thanks, Ecard," Belac said as the man crossed the room.

Shortly after Ecard left the office, Vairug returned. *It is probably better to keep those two away from each other as much as possible.* Vairug brought with him a metal fistful of dried meat in one hand and a glass of water in the other. With his teeth, he held a biscuit sticking out of his mouth. Belac grinned. *We might need to work on Vairug's lordliness.*

Twenty-Six

Vairug set his empty glass on the desk and then refilled it from the decanter. He had moved his chair to the right of the desk, placing its back against the wall and giving him a better view of the room. From where he now sat, he could reach the desk only by leaning forward in his chair. He picked up the glass with his gray skinned hand, and a strip of deer jerky with his metal one. As he leaned back, he took a bite of the jerky, followed by a sip of the amber liquor.

After swallowing, Vairug complained, "These humans have ruined this meat." He scowled at the jerky held in his mechanical hand. "If it were not for this," he raised his glass, "the meat would be inedible."

Belac, still seated in the corner of the office, gnawed on a strip of jerky that the orc had given him. "I think it's good," he said with his mouth full. *And the biscuits were not as bad as I thought they would be.*

Earlier, Craig had brought Belac both a biscuit to eat and half a bucket of water to drink with it. The biscuit had been so dry, Belac had worried that half a bucket of water might not be enough to wash it down.

Belac gestured with his jerky. "I bet they will let you have another biscuit if you want one."

Vairug shook his head. "I need the meat."

As Belac ate, he became more and more aware of the consequences of drinking so much water. By the time he had finished eating the strip of meat, he had decided that he had a problem he could no longer ignore. He looked down at his bare foot, debating whether or not it was worth squeezing it back into his boot. Urgency made the choice for him. He stood from his chair and reached for his swords.

Vairug glanced at the elf's foot. "You are not supposed to walk on that."

Belac slung his swords onto his back. "It is either that, or I explode."

Vairug frowned. "You need to grow a larger bladder."

"Look at me." Belac gestured to his own slender frame. "Where would I put a bigger bladder?"

Vairug took a sip from his glass and continued to stare at the elf.

Belac swatted the air in the orc's direction. "I will be right back."

Belac limped out of the office and into the gathering hall. The escaped prisoners sat in the pews, talking to each other as they leisured. *It looks like they plan to sit around until someone tells them what to do.*

Belac halted in front of the podium. "The day is not over yet." He waited while the hall grew quiet. "We still need to search the village. Trouble is going to find us one way or another, and we need to be prepared for it. Take your spears, stay in groups, and remember that there are things out there that want to kill us."

Simon's deep voice resonated through the gathering hall. "You heard him. Let's go."

Belac limped past the men as they rose from the pews. *It's crazy how fast humans can forget that they are in danger.* He left the gathering hall and found a place outside to relieve himself. When he returned to the office, an angry dwarf was waiting for him.

Rolan was holding a rock in one hand and an open vial of pink liquid in the other. He looked down at the elf's booted and unbooted feet. "That is not making things better, Belac."

Vairug nodded. "I told him not to go," he said as he refilled his glass from the decanter.

Belac removed his swords and placed them behind the chair in the corner. "It could not be helped." He then sat down, glad to be off his ankle again.

Rolan knelt down in front of the elf. He set the rock on the floor and held the vial up. "Here. Hold this." As the elf took the vial, Rolan added, "Don't drink it."

Belac looked at the small vial, taking note of the wooden stir stick protruding from the pink liquid inside. He stirred the concoction with the stick and then sniffed the vial. Wrinkling his nose at the strange chemical smell, he moved the offensive thing away from himself. "This smells awful."

Rolan glanced up at the elf. "Then, don't drink it."

Rolan dragged Belac's water bucket closer and then positioned it under the elf's injured foot. While there was not much water remaining in the bucket, Rolan scooped up what he could and splashed it onto Belac's foot. Belac winced as the dwarf began to rub the grime away from his ankle.

When Rolan was satisfied that the ankle was clean enough, he picked up his rock and held it out to the elf. "Here. Trade me."

Belac took the rock and then handed the dwarf the glass vial. "What's the rock for?"

Rolan nodded toward the door. "Hand it to him," he said as he took hold of the elf's foot.

Belac turned in his seat, wondering who was in the doorway. "Ow!" he exclaimed as pain lanced through his ankle.

Belac attempted to yank his foot away, but Rolan held it firm. In his pain, Belac thought about hitting the dwarf in the head with the rock. *Sneaky dwarf!* Pain clawed its way through the elf's ankle, leaving behind trails that felt like molten fire. *He stabbed me!*

With his left hand locked around the elf's ankle, Rolan had the glass vial palmed in his right. In his fingers, he held a tiny wooden spear that had been mistaken for a stir stick. "Calm down," he said dispassionately.

Belac gripped the rock and once again considered hitting the dwarf in the head. "You could have warned me!"

Rolan shook his head. "You would have tensed up. I needed your ankle relaxed." He flicked the tiny spear to the side and then dribbled pink liquid into the wound he had created. With his left thumb, he began to rub the puncture.

Vairug laughed. "I bet you won't hit him."

Belac narrowed his eyes at the orc and considered throwing the rock at him. *He would probably just catch it in his shiny metal hand and crush it.* As Rolan continued to work his medicine into the wound, Belac's foot began to slowly go numb.

Belac looked down at the dwarf. "It stopped hurting."

Rolan nodded. "This should work, but you are going to have to stay off your feet until this heals."

Belac wiggled his toes. "So, you fixed it?" he asked optimistically.

Rolan frowned. "I am serious, Belac. Unless you want to go through life gimped, stay in that chair or have someone carry you."

"But what if I…" Belac began.

"Have someone carry you," Rolan repeated forcefully.

Belac nodded dejectedly. "Yeah, okay." He looked down at the dwarf. "But if a herd of angry owls come looking for me, you are on your own."

Rolan pushed the water bucket to the side. "Deal." He stood and then crossed the room, walking around to the other side of the desk. He grabbed the back of the unoccupied chair there and dragged it over to the elf. "Here. You can put your foot up if you want to." He repositioned the chair. "It is probably better if you do."

Belac put his foot on the seat, half worried that the dwarf would try to tie his leg to the chair. "How long do I have to sit here?"

Rolan shrugged. "I am not sure how well this is going to work. Just stay put until I come back and check on you."

Come back? Belac looked from his foot to the dwarf. "Where are you going?"

"I need to go see what all we have to work with," Rolan replied. "But first, I need to get some more details from you."

"What kind of details?" Belac did not want to waste time guessing.

"I need a better idea of what we are up against," Rolan explained. "I need the size and disposition of the forces, both theirs and ours. I need to know how soon you expect an attack and what you think is the most likely scenario. You said that there are only two elves. Do they make up the entirety of the leadership? If so, do you know their motivations or their goals?" His professional tone took on an edge. "Lastly, I need to know our objective. Are we here to save a village, or to kill monsters."

Belac forgot about his foot. "Wow… Ah… That's a lot."

Rolan did not apologize. "You have raised forces, you've taken over a village, and you are having people call you a lord. If you are not serious about this, we should leave while we can."

Belac shook his head. "Those exiles are not just insane, Rolan. They're evil. I have to stop them."

Rolan was unmoved. "There are evil people doing evil things everywhere. At a minimum, you are going to have to learn to prioritize. You want to be a dragon slayer? Fine. But there are no dragons here. There is no reason for us to get involved. Let the humans solve their own problems."

Belac shook his head again. "You don't understand. I," he tapped his chest, "I have to stop them. Those exiles are claiming to represent The Elves. All elves. Me. If someone claims to represent you, and you don't try to stop them, then they do represent you. If you don't punish them for daring to invoke you, if you don't show the world where you truly stand, then the villains do represent you."

Belac moderated his voice though his pulse continued to increase. "I will not let them commit evil in my name. I will not let them start a war with the very people I live amongst. I will not hide and try to go unnoticed. I will not wait and secretly hope that I somehow benefit from what the villains do. I will not!" Belac's closed fist slammed against his chest. "I will stop them."

Rolan frowned. "That's a good reason."

Vairug held up his glass. "I'm in."

Twenty-Seven

Belac was awakened by the smell of manifest damnation. "Ugh! Vairug, did you die?" He fanned his hand in front of his face.

Vairug laughed from where he lay on the floor of the office.

Belac took his bare feet off the chair in front of him and set them on the floor. He stood, fanning the air and trying not to breathe more than he absolutely needed to. Though he grabbed his swords from behind the chair, he decided that his boots would simply have to be left behind. *I need out of this room!*

As he swung the door to the gathering hall open, Belac called back, "I am leaving the door open, Vairug." *Or it will never be safe to come back and get my boots.*

The gathering hall was empty of people despite the morning sun that crept in through the windows. *I can't let the humans just stay underground forever.* As he went outside and delt with his morning concerns, Belac wondered what the people in the cellar were doing for facilities. *Maybe I don't want to know.*

The morning air had a damp ashy taste to it. Groups of men dressed in brown moved about the ruined village; some on patrol, others preparing for the day ahead. Birds chirped in the distance, announcing that life had not yet abandoned Gofell.

A village is more than lumber and stone. Belac stood outside the gathering hall, hoping that his plan to rescue Gofell would succeed.

Belac narrowed his eyes at a group of four men. *Where did they get boots?* He knew that there were clothes in the cellar, but he had not seen any boots. Barefoot, he walked over to interrogate the men. To him, it did not seem fair that everyone else now had footwear, while his were trapped in an orcish miasma.

Belac halted in front of the men and pointed low. "Where did you get those?"

None of the men seemed to know what to do with the question. One of them looked to his friends and then held up the felling axe that he carried. "Rolan told us we should take them," he said as if he were worried that he had done something wrong.

Belac looked from the axe to the other men. They had all traded their spears for axes. One of the men even had a short sword hanging from his hip. *I probably should have noticed that.* Belac nodded as if that had been his question all along. "And what about the boots?"

The spokesman for the group answered again. "Rolan told us that we should take them too." He looked down at the elf's bare feet. "We did not take yours. I promise!"

Belac waved the concern away. "Then, where did Rolan get boots?" *I swear. If someone tells me that magical elves made them…*

"Oh," the man said, now understanding. "We found weapons and clothes a little ways west of the village. Those filthy…" he stopped himself as he remembered who he was speaking to. "Those elves stripped the prisoners naked before they carried them off. Rolan had us move everything to the factorage." He pointed to one of the few buildings left standing.

Belac considered the stone building. "I should probably go take a look." *Maybe the merchant trades wine.* As he began walking toward the factorage, Belac called back, "Don't let owls steal your boots!"

"Owls stole his boots?" one of the men muttered.

Though Belac was sure that the factorage must have had a store front on the other side, he did not bother walking around to it. Instead, he headed straight to the half burned loading bay doors on the side that he could see. As Belac approached the building, a man dressed in a blue doublet walked out smoking a long-stemmed pipe. *This guy…*

The merchant lowered his pipe and bowed. "Good morning, Lord Belac," he said with a smile. "I would like to apologize for my behavior yesterday. It had been a rather trying day and I was unaware of who you were."

Someone needs to teach humans how to actually apologize. Belac stared at the merchant, suspicious of the man's sudden conversion.

The merchant took a draw from his pipe and then blew the smoke away to the side. He smiled again. "Though I imagine it is possible that you did not know who I was either," he said as if making an understatement. He took a step back and bowed again. "Harris Lud, at your service."

…Right. Belac crossed his arms and wondered what the merchant was about to try to sell him.

Harris continued, "Though your prestige had yet to reach Gofell, I am certain that I would have heard of you when next I sojourned in Harbridge." He pointed with the stem of his pipe. "Someone with your connections is not to go unnoticed."

What did Rolan tell this guy? Belac checked his surroundings, half worried that the merchant might be trying to distract him.

"Are you looking for Master Rolan?" Harris asked with a tone that suggested he was attempting to be helpful. "He is inside, appraising his most recent of acquisitions."

Belac raised an eyebrow. "What did he buy?"

Harris gestured grandly to the factorage. "Everything."

I guess that is one way to deal with the merchant. When Rolan had said that he would handle the merchant, Belac had expected something less polite.

Rolan walked out of the loading bay carrying an axe in one hand and two sheathed knives in his other. He stopped in front of the elf and frowned. "I just fixed that yesterday," he said, pointing the axe at the elf's foot. "Are you trying to ruin your feet?"

Belac glanced down at his own bare feet. "No. I… Ah…" He looked up at the dwarf. "I was kind of in a hurry."

Harris stepped away, speaking in a friendly tone. "I will leave you two gentlemen to plan your day." He began strolling toward the gathering hall, granting the other two their privacy.

Rolan ignored the man. "You don't look like you are in a hurry," he said to the elf.

Belac leaned forward and spoke in a lowered voice. "Vairug stunk up the room."

Rolan's stony gray eyes were disapproving. "You fed deer jerky and bourbon to an orc. What did you think was going to happen?"

Belac shrugged angrily. "I didn't think that it was going to rot his insides."

Rolan held out the axe and knives. "Here. Take these." As the elf took the items, Rolan continued to issue orders. "Go back to the office. Give Vairug the axe and one of the daggers. You keep the other one." He gestured at the elf's bare feet. "Then put on your boots."

Belac held up the knives. "Which one do I give him?"

Rolan shrugged. "It doesn't matter. They are both good blades. Just pick one."

Belac nodded. "I can do that."

Rolan pointed to the factorage with his thumb. "I am going to keep getting things ready for you and your team. I should have everything together in time for you to set off after lunch."

Belac glanced at the building. "Did the merchant have what we need?"

Rolan nodded. "Fortunately, he imported tools for the village as well as managing timber shipments. If the plan fails, it will not be due to a lack of tools."

Belac held up the axe. "I will get this to Vairug, then."

"Let him know that I have a job for him," Rolan added. "The hunters that we sent out should be back soon and I want Vairug to help with the hides."

Belac glanced over his shoulder at the gathering hall. "You want him to spit on them?"

Rolan nodded. "It's the fastest way to treat the hides. We need all the resources that we can get. I do not know what the hunters are going to bring back, but I am sure we can find a use for the leather."

Belac decided to leave before the dwarf could make a joke about cobbling shoes. "I'm on it," he said and then hurried away.

As Belac neared the gathering hall, he heard Simon speaking to someone inside. The man's words were forceful, but Belac could not immediately make them out. Josey answered, her voice no less forceful than her husband's. The conversation became clear as Belac entered the hall.

"I have to go," Simon told his wife.

"No, you don't," Josey argued as if her words were law.

"You don't understand, Sweetheart," Simon insisted. "Those men that were taken..." he could not finish the thought. "We can't leave our people to those demons."

"It does not have to be you that saves them," Josey said, caring only for her husband.

Simon's tone became angry. "You would have me hide in the cellar while the men go off to war?" He thrust his hand toward the door that led down to the women and children. "What would that make me?"

Scorning her husband's pride, Josey shouted, "It would make you alive, Stupid!"

Despite the size of the gathering hall, Belac did not want to be in there with the couple while they fought. *I am not getting pulled into a fight with a pregnant woman.* Staying close to the wall on his right, Belac began to tiptoe around to the office.

The elf's attempt at stealth only exaggerated his movements. *Don't see me. Don't see me. Don't see me.* Bringing each knee up to his chest before reaching out with his toes, he found himself glad that he was barefoot.

Twenty-Eight

When Belac finally snuck into the office, he discovered that Vairug was up and about. Filling his glass from a newly opened bottle of liquor, the orc turned his head as Belac entered the room. *I need to learn how to sneak better.*

Vairug set the bottle on the desk. "I do not like your plan."

"Well, good morning to you too," Belac replied.

Vairug frowned at the elf. "I should go with you."

Belac shook his head. "I need you on the other team."

"Bah!" Vairug swiped his gray hand through the air, dismissing the importance of his role.

Belac held out the felling axe that he carried. "Here. You can show the humans that you know how to swing an axe."

Vairug accepted the axe with his mechanical hand and then transferred it to his one of flesh. "This is a nice axe." He rotated the haft. "But the handle is too long."

"It is designed to chop down trees," Belac explained.

Vairug seemed not to hear the elf. "I will need to cut it down and reshape it." He tapped a point approximately one third away from the bottom of the handle. "Right about here."

Belac set one of the sheathed knives on the desk. "Here. Maybe this will help."

Vairug's metal hand patted his crimson sash. "I have a knife."

He must be hiding one. Belac left the knife on the desk. "Now, you have two."

Vairug did not look away from the axe. "I will need to see if Rolan can find me a saw."

"You should go do that now," Belac advised as he walked to the chair in the corner. "Rolan has something he wants you to do anyway."

Vairug lowered his new axe and looked at the elf. "What does he want me to do?"

Belac sat down on the edge of the chair's seat, careful to keep his swords from banging against the wall. "We have some hunters due back soon. He wants you to orcify the hides for him."

"Orcify?" Vairug asked.

Belac reached for one of his boots. "He wants you to spit on the hides for him."

Vairug looked up and away. "Orcify. Pronounced: orc, if, eye. Definition: To improve upon the nature of a thing." He nodded approvingly. "I like it."

That is really not what I meant. "Yeah, okay." Belac began putting on his boots.

Vairug picked up his glass with his mechanical hand and drank the amber liquor inside. Once finished, he set the glass back down on the desk. Belac was again impressed with how well the Vairug could control the prosthetic. *I wonder if he practices when no one is looking.*

Vairug grabbed his new knife, his metal fingers gripping the leather sheath gently. "First, I would like to get something to eat."

Belac pointed his thumb at the door. "I think that there are still some biscuits left in the box. I know they don't taste great, but they should keep you full until the hunters get back with some real food."

Vairug turned. "Is there any of the dried meat left?"

I hope not. While the air in the office was breathable, Belac did not want it to get any worse. "There might be some more downstairs, but you would have to go look."

Vairug shook his head. "It would be better if I waited for the humans to come up and see me outside. It will be difficult enough as it is to convince them that I am not going to eat them."

Belac nodded. *I should have considered that.* He imagined Vairug walking into the dim light of the cellar and saying, 'I need meat.' *That might not go so well.*

Belac stomped his feet down into his boots and stood up. "I will go see what I can find."

Vairug nodded his thanks. "I will meet you at the merchant's building."

Belac grinned. "It is not the merchant's anymore."

Vairug gave the elf a curious look.

"I think Rolan bought it," Belac explained.

Vairug shrugged dismissively. "That is not how I would have delt with things, but I am sure Rolan knows what he is doing."

Belac went to the door and poked his head out of the office.

"What are you doing?" Vairug asked, moving closer.

Belac scanned the empty hall. "Avoiding a woman's wrath."

Vairug leaned past the elf and looked out into the gathering hall. "Then, you grow wiser by the day."

Belac stepped out of the office. "She may have gone back downstairs."

Vairug followed the elf into the gathering hall. "Then, while you go look for food, I will go outside. This way, at least one of us will survive."

Belac smiled, once more happy to have his friend back. *It's a shame that we will have to split up again.* He gestured to the main entrance. "Go. Tell the world that I died bravely."

"You should be so lucky," Vairug replied as the elf walked away.

As Belac made his way down into the cellar, he wondered if he would have the courage to die bravely. *When the time comes, what direction will I be running? Away from the danger, or toward it?* He decided that it was a question he would prefer never have answered.

Once he was in the candlelit sub-level, Belac began to look for Josey. He debated whether or not he should ask her for help, but was saved from having to make the decision. *I don't think she is here.* Belac smiled. *Maybe Vairug found her.*

Belac walked over to a matronly woman that was sitting alone. "Hello. I was wondering if you could help me find something."

The woman crossed her arms. "That depends on what you are looking for." Her dark eyes regarded the elf sternly.

Belac smiled as charmingly as he could. "I am looking for something to eat that is not deer jerky or biscuits."

The woman continued to stare at him through the candlelight. "So, you're an elf," she said instead of offering food.

Belac gestured to one of his pointed ears. "Yep." *Now, about that food...*

"Biscuits and jerky are not good enough for elves?" the woman asked like a disapproving grandmother.

Belac shook his head quickly. "It's not for me." He pointed toward the stairs. "It is for my friend." *Go yell at him.*

"Lord Vairdoe?" the woman asked, her tone completely different.

Belac nodded. "The jerky does not agree with him."

"Oh! Well, bless his heart." The woman stood up. "Let me find you something he can eat."

What?! She likes the orc? She has not even met him! Belac followed the woman, confounded by her values.

"That poor man," the woman muttered as she led the elf to a shelving unit toward the back. She reached up and pulled down a large cylindrical tin. Then she turned and pushed the tin into the elf's arms.

Belac tried to hold the tin without crushing the sides or dropping his new knife. "What's in it?" *This thing is a lot lighter than it looks.*

The woman twisted off the lid of the tin, revealing what was inside. "Pork rinds."

Belac was struck by the sick, salty smell of the things. He pulled his head away from the tin. "Okay, okay, close it, close it!" He struggled as he attempted to get his head farther away from the smell.

The woman reached into the tin and pulled out one of the curly yellow strips. "They taste better than they smell," she said as she twisted the lid back on the tin.

I am not going to taste this stuff! Belac was not convinced that even Vairug would eat the foul smelling things. "Are you sure this is really food?"

The woman bit into the pork rind and let it crunch in her open mouth. She made a show of swallowing. "See?"

I see that you are a crazy person. Belac pitied anyone that would have to talk to the woman now. He smiled unconvincingly.

The woman chuckled and then walked away.

Belac considered putting the tin back on the shelf and leaving it there. Even if Vairug would eat the pork rinds, Belac did not know if he wanted him to. *At least I won't have to be there when he wakes up tomorrow.*

As Belac turned to leave, he remembered the biscuit and strip of jerky that he had left behind the previous day. Instead of leaving, he moved deeper into the cellar, intent on a breakfast that he could stomach. Fortunately for the hungry elf, both of the dry rations were still on the shelf where he had left them. *I bet no one even noticed that they were here.* He stared at the food, realizing that he was going to have trouble carrying everything. Once again, he seriously considered leaving the tin behind. *No. Vairug needs to eat too.*

Belac set the tin down on the floor and tucked his new knife into the waist of his trousers. As he did, he found himself facing the box filled with old belts. *New plan.* He pulled the knife and its sheath out of his trousers and set it on a crate of clothes. *I needed a belt for the knife anyway.* He wiggled the lid off the box and then leaned it against the side.

There were too many belts for Belac to inspect them all, but he quickly found one that he could make work. Though the end of the belt's tongue had been torn off, Belac was thin enough that a new eyelet would be all it took to make the belt fit him. He laid the belt out on the edge of the box and used his new knife to dig out a crude hole in the leather. Then he put the knife in its sheath and the sheath on the belt.

Belac looked at the heap of damaged belts. *These things have got to be useful for something.* He frowned in thought and then smiled. He tossed his belted knife to the side and began pulling out the strips of worn leather.

Twenty-Nine

With the large cylindrical tin tucked under his left arm, Belac gnawed on the strip of deer jerky in his other hand. He strolled through the burned doors of the factorage's loading bay, pleased with his own ingenuity. Inside, he found Rolan and Vairug facing each other in focused debate.

"…do not care. He should be told," Vairug asserted.

Rolan scowled up at the orc. "That is not what we agreed to. We have to trust him."

Belac thought that interrupting would be more polite than eavesdropping. "What's the problem?"

Rolan frowned at the elf and then gestured to the orc. "Vairug does not like the plan."

Vairug crossed his arms and said nothing.

Belac remembered the orc's previous objections. "I will be fine, Vairug. Things need to be this way if any of this is going to work."

"He's right," Rolan agreed.

If Vairug had not been an orc, his demeanor may have been described as pouting.

Belac brought his jerky up to his mouth so that he could hold the strip of meat with his teeth. Then he used his free hand to reposition the tin and hold it out to the orc. "Here. Take this," he said around the jerky clenched between his teeth.

Vairug uncrossed his arms and took the tin. "What is it?" He shook the container, causing the pork rinds inside to shift audibly.

Rolan put a hand to his forehead and pinched his temples. "If you don't know what's inside, then you probably shouldn't shake it."

Vairug lowered the tin and looked to the elf. "Would you give me something that I should not shake, and not tell me?"

Belac took the jerky out of his mouth and smiled. "If I thought it would be funny."

Vairug frowned at the tin. "Then… Is it safe to open it?"

No. Not even a little. Belac took three steps back. "Sure. Go ahead."

Vairug looked at the elf and then turned to the dwarf.

Rolan met the orc's eyes and then turned to the elf.

Belac tilted his head to the side, indicating to the dwarf that he should step away.

Rolan moved like he thought the tin might explode. He hopped and then shuffled back farther than the elf had. "I think you should open it," he said after a pause.

Vairug's dark eyes darted from the dwarf, to the tin, to the elf. "Belac?"

Belac smiled and gave an exaggerated shrug.

Vairug frowned at the elf. Then he set the tin on the floor and held it in place with his feet. He twisted the lid off the tin and pulled it back, holding the lid like a shield between himself and whatever might be inside the tin. When nothing shot out and tried to kill him, he slowly peered around the edge of the lid.

Vairug took a deep whiff and then looked up. "It's food!"

If you want to call it that.

Vairug sent the lid flying to the side, where it bounced off a wall before clattering onto the floor. Then he sat down cross legged with the open tin in front of him and began to munch on the crinkled strips of fried pork skin. When Rolan walked over and took one of the pork rinds, Vairug growled at him.

Rolan ignored the growl. "Why would you give him these?" he asked, laughing.

Belac shrugged. "I'm not going to be here."

Rolan chuckled and then popped the pork rind into his mouth. He pointed at the elf as he chewed. "What are you wearing?" he asked as if seeing the elf for the first time.

Belac held out his arms and spun around, displaying the strips of leather that he had wrapped around his forearms, abdomen, and shins. "Behold! The armor of the Evil Empire of Belts!"

Rolan shook his head. "You look ridiculous."

Belac stood tall and held his head up high. "I look like an elf prepared for war!" he replied playfully.

Rolan gestured to the elf's improvised armor. "What do you think that is going to do? You are going into a forest. Those straps are just going to get snagged on things."

Belac looked at his own leather belts and then the ones strapped all over the dwarf. "You have leather straps too!"

Rolan held out his arms. "Mine are holding things on!"

Belac brought his hand up to his face and pointed a slender finger at the dwarf. "You are just jealous that I have more straps than you now."

Rolan took a deep breath and let the matter drop. "I have your team's gear ready," he said, changing the subject. "But, there is a problem. We lost two men last night."

"How?" Belac asked before the dwarf had time to explain.

Rolan frowned. "Desertion. Neither of the men were from the village. They must have figured that this was not their fight."

Belac was not entirely surprised by the development. Its possibility was one of the reasons that he wanted to enact his plan as soon as he could. He knew that the longer the men waited, the more likely they were to change their minds. Attrition was already working against him. Belac did not know how fast Kaelem could turn humans into briar men, but every enemy gained would be another ally lost. *We are outnumbered too much as it is.*

Vairug stopped eating long enough to say, "We are better off without the cowards."

Rolan did not agree with the orc. "Cowards can still be useful if managed properly."

Vairug did not bother arguing.

Belac chose not to dwell on the loss. "I will just have to make do with the men that I have."

Vairug looked up from the tin, his thoughts obvious.

Belac pointed at the orc. "No. You can't come with me."

Vairug frowned and went back to eating pork rinds.

Rolan attempted to console the orc. "The plan works better if you are not there."

Vairug looked at the dwarf sideways. He was not consoled.

Ecard walked into the loading bay. His dark hair had been combed and pulled back into a tail, and he had even taken the time to trim his beard. "Ah. You are here."

Belac assumed that the man was speaking to him. "Is something wrong?"

Ecard gave the elf a comradely smile. "Quite a lot, I would imagine."

Belac nodded, finding the pessimistic humor tedious.

Ecard turned toward the dwarf. "The men are back from their hunt. They are preparing for the social now."

Rolan accepted the news with a nod. "What did they bring back?"

"Hog," Ecard said, holding up two fingers. "Two of them. And they are rather large, I must say."

Belac glanced down at the pork rinds. *It would be more pig.* "Are we going to roast them?"

Ecard shook his head. "Roasting them would take far too long. They will need to be butchered. Though, I doubt it will be expertly done. This will allow us to cook the meat faster and have everything prepared within your time frame."

Belac pointed with his thumb. "We still need to get those people to come out of the cellar."

Ecard nodded. "That was my very next destination. Would you care to accompany me?"

Belac shook his head. "I think it's better if you handle it. Try to keep everyone focused on the preparations. I know that it is going to be hard, but do your best. Get Simon to help you. Once you have everything ready, come and get us. You can introduce us to the village and then we can all eat. Hopefully, everyone will be too hungry to freak out when they see Lord Vairdoe."

Ecard eyed the elf suspiciously. "You want to establish me as an authority."

It's good that he noticed that. Belac nodded. "It will make the other elements of my plan work better." He paused and then added, "You are important, Ecard."

Ecard stood taller as his posture improved. Groomed, fed, and rested, the man finally looked the noble he was. "Then, I will see to it." He gave a crisp nod and then left, a man on a mission.

Once the lord had left the building, Belac realized that his friends were staring at him. "What?"

Vairug went back to eating.

Rolan scratched the stubble on his cheek.

"What?" Belac asked again.

Rolan shook his head and shrugged.

After a moment of awkward silence, Vairug inquired, "Is the party merely a way to place Ecard in command?"

Belac shook his head. "No. We need those people to come out of the cellar, and I want the men to have at least one good meal before we head back into the forest. The party acts as a distraction while I fit everything together."

"And Ecard?" Rolan asked without judgement.

Belac welcomed the question. "I do want Ecard in a leadership role. He's a general, and I think that he is technically still a lord. The humans are going to need a human that they can look to." He gestured to himself with both hands and then swept them out toward his non-human friends.

Vairug considered the elf's words and then smiled, his tusks jutting from his mouth. "You know what that means? It means that Rolan is the only one in command that is not a lord."

Rolan scowled at the orc.

Vairug pointed at the dwarf. "That is insubordination."

Thirty

"What were the clothes made from?" Vairug asked into the silence of the loading bay.

Lying on his back, staring up at the rafters, Belac had no idea what the orc was talking about. "You are going to need to be more specific."

"The elves," Vairug offered as clarification.

Why would that matter? Belac thought back on what the Elven exiles had been wearing. "It was just some kind of ugly gray cloth. A sleeveless tunic and some loose trousers."

Vairug did not seem content with the answer. "Are you sure? Things would make more sense if their clothes had been made from leather."

"What?" Belac rolled over and looked at the orc. "Why?"

Vairug frowned from where he sat leaning against the wall, whittling the haft of his axe. "If the orcs were starving, they might be willing to eat clothes made out of leather." His frown deepened. "Though, I do not know why they would not simply eat the elves."

Belac closed his eyes. *He is talking about that stupid cobbler story.* The elf opened his eyes. "Maybe the orcs took the clothes while the elves were bathing in a river."

Vairug pointed his knife at the elf and nodded. "But that does not explain why the orcs would eat the clothes."

Belac shook his head. "Maybe the clothes were soaked in blood."

"That's brilliant!" Vairug exclaimed. "That would even explain why the elves were bathing!"

Belac held up a hand in lazy congratulation. "Seems as though you solved it."

"The pack of vicious elves must have raided an orcish tribe," Vairug said as he began to detail the events. "The elves must have slaughtered everyone. Otherwise, they would not have had so much blood on their clothes and then still have survived the encounter." He pointed with his knife again. "That means, that the elves must have struck at night."

"The pack of vicious elves?" Belac asked dryly.

Vairug continued as if he had not heard the elf. "Sneaking through the darkness like jackals, they murdered the tribe while it slept. The males and the females; the young and the old. I bet the elves danced after they did it."

"The elves?" Belac asked again. "The shoe making elves?"

"Once they were finished," Vairug continued, "they would have slunk back into the night like the cowards they were."

At least that's the end of the story.

Vairug had not finished telling the story. "But what the elves did not know, was that a band of orcs had been out hunting. When the hunters returned, they did so to silence and blood. They would have looked upon the dead and known that they themselves could not live in a world where such a thing could go unpunished." There was heat in Vairug's words.

Belac looked at his friend uneasily.

Vairug took a moment to collect himself and then added, "The hunters must have tracked the blood."

Belac cleared his throat. "It was… ah… no one I knew."

Denis and another man entered the loading bay through the half burned doors that hung open toward the gathering hall. Each of the men carried a fresh hide covered in blackish brown hair. Though Belac recognized the second man, the elf did not know his name.

As the two men walked toward the orc, Denis declared, "Lord Ecard told us that we should bring these to you." Both of the men were hesitant in their approach.

Vairug rose from the floor, his axe clutched in his metal hand and his knife held in his other. He attempted a reassuring smile and then gestured with the knife. "You can leave them on the floor here."

Neither of the men seemed reassured by having an orc smile at them.

Denis dropped his hide first. "Rolan told me that I am going to be on your team," he said, stepping out of the other man's way.

Vairug glanced over to where the elf lay on the floor. "Both teams will need men of courage."

Belac rolled backward onto his shoulders and then kipped up onto his feet. *It is really nice to have two working feet again.* He left both of his scabbarded swords on the floor, stepping over them as he moved toward Denis.

Belac clapped the man on the shoulder. "Denis won't let you down." He nodded to the second man. "I once saw these men stand and face an angry-feather-bear. They were half starved, half naked, completely exhausted, and they had nothing but sharpened sticks."

Both of the humans stood taller.

"An angry-feather-bear?" Vairug asked skeptically.

"It was way scarier than it sounds." Belac gestured to the two humans. "They called it a kuma. It was a giant bear covered in feathers." He shrugged. "And it was angry." Then he added, "I mean, like really angry."

Vairug appraised the faces of the two humans. "And what became of the kuma?"

Belac wanted to be honest without taking away from the humans' contributions. "They helped me kill it."

Vairug nodded. "Then, I welcome your valor."

The second man set his hog hide down, moving as if afraid to draw attention.

Belac did not want the man to go unnoticed. "What is your name?"

The man blinked, startled by the question. "I'm Philip."

I need to make sure that he goes with my team. Belac's smile was far more reassuring than the orc's. "Are you ready to go with me, Philip?"

Philip nodded quickly. "I will be, Sir. Ah… Lord?"

Belac swept his hand, dismissing the issue. "I don't need a title. There are 'Sirs' and 'Lords' all over the place. If you need to get my attention, use my name."

Philip nodded again.

Denis waved for the other man to follow him. "Come on, Phil. We need to get back to work." He nodded to both the elf and the orc. "Lord Belac. Lord Vairdoe."

After the humans had left, Vairug said, "I think they like you better than me."

Belac grinned at the orc. "That's just because I know how to keep my teeth on the inside of my mouth."

Vairug contorted his upper lip, tucking his tusks into his mouth. "Isthisbetter?" he mumbled through his bulging lips.

Belac laughed. "You have got to show that to Rolan."

Vairug's tusks popped out of his mouth as he smiled. "He may see it as a challenge and decide to build himself a mechanical jaw."

Belac imagined how the dwarf would look with a metal wolf's muzzle strapped to his face. "I take it back. Let's not give him any ideas." He went back to his swords and laid out on the floor next to them. "Though… I wonder if I could get him to make one for me." *It would look better on me anyway.*

Vairug sat down next to the hides. He set his axe and knife to the side and then reached for one of the harry hog skins. "Would you really want metal teeth?"

Belac thought the question sounded like a trap. "I would not want to give up my real ones for them."

Vairug held up his prosthetic hand. "I can understand that." He spat on the inside of the hide, folded it over, and then began to rub the hide against itself.

Belac continued to consider the idea of a mechanical jaw as he gazed up into the rafters. "Maybe I could get him to make me a whole mask. Something that could protect my face." *I really don't want to lose my teeth.*

"I am certain that he could craft something fearsome." Vairug looked up from the hide. "That dwarf has a violent mind." He unfolded the hide and looked down at his work. He frowned.

Belac tried to imagine what he would want his mask to look like. "What kind of a mask would you want?" he asked, searching for ideas.

Vairug did not answer.

Belac turned his head to look at the orc. "Vairug?"

Vairug seemed to not hear the elf. He spat on the hide again, folded it over, and then rubbed vigorously. Then he opened the hide and stared down at it.

Belac saw fear in the orc's eyes. "Vairug, what's wrong?"

Vairug tossed the hide aside. "Maybe I just need something to drink," he said to himself as he rose to his feet.

Belac's concern grew as Vairug hurried over to a bucket of water sitting next to the burned doors. The orc picked up the bucket and began to drink greedily, spilling water onto his chest. Then he dropped the bucket and went back to the hides. He picked up the hide that he had been working on and began to spit forcefully. When he rubbed the hide again, his movements seemed frantic.

Vairug opened the hide and stared down at it. After a moment of disbelieving silence, he looked up. "Rolan!" he shouted toward the factorages offices. When the dwarf did not magically appear, Vairug shouted again, "Rolan!"

Rolan rushed into the loading bay with a knife drawn, his stony eyes scanning for threats. When he did not see anything that needed to be stabbed, he sheathed his blade. "What?" he asked the orc irritably.

Vairug held out the hide, its inside facing the dwarf.

Rolan gestured to the hide. "I don't know what that means," he said impatiently.

Vairug's eyes begged the dwarf for help. "It doesn't work."

Rolan's tone softened. "Your saliva?"

Vairug nodded. "There is something wrong with me."

Rolan shook his head. "Not necessarily."

Vairug thrust the hide at the dwarf. "It's not working!"

Rolan nodded. "It could be something environmental. Maybe dietary." He tilted his head and looked down in thought. "Orcs don't cross The Divide all that often. When they do, it's not for very long. It could be that you need to eat something that only grows in your homelands."

Vairug calmed as he considered the dwarf's words. He lowered the hide and asked, "What can be done about it?"

Rolan let out a breath and shook his head. "I don't know that there is anything to be done. If this is just a matter of you not getting something that you are used to, then it should fix itself when you go back home." He shrugged. "If it's something else... Well, lots of people do just fine without spit that can tan leather."

Vairug threw the hide down and then walked back to his axe. He sat down, crossed his arms, and refused to look at his friends. Though he was an orc, no one could have mistaken his behavior for anything other than pouting.

Thirty-One

When the time came to join the humans for lunch, Vairug was still in a mood. "Why can't I bring my axe?"

Belac did not understand the orc's sudden attachment to the weapon. "Because you are scary enough without it. Part of why we are doing this is to help the humans not be afraid of you." He gestured to the axe that the orc had spent the morning reshaping. "That thing is not going to help."

Vairug gave no indication that he would be surrendering his axe. "I should be allowed to bring a weapon."

Belac attempted to mollify the orc. "Look at it this way: you are a weapon."

"I am not!" Vairug replied vehemently. "A weapon is a tool. A thing created, used, and discarded. A thing wielded by the hand of another. A thing without agency or will." He pointed the head of his axe at the elf. "I am not a tool."

Belac held up his hands in placation. "I was just saying that you're dangerous." *How am I going to get out of this?* He gestured to the orc's metal hand. "That hand has to count as a weapon."

Vairug gazed into the palm of his mechanical hand. "I suppose you're right."

"See?" Belac moved his hands out to his sides and then dropped them. "Problem solved." He did not believe that the problem was solved.

Vairug shook his head. "I should still be allowed to bring my axe."

Rolan finally decided to weigh in. "Just leave the axe. We are going to a picnic."

Vairug thrust the head of his axe toward the elf. "What about him? He gets to bring two swords, but I am not allowed one axe?"

Rolan waved dismissively. "Belac's an elf. He is too pretty to scare anyone, no matter how many swords he has."

Belac did not know how to feel about the comment. *...I guess I am pretty.* He wondered if now would be a good time to bring up the mask that he wanted the dwarf to make for him. He considered the obstinate orc. *No. I need to deal with this first.* Belac did not like asking Vairug to go without his weapon, especially when there were monsters that wanted to kill them all. *I am sure that the humans are doing their best, but something could sneak past the patrols.* Belac turned toward Ecard. The lord looked content to keep his thoughts to himself.

Belac gestured to the lord. "Let Ecard carry your axe for you. After we introduce you and everyone starts eating, you can have the axe back." *This way, the axe will be close by if Vairug needs it, but he will be less likely to accidentally threaten anyone with it.*

Vairug regarded the lord speculatively.

Ecard smiled uncomfortably. "I would be honored to carry it for you."

It was obvious that Vairug disliked the viability of the plan. "Fine. But I am keeping my knives."

Rolan raised his arms out to his sides, displaying the various knives strapped to his stocky body. "Good. I am keeping mine too."

Vairug frowned at the absence of argument.

Ecard stepped forward and held out his hands to accept the orc's axe. "I realize that the event is less formal than a gala, but this would make the people more comfortable."

Vairug surrendered his axe without further complaint. It would have been unwise for anyone to have accused him of pouting.

"Great," Rolan said disingenuously. "Now let's get this over with." The second part he clearly meant.

Together, the four of them left the loading bay and began walking toward the gathering hall. The lunch was set up on the back side of the building in hopes of using its large stone walls to block the view of the burned village. As they walked around to the other side of the building, Belac fiddled with his leather straps, attempting to ensure that they looked like proper armor. Once he was satisfied with his own appearance, he reached over and adjusted the orc's crimson sash.

Vairug glanced at the elf, but said nothing.

Belac found himself disappointed by the affair that Ecard and the other humans had arranged on the back side of the gathering hall. In his mind, the elf had envisioned bright pavilions and feast day spreads. The reality turned out to be crude firepits and bland food laid out on tables fashioned from repurposed shelving units. None of the people looked like they wanted to be there. *Worst. Party. Ever.*

Belac took in the loose crowd of women and children. "How many are there?"

Ecard answered, "I do not have an exact count, but I estimate close to a hundred women. Not counting the children."

Belac nodded to the lord. "Go ahead and introduce us."

Ecard took a step forward. "People of Gofell!" Though at volume his voice projected a damaged sound, it carried over the murmuring of the villagers. "I would like to introduce you to the three men who have come to aid you in this time of tribulation." He stepped to the side and gestured to the elf. "You already know Lord Belac Melavar, The Dragon Slayer."

Belac held up a hand and waved.

No one waved back.

Ecard's arm lowered slightly as he indicated to the dwarf. "With him, is Master Rolan. He will be the chief architect of the village's defenses."

Rolan did not wave.

Ecard then moved to stand next to the orc. "And this is Lord Vairdoe of Enevic. You know his tragic story. As well as my own."

Vairug stood proudly, though he too offered no greeting.

Belac frowned at the quiet reception. *Well, don't everyone cheer at once.* He considered forcing a smile, but decided on a different tact. "Your homes have been burned!" he said loudly and then let his words hang in the air. "Your men have been taken," he continued, matching his own tone. "Monsters have risen in the forest." He followed the rhythm with, "And evil would claim you as its own."

All the murmurs had stopped. Children clung to their mothers, frightened by the elf's words. The few men among the villagers attempted to comfort those around them. Worry built as everyone remembered the devastation on the other side of the gathering hall. Even Belac's friends looked upon him with concern. *It is not 'happy' that these people need.*

Belac shouted into the suspense, "But this is not the end of Gofell!" His own conviction empowered his voice. "Your story will not be one of tragedy and despair!" *They need hope.* "A village is more than lumber and stone. We will take back what was taken. We will throw down what has risen. And we will show evil that we are not its to claim!"

Belac was breathing hard by the end of his speech. His heart pounded in his chest, healthy and ready for war. The gestalt of the village hung over a precipice. It was time to see if they would fall or fly.

Many of the men nodded to themselves, unaware that they did so in unison. The villagers looked to each other, communicating silently with familial glances. Before long, every human there was gazing out toward the forest. The villagers knew that they could not abandon their people to the evil that grew there. Just as Belac knew that he could not allow the evil to grow. *The dragon can wait. I have demons to slay.*

Vairug surprised everyone by speaking. "Do you know what mistake our enemies have made?" he asked the villagers, gathering their attention.

Vairug reached over with his gray hand and took his axe from Ecard. The lord relinquished the weapon without a struggle, then looked to the elf for guidance.

Vairug did not give his friends time to argue. "When the villains made their monsters out of wood," he thrust his axe above his head and shouted, "they forgot what woodsmen cut!"

Every forester threw a fist into the air and shouted wordlessly. Though their numbers were relatively few, there was an undeniable fierceness to their pride.

Oh. So, now they cheer. Belac narrowed his eyes at the orc. *My speech was so much better than his.*

As the villagers discussed their roles in the upcoming plans, Belac went to get something to eat. *Stupid axe.* One of the makeshift tables was covered in an assortment of wooden cups while another held trays of food. Though the size and shape of the trays varied, they had all been loaded with the same cuisine. Luckily for the elf, the chunks of pork and root vegetables skewered on wooden sticks looked appetizing. He picked up one of the kabobs and began to nibble on it as he considered the people of Gofell. He had plans for them all. Men, women, and children, they would all have a role to play. *They won't survive without my help.*

The children were still scared. However, their fear was a product of confusion. They did not understand what was happening or why. The women who cared for them forced smiles with a feminine strength that tore at Belac's heart. The men attempted to offer reassurance, but even they were unable to completely hide their worry. *I just need them to have faith in me for a little longer. Once we rescue the other villagers, it will be proof that we can win.* The elf grinned. *I never would have guessed that my answer to a problem would ever be, 'more humans.'*

Belac quickly learned that standing in front of the food was a good way to get run over by hungry villagers. He grabbed two of the kabobs and then shuffled out of the crowd. *Hopefully, the food distracts everyone from the fact that I might get us all killed.* He leaned against the stone wall of the gathering hall and continued to study the humans as he ate.

Ecard joined the elf, asking, "Should we encourage our friends to mingle?"

Belac caught the not-so-subtle suggestion in the question. "No. For now, it is probably better that we don't. We need these people to know who Lord Vairdoe is and that he is not a threat." He grinned at the orc. "At least, not a threat to them." He gestured to the villagers. "As soon as the men are finished eating, we need to leave."

There was genuine concern in Ecard's reply. "Do be careful, Belac."

Belac smiled at the lord. "I can't. The plan won't work if I'm careful."

Thirty-Two

"I'm married!" a young woman screamed and then threw her drink.

The wooden cup bounced off a man's head. He stumbled back two paces and then shouted, "It's not my fault that your husband can't afford to buy you a shawl!"

The woman shrieked and rushed at the man, her fingernails pointed at his eyes.

Denis wrapped an arm around the woman's waist and held her back. "Enough, Fiona."

Fiona continued to struggle for a moment and then turned, tears in her eyes. "But Daddy, he…"

"He is not the one that is supposed to be wearing a shawl," Denis interrupted. He gestured to his daughter's flowing hair. "How is a man to know?"

Fiona's mouth went slack jawed.

An older woman, her hair held back under a thin cloth, took the younger woman's arm. "Come with me, Sweety."

The offending man held out his arms as the young woman was led away. "I could buy you a shawl," he taunted.

Denis struck the man in the face, knocking him into the dirt. Denis pointed down at the man and warned, "Shut your mouth or I'll break it."

Belac looked away from the scene and raised an eyebrow at the Enevician lord standing next to him.

Ecard frowned and gestured to the villagers as a whole. "It is a custom of Harbridge. Married women are expected to cover their hair with a shawl as to not invite the attention of other would-be suiters."

Belac appraised the women of Gofell. "I thought more of them would be married."

Ecard shrugged. "Most of them are. It appears as though they do not enforce their cultural norms as strictly out here as they do in the capital."

Belac had noticed women wearing shawls before, but he had never questioned if the garments might have a meaning. *That might explain a few of the slaps that I have gotten.* He could understand why humans might need such a system. The Elves would never tolerate the licentious lifestyles that the humans seemed so fond of. Lineage was simply too important for such behavior to be allowed. It was one of the reasons why Belac like living among the humans so much. *Frivolity is definitely an advantage of a short life.*

Ecard's explanation turned into speculation. "I suspect that the tradition is due to how much time the men of Harbridge spend away from their wives. Whether on a military excursion or a ship at sea, the men are frequently gone for extended stretches of time. The shawls likely reduce… misunderstandings." He shrugged and expounded, "So, young girls keep their hair in ribbons, eligible women let their hair down, and married women are to don a shawl."

Belac pointed a finger blanketly toward the villagers. "Then, why are they not wearing shawls?"

Ecard held up a hand in resignation. "Not everyone values the wisdom of their ancestors."

Belac wondered if that was a disadvantage of a short lifespan. He decided that it could be just as much an advantage as a disadvantage. *In my experience, what people think of as wise is often not. Especially when humans think it.*

Simon approached, motioning toward where the incident had taken place. "I'm sorry about that. Darrel is drunk."

Belac thought that the man being drunk was of less importance than where he had procured the alcohol. "Find out where he got the booze. Make sure Rolan knows."

Simon looked to where Rolan and Vairug stood. The two had taken the backside of the food table for themselves and were in the deliberate process of eating as much as they could. *At least Vairug is not growling at anyone.*

Belac added, "And make sure that Darrel is on my team." *That's another person that I need to keep separated from Denis. If this continues, I am going to have to make a list of who needs to be kept away from who.*

Simon nodded. "I will take care of it." He hurried away to investigate.

Belac revisited the food table and then watched the villagers as he ate. Once he saw that the humans were talking more than eating, he decided that it was time for his team to depart. *If I wait any longer, the men are going to start finding reasons to stay.*

Belac raised his voice above the growing hum of the villagers. "Listen up!" He waited for the crowd to quite before he continued, "Everyone on my team needs to head over to the factorage now. Rolan will issue equipment, and then we leave. Make sure you wait in the loading bay. If one of you wanders off and we have to come looking for you, no one is going to be happy about it."

Belac wanted to give the men more time to say goodbye to their families, but he knew that if he did, the farewells would stretch on too long. As they delayed, people were dying and the opposition was growing. Also, the longer they delayed, the harder it would become for the men to leave their families again.

Belac turned his head and lowered his voice. "Ecard, I am going to head over there and start organizing the men. Would you stay here and make sure that no one on my team forgets it's time to leave?" He met the lord's eyes. "Or gets lost."

Ecard nodded. "Once you are gone, I will go around and remind the men that you are waiting for them."

Belac clapped the lord on the shoulder. "Good man."

Rolan and Vairug had already moved away from the crowd. Belac joined them, taking a wooden cup of water with him as he passed by the refreshments table. *This would all be a lot easier if Rolan still had his springer. I could just have him sneak out there and put a tiny little hole in Kaelem's bald head.* The thought of blood trickling from the exiled elf's skull pleased Belac immensely.

As expected, the foresters tarried behind Belac and his friends. Though he worried that more of the men might yet abandon their cause, he did not truly believe that they would. However, with or without the humans, Belac was committed to his plan. *I will go alone if I have to.* He turned his thoughts to preparation.

Vairug interrupted the elf's thoughts. "Hey, Belac." He grinned at the elf. "I think the villagers liked my axe."

Belac narrowed his eyes at the orc. "That is only because I fixed your sash."

Vairug's laugh made him sound like he was choking. "What!?"

Belac attempted to make sense of his own nonsense. "The pretty red color distracted them from the fact that you were waving an axe around like a crazy person." He nodded, mostly to himself. "I am good at distractions."

Vairug continued to laugh silently, but he did not argue.

Rolan had a different take. "We should have considered that the foresters would not think of an axe as a weapon."

While Belac agreed with the dwarf, he worried what that might mean for the foresters. "They are going to need to change the way they see the world. Everything is a weapon." He nudged the orc. "Except for you, Vairug."

Vairug grinned fondly at the elf.

As they walked into the factorage's loading bay, Rolan began to explain how he wanted things done. "Have everyone line up in here." He pointed his hand at a door on the far side of the loading bay. "Then send them through that door one at a time. We can load them up and then move them out the front door. You can stack them up in whatever formation you want on the other side of the building."

Belac had not planned on establishing a formation. He did not think that such a level of discipline would be feasible for men without military training. "Trying to keep those men in a formation would be a waste of effort. Besides, I would rather have them paying attention to the forest, than worrying about where they are in line."

Rolan shrugged. "You will still need to assign someone to pull the handcart."

Belac nodded. "I am going to have them take turns as we go." *I think I will have Darrel go first. Once he sweats himself sober, I can just pick whoever is annoying me the most, and make them go next.*

Rolan went through the doorway that he had indicated to, waving for Belac to follow him. "Let's get you outfitted first."

Vairug took it upon himself to remain in the loading bay. "I will stay here and inform the men that they should wait here."

Belac followed the dwarf through a short hallway and into a large storage room with crates stacked against the walls. Piles of equipment had been laid out on the floor, staged for Belac's team. Beige canvas wrapped around tools and provisions, the tied bundles contained nothing that was not necessary for his team's mission. Each of the bundles had been bound with a rope that would also serve as a carrying strap. To Belac, it was obvious that the utilitarian packs were not assembled with comfort in mind.

Rolan picked up one of the packs and held it out to the elf. "Here. Put this on."

Belac took the pack, but then frowned. "This feels light." He hefted the pack. "Why are there no tools in it?"

Rolan reached into an open crate and pulled out a compact, leather pouch. "You're in charge. That means that you have different burdens than your men." He held out the pouch.

Belac downed the rest of his drink and then set the wooden cup on one of the crates. He reached out, accepting what he suspected was a tinder kit.

Rolan continued, "If you really want to swing an axe, borrow one of theirs. It'll give them a break. It will also make them focus on the fact that you are working for them."

Belac grinned slyly. "That is pretty manipulative, Rolan."

Rolan frowned at the elf. "What do you think being in charge is?"

Thirty-Three

Though the storefront side of the factorage had once been sheltered by a wooden porch, fire had destroyed it. Men had moved the charred remains away, creating space for operation to continue. The soot blackening the stone walls blended with the black iron lattice that covered the shops display windows, the complementary coloring almost adding a sense of charm to the building. *If that dwarf has this shop open for business by the time I get back from my mission, I am not going to be even a little surprised.*

Sixteen men stood ready for departure, all of them outfitted with a canvas pack and a waterskin. Some of the men had wanted to bring swords, but Belac had denied them. The people of Gofell were untrained in the ways of war, and Belac worried that the blades would only hamper the men's movements and get them killed. Fire hardened spears had been the elf's answer. Simple and effective, the spears would serve the men better. Vairug had found Belac's decision hilarious.

Rolan approached the elf and clapped him on the arm. "Don't die. You still owe me a boat."

At first, the statement confused Belac. Then he remembered that Rolan had claimed it had cost a ship to rescue Vairug and him from the prison in Harbridge.

Belac shook his head. "No." He pointed at the dwarf. "I already got you a ship."

"What?" Now, Rolan was the one confused. "You did not."

"I did too," Belac insisted, nodding. "I stole it from the water worshiping cult people and brought it straight to you."

Rolan held both hands up to stop the elf. "You crashed that one into the docks!"

Belac held his hands out to his sides and shrugged. "It was still a boat."

Rolan chuckled. "Still. Maybe try not to die anyway."

"I don't know," Belac smiled and gestured to the factorage, "Vairug told me to die bravely."

Rolan nodded. "I can just about guarantee that you will be happier if you don't."

"Don't worry," Belac patted the leather straps wrapped around his abdomen, "I am wearing my armor."

Rolan sighed gruffly.

Belac placed a hand on the dwarf's shoulder and then walked away. "Let's go!" he shouted to the men that had pledged to follow him to war.

Belac turned around and walked backward so that he could make certain all of his men were still with him. Their mission was arguably the most dangerous, and the elf would need to account for anyone he lost. Sixteen men still followed him, one of which was unhappily pulling a handcart. *Darrel looks like he already regrets getting drunk.* Belac knew that the cart would be a hardship on his men, but without the barrel it carried, his plan would not work.

Belac turned back around and continued to lead the men to the southwest side of the village. There, he found an old road that few living had ever traversed to the end. Though it appeared well traveled, the dirt road was reported to become more overgrown the farther it was followed into the forest. Belac was prepared to transfer the barrel to a litter if the road proved to be unnavigable. However, his hope was that the road would remain clear enough for easier travel.

A short distance from the village, Belac and his team came upon a wide creek that flowed to the south. Fortunately, the old bridge that spanned it had been well maintained. While the bridge's moss covered stone supports appeared ancient, the wooden planks that ran across its deck had been recently replaced. The wheels of the handcart rolled loudly on the wood as Belac's team crossed over the water.

Belac was reassured by the quality of the road on the other side of the bridge. It was obvious to him that at least this part of the forest was frequented by villagers. A sinuous trail led off from the side of the road, circling back toward the creek and down to a spot that Belac assumed had been set up for fishing. Despite the green of the forest, he did not expect to encounter anything in the immediate area that would attack him or his men. *It feels like the forest knows that it should not provoke the village.* He decided that the greatest threat to his men at the moment was doubt.

Belac turned around and began walking backward as he studied the men who followed him. *They look more bored than frightened.* Once again, Belac marveled at how quickly humans could forget that they were in danger. *I guess I should make use of the time.* He considered the man that was closest. *Charles might not be from Gofell, but I bet he can manage following a road.*

Belac turned and pointed his hand down the road. "Charles, keep moving forward."

Concern showed on Charles's face, but the man's only reply was to nod.

Belac raised his voice. "Listen up! I want to get a head count. When I point to you, sound off with your name." He knew that it would be easier to get a count by having the men sound off with numbers, but what he actually wanted was to learn their names.

Though Belac already knew Charles's name, the elf started with him. Using his whole hand, Belac began pointing to each of the men as he worked his way to the back of the group.

"Charles." *Avenging murderer.*

"Ben." *Kind of stupid, but he helped me with the spears.*

"Vaun." *The scabbard thief.*

"Craig." *That's the guy that keeps bringing me water. ...I hope he is not poisoning me.*

"Philip." *Shy. Kind of young.*

"Halex." The man smiled. *How does someone live without any teeth?*

"Jeffery, but you can call me Jeff." *I think that someone might have dropped him on his head as a baby.*

"Lochlin." *If the top of my head were bald like that, I would wear a hat.*

"Bartell." *I will remember the name if not the man.*

"Corry." Scars ran through the man's beard and across the bridge of his nose. *Do not ask that man's sister for a dance.*

"Wallace." *That guy is more beard than man.*

"Keith." *Uhm... Looks like a human.*

"Shane." *Also looks like a human.*

"Matt." *I am starting to see a problem.*

"John." *At least this one has big ears.*

The last man was the one who pulled the handcart. "Darrel," he said as if cursing at the elf. *He looks like he is about to die.*

Belac did not think that he would be able to remember who was who. All of the humans were dressed in browns. They all had wild, brown hair and thick bushy beards. It even seemed as if each of them was missing at least one tooth. *I don't think I can remember a man by what teeth he has left.* Belac imagined himself grabbing men by the jaw and inspecting their teeth like a farrier would a horse. The elf decided that he would simply have to do the best that he could. *It is not my fault that all the humans look alike.*

Belac spoke to the man with big ears. "John, take the cart from Darrel. When it gets too hard for you, have one of the other men take over." *Maybe he can remember everyone's name.*

John smiled. "Then, you can all watch me put Darrel to shame. Pulling that cart is never going to get too hard for me!"

Belac grinned at the braggart. "Yeah, alright."

As Belac returned to the front of the group, he realized that he had not kept a count of the men. *Oops.* He glanced back and made a quick count. *Yeah. That's sixteen.* He frowned. *I am supposed to have sixteen, right?*

Thirty-Four

Belac awoke from a dream in which a headless spriggan had been chasing him through a dark forest. *It's trying to steal my head!* Drenched in sweat from the nightmare, he threw off his canvas covering. Though stars sparkled between the branches of the trees above, the moon was nowhere to be seen. *I am making sure that the next spriggan I kill is really dead.*

Belac sat up from where he had lain down by the side of the road. *Maybe fire. Fire kills just about everything.* He pictured a burning spriggan running toward him. Wreathed in flames, its claws reached for him. Belac shook his head. *Nope.* He decided that he would need to find another way.

Though he knew that sleep would soon be precious, Belac reached for his boots. *Maybe one of the men on watch can sleep without getting chased by monsters.* Once he had put his boots on, he began to reroll his canvas pack. He set one of his rations to the side as he arranged the rest of his gear. After retying the heavy canvas, he left the pack lying there on the ground. His swords, he took with him.

Belac slipped his swords onto his back as he stepped out into the road. Two men stood guard next to the handcart, but the night was too dark for him to make out who they were. The rest of the men slept in rows on either side of the road. Fortunately, none of them snored.

The two men on guard were arguing, their young voices whispering in the darkness.

"I am telling you, you can't build a house out of dirt."

"Not dirt. Mud. I could shape it while it's wet, and then move in once it dries."

"But what about when it rains? Your house is going to melt!"

There was a pause.

"What if I build a big roof that covers up the little roof?"

"You mean, like a house inside a house?"

"That's right."

There was another pause.

"That might work."

I don't understand how these people survived before I got here. Belac shook his head. "Why not just build a house like a normal person?"

Jeffery and Ben both jumped. Somehow, the two least competent men had ended up on watch together. *I can't believe the others trusted these two to watch over them while they sleep.*

Once he had recovered from his startlement, Ben answered, "We want a house that won't burn up."

Jeffery added, "You can't burn dirt."

That is less stupid than I thought it was. Belac gestured up the road. "I am going to go use a tree. Maybe the two of you could actually keep watch while I'm gone."

"You want us to watch?" Jeffery asked, misunderstanding the instructions.

Ben followed the other man's line of thought. "I think it would be too dark for us to see anything."

"No. That's..." Belac shook his head. *We are all going to die.* "Just stay here and guard the cart."

Belac went and found his tree. When he returned, the two men were debating on how to best make a roof out of dirt. Belac felt his mind being pulled into the discussion. Desperately wanting to change the subject, he asked, "Are either of you from Gofell?"

Jeffery turned away from the handcart. "We both are."

"It's where I was born," Ben professed. "And I hope that I get married and die there."

Those are awful things to hope for. Belac tried to not sound discouraging. "Well, you are going to be a hero after this. I bet that helps convince the woman that you have in mind. Women like heroes."

Ben shook his shaggy head. "I don't know who I am going to marry yet." He gestured to the other young man. "But Jeff here is sweet on Ellen."

Jeffery's reply sounded both insecure and frustrated. "I don't know. She says that she does not want to wear a shawl." His tone became more frustrated. "I think that if a woman wants to get married, she should want people to know that she's married."

Belac thought he understood both sides of the issue. To him, the solution was simple. "Then, you should find a woman that wants to wear a shawl."

Jeffery did not think the solution was that simple. "But Ellen is the prettiest woman that I've ever seen. I can't look at her and not want to marry her."

Belac did not understand how humans could get things so wrong. "Would you rather spend your life with someone that is pretty, or someone that shares your values?" *Talia is super pretty, but there is no way I am ever going to marry that crazy woman.*

Evidently, Jeffery needed time to consider the question.

Wow. Humans are stupid. Belac tried to think of something that might help the man make the right decision. "Women don't usually stay pretty." *At least human women don't. Talia would be gorgeous forever…* He forced himself to stop thinking about what the exiled elven woman would look like with long, black hair.

Jeffery gasped. "I never thought of it that way."

Ben reached over and slapped the other man on the arm. "See? Lord Ecard told us Lord Belac was smart."

And just like that, two new acolytes for The Order of the Stubbed Toe. Belac tried to imagine what the two men would look like wearing giant shoe hats. He leaned in. "You know? There are some women that will sleep with you even if you don't marry them."

Both of the men laughed as if the elf had made a joke.

Belac realized that he could see the men's eyes. He looked up into the sky, registering the faint gray of early dawn. *There is hard work ahead. I should let the men laugh while they can.* He redirected his gaze onto the two men. "What is the most annoying song you know?"

"Bacon in the Evening?" Jeffery asked more than answered.

"The Bunny Chased My Dog?" Ben suggested.

Belac did not recognize either song. "It needs to repeat," he qualified.

Ben nodded. "How Many Fish in the Barrel." He was sure of his answer.

Belac glanced at the barrel in the handcart. "That will do." He motioned for them to begin.

The two men began singing hesitantly, though the song had obviously been composed with the intent of being belted by drunks.

"We have a barrel,
A barrel full of fish.
We should fish the barrel,
To find out if we're rich.
Reach into the barrel,
Pull out a single fish.
Drop it next to the barrel,
And now we have one fish."

Belac grinned. "Louder."

The two men began to sing loud enough for their voices to echo through the forest.

"We have a barrel,
A barrel full of fish!
We should fish the barrel,
To find out if we're rich.

Reach into the barrel,
Pull out a single fish.
Drop it next to the barrel,
And now we have two fish!"

Keith yelled, "Shut up!" and rolled over in his canvas bedding.

Belac took up the shanty, encouraging the two men on watch to sing louder. "We have a barrel, A barrel full of fish! …"

Groans issued from the men still trying to sleep.

Belac smiled at the watchmen and then raised his voice to a shout. "We have a barrel, A barrel full of fish! …" He began pacing up and down the road as he sang. The rhythm of the song broke down at thirteen, but still the shanty continued. "We have a barrel, A barrel full of fish! …" *It just makes the song more annoying.*

Vaun crawled out of his bedding, stood, and then joined in the shanty. "We have a barrel, A barrel full of fish! …"

One by one, the other men took up the shanty until Keith yelled, "Fine! I'm awake!"

The shanty only grew louder. "We have a barrel, A barrel full of fish! …"

Belac stopped singing, but he let the shanty go on as he walked back to his pack. He smiled as he sat down next to the ration that he had set aside. *I am never going to get this song out of my head.* He glanced at the men singing as they went about their morning. In their merriment, none of the men were thinking about the horrors that they would soon face. *Worth it.*

Belac picked up his ration and untied the cloth wrapping. Dried meat and a dry biscuit, the food was substance without satiation. Belac hummed along as he ate, but the shanty died as the men began to eat their own breakfasts. However, he could still hear the song in his head. *"We have a barrel, A barrel full of fish!"*

Thirty-Five

The condition of the second bridge tested Belac's optimism. "Would you call that 'dilapidated?"

Charles nodded dispassionately. "I would be tempted to, yes."

Though the bridge's moss covered stone supports still stood strong, every wooden element showed signs of rot. A river flowed between the supports, its current fast enough to be heard from above. The light of the afternoon sun shimmered along the rushing surface of the water, throwing playful flashes up into the forest dim. Too wide to be crossed without being washed away, the river was a clear boundary between Belac and his destination.

Belac studied the rotting bridge. Holes and warped lumber made up the entirety of its decking. While the planks that ran across had once been treated, the dark splintery wood was now falling apart. Even the thick girders underneath appeared suspect. Crumbling where exposed, the beams offered no promise of support. *I could really use a flying carpet right about now.*

Vaun suggested, "We could always make Darrel go first."

Darrel disliked the idea. "Don't you think that it would make more sense if we sent the shortest person first?"

Everyone looked at Vaun. He obviously regretted having said anything.

Belac sighed. "I'll go first." He gazed out along the bridge. *The left side looks like it might be safe enough to cross.* "Once I am across safely," *If I can cross safely,* "you can all follow after me one at a time. We can just leave the cart here for now."

Lochlin ventured, "We could might try and repair the bridge a little."

Belac shook his head. *We don't have time for something like that.* "It is better if we don't. I think it probably looks worse than it is." He did not think that at all.

Staying to the left side of the bridge, Belac began his crossing. He moved slowly, testing each plank before transferring his full weight to it. He had expected the wood to creak as he crossed, but the only sound was the rushing of the water below.

When the elf was about a quarter of the way across the bridge, Vaun called out, "Maybe you should take a rope."

Belac stopped and narrowed his eyes at the short man. Pointing, Belac yelled back, "You cross next!" *I should have made him go first.*

The elf resumed his crossing, growing more confident the farther he went without falling into the waters below. Despite the condition of the bridge, he thought that it would hold well enough for his purposes. Halfway across, he waved for the men to begin following him. Then he increased his speed, believing that the bridge was in fact sturdy enough to cross.

Though it countered Belac's original instructions, the men began to follow him across the bridge as he had indicated. Vaun followed first, the short man showing no signs of fear. The other men proceeded to follow him in closer intervals. While they began the crossing with their arms held out to their sides for balance, few of the men made it more than halfway across the bridge before relaxing into a slow walk.

When Belac reached the other side without incident, he turned and watched the men as they crossed. He had been thinking about something off and on all day, and he finally decided that he had a problem. *I can't let The Order of the Stubbed Toe wear giant shoe hats on their heads. It might remind people of that stupid cobbler story.*

He frowned to himself and tried to think of a suitably silly alternative. *Maybe something with feathers.*

Vaun was walking casually by the time he made it to the other side of the bridge. "Do you think we can bring the handcart across?"

Belac shook his head. "Let's just leave it where it is for now. If the map is right, we should almost be there."

Vaun's eyes gazed down the road. "That would give us time to get a lot done today."

Belac nodded. "We should still wait until tomorrow to start cutting down trees." He did not know how far the sound of a felled tree would carry, but he wanted his team's presence to remain undetected for as long as it could.

The rest of the men were crossing faster than the elf had. Once Wallace was on safe ground, he turned around and shouted, "Watch out, Shane! I think I see a snake crawling up the side of the bridge!" He laughed.

Shane seemed to know that the other man was lying. "Shut your face! That's not funny!" True or not, Shane began to move faster.

"You don't see it?" Wallace persisted. "It's right there, slithering around right under your feet!" He was not even trying to sound honest.

Shane began to step high so that he could look under his feet as he hurried to cross the bridge. "Stop it, Wallace!"

Belac grew worried that Shane might dance off the side of the bridge. Belac laughed, hoping that the fall would not kill the man.

When Shane finally made it across, he lunged at Wallace. Wallace jumped away with his hands held up while Lochlin and Keith held the angry man back. Philip and Jeffery simply stood there, seemingly confused. The other men were too busy laughing or crossing the bridge to intervene.

Shane yelled, "You know I'm scared of snakes, you son of a sow!"

Wallace's face looked like a laughing beard. "It would not have been funny if you weren't!"

Though Belac enjoyed laughing at the humans, he knew that it was his job to keep them on task. He waited for the last man to cross the bridge, and then Belac harrumphed to get his laughing under control. "Alright. That's enough of that. We need to get moving."

Shane stopped trying to attack Wallace. However, Wallace did not stop laughing. Amidst the lingering amusement, Belac led his team away from the bridge and further down the forest road. A short distance into the trees, the road bent to the right. Shortly after the bend, the road ended at an open field that stretched out in an almost perfect circle. Dozens of broken, white stones jutted from the grass at seemingly haphazard locations.

Belac walked out into the field of grass and considered what he saw. He had led his team to the southernmost star on Leeson's map. To Belac, it had been obvious that the white stars represented Vaquian ruins. It had been simple enough to have Simon confirm his assumption. According to the villagers, a lord had come from Harbridge long ago, intent on salvaging the ruins. The enterprising lord had commissioned the construction of the road and then overseen the removal of extrinsic stone. Though careful to take only the stone above ground, the lord had left behind little to mark the ruins' location.

The men remained on the road as Belac walked the field. The humans saw the Vaquian ruins as more than the remnants of a departed people. 'Vaquian,' was a word they did not even know. In their minds, the ancient places of power were not the domain of people, but of demons.

Belac did not entirely disagree with the humans. He knew that what lay under his feet was an evil thing. He could still remember what it had felt like in the deep delve that he had been marched down into. He could still remember the ugly red light and the smell of burning herbs. Though he had seen nothing that he would have categorized as a demon, he thought that the misnomer was more than reasonable.

The picturesque clearing made Belac's skin crawl. *The trees won't grow here.* In the absence of the collapsed ruins, and in the course of time, trees and underbrush should have claimed the clearing. Instead, the forest had been held back as if curated. *I wonder if it is magic, or just the pure evil of this place.*

Belac did not know what was at the bottom of a Vaquian stronghold. Nor did he know if the three sites depicted on Leeson's map were connected underground. He did not even know if the stronghold he stood above would be accessible. What he did know, was that whatever was down there, it would be something that Kaelem feared.

Belac walked toward the eastern side of the clearing and tapped his foot on the soft soil. "Here."

Thirty-Six

Belac gazed up at the partially constructed crane that had been erected by his men. Though shorter than he would have liked, it was as large as the foresters thought they could build it safely. Hastily assembled with ropes and felled trees, the heavy frame did not reach much higher than a single-story cottage. *At least it looks like a crane.*

Most of Belac's men were stretched out on the grass, resting as the sun passed by above. They had worked late into the evening the day before and then rose early in the morning to continue working. The almost constant hard work had exhausted them beyond their concern for demons.

Belac had found overseeing the men no easy task. In between managing the patrol, he had taken over for each of his men, giving them a break as he did their work for them. Despite the challenging exercise, Belac was careful not to overexert himself. He knew that his first responsibility was to make decisions, and that exhaustion could cause him to make a mistake. Also, if his plan were to succeed, he would need to reserve his strength.

A bonfire of brush, branches, and small trees burned in the clearing's southwest. Fortunately, the winds were tame enough that the thick smoke traveled high into the sky before being blown away. *This would all be a lot more difficult if we had to do it in a cloud of smoke.*

Belac glanced at the empty handcart, glad once more that they had been able to get it across the bridge without losing it to the river. The wooden cart had proven itself even more useful than he had expected.

Corry and Matt ran into the clearing from the western side. The two men had been deployed to watch the forest to the north. That they had returned without being relieved could only mean one thing.

Belac did not wait for his scouts to reach him. "Everybody up!" he ordered. "If Keith is sleeping, start kicking him until he is not."

With a groggy voice, Keith asked, "How is that fair?"

Wallace had no sympathy for the man. "You sound like my niece."

Lochlin answered, but his retort was gruff. "If you want fair, you should go dig your own grave so that we don't have to do it. Then you can go back to sleep."

Keith climbed to his feet. "I think I've done enough digging."

Corry ran up to the elf and then halted, placing his hands on his knees. Between haggard breaths, he reported, "They're coming. From the north. Just like you said." He looked up and met the elf's eyes. "There's a lot of them, Belac." He gave a wheezing laugh that verged on hysterical.

Belac nodded. "How many spriggans did you see?"

Corry replied, "I didn't see any." He turned his head to look at the other scout.

Matt shook his head. "We ran as soon as we saw the little, wooden, demon men."

Belac almost asked if they had been spotted, but he decided that the answer did not matter. *The exiles know that we are here.* The smoke and sounds were sure to draw attention sooner or later.

Philip, his voice already scared, asked, "Do we have to stand?"

Belac gazed toward the norther tree line. "That depends on how many spriggans there are."

The men began to stretch, limbering up for whatever was to come. Belac continued to watch the forest. Of all that he and his men would face, Belac believed that the spriggans posed the greatest danger. Wooden juggernauts of hate and rage, the spriggans would be able to tear through any defense that was presented. Belac did not expect both of the exiles to come. Also, he did not think that either Talia or Kaelem would stay behind without at least one spriggan to protect them. Therefore, assuming Belac was correct and there were only three spriggans left, there should be no more than two spriggans on their way to kill him.

I don't know if I can handle two of the spriggans at the same time. Belac shook his head. *Especially not without a lot of the men being killed.* Though it shamed him, Belac recognized that another dead spriggan might be of more strategical value than a dozen living foresters. He turned his gaze on the bearded men who had pledged themselves to his cause. *I will not sacrifice these men.* He looked back to the forest. *The sacrifice of humans is what I am here to stop.*

Belac heard the briar men before he saw them. The clattering of sticks announced their approach. Then dull garnet lights began to pulse in the tree line. A slender figure in heather gray strode forth from the forest's shadows. Accompanied by a single spriggan, the exile halted and surveyed the field. *I can't tell if that is Talia or Kaelem.*

Belac removed his dwarf-sword and then thrust the scabbarded blade above his head. "To arms!" he yelled as loudly as he could. *I can't give anyone time to think.*

The foresters had left their spears in a line on the grass, the tips pointed north. To a man, they rushed for their spears. Belac lowered his sword and walked behind the line as the men took up their weapons. He glanced at the rickety crane. *It's time to find out how much they don't want me digging here.*

Belac halted behind the center of the defensive line. Raising his sword once again, he shouted, "Let them hear that we are not afraid!" Belac was afraid.

The foresters shook their spears in the air and roared. Belac had no idea if the briar men could hear anything, but he knew that the exiled elf would. Briar men began pouring out of the tree line, their twisted forms sprinting toward the foresters. Belac had no way of knowing how many of the monsters there were, but he thought it must be hundreds.

Philip dropped his spear and ran away from the nightmarish army.

Though furious with the man, Belac let him go. "Hold!" he shouted at the other men.

Before the first of the briar men could reach the line of spears, the ground fell out from under the monsters. Momentum caused more of the briar men behind to continue spilling down into a trench littered with sharpened spikes. Though many of the briar men were impaled, few of them were killed by the fall. Undeterred, the brushwood monsters began to claw over each other and toward the other side.

Belac grinned as the briar men fell into the trench that his men had dug and then covered with canvas and grass. "Retreat!" he shouted to his men. It was only a matter of time before the briar men began climbing over each other to get out of the trench.

The foresters turned and ran, many of them dropping their spears in their haste to get away. Belac did not drop his sword, but he did turn and run. The briar men were already spreading out on the other side of the trench, searching for a way around.

A woman screamed in the distance, her voice filled with virulence. *And that would be Talia.*

The spriggan charged forward, shoving its way through the flood of briar men. When it reached the trench, the spriggan leapt into the air. The wooden horror flew over the gap and landed on the other side with a thump that drew backward glances from the fleeing men. Matt stumbled at the sight of the oncoming spriggan. He fell, tumbling through the grass as he lost his footing. First scurrying on his hands and feet before lurching forward into a run, the man's terror drove him on.

A massive wooden hand grabbed the back of Matt's head and lifted him into the air. The man's legs swung out from under him as he was yanked back and around to face the spriggan. The hooked claws of the spriggan's other hand sank into the man's upper chest and then tore through his ribcage. Chunks of lung, heart, and bone ripped away in a spray of gore. Then the spriggan threw the dead man at the back of another fleeing forester.

The corpse slammed into Jeffery, sending him crashing forward onto the ground. Before the man even understood what was happening, a foot of tangled roots stomped down on his skull. The spriggan's feminine face looked up from the dead man. Though the spriggan had no voice, no words could have better expressed its contempt.

John screamed in anger, "No!" drawing the attention of the elf.

Belac glanced back and saw the spriggan. *I could keep running.* The thought did not feel like his own. Despite his fear, it took Belac no time to calculate. The spriggan needed to die. And he was the only one who could kill it.

The elf's boots dug into the soil as he stopped and turned around. Dropping his dwarf-sword onto the grass, he removed his one of starmetal. His thumb unsnapped the scabbard, and then he drew the milky white blade. *I am going to make sure that this one stays dead!* Belac charged toward the spriggan.

Thirty-Seven

John lunged at the spriggan, the tip of his spear striking against the horror's masculine chest. The wooden spear deflected harmlessly as the spriggan turned to face the enraged forester. Reaching out with its hooked claws, the spriggan grabbed the man's right shoulder. John cried out in pain as the claws dug into his back and chest. Lifting the man up, the spriggan grabbed his left hip with its right hand, the claws puncturing into his pelvic bone. John screamed as the spriggan held him aloft. Then the spriggan tore the man apart.

The spriggan stood tall, clutching the forester's right arm, shoulder, and a portion of his upper torso in one massive hand, while the rest of the man's body hung limply from its other. Blood leaked onto the grass next to the spriggan's feet. From beneath a crown of pointed roots, glowing red eyes stared out at the charging elf. The spriggan's eyes held only hate. It did not fear the elf. It should have. Azure eyes could hold hate as well.

The starmetal blade cut into the spriggan's right cheek and then sliced upward at an angle between its glowing eyes and out the top of its crowned head. Belac followed the backhanded slash with his left shoulder, slamming into the spriggan at speed. The impact shot through Belac, but he did not care. He crashed to the ground on top of the spriggan, his legs straddling its unyielding abdomen.

Scabbard still in hand, Belac pressed his knuckles against the spriggans chest and pushed himself up. Raising his starmetal sword above his head, he glared down at the wooden horror. A single unlit eye socket stared up from what remained of the spriggan's head. Belac roared at the lifeless thing, wanting it to rise so that he could kill it again.

"Belac!" a man shouted urgently.

Belac turned, ready to kill the man too.

Charles pointed his spear toward the army of briar men. "We have to go!"

Belac swayed his head side to side, attempting to regain his senses. Charles began running as the elf climbed to his feet. His clothes stained with human blood, Belac stumbled away from the spriggan. He slid his starmetal blade into its sheath and then snaped it closed. As he began to run, he swung the scabbarded sword onto his back. He ran to his dwarf-sword, slowing as he reached down for the discarded weapon. In his haste, he tripped over his own feet. Rolling over the starmetal sword on his back, the elf came to his feet running with the dwarf-sword in hand.

"I totally meant to do that," Belac lied perfunctorily.

None of the other men had stopped running. Belac did not blame them. He ran for the road, the clattering sounds of briar men spurring him on. The briar men had found their way around the trench and would be tireless in their pursuit. Shortly after Belac and Charles reached the road, the forester began to falter. Though Belac wanted to run faster, he refused to leave Charles behind.

Belac grabbed the man's arm, urging him on. "Move or die!"

Charles dropped his spear and struggled to run faster. Trees flashed by as they ran down the road. Beams of light slipped between the branches and cut through the shadows of the forest. Running through the lights, Belac pulled the man along.

When they reached the bridge, Belac pushed the man forward, shouting, "Go!"

Charles began crossing the dilapidated bridge, careful of where he stepped. Though no longer running, the man hurried still.

Belac followed after him, trusting that the rest of the men had already crossed. Halfway across the bridge, Belac looked back and saw that the briar men had rounded the bend in the road. Garnet lights pulsed in the shadows as the brushwood bodies rushed toward the bridge.

"You need to move faster!" Belac said with the utmost sincerity.

Charles glanced back, his eyes widening at the sight of the oncoming briar men. Despite the precarious situation, he did indeed move faster.

The briar men reached the bridge before Belac made it to the other side. Though some fell through holes in the deck, the briar men continued to swarm onto the bridge. When Belac finally reached the other side, Lochlin handed him a lit torch.

Belac turned toward the bridge. Singing to the tune of 'How Many Fish in the Barrel,' he called out, "We have a barrel! But it's not filled with fish!" He tossed the torch onto the bridge.

Fire erupted from the black accelerant that Rolan had prepared for them. Flames raced across the bridge, engulfing the briar men. The bridge caught fire almost immediately, its wood primed for consumption. The briar men on the bridge continued to give chase, their misshaped forms pushing through the blaze. Belac and his men stepped back, suddenly less confident in their trap.

Belac gripped the hilt of his dwarf-sword, preparing to draw the blade. However, as the briar men pressed forward, their movements began to slow. Burning fingers made of sticks reached toward the humans. Then the monsters began to fall. Collapsing onto the bridge, the briar men became nothing more than kindling.

Belac turned around and addressed his men. "We did not set this thing on fire just to watch it burn." He gestured with the hilt of his sword. "Let's move."

The foresters hurried down the road to where they had unlit torches and waterskins laid out. Four of the torches would go unclaimed.

Belac slung his dwarf-sword onto his back and then picked up one of the waterskins. "Don't leave the extra waterskins behind."

Keith understood why there would be extra equipment. "Wait. Where is John?"

Walking past the men, Belac attempted to keep emotion out of his voice. "John, Jeffery, and Matt are dead. Philip fled."

Shane asked, "Why didn't Phil run here?"

Ben speculated, "Maybe he got lost?"

Angry, Darrel asserted, "The coward knew not to show his face."

Past the staged equipment, waited the barrel they had brought. Now empty of accelerant, the barrel had been flipped upside down so that it could be used as a pedestal. Atop it, sat a rigid leather satchel. Belac slipped the strap of his waterskin over his head and then reached for the satchel.

Vaun stepped close to the elf and asked, "Shouldn't we look for Phil?"

"No," Belac answered without explaining. He and his men were not yet safe, and Belac did not like the idea of risking the lives of brave men to save a man that had abandoned them.

The other foresters began gathering around the barrel, all keenly aware that an army of monsters still amassed on the other side of the burning bridge. The next part of the plan had not been Belac's idea. *I hope Rolan is right about this.* The elf opened the satchel and took out a tiny vial that had been wrapped with a scrap of brown cloth.

Belac held the vial out. "Take the first dose now."

Vaun took the cloth wrapped vial, pulled out the stopper, and then downed the contents. His eyes immediately dilated. "I want more of that!" He no longer seemed concerned about the missing forester.

Belac waved the man away and continued handing out vials. Rolan's instructions had been firm. One dose at the bridge, and a second once they were all halfway back to the village.

Belac himself was not to take the potion. What was inside the vials was not magic. While Rolan knew how the potions would affect humans, he worried what such a drug might do to an elf.

"Sun shine on me!" Shane exclaimed. "I will dig two trenches for more of that!"

Bouncing on his toes, Corry suggested, "If we run the whole way, we can get our second dose sooner."

After giving each of the foresters their first dose, Belac closed the satchel and then hung it over his shoulder. He appraised his men, disconcerted by their euphoria. No longer did the foresters seem troubled that an army of monsters was searching for a way to murder them at that very moment. Even the death of their friends seemed to have been forgotten. *Maybe it is for the best.* Though the drug had not been provided to bolster morale, its effects would allow the men to process their losses at another time. Belac was willing to grieve alone if it would help his men survive. *I have different burdens than they do.*

Thirty-Eight

The drugs that Rolan had provided worked well. The dwarf had worried that the foresters would be too weak to escape without aid. Swift travel and hard labor could exhaust even the strongest of men. As recent captives, the foresters would have struggled to outpace pursuit. The drugs granted them not only energy, but the ability to continue on through the night. Staggering the use of their torches, Belac's team pressed through the darkness, needing only brief and infrequent stops.

Belac did not know if Talia would give chase or not. His hope was that she would waste at least a day trying to figure out what he had been searching for. If he were lucky, she might even attempt to dig where his men had set up the unfinished crane. Belac was fairly certain that she would find nothing but dirt and frustration for her efforts.

By the time that Belac and his team reached the village, they all looked dead on their feet. For most of their journey, the elf had acted as something like an anker, slowing the men down as they returned to Gofell. Now, it was Belac that lagged for his men. He had considered handing out the extra drugs he carried in the satchel, but he decided against it. Rolan had insisted that the men only be given two doses. Belac did not know what would happen if he disregarded the dwarf's instructions, but he did not want to risk losing any more of his men.

In his mind, Belac saw the bearded faces of the men he had lost. *I hope the distraction was worth it. If Vairug's team does not free the other men…* He shook his head and then forced himself to focus on the moment. Beyond the burned remains of Gofell, campfires lit a new hamlet of off-white tents. Erected in the field north of the gathering hall, the tents spread out to the east, away from the forest. A long mound of dirt walled the eastern side of the encampment, creating a defensive berm that continued around on the northern side. Shadowed shapes moved inside the encampment as the villagers prepared for the day ahead.

The tents gave Belac hope. *It's like they built a new village on the ashes of the old.* The new encampment represented a resilience that the elf had hitherto not attributed to humans. Short lived and prone to disease, humans were something that was easy to underestimate. *How many times have the humans fallen, only to rise again?* Belac thought that there might be a reason that the briar men needed a human heart.

Though Belac's team had only two torches lit, the flames were sufficient to announce their arrival. As he and his men neared the gathering hall, two women approached from the west. One of the women held aloft a burning torch of her own, while the other carried a spiraled instrument that looked to have been made from the horn of a goat.

As the women intercepted, the one bearing a torch called out questioningly, "Wallace? Wallace, is that you?"

Wallace stepped away from the other men. "What, did you think that I was a ghost?"

The woman moved her torch to the side and then slapped the forester in the face. "Do you know how scared I was?" Her eyes began to tear.

Wallace's voluminous beard seemed to have absorbed most of the blow. He chuckled at the woman before replying, "How am I supposed to answer that? What, do you want a number? Twelve. I thought you were twelve scared."

The woman threw her arms around the forester, careful to keep the torch away from his beard. Weeping with relief, she said, "You are not funny."

Wallace wrapped his arms around the woman. He kissed the shawl covering her head and said, "Sweetheart, I love you. But I am really tired."

The woman untangled herself and stepped back, sniffling. She stood next to the other woman and then straightened her spine. "Right. Well, I am on guard anyway. You should go get some sleep."

Wallace looked taken aback. "They have women guarding the village?"

The woman's eyes became fierce in the firelight. "That's right. Who else is going to do it?"

The other woman added her voice, "Really, Wallace. Did you want us to hide in the cellar forever?"

Wallace's wife focused on the other woman. "Oh, shut up, Jaclyn."

Belac noticed that Jaclyn was not wearing a shawl. *I wonder if she is married and just doesn't like her shawl.* Then it occurred to him that regardless of whether or not the woman was married, she would have loved ones that were missing. Spouse, sibling, parent, or even neighbor; every person lost would harm the village.

Belac pushed his pity away, not wanting it to infect the humans. "Jaclyn, do you know where Rolan is?"

Jaclyn nodded. "He has been sleeping in his office."

Belac assumed that she was referring to the offices in the factorage. "Thanks." He turned and gestured to the forest. "There have been no signs of pursuit, but there is an army behind us." He looked back to the woman and smiled. "I guess it's a good thing that women pay more attention than men do." He was not sure that was true, but he thought it sounded good.

Jaclyn smiled like a cat.

Wallace's wife elbowed the smiling woman's arm.

Jaclyn turned her head and glared at the other woman.

Belac grinned at the exchange. "Come on, Wallace. Let's go. I think you have distracted the women enough."

"Me?!" Wallace asked incredulously. "I am just a victim in all this."

Wallace's wife took a step forward and swatted her husband's arm. "Go. Get some sleep."

Belac led his team past the two women and to the edge of the encampment. He gestured to the off-white tents. "If you have wives, you should let them know that you are not dead. But don't let them keep you awake. You all need sleep. You may have to ask around, but there should be a place set up for you." He shook his head tiredly. "I still need to go report." He considered the men that had followed him to war. "You all did well out there. No matter what happens with Lord Vairdoe's team, every one of you is a hero."

The foresters glanced at each other while simultaneously trying to hide their own pride. Grinning behind their bushy beards, the men felt the satisfaction of success despite their exhaustion.

Belac turned toward the factorage and left the foresters behind. He had grown fond of the ugly, bearded humans, but he had work to do. *Rolan needs to know I'm back.* Drifting through the shadows, the tired elf made his way to the factorage. Though dawn had yet to come, the encampment felt bright after so long in the forest.

Belac entered through the open doors of the loading bay and crossed the darkened space inside. He opened the door to the factorage's offices and then made his way through a lamplit hallway. Though he knew that he was welcome in the factorage, Belac knocked before opening the door to Rolan's office.

"Rolan?" Belac called through the door. "Don't stab me," he said, pushing the door open.

As the door opened, Belac saw that no one sat at the desk to the right. He stepped into the room and looked left, finding Rolan sitting on a cot that had been set up behind the door. A lamp hung from the far wall, illuminating the office and the scruffy dwarf.

Rolan finished putting on his boot and then gestured to the chair on the other side of the desk. "Close the door and sit down. You look half dead."

Belac closed the door. *At least I don't look like a dwarf.* He walked to the other side of the desk and sat down on the chair's padded seat. He thought that he might fall asleep right there. "The plan worked."

Rolan shook his head. "We don't know that yet." He reached under the cot and dragged out a metal bucket. "We won't know if the plan worked until Vairug gets back and we don't all die." He pulled a wooden cup out of the bucket and began drinking from it.

Belac squirmed in the chair, trying to change where his scabbarded swords pressed into his back. "Well, my part of the plan worked."

Rolan set the empty cup on the floor. "How many did you lose?"

"Three," Belac said and then corrected himself. "Four, if you count the one that ran away."

Rolan drew a knife and tested its edge with his thumb. "Did the fire work on the wicker men?" he asked and then began to scrape the hair off his face.

"They are called briar men," Belac said instead of answering.

Rolan lowered the knife. "Oh? Excuse me. I would not want to offend the soulless monsters that want to kill us and rip out our hearts," he replied sarcastically.

Belac grinned. "There is a reason we give things different names."

Rolan frowned at the use of his own argument. "Fine. Did the fire work on the briar men? I am guessing that it at least took out the bridge. Otherwise, I would expect to hear a lot more screaming right now."

Belac nodded. "Whatever you put in that barrel took out the bridge and a bunch of the briar men with it." He met the dwarf's stony eyes. "But there are still hundreds of them, Rolan."

Rolan dipped his knife into the metal bucket and swished the blade through the water. "Did they bring any of those big spriggan things that you were talking about?"

Belac nodded again. "One. I don't know if fire works on them, but chopping through their skulls seems to do the trick." He looked down at the dwarf's water bucket, knowing that there would be tiny, black hairs floating in it. "You are not going to drink that, are you?"

Rolan frowned. "No. Why? Do you want it?"

Belac's mind tortured him with the thought of tiny hairs stuck to the back of his throat. "Yuck!"

Rolan chuckled. "What if I pour booze in it?"

Belac forgot about the tiny, black hairs. "What kind of booze?"

Thirty-Nine

If Belac dreamed, he slept too well to remember. The sound of knuckles on wood echoed around him, calling him from his slumber. He awoke in a small storage room next to a stack of wooden casks. Rolan had been insistent that the elf not try to drink them. The canvas cot that Belac had slept on was stretched in odd places and was far too similar to a hammock for his liking. However, exhaustion had proven itself superior to discomfort.

"Lord Belac," a muffled man's voice spoke through the door. "Rolan wants us to move the casks. Is it okay if we come in?"

Belac lolled his head side to side and then sat up. "Yes." He felt like his mind was mud.

The door bucked in its frame as the man outside attempted to push it open. "I think you have it locked."

Belac glanced at the door. Light leaked around its edges, revealing that a knife had been hammered into the frame. *Oh, right.* "Yeah. Just a moment."

Belac turned and placed his bare feet on the floor. The grain of the wooden boards pressed into the soles of his feet as he stood. The room lurched around him as he stumbled to the door. He leaned his forehead against the door and took a deep breath. *Why does my head hurt so much?* With his eyes closed, he gripped the hilt of the knife and worked it loose. When he finally swung the door open, the fresh air that rushed in was invigorating.

Four men that the elf did not recognize were waiting in the hallway outside. Belac waved the men into the room and then stumbled back to his cot. He sheathed his knife and sat down, staying out of the way as the men entered the cramped space.

The first man to enter was the one who had spoken through the door. He ran a hand down his neatly trimmed beard and said, "We are sorry to wake you, Lord Belac. We were told that you would understand."

Belac nodded, his mind still trying to make sense of the unrecognized men. *Vairug's team must have succeeded. Now, the village has its men back.* All four of the men were dressed in browns and each had on a pair of boots. Belac hoped that they had been able to find enough clothes to dress all of the rescued men. *The hard part comes next.*

Each of the four men took a cask and carried it from the room. Once the men were gone, Belac closed the door and used the chamber pot. He was quick to open the door again once he was done. Still dressed in his bloodied browns and leather straps, Belac sat on the edge of the cot and put on his boots. *I need a bath.* He gazed at where his scabbarded swords leaned against the wall. *I bet even my swords stink.*

Belac untied his long, black hair and began running his slender fingers through it. *I might not be able to have a bath, but I can at least fix my hair.* He had to struggle with a particularly unruly tangle. *I don't understand how those foresters run around with their hair sticking out all over the place.*

Once he was satisfied with the state of his hair, Belac retied it and then stood. The movement brought his headache back into focus. *This does not seem fair. Rolan would not give me anything to drink. No one should have to feel hungover without getting to be drunk first.* He strapped on his swords and then walked to the door. Stopping in the doorway, he looked back at his chamber pot. *No one is going to empty that for me.* He walked back into the room and retrieved the chamber pot, trying to think of a reason why it was unfair that he needed to empty it himself.

Holding the chamber pot out away from himself, Belac walked out into the light of the hallway and turned left. Fortunately, the men who had carried away the casks had left the door to the loading bay open. Belac made his way through the shadowed loading bay and out into the evening sun. Across the road, men were saying goodbye to their families before the women and children returned to the safety of the gathering hall. *The attack could come at any time now.*

Belac gazed off to his left. The defensive berm now surrounded the tents. The hope was that the exiles would see the tents as a target and ignore the buildings that had survived the fire. Belac looked back to the women and children. *Whatever happens, there is nowhere safer to hide them.*

Belac turned to his right and began walking into the burned village. He did not know where he was supposed to empty his chamber pot, but he did not think that anyone would notice if he sloshed the contents into the burned wreckage. With his emptied chamber pot in hand, he returned to the factorage.

After retracing his steps, Belac slid the empty chamber pot into the storage room before continuing on to Rolan's office. *I think chamber maids deserve their own day of celebration.* The door to the office was open, allowing Belac to catch the last part of a conversation.

Vairug's voice sounded pensive. "…the spriggan dragged the man away. I know it was the right thing to do, but it felt wrong all the same."

"We can't save them all." Rolan stated plainly. "That man was dead either way. Focus on all the men that you did save."

Though the dwarf's voice was hard, it was obvious to Belac that Rolan was attempting to console Vairug. *Vairug must have let a spriggan take one of the prisoners to buy the time he needed to save the others.* Belac wondered what he would have done in the orc's place. Though one of Vairug's hands was magical, the weapons he wielded were only wood and steel. Without a starmetal blade to cut the spriggan, the supernatural monster could have slaughtered the entire rescue team. *I don't know what I would have done. But I am glad that Vairug made the choice he did.*

Belac walked into the office and said, "I'm glad you're not dead."

Vairug's tusks jutted from his mouth as he smiled at the elf. "It was a good plan."

Rolan frowned. "We don't know that yet."

Belac ignored the dwarf's grumpiness. "I am good at distractions."

Rolan stepped away from his desk and examined the elf's face. "You look sick. I told you to leave the door open if you were going to sleep in that room. Those casks are sealed fairly well, but it is not great for you to breathe in the fumes."

Belac vaguely recalled the dwarf saying something to that effect. He narrowed his eyes at the dwarf. "Then, why did you put a cot in there?"

Rolan shook his head. "I didn't. I put the casks in there."

Belac tried to narrow his eyes at the dwarf harder, but the effort hurt his head.

Rolan continued, "You should be sleeping in the tents anyway."

Belac shrugged. "There are bugs out there."

Vairug grinned. "Are you sure that you are not just hiding from the green of the forest outside?"

Belac pursed his lips at the orc. "Die in a fire."

Rolan did not seem to appreciate either explanation. "The tents were your idea, Belac."

Belac nodded. "I know," he acknowledged before attempting to offer a better excuse. "But the trench was not even finished when I went to sleep."

Rolan crossed his arms and frowned at the elf. "Women and children do not dig as fast as men. I had to have them use the dirt from the trench to build a wall on the other side. Even then, I was worried that we would not have it ready in time."

Belac grinned at the dwarf's defensiveness. "Isn't there an old saying about how it's a poor craftsman that blames his tools?"

Rolan's frown deepened. "I got it done, didn't I? Besides, I guarantee that whoever said that nonsense was a man with quality tools."

Still grinning, Belac asked, "Did you get the catapults built?"

Rolan nodded. "Yes. But they are a chore to aim, and we are not going to be able to reposition them in time if the attack does not come from the west."

Belac understood the dwarf's concern. "We are not dealing with strategical masterminds. I think those exiles really are just crazy." His voice took on a speculative tone, "If it were me, I would split off two thirds of the army and have Talia move them north and then east to the road that leads to Harbridge. Then she could follow it back to Gofell. That way, the army could approach from the direction we are least likely to be prepared for. They would also be able to sweep up any of the humans that were attempting to flee to the capital."

Belac had not yet visually inspected the village's defenses, but he continued to outline a general plan. "I would have the briar men bang sticks together constantly while I sent the spriggans in to hit and run. Once the humans showed signs of demoralization, I would have the briar men go silent. I would let the anticipation caused by the silence to build, and then I would order Talia's forces to attack."

Belac nodded to himself. "The briar men that I held in reserve, I would have covered with cloth or mud to mute the glowing in their chest. Then I would have staged them in the forest with Kaelem, ready to attack from the east once the defenders had moved west."

Belac frowned and shook his head. "But that is only if I had no choice but to directly assault the village. If I had more time, it would open up better options."

Vairug gave the elf a scrutinizing look. "If it were you?" he asked dryly.

Belac nodded and then shook his head. "But I don't think that is what they will do. I think they will bring everything they have and hit us from the west. They may not send in the spriggans at all, but if they do, it won't be until after the briar men have triggered all of our defenses." He looked from the orc to the dwarf. "Don't try to fight the spriggans. Either throw fire at them, or let me deal with them. I don't think we have anything other than my sword that can cut through their skulls."

Vairug questioned the elf's advice. "Are you certain that you can defeat two of those monsters?"

Belac did not like the question. *Of course, I don't know if I can beat them. I don't even know if I can survive them!* "I don't see any other options." He shrugged. "But the starmetal sword is not my only advantage. The spriggans don't bother with defense. Whatever it is that animates those things, they don't seem to realize that they can be destroyed."

Vairug was not reassured. "That makes them more dangerous."

Belac shook his head. "No. That makes them wrong."

Forty

Horns sang through a fog of dreams. Shouts followed, the words making no sense to the sleeping elf. The horns continued to call out. Belac disliked the insistence of the horns despite the clarity of their sound. *Don't they realize that people are trying to sleep?* The thought pulled him closer to consciousness. *I need to get a dog and train it to bite people that play horns.* It occurred to his sleep addled mind that dogs were known to bark. *Not a dog, then. Maybe a big cat. One of those panther things. Or a horse. Could I train a horse to bite people?* The sound of bedlam intensified.

Belac shot up from his bedroll angrily. "Don't make me get my horse!" he shouted at the empty tent.

"Western battlements!" Ecard's voice called from outside the tent. "If you are not assigned elsewhere, you had better be moving!"

In his mind, Belac imagined a pale morning blanketed with clouds of mist. Garnet lights pulsed as the twisted forms of the briar men slowly approached. Then, Kaelem rode forward on a horrific wooden horse, the exiled elf brandishing a flaming sword. Belac shook the image from his mind. *He stole my horse idea!*

As the elf moved to put on his boots, Simon's deep voice called out, "James, help me pull up the bridge."

Once his boots were on, Belac snatched up his swords and then stood. *If I don't hurry, I am going to miss my own war.* He rushed out of the tent, hoping that Kaelem did not really have a magic horse. Despite the advancing dawn, fires still burned from the night before. Belac searched the bearded faces of the men around him, finding few that were familiar. *If this battle is decided by which army has the most hair, we are definitely going to win.*

Belac slung his starmetal sword onto his back as he followed the flow of men west. Once past the tents, he strode between the two catapults and to the western berm. Though the berm was still mostly dirt, poles had been added to the sides to reinforce the walls. The top of the berm had been flattened, allowing for a stable platform along its ridge. To access the upper area, wooden planks had been set into the dirt, creating steps that ran up the side of the berm in multiple locations.

Rolan stood center of the western battlement. Arms crossed and feet set wide, the dwarf stared out toward the forested hills. Somewhere, he had acquired a new rucksack. And while the leather bag had no frame, its traditional design still suited him well. *Rolan looked kind of naked without a backpack.* An image of the dwarf standing nude in a storehouse flashed in Belac's mind. *Okay, maybe not actually naked.*

Belac climbed up the side of the berm and stood next to the dwarf. Horns continued to bray in the distance, though their sounds seemed to be getting closer. Beyond an open field of grass, the forest was deceptively calm. *All that green is not going to trick me.* He glanced back and to his left, reassuring himself that the bridge had been raised. He saw that Vairug was stationed on the southeast corner, prepared to take command if the exiles proved more competent than Belac believed them to be.

Rolan spoke loud enough to be heard over the hustling of the men taking their positions on the battlement. "At the first sign of artillery, take cover behind the wall."

Belac shook his head dismissively. "I don't think they are going to have artillery. The briar men are not smart enough to use bows." He considered the greater threat. "But I guess the spriggans might throw rocks or something at us."

Rolan nodded, not arguing. "Let's hope that they don't expect us to have artillery either."

Belac shook his head again. "They are not going to care. They want me dead, and they want the village erased. Even the women and children would be killed at this point. We have bested them too many times for the exiles to tolerate anything less."

Rolan gave the elf a curious look. "Still. Even if it is just a rock. Get out of the way."

Belac raised his voice over the sounds of the other defenders. "Maybe I will just hide behind Wallace's beard!"

Scattered laughter moved through the line of men.

Ecard climbed the berm and took his place next to the elf. "I believe we are as prepared as we can be. It is impressive how quickly the men have taken direction. Their willingness to fight might very well be what makes the difference."

The villagers understood their situation. There was simply no way to move their families faster than the packs of supernatural monsters that would hunt them. There would be no better place to stand. There would be no other chance of survival. *If the exiles had been smart enough to wait, they could have picked off the families that attempted to flee. Even a short siege would be to their advantage.* A dark suspicion gripped Belac. *What am I missing?*

Shadows began to take shape on the other side of the berm as the morning sun broke the horizon. *At least the sun won't be in our eyes.* Belac did not expect the glare of the sun to deter the exiles. The briar men were without eyes, and the hate that burned in the spriggan's would not be quelled by radiance.

Two men ran from the tree line and into the field. Then four more men fled the forest from two other locations. Six in total, the scouts raced across the clearing and toward the south of the encampment. Belac did not know if the men had a way to get inside the defenses, or if the men were to hide in one of the buildings. Movement from the forest drew his attention away from the scouts.

There was no amassing of an army, no display of militaristic threat. A horde burst from the forest. Twisted, wooden berserkers sprinted into the clearing, their chests pulsing with garnet lights. The sound of their misshapen feet trampling the ground grew thick in the morning air. There were more briar men than Belac had imagined. He stared at the flood of wooden monsters and wondered how many other villages had fallen to the exiles.

Rolan held up a fist and then thrust his hand forward. The mechanical release of the twin catapults sounded from behind him. Two casks soared high over the western berm and out above the clearing. *It's Kaelem's turn for a headache.* Thunder and light erupted where the casks struck the field. Force and debris ripped through briar men, sending wooden flack into the air.

While Belac had expected an explosion of flames, he was not disappointed by the damage done to the briar men. The ones not immediately killed by the blast were broken and strewn on the field. However, the horde continued to charge the encampment without temporization. Belac worried that the artillery would not be able to thin the monster's numbers enough for the defenders to survive the coming onslaught.

The men operating the catapults immediately began to reload and adjust their aim. They were only able to get one additional salvo off before the first of the briar men reached the trench. Though wooden spikes lined the bottom of the trench, they did little to slow the briar men. Belac drew his sword as another cask flew overhead.

Clattering against each other, the briar men poured into the trench and rushed toward the battlement. Clawing at the dirt and climbing over each other to reach the top, the swarming monsters pursued a single goal. *They want to kill us all.* Belac's grip on his sword tightened. The clearing had filled with erratic garnet lights and there was no indication that the flood would stop.

The men atop the battlement began thrusting wooden spears down at the monsters. Few of the defenders were accurate enough to strike a glowing heart, and some even lost their spears. While the lost weapons were quickly replaced, the fallen briar men were replaced faster. To Belac's right, the edge of the battlement crumbled, spilling two of the defenders into the trench. Briar men tore the two humans apart as more of the monsters swarmed past.

Belac turned away from the bloodied briar men and faced the interior of the encampment. He raised his sword over his head and shouted, "Call the burn!"

A hornsman blew two short notes and then a long third. Men at the base of the berm threw flaming torches over the wall of dirt. Fires erupted on the other side as the accelerant coating the bottom of the trench was ignited. The fires spread rapidly, creating a blazing ring around the encampment. Though the briar men in the trench were engulfed, still more of the monsters poured into the inferno.

Elated voices cheered over the sound of the roaring flames as humans pumped their fists and shook their spears. *It's not over yet.*

Rolan grabbed the elf's arm and pulled him close. "The south catapult is not launching."

Belac nodded. "Go! I've got this." He turned back to the trench and stared through the dark smoke rising from it. *I really hope I've got this.*

The briar men had stopped throwing themselves into the burning trench, but more still crowded into the clearing, spreading out to the north. A cask crashed down on the briar men, its blast scattering wooden body parts. Belac reminded himself that he was now at one of the safest locations in the encampment. The briar men burning in the western side of the trench would keep the fire fueled longer than the accelerant alone. When the ring of fire began to dissolve, the briar men would be able to resume their attack from the other sides. It would be Belac's job to redirect the defenders to where they were needed. *I am not out of tricks yet.*

Forty-One

Belac stared out at the sea of pulsing garnet lights. The briar men were not doing what he had expected them to do. They had continued to flood into the clearing, and then inexplicably, they had frozen in place. Instead of searching the encampment for locations of possible ingress, they waited motionlessly on the other side of the burning trench. When a cask fell on the horde of silent monsters, they did not seem to notice the explosion, nor the ensuing loss of numbers.

Belac frowned. "Maybe they will just stand there and let us kill them."

"I think that is unlikely," Ecard replied without feeling.

Those things are really kind of ruining my plans here. Belac wondered if he should have the men moon the monsters.

A dull pounding sound began to emanate from the forest, and then something stepped out of the tree line. Easily four times the size of a spriggan, the lanky humanoid that emerged towered over the briar men. Despite its shape, the monster's body was completely covered with dark, gnarled bark. *It looks like a walking tree!* Even from across the clearing, the mote of red fire burning in the center of its forehead could be seen.

Belac pointed with a finger of the hand holding his scabbard. "They are not supposed to have one of those."

Ecard could not hide his dismay. "What is it?!"

"It's... Ah... Uhm..." Belac knew that he needed to give an answer. "It's a giant-evil-tree-person." He turned his head to the side without looking away from the monster. "Rolan!"

The giant-evil-tree-person waded through the briar men as it moved directly toward the elf. Belac could feel the thing staring at him. Thunderous footfalls began to shake the battlement as the monster neared the encampment. A terrified silence had seized the defenders. No one knew what to do. There was no contingency for such a thing. The pounding of the giant-evil-tree-person's steps continued to grow louder.

Belac tore his gaze away from the red ghost flames rising from the monster's forehead and turned toward the southern catapult. "Rolan!" He pointed his sword at the monster. "They have a giant-evil-tree-person!"

Belac returned his attention to the monster in time to see it raise a bark covered foot and begin to kick out toward where he stood on the battlement. Belac dropped his scabbard, wrapped an arm around Ecard's waist, and jumped off the berm. Dirt exploded from the wall behind them as the two fell toward the ground. Ecard's back slammed into the ground with Belac still on top of him. Though Ecard's body softened Belac's fall, the impact knocked the lord unconscious.

Belac pushed himself off of the unconscious man and looked back toward the battlement. One of the giant-evil-tree-person's long legs stepped over the broken wall. Then the other followed and the monster was inside the encampment. Belac suddenly recognized the thing's face. Even covered in bark, the lines of Talia's elven visage shown through. And while her eye sockets were empty, the mote of red fire on her forehead burned with feminine scorn. *I am so glad that I didn't marry her.*

Belac climbed over Ecard, grabbed the back of the man's tunic, and began dragging him away from the berm. *I need to get him away from the giant-evil-tree-Talia.* He glanced at the unconscious lord's face. *I really hope I didn't kill him.*

The giant-evil-tree-Talia turned around and began pushing the berm into the trench on the other side. Dirt smoldered the flames as she created a narrow bridge for the briar men. Belac continued to pull Ecard away. *If he is dead, I am totally going to blame it on Talia.* He glanced back at the giant-evil-tree-Talia. *Only a woman could mess up my plans this much.*

Once the lord was out of immediate danger, Belac let go of the man's tunic and then turned around. *I need a new plan.* A forester that had found his courage hacked at the giant-evil-tree-Talia's leg with an axe. The heavy steel head broke through bark and tore away chunks of soft, rotten wood. The giant-evil-tree-Talia backhanded the man, sending his broken body flying into the tents. Men began abandoning the battlements and charging at the giant-evil-tree-Talia. The superficial damage of their wooden spears was answered with contemptuous kicks that shattered bones.

Maybe Rolan has a plan. Belac looked toward the southern catapult, searching for the dwarf. Rolan stepped away from where he had been repairing the catapult, grabbed the release lever, and then threw it forward. The catapult's arm swung up, launching a cask that flew past the giant-evil-tree-Talia. An explosion sounded on the other side of the berm.

Belac turned and began sprinting toward the norther catapult. *I am stealing Rolan's plan.* The catapult was aimed at the giant-evil-tree-Talia, but the four men who were to operate it cowered on the back side of the device.

Belac pointed his free hand at the giant-evil-tree-Talia and shouted, "Shoot her!"

One of the operators shouted back, "There are no more casks!"

Belac looked back to the giant-evil-tree-Talia. Briar men had begun to flow past her legs and into the encampment. Defenders rushed to stop the monsters, but none could withstand the giant-evil-tree-Talia's kicks. *We are going to lose.* After eradicating the villagers of Gofell, the exiles would go on, feeding village after village to their army of nightmares.

Belac tossed his sword up and caught it in an underhanded grip. *The humans are not food.* He turned and then climbed up onto the catapult. Balancing his feet on the bucket, he stood and faced the giant-evil-tree-Talia.

Vairug's voice called out from the elf's left. "Belac, don't!"

Belac swept his blade up, slapping the throw lever as he raised his sword above his head. He felt his spine compress as the catapult's arm swung forward. His plan had been to fly straight at the giant-evil-tree-Talia and stab the fiery mote on her forehead. However, the angled momentum of his rising sword caused him to rotate in the air to his left until he was flying horizontally.

Belac roared as he flew over the battle, intent on stabbing the giant-evil-tree-Talia regardless of his orientation. The tip of his blade sank into the giant-evil-tree-Talia's left eye socket as he passed over her shoulder. The giant-evil-tree-Talia's upper body twisted to her left as Belac's weight hooked her head around. Her giant legs tangled under her, causing her to fall toward the berm as she spun.

The world lurched around Belac as he clung to the hilt of his sword with both hands. The giant-evil-tree-Talia's back slammed into the ground on the other side of the berm, her legs lying over the burning trench. Shock lanced through Belac's body when his boots hit the ground, but still he held tight to his sword. Standing to the left of the giant-evil-tree-Talia's massive head, he jerked his sword free, raising it high so that he could stab her again. The red glow of the giant-evil-tree-Talia's flaming third eye lit Belac's face as the sword moved above his head. Roaring down at the hellish red light, he looked like one of the demons that the Vaquians were believed to have been.

Belac's sword plunged down into the fiery eye, ghost flames climbing his arms and chest. A shadow rose above him, warning the elf of danger. *Not dead.* He jumped out of the way, leaving his dwarf-sword sticking out of the monster's flaming third eye. The ground thundered behind Belac as he flew. When he landed, he rolled onto his feet and then scurried away as giant fingers dug furrows in the dirt.

The giant-evil-tree-Talia rolled onto her chest, crushing the briar men in her way. She climbed onto her hands and knees and then began pounding her fist onto the ground as her legs continued to burn. Belac staggered away from the giant-evil-tree-Talia. *I think I made her angry.*

The giant-evil-tree-Talia stood, inciting the flames to climb higher up her legs. Then she began stomping her foot blindly, guessing at where Belac might be.

As the giant-evil-tree-Talia crushed unfortunate briar men, Belac suddenly realized that the twisted wooden men were ignoring him. Staying out of sword reach, the briar men moved around him as they crowded toward the breach in the berm. He did not know if it was because he was an elf, or that he was simply on the outside of the encampment, but the briar men's orders obviously did not include him. *How do I use this?*

A cask slammed into the giant-evil-tree-Talia's shoulder, the explosion tearing off bark and knocking her to the ground. More of the briar men were crushed as she crashed down on top of them. The fire that had climbed from her legs to her torso now spread to the field of grass. *I can't get near her.* Belac glanced at the breach. *If the opening stays narrow, the humans might be able to hold it.* His head turned toward the forested hills to the west. *I think it's time to find out what happens to all the tree people when I kill Kaelem.*

Forty-Two

Briar men moved out of Belac's way as he ran toward the forest. *I need to find Kaelem before he tells these things to kill me.* He began moving along the tree line, searching for the best way up. Trails wove through the forest in a tangled maze that offered Belac no clues. Even the early sunlight did little to show him where Kaelem might be hiding. Belac may never have found the exile, had he not seen the glowing red eyes of the spriggans.

Hidden in the shadows of the trees, Kaelem stood on a rocky shelf overlooking the battlefield. He now wore a sword on his hip, its wooden basket hilt made of thorny vines. To either side of the exiled elf, a spriggan waited protectively.

Belac's pace slowed to a determined stride as he followed a trail up toward the side of the shelf. He removed his starmetal sword, thumbed the snap, and drew the milky white blade. Belac decided that Kaelem would be his first target. *He needs to die.*

When Kaelem spotted Belac stalking through the forest, the exile stumbled back in fright. *That's right, Kaelem. You are going to die.* Kaelem pointed, shaking his finger at the approaching elf. Then the exile turned and ran. *Fine. I will kill the spriggans first.*

Belac dropped his scabbard and charged toward the spriggans, his blade pointed out behind him. Both spriggans turned as one, directing hate filled stares at Belac. The elf snarled at the things that thought they could stop him.

The closer of the spriggans reached for Belac with its monstrous wooden hand. He dodged under the claws and to his left. The back of his blade swept forward, slicing through the roots of the spriggan's right leg, and causing the wooden horror to crash onto the rocky ground. Belac's feet slid across the rocks as he redirected his momentum, turning to face the spriggan with his sword held over his left shoulder. Before the spriggan could rise from its hands and knees, Belac darted forward, slashing out with his sword at an angle that cut through the back of the spriggan's crowned head.

The upper portion of the dead spriggan's head fell away as Belac recovered from the swing. Gazing over the back of the hardened corpse, he looked into the glowing red eyes of the last spriggan. *You were right to hate me.* Belac leapt forward, placing his left hand on the dead spriggan's back as he vaulted over. The starmetal sword rose above the elf as his legs swung over the corpse's decrowned head.

As Belac's blade descended, the spriggan attempted to backhand him away. The impossibly sharp edge of his starmetal sword sliced through the wooden forearm and scored the spriggans chest. However, the severed hand still struck Belac in the head. Light flashed through the elf's vision, and then he found himself face down on the ground. *Lesson learned.*

Knowing that he was still in a fight, Belac rolled to his right. A foot made of tangled roots stomped down where he had been. He used the roll to come to his feet and then faced the wooden horror. Keeping away from the ledge on his left, Belac backed away from the spriggan. A grassfire raged in the field below, but he had no time to appraise it. The spriggan pressed its attack, leading with the hooked claws of its remaining hand.

Belac dodged to his right, turning left as he slashed downward with his sword. The starmetal blade hacked through the thick tangled roots of the spriggan's elbow, taking away its remaining hand. The spriggan pivoted toward Belac and punched with the stump of its right forearm. Belac leapt forward, grabbed the wooden forearm with his left hand, and then pulled himself closer as he thrust with his sword. The spriggan's glowing red eyes blinked out as the starmetal blade sank into the monster's skull.

Belac put his right foot on the spriggan's chest and pushed himself away. He landed with his right foot back and his sword pointed away from the spriggan as it toppled backward. Belac looked from one dead spriggan to the other. *I want to see Vairug do all that with just an axe.* He turned away from the ledge and the war that waged below.

Belac ran into the woods, chasing after the exiled elf that had fled. *I'm coming for you Kaelem.* The trail that Kaelem had taken was narrow, but Belac had no problems following it. At the top of the forested hill, he found a trapper's camp that the exiles had appropriated for themselves. On the other side of an unlit firepit, Kaelem was helping Talia rise from a wooden litter. Blood dripped from the elven woman's eyes and ran down her face as she clung to her brother's arm.

Kaelem dropped his sister when he saw Belac step out of the trees. Talia fell to the dirt, blood still dripping from her eyes. Kaelem glanced away to the west and then looked back to Belac. *If you leave her, I am going to kill her.* Kaelem could read the other elf's thoughts on his face.

Kaelem stepped away from his sister and drew the sword that hung from his hip. "Then it will be decided here," he said in Elven.

Belac's eyes locked on the shimmering silver blade. Though it could have been made from the same metal as Vairug's mechanical hand, Belac knew that it was not. Perfectly straight and doubled edged; Belac knew the sephen blade for what it was. *He should not have one of those.*

Kaelem smiled at the other elf's obvious interest. "You thought you were the only one with a wondrous sword?" he taunted in Elven.

Belac knew that no exile would be allowed to take a sephen blade. He held up his starmetal sword, the side of the dragon claw cross-guard facing the other elf. "I did not steal mine."

Kaelem shouted in Elven, "I take my due!"

Belac stared into the madness of Kaelem's amethyst eyes and suddenly understood the idiocy in the act of exiling. No delegation could ever undo the damage this one elf could do to the reputation of the Elves. Instead of ridding themselves of a problem, the Elves had given it a place to grow.

Belac voiced his understanding. "The Elves should have killed you." He moved to the right of the firepit. "I will correct their mistake."

Kaelem's face hardened as he advanced. He raised his sword above his left shoulder and then slashed down at Belac. Belac's blade swept up to meet the attack. The starmetal sword, a product of Giant, Dwarf, and Man, clashed with the elegant Elven blade that had been profaned with Vaquian iconography. As soon as the blades touched, both elves settled into the movements of an Elven blade dance.

The edges of their blades rotated down until the flats slapped against each other. Swords crossed between them, the two elves began to circle one another with their left hands held out to their sides. Over their blades, the azure eyes of renegade stared into the amethyst of exile. Though both men had left their home behind, they would now determine the fate of their people.

The early sun gleamed through the trees, causing the forest to sparkle as a southern wind blew across the leaves. Agile footing moved the elves over the barren dirt of the campsite as they danced in the sparkling light. The blades of their swords slid up and down each other, both elves searching for an advantage. Their bodies shifted from the beginnings of one stance to another in a fluid rhythm as they each responded to the other.

It had been decades since Belac had last engaged in a blade dance. The sophistication of the duel rarely reached beyond the Elven courts. Kaelem was not only older and more experienced, he had also been at court far more recently. Though the signs were too subtle for anyone other than an elf to notice, Belac was losing the dance.

Kaelem smiled villainously at his own impending victory. The exile suddenly stopped circling and then flowed into an oscillating press that forced Belac to devance. Belac's bladework became more strained as he struggled to maintain his footing. If not for the sound of the daggers being drawn from their sheaths, he would not have known that Talia had risen behind him. He rotated the edge of his blade toward Kaelem and then shoved forward with the hilt of his sword. The dragon claw cross-guard caught the sephen blade and pushed it up and to Belac's left. Spinning to his right, Belac danced away from Talia as one of her daggers raked the air where he had been.

Belac's blade swept out in a horizontal arc as he spun to face the other elves. Kaelem evaded the milky white blade lithely and then flowed into an aggressive slash. Belac's sword followed the momentum of his spin and then whipped over his head as he lashed out at the sephen blade. The two blades clashed again, and then the blade dance resumed once more.

Kaelem immediately attempted to circle Belac in an obvious effort to expose the other elf's back to Talia. Belac denied him, instead trading advantage for relative safety. Talia juked side to side, attempting to get around her brother as the other two elves danced. *I can't win like this.*

Belac stepped forward with his left foot, rotating his shoulder in as he drew his knife in an underhanded grip. Stabbing upward, he drove the knife up between Kaelem's thighs. The knife's blade slid up into the exile's pelvis, causing the elf's body to seize. Then Belac ripped the blade free and danced away.

Kaelem released the thorn covered basket hilt of his sword, letting the sephen blade fall to the ground as his hands moved to cover his groin. With his knees pressed together, he attempted to walk away.

That might not have been exactly honorable, but neither is having your sister try to stab me in the back. Stumbling forward, Kaelem fell to his knees. Anguished sounds escaped the elf as he collapsed onto his face and then his side.

Belac began to laugh hysterically. Talia looked from her fallen brother to the laughing elf, her amethyst eyes filled with outrage. Belac struggled to speak, but he could not get the words out. As Talia moved toward Belac, he swiped back and forth with his sword, barely able to put up a defense. He could not stop laughing.

Talia backed away and glanced down at her brother. "Kaelem?"

Belac pointed with the hilt of his bloodied knife, forcing his words out through laughter. "Well, Talia. I guess you do have a sister, now." He almost dropped his sword laughing.

Talia screamed and rushed at Belac with both of her daggers held above her head. *Ut-oh.* Despite the daggers pointed at him, Belac was still struggling with his laughter. He turned right, threw his knife at Talia's face, and then stepped backward out of her path. Though the blade of his knife did not cut her, its hilt broke her nose. As Talia stumbled past him, Belac slashed the back of her right calf.

Talia spilled into the dirt, losing her daggers as she stopped her fall. On her hands and knees, she looked back, unable to hide her fear. Belac's laughter had become an unruly chuckle. *What am I going to do with you Talia?* The elven woman glanced to one of her daggers and then looked back to Belac. Then she rolled over onto her backside, untied the rope around her waist, and began applying it as a tourniquet. *Maybe she is not just crazy.*

If the currents of time had flown another way, Belac may have actually married Talia. Had they both stayed in the Elven Lands, they may have found each other there. Despite his unknown linage, she may have seen his worth. *Happiness hides behind our own choices.* Belac thought of all the women that he had met; from the beauty of golden hair, to the ugliness of a goblin. His mind fixed on a giantess, nude and covered in gore.

"I want to let you live, Talia," Belac said as he stepped close with his sword held ready.

Talia looked up, her face masked in blood, eyes filled with defiance.

Belac could still see her beauty. "But I respect you." His blade slashed through her throat.

Forty-Three

Belac considered sharing his thoughts with Kaelem as the exile bled out. He considered explaining the mistakes that Kaelem and the Elves had made. Belac even considered offering his condolences for the death of the other elf's sister. *Why bother?* Belac thrust his starmetal sword into Kaelem's back. The milky white blade found the exile's heart, ending his suffering.

Belac pulled his sword out of Kaelem's back and knelt beside the corpse. He used the dead elf's heather gray tunic to wipe the blood off the white starmetal blade, and then set the sword aside. Leaning over the corpse, he placed his left hand on the ground and began straightening Kaelem's legs. Once Belac had pulled the corpse out of the fetal position, he rolled the dead elf onto its back. Ignoring the dead stare of Kaelem's amethyst eyes, Belac removed the exile's sword belt.

Belac was less happy about the death of the exiled elves than he had expected to be. Now that they were no longer a threat, Talia and Kaelem somehow seemed almost tragic to him. *If they had just made different choices…* Belac shook his head. *If they had made different choices, they would have been different people. And then, maybe I would not have needed to kill them.*

Leaving the belted scabbard lying on top of Kaelem's chest, Belac stepped one leg over the corpse and reached for the sephen sword.

His hand froze before touching the thorny basket hilt. *What if those vines come to life and try to eat me?* He finished stepping over the corpse and then picked up Kaelem's scabbard. Belac twirled the scabbard, wrapping the leather belt around its plain, wooden sides. Then he took hold of the wrapped leather like a handle, and poked the scabbard at the thorny vines of the sephen sword's basket hilt. The vines did not try to eat him.

Belac leaned closer and struck the basket hilt, the hollow scabbard clacking against the wooden vines. *I hope that I'm not just making those things angry.* He held the scabbard up over his head, ready to use it as a club as he slowly reached for the basket hilt with his left hand. *Please don't eat me. Please don't eat me. Please don't eat me.* Belac's hand gripped the hilt of the sword. The sword did not try to eat him.

With the sword and scabbard in his hands, he stood. His eyes traced the simple lines of the sephen blade. Elegant in its utilitarianism, the silvery blade was slimmer and much lighter than an arming-sword. Though Belac had held a sephen sword only once before, they were the blades that most Elven swords were patterned from.

"Oh, I'm keeping you." Belac narrowed his eyes at the sword. "But don't bite me."

He slid the scabbard onto the sword and then walked over to his knife. He frowned down at the small blade. Dirt had powdered the exile's blood, creating a sticky looking mud that would need to be cleaned off. He picked up the knife and carried it over to Talia's corpse. *She looks a lot less pretty now that she is dead.* Though Talia's tunic was bloody, Belac thought that he would be able to find enough dry cloth to wipe the mud from his knife.

Belac looked past the elven woman's corpse to where one of her daggers lay in the dirt. *Maybe I should just take hers.* He dropped his knife next to the bloody corpse and walked over to the dagger. As he reached for the dagger, he saw the blade for what it was. *It can't be.* He picked up the dagger and inspected its perfect edge. *There are no sephen daggers.*

Belac glanced at the other dagger, suddenly recognizing the importance of its twin. A sephen sword was nigh indestructible. Its edge would never dull, its blade would never warp or break. Yet somehow, something had broken one. Somehow, someone had reforged a sephen sword into daggers.

The art of forging sephen had long ago been lost to the Elves. Thirteen swords were all that was said to remain. Symbols of prowess and prestige, the sephen blades were entrusted to only the most worthy of elves. Belac did not understand how the exiles had successfully stolen two.

Belac collected the second dagger and then returned to Talia's corpse. *I hope I don't get too much blood on my new sheaths.* He knelt down, set all three of the sephen blades to the side, and began removing the belts that held the leather sheaths strapped to Talia's thighs. *I wonder if I am going to get into trouble for having these.* He imagined elves swathed in loose, black cloth pouncing from the shadows to strike at him with poisoned knives. *I think maybe I just won't tell anyone.*

Once Belac had unbuckled the belt from around Talia's waist, he rolled her over to free the harness. He stood and buckled the belt around his waist, thinking that Vairug would give him a hard time for wearing a woman's belt. *Stupid orc.* He buckled the straps that held the sheaths against his thighs and then knelt down to retrieve the sephen daggers. *The back of Talia's tunic has less blood on it.*

Belac slid his new daggers into their sheaths and picked up his knife. He cleaned the knife on the back of the dead woman's tunic and then sheathed the blade. *Is that smoke?* He sniffed the air. He could smell burned tree sap in the faint smoke. *The forest is on fire!* Moving half bent over, he grabbed the sephen sword and hurried back to Kaelem's body. After snatching up the hilt of his starmetal sword, Belac reversed course and ran back to the trail he had traveled up.

Belac followed the trail down to where he had fought the spriggans. From the vantage of the overlook, he could see that the grassfire had spread to the eastern side of the forested hill. *I am not going that way.* He sprinted to the scabbard of his starmetal sword and then took a knee. He set the sephen sword down and grabbed the empty scabbard. He slid the starmetal sword's milky white blade into its scabbard, snapped the securing strap, and then slung the scabbarded sword onto his back. *I might have too many weapons.*

Belac grabbed the sephen sword with his left hand and then raced into the woods. *I am feeling kind of conflicted here.* He liked the idea of all the green being burned down, but he did not want to die in a fire. *It's like a bad joke! How did the dragon slayer die? In a fire.* Moving south through the trees, Belac attempted to outpace the fire's advance.

While it would have been safer for Belac to run away from the fire, he did not want to get trapped in the forest. *With my luck, another angry-feather-bear would try to eat me. Or a pack of owls.* He nodded to himself. *It would be a pack of owls.* He did not know what had happened to the army of evil tree people, but if the war still waged, Belac would not run from it. Not only were his friends on the other side of the fire, there was an entire village of people that had trusted him.

When Belac burst out of the trees and onto a road, he turned left and began following it east. Now running downhill at a breakneck speed, he focused on getting to the village before the fire spread to the road. As he neared the bottom of the hill, he began to feel traces of smoke being pulled into his lungs. Haggard of breath, the elf hurried into the burned village.

Slowing to a stumbling walk, Belac looked back to the forest. The fire continued to spread in his direction, but the majority of the smoke was being carried north by the wind. *I should be safe here.* He glanced at the charred remains of the village. *There is nothing here left to burn.* He moved through the empty roads of Gofell, making his way toward the encampment. What he saw there surprised him. Men in red doublets and steel hats walked the battlements. *When did they get here?*

Belac stood on his tiptoes and hopped into the air to get a better view of the battlefield. Motionless briar men lay on a blackened field of burned grass. Though many of the monsters appeared to have been set on fire, most looked to have simply stopped moving. Belac saw not one garnet light. The giant-evil-tree-Talia smoldered on the field. Though her bark skin had burned easily, her rotten core had resisted.

Belac continued on to the factorage. He did not expect to find the dwarf inside, but he thought that he should check Rolan's office anyway. Belac went into the factorage through the front and peered into the offices as he moved through the building. Finding no one inside, he continued out through the loading bay. On the road outside, he turned left toward the encampment.

The bridge had been lowered, and more of the men in red doublets were now in the process of carrying dead bodies from the encampment. *Those are Cavascan soldiers.* Belac frowned at the unexpected reinforcements as they carried the dead toward him. *How long was I gone?* He stepped aside, allowing the soldiers to transport the dead into the factorage. Despite their burdens, the soldiers nodded to Belac as they passed him by.

Keeping to the right of the road, Belac continued on toward the encampment. *The Cavascans are on their way to Harbridge. They have no choice but to pass by Gofell. I should have thought of that.* He wondered how long it would be before the rest of the refugees arrived. Then he wondered how they would react when they beheld the battle's aftermath. *Will they be reminded of what happened to their own homes?* He realized that their empathy could work to his advantage.

As the elf entered the encampment, he heard Vairug shout, "We have to go look for him!"

A rich, familiar voice replied calmly, "I do not believe that will be necessary."

Rolan added, "We know he's not dead. It had to be him that made the briar men stop."

Vairug pointed to the burning forest. "We still need to go look for him!"

Ecard stepped forward. "I will go with you."

Serath grinned as the elf walked over to the group.

Belac halted behind the orc and asked, "Who are we looking for?"

Forty-Four

Beyond the blackened field of burned grass, fire still blazed in the forest. Smoke rose from the mounds of cremated briar men scattered about the burned field, a southern wind carrying the smoke north to chase after the departing forest fire. The village had acted as a fire break to the south, but the grassfire had spread in every direction north of the main road. Cavascan soldiers now patrolled the village and the surrounding area, ensuring that no monsters remained to threaten the exodus. The people of Gofell had been grateful to relinquish the responsibility.

Belac stood inside the loading bay of the factorage, gazing down at the bodies of the fallen. A total of thirty-two dead men were laid out in four rows. *This is too many.*

Once the battlement had been breached, the briar men had swarmed into the encampment. Belac knew that there were men who could have led better than he had. Even among the humans, there were those who had mastered tactics and strategy. *I need to be better.* The dead before him were a painful lesson. He silently vowed to seek out an education that would not cost the lives of others.

Of all the men laying on the floor, Belac knew the names of only three. Vaun, Lochlin, and Ben; three of the sixteen foresters that had followed him to the southern ruins and back. Had the Cavascan forces not arrived in Belac's absence, the numbers may have been far greater.

"I'm sorry," Belac said softly to the assemblage of dead men. Then he turned and strode into the hallway that accessed the factorage's offices.

When he got to Rolan's office, the door was already open. Belac walked through the open doorway without knocking.

Seated behind his desk, Rolan raised his head from the correspondence that he was in the process of drafting. He took one look at the elf and said, "You want something."

Belac nodded, "Yes. But it's not anything too crazy."

Rolan frowned. "That statement is not as reassuring as you might think it is."

Belac grinned, though his heart was not in it. He stepped over to the desk and held out the sephen sword. "I want you to turn this into a dwarf-sword."

Rolan dropped his quill in its inkwell and then took the scabbarded sword. "You want a longer handle on it?" he asked in a professional tone.

Belac nodded again. "I want everything except the blade replaced." He waved his hand at the sword. "Get rid of all that evil Vaquian stuff. We should probably burn it." He leaned over the desk and held a hand out past the bottom of the thorny basket hilt. "Make it long enough that I can use it with two hands, but don't weight the pommel too much." He moved his hand above the hilt, extending his thumb and forefinger for measure. "Keep the cross guard small. All it needs to do is stop my hand from sliding up onto the blade." *And that way, it won't poke me in the back as much.*

Belac straightened his posture, but then held up a finger as one thought led to another. "And I need a scabbard that will ride on my back. Maybe you can add one of those thumb snap things to keep it from falling out like you did for the starmetal sword."

Rolan drew the sword and then set its wooden scabbard on his desk. He furrowed his brow as he appraised the silvery blade. "What is this?"

"It's... Ah..." Belac considered lying and then decided not to. "It's sephen."

Rolan gave the elf a questioning look.

Belac shrugged. "Magic-elf-metal."

Rolan chuckled and then tested the balance of the sword. "This blade is a lot lighter than that one." He gestured to the hilt riding above the elf's right shoulder.

Belac glanced back at the hilt of his dwarf-sword. Ecard had returned the scabbarded blade himself. Among the humans, there was a growing belief that the sword was magical. After being pulled from the giant-evil-tree-Talia's forehead, the soot covered blade had been treated with something akin to reverence.

Belac rolled his shoulders. "I have more experience with lighter blades." He nodded significantly to the sephen sword. "Especially, that style of blade."

Rolan scratched the stubble on his cheek. "So, what you are saying," he smiled, "is that you want an elven-bastard sword?"

Belac could not help but grin. "I guess it's fitting." He pointed at his friend. "But I am still calling it a dwarf-sword."

Chuckling, Rolan nodded. "Fair enough." He picked up the wooden scabbard and slid the sephen blade inside.

"Rolan," Belac said seriously and then waited for the dwarf to look at him. "Don't show that to an elf."

Rolan raised an eyebrow.

Belac added, "And don't tell anyone what it is."

Rolan reassessed the scabbarded sword. "It's stolen?"

Belac did not think that 'stolen' was the right word to use. "Let's call it confiscated."

Rolan smiled knowingly at the elf. "So, you want to hide it by making it look Dwarven."

Belac squirmed like a child caught stealing cookies. "I mean... Ah..." He held up his hands. "More than one thing can be true."

Rolan harrumphed deeply with amusement. "Between Vairug's hand and your swords, if there is ever an anti-interracial coalition, we are going to be their first targets."

Belac laughed. "Well, when they come for us, maybe we don't tell them that my dad is a dragon."

Rolan nodded approvingly.

Belac glanced at the open door, suddenly worried that he may have been overheard. He walked over to the doorway and poked his head out, searching the hallway for spies. Finding no one, he stepped back into the room and asked, "How long until the rest of the Cavascans show up?"

A rich voice answered from behind the elf. "They should begin arriving shortly after noon."

Belac jumped at the sound of the wizard's voice. Startlement gripped Belac's heart as he spun to face the man. *How did I not see him?!*

Leaning against the far-left wall with his arms crossed, Serath offered the elf a friendly smile. The wizard's green eyes were bright in the dim of the room.

Belac put a hand to his chest and pointed at the wizard with the other. "Have you been there the whole time?!"

A grin twisted Serath's neatly groomed beard. "In time, I have been many places."

Belac narrowed his eyes at the wizard. *Sneaky wizard thinks he's smart.*

Serath continued to grin pleasantly.

Belac crossed his arms as he regarded the wizard. "I needed to talk to you anyway."

Serath nodded, holding his grin. "Then, it seems as if you have rather exacting needs."

Belac ignored the banter. "I want to know if you can magic something for me."

Serath's grin slipped away. "You cannot have a magic carpet."

Belac shook his head. "It's not that." He pointed at the wizard. "But why can't I have a magic carpet?!"

Serath's head swung side to side as he exhaled.

"Whatever." Belac waved the matter aside. "I need to know if you can magic my voice loud enough for all the Cavascans to hear me. Like the way that you did when you warned them about the volcano."

Serath shook his head. "I made use of the fountain in Cavasca. Even then, I doubt that all who were in Cavasca could hear me."

Belac held up a finger. "I thought of that." He smiled at his own cleverness. "What if I lay out a row of buckets filled with water? It might not be as loud as the fountain, but at least more people would be able to hear me."

Serath frowned thoughtfully and then nodded. "I believe I could manage that." He grinned at the elf. "Do you have an announcement?"

Belac nodded. "I want to give Enevic to the Cavascans. They can take the villagers with them."

Rolan began choking on his own laughter.

Serath smiled broadly. "And you believe that Enevic is yours to give?"

Belac shrugged. "It will be once I kill the dragon." He pointed over his shoulder, uncertain what direction he was indicating to. "Harbridge is not going to let an entire city of people use its pond. These people are going to need to walk the whole way to Enevic. By the time they get there, Enevic should be dragon free."

Serath continued to smile. "You would rearrange the peoples of the world," he mused.

Belac shrugged again. "Why not?"

Still laughing, Rolan asked, "How do you think you are going to get all those people to move to another country?"

Belac looked over his shoulder toward the dwarf. "I am going to offer them a new home." He turned his focus back to the wizard. "A lot of those people probably still believe that Agadon was a dragon. If a dragon took their old home, maybe they would be willing to make a new one in a place taken from a dragon. They might see it as a sort of justice." He held his hands out. "Besides, where else are they going to go?"

Serath's head tilted slightly to the side. "What you propose will travel beyond the borders that you know." He began to nod appreciatively. "I approve of this plan."

Forty-Five

Standing on the eastern battlement, Belac gazed out over a sea of dirty faces. *There are more people staring at me now than there were briar men trying to kill me this morning.* He gulped. *I hope the speech that Serath gave me does not make them angry.* The sun shown behind the elf, outlining him on the ridge. Though the war was over, he could still taste smoke in the air.

Thousands of people had gathered before the elf, leaving their wagons and belongings to be protected by the Cavascan guard. Men, women, and children; there was a vibrancy to the people despite their travel stained attire. Speculative discord created a blanket of sound that Belac would need to cut through if he were to reach the crowd.

Belac turned away from the people and looked down at the base of the berm, wondering if Ecard was as nervous as he was. The Enevician lord stood with his feet shoulder width apart, his hands held behind his back. If the man was experiencing any anxiety, his military bearing prevented it from showing. *Of course, he is not worried. He is hiding on the other side of the wall.*

Serath approached from the south, his black coat brushing against his legs. He too appeared unconcerned. With a kindly nod to the Enevician lord, the wizard climbed the battlement. Seeming to ignore the audience, Serath halted next to Belac and studied him for a moment.

Serath smiled at the elf. "Are you ready?" he asked above the noise of the crowd.

Belac squared his shoulders. "I hope so."

Reaching out with a gloved hand, Serath placed two fingers on the hollow of the elf's throat. Warmth spread into Belac's throat, the sensation lingering even after the wizard removed his touch. Belac found himself unexpectedly excited at the prospect of using magic. Serath gripped the elf's shoulder and then released him before stepping down from the battlement.

Smiling brightly, Belac turned toward the crowd. He opened his mouth to speak, but then stopped. He closed his mouth. *I almost forgot.* He dug into the pouch on his right hip and pulled out two tiny wads of waxy cloth. His azure eyes ran over the metal buckets on the other side of the trench as he crammed the wads into his ears. *That could have been unpleasant.*

Once he had the cloths stuffed into his ears, Belac tested his magical voice. "Hello?" His voice boomed from the buckets.

The people standing closer to the buckets covered their ears and shied away from the sound. Those not pained by the volume, were awed by the obvious magic. The elf unquestionably had the audience's attention. *Wow! That will work.*

Belac straightened his posture and then raised his voice. "Noble People of Cavasca!" He noticed that his voice was the same volume regardless of how loudly he attempted to speak. He shrugged his shoulders and continued to give the speech that the wizard had helped him prepare.

"You are Cavascans no more," Belac said in a somber tone. "For Cavasca is no more." Strength gradually crept into his voice as he continued, "Fire rose from the depths, and consumed your homeland." He gestured to his right. "Behold this village. And be reminded." He paused, allowing the crowd to consider the burned remains of Gofell. "In your suffering, you are united."

Belac paused again, allowing a sober air to grow among the crowd. Then he shouted, "And where was Harbridge?! Where was Harbridge when Cavasca and Gofell burned?!" Then he asked calmly, "Where are they now?"

Though the crowd was silent, Belac could feel the emotions building in it. He held his left hand out forward, pointing east. "Harbridge is there. Lounging by the shore." His words broke the people's silence. Belac did not know if they were agreeing with him or arguing, but he continued on as if he did not hear them. "You can go there. You can beg for the aid that you should have already been sent."

Belac's own emotions began to color his words. "You can live in the shadow of the city that abandoned you! You can eat their scraps. You can clean their streets. You can work in their brothels." He brought his hand up and then pointed forcefully to his left. "Or you can travel north! You can march past the city that abandoned you! You can find a kingdom waiting for you! Beyond the boundaries of Harbridge, lies Enevic. A kingdom in need of a people. A kingdom that could be yours." There was silence once again.

Without turning away from the crowd, Belac waved Ecard up to join him. Ecard climbed the steps and took his place on the battlement. Feet shoulder width apart, hands behind his back, the lord made it clear that he was a soldier.

Belac gestured to the man. "This, is Lord Ecard von Leos. A Lord of Enevic, and general of its armies. Through birth and service, he holds claim to Enevic." Belac removed his dwarf-sword and drew the blade.

Ecard eyed the elf without turning his head, keenly aware that death would end any claim he had to the kingdom.

Belac held his sword high, the tip of the blade pointed toward the cloudless sky. "With this sword, I faced the fires of Agadon! With this blade, I struck down the monsters that would feast on the children of Man!" His eyes took on a fierce light. "I am The Dragon Slayer! And I have carried this sword for you!"

The crowd roared, caught up by the elf's passion. A chant began to form. "Mel-la-var! Mel-la-var!" The collective exclamations of the people were louder than the elf's magically projected voice. "Mel-la-var! Mel-la-var!" *I'm glad we plugged our ears.* "Mel-la-var! Mel-la-var!"

Belac lowered his sword, and the crowd began to quiet. He turned to the man standing at his side. "Face me, lord of Enevic."

Keping his hands behind his back, Ecard turned toward the elf.

Belac slid the dwarf-sword into its scabbard, and then held it out to the lord. "Lord Ecard von Leos, will you carry this sword? Will you protect these people? Will you lead them to their new home?"

Ecard reached out with both hands, his palms facing upward. Gingerly, he accepted the sword; and the burden that came with it. He met the elf's eyes and vowed, "I will." His voice boomed loud and strong from the water.

The crowd erupted in cheer. Belac released the sword and leaned away from the roar. He realized that the wizard's magic was more than sound. The words that Serath had given him held more power than the enchantment that had projected them. *I just changed the world.* Something within Belac shifted. He felt aligned in a way he could not have explained. A new future had been set in motion.

Belac turned toward the cheers of the crowd and held his arms out to his sides. "Rejoice!" He doubted that many could make out what he said, but he felt confident that everyone would get the message. "Celebrate the new home that awaits you!"

Belac lowered his arms and stepped back. Then he turned around and walked down the steps, leaving Ecard to stand alone on the battlement. *There is no backing out now. Now, I absolutely have to kill that dragon.*

Serath smiled at the elf proudly. "Well done."

Though Belac could not hear the wizard's words over the cheers coming from the other side of the berm, he was able to guess their meaning. He opened his mouth to respond, but then closed it. He pointed to his neck.

Serath nodded and then tapped the elf's throat with a gloved finger.

Belac's throat did not feel any different, so he tested his voice by saying, "Ahhhhh." His voice was no longer projected.

Ecard waited for the cheering to lessen and news to be relayed to those who may have been too far away to understand what had been said. Then he spoke. "People of Cavasca." They quieted to hear him. "People of Gofell. Those who would be of Enevic. There is much work ahead." He held up a hand to forestall concern. "However, the lands I would lead you to offer bounty and beauty beyond compare."

I doubt that bit. Belac's attention was pulled away from the lord's speech by a bearded forester. Arms held out to his sides disgruntledly, Simon stormed toward the elf. Though Belac could not make out what Simon was saying, the man was shouting at him.

Belac touched Serath's arm and gestured up to the battlement where Ecard was expounding on his expectations. Then Belac pointed to his own eye, indicating that he wanted the wizard to watch after the lord.

Serath nodded.

Belac nodded his appreciation and then left the lord in the wizard's care.

Simon halted when he saw that the elf was moving toward him. Belac walked past the angry forester, waving for the man to follow him. Ignoring Simon's attempts at conversation, Belac led the forester to the gathering hall. Once inside, Belac proceeded through the empty hall and into the side office.

Hoping that the stone walls would protect his hearing, Belac removed the waxy plugs from his ears and asked, "What?"

Simon began gesticulating angrily. "You expect us to just leave?! Just pick up and leave?! After all this?! After all we have been through?!"

Belac did not care for the man's tone. He waited for the forester to calm, and then answered, "Yes." He let the word hang in the air for a moment, then he continued before the forester could formulate a reply. "If you want to stay here with the ash, and the death, and the blood soaked soil, then that is on you. You can stay, and you can try to rebuild what you have lost." He pointed to the northeast. "Or you can go, and you can help to build something better."

Belac lowered his arm and shook his head. "You don't understand what is being offered. Your child could be anything in Enevic."

Simon's anger drained at the mention of his unborn child. He crossed his arms in contemplation. Finally, he complained, "You said, I was king." As the man was clearly not an orc, it would have been completely acceptable to suggest that he was pouting.

Belac shrugged. "You turned down the job."

Forty-Six

If there was one thing that the Cavascans knew how to do well, it was celebrate. Though the sun had fallen, music still played as exuberant people danced around campfires, the fluttering flames seeming to dance with them. The Cavascans had shared their wine while the villagers roasted hog. The woodland wildlife had fled from the blazing forest, making it difficult to find game. However, a loose sounder of domestic hogs had remained close enough to be found. Though the fresh meat was appreciated, there was nowhere near enough for the thousands of celebrating people. When it became evident that the pork would be too limited, the villagers had turned out their stores.

Leaning against the back of the gathering hall, drinking from a wooden tumbler filled with wine, Belac ruminated on how fire could bring life and joy as easily as it could destroy. Vairug and Rolan stood nearby. Neither of them had wanted wine, but they had both claimed more than their fair share of meat. Vairug had helped in the hunt, tracking the hogs into the forest south. The orc felt intitled to his fill.

A young girl squealed and ran toward Belac's group. Belac smiled at the little girl's floppy pigtails as he pushed himself away from the wall. He held his arms out, stepping forward to embrace her.

Gwen, however, ran straight to Vairug, throwing her skinny arms around the orc. Belac narrowed his eyes at the little girl.

With a hand of gray flesh and one of exotic metal, Vairug picked the little girl up and went, "Rawr!"

Gwen stuck out her lower jaw and replied, "Rawr!" The four tiny teeth beginning to grow in between her canines only made her look more like an orc.

Vairug hugged the little girl to his chest, and Gwen wrapped her arms around his thick neck. Standing off to the side, Marsha clutched her hands against her chest and smiled at her daughter.

Belac drank the last of his wine as he walked over to the flaxen haired woman. "Hello, Marsha."

Marsha gave a shallow bow. "Lord? Belac."

Belac shook his head. "Just Belac."

Marsha nodded. "Thank you again for what you've done."

Belac shrugged and glanced at the happy little girl in the arms of an orc. "I'm just glad that she is safe."

Marsha put a hand on the elf's arm. "Thank you," she said again.

Belac met the woman's eyes and nodded, uncomfortable with the amount of sincerity in her gratitude.

Marsha smiled. "I'm sure that Debra would like to thank you also." Her tone suggested that the other woman might offer a reward.

Belac thought he might enjoy that. "Where is she?" He looked around, searching the crowd.

Marsha shook her head. "She is still in her wagon with Brandon. She hardly ever comes out anymore. She just looks down at him and cries. If not for George, I don't know what we would do."

Belac frowned. "Who is George?"

Marsha grinned and shook her head again. "He is just a boy. Well, not a boy. But he is too young for her. He has been driving the wagon for Debra so that she can look after Brandon."

Belac nodded, accepting the woman's assessment. "Where can I find them?" *I should see if there is anything that I can do for Brandon while I'm there.*

Marsha pointed toward where the caravan was parked south of the main road. "She is probably about a third of the way down. George usually moves her wagon away from the others to give Debra more privacy." She leaned in. "I think the boy is hopeful."

Belac grinned as he remembered the barmaid. *I guess I can't blame him for that.* He suddenly recalled another boy that ought to be following the woman around also. "What about Frank?"

Marsh sighed with mild exasperation. "We all try to look after him, but he refuses to listen to anyone anymore."

A tiny finger poked Belac's thigh. He turned and looked down, finding Gwen smiling up at him. He grabbed at the little girl's nose, intentionally coming short of her face. Giggling, Gwen swatted at the air with both hands. Then she threw her arms around the elf and hugged him tightly.

Belac pet the top of the girl's head. *I refuse to regret saving this little girl.*

Gwen looked up at the elf. "Belac, are you going to take us to Enevic?"

Belac shook his head. "I have to go make sure that it is safe for you."

"Okay." Gwen lowered her head and squeezed the elf tighter. "Thank you." Then she let go and stepped back.

Marsha held her hand out to her daughter. "Okay now, Gwen. It's time to get you to bed."

Gwen took her mother's hand. "But Mom…"

Marsha shook her head sternly. "You agreed." She smiled at the elf. "Besides, Lord Belac has someone he needs to go see."

She is right. I leave tomorrow. If I want to check on Debra and Brandon, I need to do it tonight. Belac nodded. "I will go see her now." He turned toward the dwarf. "Hey, Rolan." When he was sure that he had the dwarf's attention, Belac tossed his empty tumbler to him. "I will be back before morning."

Rolan frowned. "Tomorrow is going to be hard enough without you being hung over."

Belac shook his head. "I'll be fine."

Rolan huffed at the elf.

Vairug's dark eyes twinkled as he asked, "Do you need a bribe?"

The question confused Marsha. "A bribe?"

Belac shook his head vigorously at the orc and then turned to the confused woman. "Inside joke. Totally unrelated. It's one of those lord people things." He glared at the orc. "We can talk about bribes later."

Vairug laughed silently.

Belac began backing away from the group, waving to the little girl and her mother. "Bye, Gwen. Tell Ecard, I said he should look after you. I will see you in Enevic." He turned and hurried off. *Stupid orc.*

Once away from the group, Belac set himself to searching for Debra's wagon. He had to ask nine people for directions before he was able to find it. Three of the Cavascans were of no help, and one of them sent him in the completely wrong direction. When Belac finally found the wagon, his first thought was that it had been pulled too far away from the others. Though the glow of campfires reached the wagon, the moon above provided more light.

I don't see any sign of that George guy. Belac considered the unhitched wagon. *Maybe he is taking care of the horses.* As he approached the lonely wagon, Belac began to smell why it might be so isolated. *It smells like bad honey and unwashed feet.*

Belac walked around to the back of the wagon. "Debra?" he called out loud enough to be heard inside the wooden cabin.

Someone inside moved abruptly, causing the wagon to rock. *Surely Debra is not in there celebrating with George.* Belac made a disdainful face. *I mean… there is a kid in there.*

Belac knocked on the door. "Debra?" he called out again.

There was no answer. No one moved inside.

I did not come all this way to stand out here and breathe in stink. Belac opened the door. As the wood panel swung out, a waft of stench hit the elf. He turned his head away in revulsion. "Ugh!"

When Belac looked back to the cabin, he found a pair of wide, gleaming eyes staring at him. The dark interior of the cabin drank the moonlight, granting sinister life to the thing crouched motionlessly on the bed inside. In the back corner of the cabin, a woman's body had been broken and contorted. Bites had been taken out of her face and exposed flesh.

Belac backed away from the wagon, suddenly recognizing the underlining scent. It smelled like rotten fruit. The thing inside crawled off the bed and then out of the cabin, its movements jerky and unnatural. It stopped just outside the wagon, crouching in the moonlight as it regarded the frightened elf.

Belac gaped at the thing that had once been Brandon. Though childlike in size, it no longer looked human. Shirtless and wan, its belly protruded grotesquely. Under a wild mane of filthy hair, black eyes bulged out of its gaunt skull. Its thin lips were pulled back in a rictus grin that split the skin above the back of its gumline. The mouth was covered in blood. *What do I do?*

Belac's mind flashed back on an underground hamlet. He witnessed once again as a nightmarish hobgoblin stabbed the pointed tip of its elongated finger into a frail child's eye socket. *They did this to him… He is half-hobb.*

The half-hobb child began to laugh, the sound an inhuman mockery of mirth.

Though Belac did not remember removing the sword or drawing its blade, he held the starmetal sword in one hand and his empty scabbard in the other. He took a step back with his right foot and pointed the mouth of his scabbard at the laughing half-hobb. "Brandon," he said threateningly, still not accepting what he would need to do.

With a sudden start, the half-hobb shot forward and to Belac's right. Then it stopped, its hideous laughter continuing as it stared at the elf like he was food.

Belac backed away, keeping his scabbard pointed at the thing. He knew what he would have to do. He began to beg. "Please, don't make me do this."

The half-hobb continued to laugh at him.

In Belac's mind, he saw a pack of laughing hobbs tear a man and his son to pieces. *Please, don't make me do this.* Belac's eyes pleaded with the laughing thing crouched before him. "Please, don't make me do this."

The half-hobb leapt at him, its arms raised high and wide. Belac pivoted forward on his left foot, his sword arcing up and then down. The milky white blade cut into the thing's chest where its shoulder met its neck. The blade sliced through the half-hobb's heart and then out its lower ribs.

Belac was weeping before the two halves of the cleaved body hit the ground. He wanted to fall to his knees. He wanted to throw his sword away and never pick it back up. Instead, he raised his head and took a deep breath. *I can't let the humans see me weak.* He lost track of time as he collected himself.

Eventually, a young man approached from the campfires. "Hello?" he asked hesitantly. "Who are you?"

Belac pointed with his scabbard. "Go get the guard."

"What?" the young man asked.

"The men with the metal hats," Belac replied impatiently. "Go get them."

The young man dropped something that he had been carrying and ran back toward the campfires. *That must be George.* Belac sheathed his sword, but he was still standing in place when the boy returned with two of the Cavascan soldiers. Both of the men carried a lit torch in their left hand and a side-sword on their left hip.

One of the soldiers held his torch over the remains of the half-hobb. Firelight gleamed off its bloody teeth. "What is it?" he asked with worried disbelief.

Belac answered emotionlessly, "It's a monster." He gestured with the hilt of his sword. "Put it in the wagon with the woman it killed, and then set it on fire."

George took a benumbed step toward the wagon. "Debra?"

The soldier looked up from the half-hobb corpse. "I don't know. I need to…"

Belac pointed to the wagon with the hilt of his scabbarded sword. "Do it now." There was no argument in his voice.

The soldier nodded. "Yes, my lord," he said quickly and then motioned to the other soldier. "Doug, get the other half." He reached down and took hold of one of the small arms with his free hand.

Belac turned to the distraught young man and put a hand on his shoulder. "Go round up some other people and have water brought. We don't want the fire getting out of hand."

George could not process what was happening. "But… Debra…"

Belac gripped the man's shoulder. "Stop thinking. Go get the water."

George nodded, trusting in the elf's words. As soon as Belac released the man's shoulder, George ran off toward the campfires. Belac turned and watched as the two soldiers used their torches to set fire to the wagon. *How many more will I fail to save?*

Forty-Seven

Belac sat in one of the two armless chairs that had been brought into Rolan's office. The starmetal sword lay on the desk. Belac did not want to touch it. After seeing to the fire, he had found Rolan and told him about Debra and Brandon. Now, Belac's mind continued to drift back to the event, searching for something he could have done differently.

Rolan seemed to recognize what the elf was doing. "You did the right thing."

Belac could not look up from the floor. "It does not feel like the right thing."

"That is why feelings should have nothing to do with decisions," Rolan replied as if it irritated him that such a thing needed to be explained.

Belac shook his head. "That thing used to be a child, Rolan. I… I could still see that it used to be Brandon."

Rolan's tone became more compassionate. "Everyone was once a child."

Belac took a deep breath, struggling to control his emotions. He stood up. "I need to get some air." He looked at his sword, debating on whether or not to take it. *It does not matter what I want. Someone else's life might depend on me having this sword.* He picked up the scabbarded sword and slung its baldric over his shoulder.

"We still need to leave at daybreak," Rolan said grumpily. "You should get some sleep."

Belac did not think that he would be able to sleep that night. He felt like he would never be able to sleep again. "I need to go for a walk."

"No," Rolan disagreed. "What you need to do, is lay down and go to sleep. You have a long day ahead of you tomorrow. The road to Harbridge is safer than some others, but there will still be plenty of things that want to kill us."

Belac did not have the energy to argue. "Thank you, Rolan," he said and then walked out of the room.

Without considering his route, Belac made his way through the factorage and exited via the loading bay. The air outside was cool, but a faint taste of ash prevented it from feeling crisp. Everything in the world felt like ash to the elf. He gazed off into the burned village. *Darkness and ash…*

Though many of the Cavascans continued to drink while sitting next to their campfires, music no longer filled the night. Feeling empty and alone, Belac began walking down the road that ran between the hopeful families and the burned homes of Gofell. *Is there no such thing as victory?*

Two men in red doublets walked up the road toward Belac. He watched the twin flames of their torches as they neared, reminded of the spriggans' eyes. The torchlight enveloped the elf, and then the soldiers halted. Belac stopped as well, responding to the men's obvious desire to speak with him.

The soldier on the left cleared his throat and then said, "Greetings, Lord Melavar."

Belac looked from one man to the other. "Is something wrong?"

The soldier who had first spoken shook his head quickly.

The second soldier laughed at his partner. "Smith just wants to be able to tell his girl that he met you."

Smith scowled. "Shut up, Jeffers."

These men helped save lives. Belac took a deep breath. *They deserve more than my bad mood.* He held out his hand. "It's an honor to meet you, Smith."

Smith's eyes widened. He reached out and gripped the inside of the elf's wrist. "The honor is mine, Sir."

Belac shook the first soldier's hand and then offered to shake the second's. "It's an honor to meet you, Jeffers."

Jeffers hopped forward in his eagerness to shake the elf's hand. "Yes, Sir. The honor is mine."

Belac gestured toward the forest. "Have you seen any signs of trouble?"

Jeffers shook his head. "No, Sir."

Smith asked, "Is there something we should be worried about?"

Besides all the green? Belac glanced at the darksome forest. "The owls are still out there."

"The owls?" Confused, Smith turned to his partner.

Two more soldiers approached from behind Belac. He stepped to the side, allowing them to join the conversation. "How about you two? Have you seen anything strange?"

Both men looked at each other and then shook their heads.

Jeffers smiled broadly. "Lord Melavar is handing out handshakes, if you want something to brag about later."

Belac shook his head ruefully and held out his hand to the closer of the new arrivals. "Thank you for showing up to the battle. You men saved a lot of lives."

The man shook the elf's hand, saying, "I only killed four of those things. You took out the whole army."

The last of the soldiers held out his hand. "I got twelve."

Belac thought that the man might be exaggerating. *It does not matter. He was there when he was needed.* Belac shook the soldier's hand. "Then, I'm glad that you will be watching out for these people when I'm gone."

Smith asked, "Do you think that we will see more of those crazy stick monsters?"

Crazy-stick-monsters! Belac pointed at the soldier. "Now, there is a man that knows how to name things!"

The soldiers laughed as if the elf had made a joke.

Smith shook his head, smiling. "I know that they're called briar men. I was just describing them."

Belac narrowed his eyes at the man. *Traitor.*

Jeffers was still worried about the crazy-stick-monsters. "Are there more of the briar men?" he pressed.

Belac shook his head. "I don't think so." His gaze shifted toward the people who would be in need of protection. "But there will be more monsters along the way to Enevic." *There will always be more monsters.* He looked back to the soldiers and smiled reassuringly, hoping that the night hid his deeper feelings. "I should let you men get back to your patrols."

Though Belac walked away, the four soldiers stayed where they were and continued to gossip. As he made his way toward the factorage, Belac wondered if he should go back and break the men up. *That is not my job. Besides, maybe they are supposed to report to each other during their patrols.*

A loud thud sounded behind the elf. Then men screamed in panic and Smith cried out, "Alarm!"

Reaching for his sword, Belac spun around to face the soldiers. A horror had emerged from the burned village. It was half again as tall as the men, and had excessively proportioned arms. Comprised of the corpses of dead animals, the horror's form was held together by twisted roots that ran through the rotting meat. Its left arm ended in a small boulder, while the other a claw of pointed roots. The upside-down head of a spriggan rested atop the simian shape, the roots of its crown digging down into the cadaveric flesh. Red eyes glowed banefully.

What the... One of the soldiers had already been crushed by the boulder. The monster grabbed one of Smith's legs, slung him up into the air, and then slammed him down against the hard packed road. The arm with a boulder swept out low and bashed a soldier's leg out from under him. Then the boulder lifted into the air before slamming down on top of the man's chest, crushing the bones of his ribcage.

Belac recognized the spriggan's hateful eyes. *I cut that things head off!* As he removed his sword, he realized how the spriggan had rebuilt itself. *It's the sneaky-lake-monster! That thing almost ate me!*

Jeffers drove his sword up into the monster's side. The vengeful spriggan palmed the man's head, its finger-like roots wrapping around and digging into flesh as it crushed his skull. With an unrelenting rancor, the monster lifted the man up and slung him away. Then its hateful, red stare turned to the elf.

All four soldiers had died before Belac could even enter the fight. *I will have to aim for its eyes.* The monster rushed forward on all fours, its disproportioned arms and legs hammering against the ground. *I'm making sure it's dead this time.*

A blur of crimson streaked gray flew out of the night and struck the charging monster from the side. Vairug's metal hand clamped onto the roots holding the rotten thing together. With an orcish roar, Vairug brought the blade of his axe down on the spriggan's head. Wood cracked loudly, and the glowing red eyes went out.

The lifeless spriggan fell to the ground, taking Vairug with it. The orc landed on his feet and then stumbled backward away from the pile of rotting carcasses. He then dropped into a defensive stance, holding his mechanical hand out in front of himself while he drew a knife with his other.

Belac walked over to the orc and then gestured to the dead spriggan with his sword. "I was going to do that."

Breathing hard, Vairug asked. "Is it dead?"

Belac made a show of looking the dead spriggan over. "Nope." He stepped forward and poked it with his sword. "Now, it's dead." He failed not to smile.

Frowning at the elf, Vairug sheathed his knife and then walked over to the dead spriggan. He reached down and took hold of his axe's handle. Wood squeaked sharply as he worked the steel bit back and forth in the spriggan's head. Soldiers began to gather in the road as the orc worked his axe free.

Once his axe was free, Vairug turned to the elf. "See? I told you that axes are better than swords." He held up his axe, displaying its steel head. "This one is not even magic."

Belac narrowed his eyes at the orc.

Forty-Eight

Belac stumbled around in the dark, collecting what little he owned. He felt guilty for how well he had slept. Loss and hardship had simply not been able to compete with the elf's physical and emotional exhaustion. Without the off-gassing casks to foul the air, the small room in Rolan's factorage had seemed almost luxurious. *I am going to miss this stretched out cot when I'm sleeping in the dirt tonight.*

Belac opened the door and stepped out into the lamplit hallway. Moist morning air had flown into the factorage, bringing with it a reminder of the ash outside. *Gofell, I won't miss.* He turned and followed the hallway to Rolan's office. The lamps inside shone steadily through the open door. Rolan was seated behind his desk, while Serath and Vairug sat in the armless chairs on the other side. The wizard held his own chin with one gloved hand while the other dragged a hinged blade across the side of his face.

Belac walked into the office and pointed to the strangely shaped blade. "What's that?"

Serath held the implement up for inspection. "It is a straight razor." He flicked his wrist and the blade swung into its own handle.

Rolan asked, "How did you think he kept his beard that neat?"

Belac shrugged. "I don't know. I guess I thought that it just kind of grew like that."

Vairug twisted in his chair to stare at the elf questioningly.

Belac held his hands out angrily. "I don't know how a wizard's beard works!" *It is too early in the morning for this.* He walked over to the dwarf's cot and sat down.

Serath slid his straight razor into a leather sleeve and then placed it in the bag he kept hidden under his coat. When his hand came back out of the bag, it held a glass flask of amber liquid. He set the flask on his lap and then began removing his gloves.

Belac had never seen the wizard's hands ungloved. "You have hands!"

Vairug gave the elf another questioning look.

Belac gestured to the wizard's well manicured hands. "I thought he had claws, or warts, or something."

Serath frowned with distaste. "I do not wear gloves because my hands are ugly. I wear them because the world is."

Vairug scowled at the wizard. "We would not want you to get your hands dirty," he said with scorn.

Serath smiled pleasantly. "No," he agreed. "You wouldn't."

The wizard picked up the glass flask and unscrewed its coppery cap. He set the tiny, metal cap on the desk, and then splashed some of the amber liquid into the palm of his hand. He set the flask down next to its cap, rubbed his hands together, and then applied the liquid to the clean shaven sides of his face. When he was finished, he picked up the flask and cap, resealed the flask, and slipped it into his bag.

Belac breathed in the smell of licorice and vanilla. "That is strong."

Serath began putting his gloves back on. "The fragrance will fade quickly."

Vairug scowled again. "Not enough," he said disagreeably.

Rolan looked up from his desk. "I've told you, Vairug, you are just going to have to get used to it."

Vairug glared at the dwarf. "It makes him smell wrong." He crossed his arms. "I don't like it."

Serath grinned at the orc's grumpiness. "Well, it should not be a problem for the next few days."

The cryptic statement piqued Belac's interest. "Why do you say that?"

Serath swept out a gloved hand. "You three will be traveling without me."

Belac did not like the sound of this new plan. "What? Why?"

"I need to remain here and see to the Vaquian ruins," Serath explained. "They need to be either sealed or destroyed. Destruction would be my preference. However, that may prove untenable."

Belac agreed that the ruins needed to be delt with, but he did not understand why the rest of them would be leaving without the wizard. "We can't finish the sword without you. I don't even know where to go." *What was next? The tears of the dead?*

Serath nodded agreeably. "I can travel faster than you can. Once I have completed my task here, I will join you in Harbridge." He smiled. "We can meet at the Lucky Duck."

Again with the Lucky Duck? Belac pointed at the wizard. "I am pretty sure that place is not lucky."

"The accommodations may change your mind," Serath politely argued.

Belac frowned. "Fine. But if I end up in prison again, I am blaming you."

Serath laughed softly. "That would seem rather unfair."

Belac pointed at the wizard forcefully. "I knew it! You think they are going to try to put me in prison again!"

Serath shook his head as he laughed. "No, Belac. You simply seem to have a propensity for incarceration."

Belac narrowed his eyes at the wizard. "How long will I have to wait at the Lucky Duck?"

Serath shrugged noncommittedly. "I will not know until I have visited the ruins." He smiled. "I wanted to see you off before I began my investigation."

Belac stood. "Well, I need to go see Ecard before we go."

Rolan held up a hand to halt the elf. "Don't be gone too long. We need to leave as soon as there is enough light."

Belac nodded as he moved toward the open doorway. "I'll be quick."

Once in the hallway, Belac turned toward the loading bay. As he walked down the lamplit corridor, he wondered what would become of the factorage after it was abandoned. *I bet the owls move in and use it as a base of operations.*

Belac was halfway through the loading bay before he noticed the three chestnut horses waiting there. Tethered to a water trough, the horses regarded the elf silently. Belac's first thought was that the horses might be working for the owls. He took in the saddles, the saddle bags, and the bedrolls, realizing that the horses must have been procured for his journey east.

Belac pointed at the horses as he continued through the loading bay. "Stay," he told the horses firmly.

The world outside was gray. Belac crossed the road, able to see well enough in the light of the early dawn.

The doors to the gathering hall hung open, allowing free entry into the shadowed space inside. As Belac walked into the open hall, he saw light shining under the door to the side office. He navigated around the empty pews and then knocked on the door. *I hope I am not interrupting anything.*

Ecard answered immediately, "Come in."

Belac pushed the door open and entered the office, finding Ecard alone. Upon seeing Belac, the lord stood from his chair behind the desk.

Ecard walked around the desk, enquiring, "Are you soon to depart?"

Belac nodded. "I wanted to say goodbye before I left."

"I will miss your company, Belac." Ecard set his hand on the dwarf-sword laid out on his desk. "But you will not be forgotten."

Belac imagined the people of Enevic constructing a monument to him in the center of the capital. He pointed at the lord. "Don't let them make my statue out of wood."

Ecard laughed at the idea.

Belac moved closer to the lord. "There is a girl that I want you to watch over."

Ecard smiled conspiratorially. "Oh?"

Belac shook his head. "It's not like that." He held his hand out low. "She is a little girl. Pig tails, missing teeth, cute as can be, but kind of bossy. Her name is Gwen. Or actually, I think it is Gwyneth. Her mother is named Marsha. I think she might be a widow. You should not have any problem finding them. I think Gwen is kind of famous now."

Ecard nodded seriously. "I will do all that I can for her."

Belac clapped the lord on the arm. "Thank you, Ecard."

Ecard suddenly looked like he had something he wanted to say but was scared to say it.

Belac frowned. "What?" he asked impatiently.

Ecard's face hardened as he made his decision. He walked around the elf and shut the door to the office. Then he returned and leaned in close. "It is about the orc."

Belac's heart dropped. *No. Not after all this...* Using his peripheral vision, he checked the orientation of the dwarf-sword on the desk. *I am faster than he is.* Belac would not allow Vairug to be lynched by the very people they had just saved.

Ecard continued as if still worried that he might be overheard. "He never gave his house," he said with significance. "No lord of Enevic would neglect to give his house." He shook his head. "At first, I thought it might be shame that held his tongue." He met the elf's eyes. "But I know that is not the reason. While his speech may be merely odd, his mannerisms are not those of a noble. In both etiquette and behavior, he betrays himself."

Belac gazed into the lord's soft brown eyes. Despite all that the man had suffered, he had somehow managed to retain his inherent decency. The lord was on a path to healing, having found strength in service to others. *I will still choose Vairug.*

Ecard spoke with confidence. "Belac, I do not know who that man was, but he was not a lord of Enevic."

Belac's entire being relaxed. *He still thinks that Vairug was a human before the curse.* Though Belac knew that he needed to tell the lord something, he did not know what lie to use. Grinning, Belac came up with a different idea. He winked.

Ecard furrowed his brow and then his eyes widened with presumed understanding. He shook his head in amazement. "You are wise."

I wonder what he thinks I meant.

Forty-Nine

Belac leaned forward in the saddle and petted the side of his horse's neck. He appreciated that as of yet, the beast had not attempted to bite him. Though the chestnut horse was not a thoroughbred, it was healthy and well behaved. Belac preferred the warmth of the animal over the lifelessness of a wagon seat. Rolan did not.

The dwarf was agile enough to mount on his own, but Belac had needed to cut new eyelets to properly adjust the stirrups for him. Sitting in the saddle with his arms crossed, Rolan looked like a dwarf that was too grumpy to grumble. Vairug, seated comfortably astride his own mount, glanced at the dwarf and laughed silently.

Straightening in his saddle, Belac made a brim with his hand and used it to shade his eyes from the morning sun as he studied the road ahead. They had finally moved beyond the blackened fields of burned grass, and into rolling hills of golden green. Belac was glad to have left Gofell behind. However, he was worried still about the people that he had left there. *I did not even get to say goodbye.* Serath had recommended that Belac depart without fanfare. Nothing would be gained by having the people focus on the fact that The Dragon Slayer was no longer with them. *Still. It would have been nice to say goodbye.* He recalled his farewell to Ecard. *Ecard!*

"Oh!" Belac exclaimed, holding up a finger. He twisted to the right and pointed the finger at his friends. "We have a problem."

Riding next to the elf, Rolan grumbled, "Of course, we do."

Belac ignored the dwarf's pessimism. "Vairug needs a last name."

Vairug leaned forward to look past the dwarf. "I have a last name. It's Lost-Wind."

How did I never ask that? Belac shook his head. "Not your real name. Lord Vairdoe's. Ecard doesn't think that you're actually a lord, because you never told him what house you are from." He held up a hand. "It's fine. He still thinks that you're a cursed human. But we need to come up with a last name for you. I'm surprised that we did not have a problem like this sooner."

It occurred to Belac that he was not in the habit of asking people for their full names. He himself had not wanted to share the name of his house, and so he had simply avoided the subject. Melavar was a name other Elves would recognize.

Vairug did not seem concerned by the development. "Serath says, it's Akknos."

Rolan nodded in agreement.

Vairug continued, "He said that if anyone asks why I do not use it, I should tell them that it would not be proper to do so while I am still an orc."

"Wha... But... I..." Belac stammered, then shouted, "I almost killed Ecard!"

Rolan shrugged. "It is probably better that you didn't."

Belac narrowed his eyes at the dwarf. *I hope your horse bites you.*

Vairug grinned around his tusks. "Do you not remember that we met a king?"

Belac redirected his ire on the orc. "Yes, I remember!" He pointed at the orc. "You never told him your last name!" He thought back. *No one ever said Lord Vairdoe's last name!*

Rolan chuckled. "And you thought what? That the king forgot to ask who the mysterious lord was that was walking around his city looking like an orc?"

Belac crossed his arms and did his best impersonation of a dwarf.

Vairug laughed silently at the elf.

Belac turned away from his friends and stared out over the rolling hills. As he crested a rise in the road, a clump of shrubs growing in the valley caught his eye. He pointed down the hill and to his left. "I'm going to go use one of those little trees over there." Belac considered riding his horse all the way to the shrubs, but decided it would be safer for the animal if he kept it on the road.

As they rode their horses down the hill, Vairug shouted, "He was a thief!"

Belac looked away from the shrubs. "What? Who was a thief?"

"The cobbler!" Vairug exclaimed. "The man was a liar and a thief! Don't you see? There were never any elves. And there were no orcs. The man was stealing the shoes! He stole shoes from the other shoemakers and then sold them in his shop. When someone questioned how he had made the shoes so quickly, he invented the story! He might not have even been a real cobbler!"

Rolan began chuckling so hard that Belac thought the dwarf was going to fall out of his saddle. Belac simply pinched the bridge of his nose and endured the story's recurrence.

Vairug's excitement waned. "Have I missed something?"

Belac brought his horse to a halt at the bottom of the hill and handed his reigns to the dwarf. "You can explain it to him while I'm gone," he told the dwarf and then hopped out of the saddle.

Belac stepped off the road and waded through the grass to the shrubs. He glanced up at the wispy clouds in the sky. Slowly, the clouds began to smear messily across the pale blue. Belac looked away, only to find the greenery of the shrubs melting before his eyes. He turned to look back toward his friends, but the world blurred into a swirl of vibrant color. *This has to be magic!* As the swirling colors began to overwhelm Belac's consciousness, "Magic is cheating!" were his last words.

Epilogue

Sigren believed that no one else could have done what he had done. He also believed that such an obvious fact would be known to others. He had no option but to flee. While he was convinced that salvation lie over the sea, transportation was a problem. The lines would not carry him off the continent, and the distance was too far for him to fly without being detected. That left him in need of a ship.

Harbridge was the logical choice. There were still those in the city that were loyal to him. Even if his supporters could not help him directly, other ships would be available. Sigren only needed to entice one of the independent captains. He felt confident that he could do so; one way or another.

Though the clouds had mostly cleared from the sky, the streets of Harbridge were wet with fresh rain. The slickened surfaces gleamed in the moonlight. As Sigren walked the empty streets, he could feel himself being hunted. Dressed in shabby browns, the man hoped that he looked nothing like a wizard. Aware that his disguise would do little to protect him, he told himself that a little might be all that he would need.

He knew that no one involved would forgive him. What Sigren had done was paramount to theft. He had followed instructions until the last moment, then deviated unpredictably. He fully agreed that the elf needed to be stopped.

However, Sigren also recognized that the elf was simply too valuable to outright destroy. Now, as he fled for his life, Sigren found himself doubting that he had done the right thing.

"The world can burn if I'm not in it," Sigren muttered to himself.

The fugitive wizard's eyes darted side to side, attempting to scan every shadow. He glanced up into the sky, reminding himself that even the heavens were not safe. He was looking the wrong way.

Sigren felt the dark presence appear behind him. He did not turn to look back. He did not need to. He knew what had come for him. Just as he knew that mercy would be no more forthcoming than forgiveness. If he had thought that surrender was an option he could survive, he would have taken it. He would have begged. He would have bargained. He would have betrayed all that he believed. But he knew that there would be no negotiation. So, he ran.

Sigren's boots splashed through puddles as his mind reached out to the moon. Though the night limited his sources, the silvery light from above could still be drawn upon. He wrapped the world around him, distorting his image painfully. The defense proved insufficient.

Fire slammed into Sigren's back, throwing him down onto the paved street. On hands and knees, he screamed. First, the flames made the world too bright for him to see, then the fire burned out his eyes. And there, surrounded in flames, the wizard died in darkness.

PART

TWO

Prologue

Shoulders slumped from the burden of time, Moasitt walked the narrow streets of a city that had long ago been abandoned. The dim light of a fading sun challenged the wizard's optimism. He pressed onward, trusting that the sun would rise again. The sleeve of his multicolored robes gathered in the crook of his arm as he ran a sinewy hand down his long, gray beard. He reminded himself that there was always light in the darkness, just as there were shadows in the day.

The wizard allowed himself to believe that life could return to the city. The people that had followed him there could use the crumbling structures to hide from the dark thing that pursued them. As their numbers grew, the city could be rebuilt. And there, sheltered from the thing that would break the world, resistance could survive.

Moasitt glanced back at the men and women that he had brought with him. People without power of their own, they had banded together in service of the natural world. Driven by their own inherent decency, they each had dedicated themself to the cause. Moasitt knew that they were still too few in number. However, from small seeds, forests could grow.

Summoning his own perseverance, the wizard took a deep breath and looked to the future. Then he felt reality shudder behind him. He spun around, knowing that the darkness he felt could only be one thing. He had failed the people he had sought to protect. The creature they had fled was not something that could be stopped. And his followers had nowhere else to hide. Still, the wizard would not forsake them.

Moasitt swept his arm up and across. The ancient stones of the building on his right ripped from their mortar and rearranged themselves into a sloping canopy that stretched over the narrow street. The men and women underneath crowded together, collectively voicing their surprise. Fire slammed into the stone shielding, amplifying the people's panic. Light bloomed above the city as the fire intensified. Crys of alarm turned into screams of pain as molten rock poured down onto the cowering people.

Moasitt began hastily backing away. He watched in horror as the liquid death rained down on his followers. There was nothing he could do to save them. He might have granted them the mercy of a quick end, but his conscience was not prepared for so heavy a choice. The wails of the dying hounded the wizard as he abandoned the people that he had promised to save.

An explosion of sound rocked the city as a distant building was blown apart. Moasitt could feel the dark thing moving to flank him from his left. When he came to an intersection with another street, he halted his retreat. Crossroads held meaning that extended beyond the physical. He decided that it was there that he would make his stand. It was there that he would allow reality to choose between a path of hope, or one of destruction.

Moasitt felt the coming of darkness as the creature approached. He reached out to a building behind him and then whipped his arm forward. Mortar dust scattered into the air as stones were ripped from the building's outer wall. The stones flew into the intersection and arranged themselves into a dome that covered the wizard. The impact of flame thundered in the enclosed space.

Surrounded by stone, Moasitt crossed his arms and pressed his clinched fist against his shoulders. With will and arcane mastery, he held back the heat of the flames that assailed him.

It only took an instant for the wizard to realize that his defenses would not hold. He struggled against the flames until they waned, then he spun in a tight circle and lashed out with his left hand. Chunks of stone shot out from the side of his protective dome, creating an opening that was large enough for him to step through. Left hand still held out, he reached back with his right and made a fist. The remaining stones of the dome floated up above the wizard and arranged themselves into a horizontal pillar that hovered in the air. Moasitt stepped forward, slinging his right arm over his head as if throwing a javelin. The stone pillar shot forward, its trajectory aligned with the wizard's will.

The soring stones exploded, and then fire rushed toward Moasitt. As the flames engulfed him, his tortured scream joined those of the people who had followed him. And then there, in the crossroad, the wizard's hope for the future died.

One

Golden hair and eyes that could have been the sky, she waited for him. Belac ran to where she stood in an open field of yellow flowers. The world was alight with a clear radiance that accentuated every detail of their fateful reunion. A breeze blew across the field, lifting yellow petals into the air and causing the woman's white gown to ripple lively. The world grew brighter as she smiled. Belac knew that the smile was for him alone. He did not understand how she was there. In that moment, he did not care. He took her in his arms and gazed into her adoring eyes. He had never felt so loved. Belac traced her face with a slender finger, marveling at her perfection.

When he looked back into her eyes, they were brown. He did not care. She loved him, and she was beautiful still. Her hair darkened to black and then changed to a dark red. She was still the most beautiful woman he had ever known. The features of her face transformed, her lips becoming fuller, and her nose small and round. Belac gazed into her violet eyes and wondered how he could ever be so fortunate.

A harsh voice spoke in the elf's mind. "I have seen what you desire. Now, show me what you fear."

Belac fell backward. Alone, he tumbled through shapes and sounds until he landed face down in the dirt. Around him, the night was bright with pale, otherworldly emanations. Humans screamed in terror, their voices rising above the roar of raging flames. Belac was back in the forest, in a place where humans were not allowed.

Belac began to crawl over dirt and dried leaves. He needed to get away. He could feel the angry heat of the fires around him. The tormented screams of the dying humans tore at his soul. There was nothing he could do for them. Whatever had come for them possessed a wrath that could not be stopped. Terror was salvation; terror and escape.

The harsh voice spoke again. "Show me."

Belac would not look. He knew that the flames would be so bright that they would appear green among the forest leaves. He would not look again.

"Show me," the voice commanded without mercy. "Show me what you fear."

Against his will, Belac was turned around to face his greatest fear. He clenched his eyes, striving to shut out the awful sight. His terror was all that gave him the strength to resist.

The voice tore through the elf's psyche. "Show me!"

Belac's eyes opened to a sea of emerald flame. Dark shapes swam in the fires as they consumed the world above him. What he saw was truth. Unfathomable power fueled the emerald flames. He wanted to turn away from the alien light. He knew that it was more than fire. He knew that it was something that should not be.

The screams around him took up a singular hymn. Then they were drowned out as the harsh voice howled in pain. For a seemingly eternal moment, there was nothing but the sound of pain and the sight of the emerald flames.

The fire really was green… The burning night faded away as Belac's mind returned to him. He stood in an opulent bedroom. A masterful painting of a snowcapped mountain range hung from a crisply white wall. Below the painting, a black robed nillanan writhed on its knees.

With its bald, faceless head turned away, the nillanan held its hands up defensively, exposing the small, toothless mouths on each of its palms. The mouths continued to scream in Belac's mind.

Belac clung to the memory of the emerald flames. He could feel them scorching his thoughts, but he was determined to suffer if it meant hurting the monster that had invaded his mind. He wanted the flames brighter. He wanted them to burn hotter. He wanted to hear the nillanan scream louder.

Human hands held both of Belac's arms. He glanced at the grips that held him in place, and saw that he had been stripped naked. He looked at the man on his right and then the one on his left, finding emotionless guards that stared away impassively. Belac's eyes ran over the blue gambeson of the man on his left, and down to the weapons on his belt. The man's ringed side-sword was too far away to reach, so Belac grabbed the hilt of the dagger on the man's right hip. Belac stepped backward and to his right, drawing the dagger in an underhanded grip as he struggled with the hands that held him.

Belac stabbed the dagger upward, sinking its blade into the guard's neck just below the chin. Teeth gritted, Belac ripped the blade out and began struggling to free his arm. Blood pumped from the guard's neck, but the man refused to let go. Belac snarled and fought harder, still feeding the emerald flames in his mind.

The guard's grip lost its strength. Belac jerked his arm free and turned away as the guard collapsed to the floor. Pulling himself in close to the other guard, Belac slashed the edge of the dagger across the man's throat. The blade cut deeply, causing blood to paint Belac's pale skin red. Stepping away from the guard, Belac began to stab at the man's forearm and wrist. *I will be free!*

As soon as the elf's arm was liberated, he spun toward the nillanan. Belac focused on the emerald flame, feeding it his rage. *You will die screaming!* He leapt at the nillanan, slamming into it and tackling it to the floor.

Rising up, Belac brought the dagger above his head and then plunged it down into the nillanan's flesh covered eye socket.

Something had been taken from Belac. He did not know what it was, but he could still feel its loss. Some part of him was no longer there. His mind had been violated, and his memories plundered. Roaring, Belac stabbed the dagger into the nillanan's skull repeatedly.

"What did you take?!" Belac demanded in rage.

The dead nillanan provided no answer.

Belac continued stabbing the hated thing. He held the emerald flame in his mind, allowing it to burn with his fury. He wanted to hear the nillanan scream again. He wanted to burn the monster's harsh voice, and breathe in its pain. He wanted to embrace the flames and give chase to the nillanan's departed soul.

Panting, Belac glared down at the crater that he had dug in the nillanan's head. His hand hurt from his grip on the dagger, but the discomfort was a distant thing. Heavy footfalls sounded from the hallway outside the bedroom door. *There are more coming.* Belac let go of the emerald flame. His rage was instantly replaced with fear.

Dropping the bloody dagger, Belac scrambled off the nillanan's corpse and stumbled to where the second guard lay dead. *I need a sword.* The golden, four-pointed star emblazoned on the chest of the man's blue gambeson did nothing to inform the elf of where he was. Belac pulled the guard's side-sword from its scabbard and then flipped the blade in the air, catching it in a forward grip as he turned to face the door. There were too many footfalls for him to guess the number of men headed his way.

As the footfalls grew closer, Belac suddenly recognized a greater problem. *There has to be more than one nillanan.* If there were more than one nillanan involved, there might be more than two. *I need to escape.* The elf rushed to the door and slammed the privacy bolt shut. Turning away, he hurried to the royal blue curtain that covered the closer of two tall windows.

Belac threw the curtain open. Though the day had shown around the edges of the thick cloth, the sudden burst of sunlight hurt the elf's eyes. As his azure eyes adjusted to the light, Belac took in a city of gray stone and vivid blue rooves. His first thought was that it could not be a human city. The smooth blocks of gray stone were too cleanly formed, and the blue tiles too uniform. *Where am I?* He flicked open the latch in the center of the two large panels of sectioned glass, and then swung them both into the room. Leaning out the window, he looked down at a verdant hedge maze that separated him from the city. *That is too far to jump.* He leaned out farther and counted the windows below him. *There is no way I can survive a five-story fall.*

A body slammed into the bedroom door, rattling it in its frame. *I need a new plan.* Belac quickly appraised the door. He knew it would not hold. Another impact shook the door. *Okay, fine. I will just make this plan work.* Belac dropped the side-sword onto the floor, then jumped up and grabbed the curtain's rod. Kipping up, he unhooked the heavy rod from its supports before landing back on the floor. While there were no shouts of alarm or command, the men in the hallway continued to batter the door.

Belac dropped the curtain rod on the floor and then gathered the long, blue cloth into the center of the brassy bar. *This is a bad plan.* He wrapped the thick cloth around his left arm. *It's either this, or I hide under the bed.* He turned his head to reconsider the large bed. *Would they find me under there?* A loud crack issued from the battered door. *No time.*

Belac bent down and grabbed the side-sword hastily. Then he faced the bedroom door and hopped backward out of the window. The cloth that he had wrapped around his arm tightened, yanking the curtain rod up off of the floor as the elf fell. The metal bar caught on both sides of the open window, creating a horizontal anchor. Belac's left shoulder slammed into the side of the building. *This is such a bad plan!* He pressed the ringed hilt of the side-sword against the gray stone of the wall, and then pushed himself away. Thrashing in the air, Belac was able to get his feet between himself and the side of the building.

Now, I just need to lower myself down. Belac looked down. *Slowly! I need to lower myself slowly.* He loosened his grip on the curtain, intending to slide down it like a rope. However, the cloth was so thickly bunched, that it began to slip out of his grasp. In a panic, he dropped the side-sword and gripped the unfurling cloth with his right hand. *I should have hidden under the bed!*

Two

Belac refused to look down. He knew that with his luck, the hilt of the fallen sword had embedded itself into the grass below. In his mind, he could see the sharpened steel blade pointed upward, perfectly angled to impale him. *It's a conspiracy!*

The door burst open in the bedroom above him. Heavy footfalls poured into the room. Hastily, Belac began to lower himself down the curtain he hung from. Hand over hand on the cloth, he walked down the side of the building until he came to the window directly beneath the room now filling with men.

Standing in the center of the window, Belac hopped away from the building. He hung in the air for a tense moment, and then swung forward toward the glass. Kicking out, he stomped on the window where its two wooden sashes met. The locking clasp snapped, and the two mullioned panels of glass swung inward, pushing away the curtain inside the room. Belac let go of the cloth he hung from as he passed through the window's frame. Twisting in air, he faced the open window before his bare feet landed on the floor.

Stumbling backward away from the window, Belac tripped into the curtain hanging behind him. Flailing as he fell, he grabbed the blue cloth for balance. One side of the curtain rod pulled free from its support, causing the elf to spin around as he fell to the floor.

Belac crashed onto the hardwood floorboards in a tangle of blue cloth. And then the curtain rod hit him in the back of the head.

Stunned, Belac found himself wondering why the curtains hated him so much. *I have always been nice to curtains. Why are these being so mean to me?* He shook his head, attempting to focus his thoughts. *I can't let the curtains win.*

"Let me go!" Belac scolded the curtains as he clumsily pushed them away.

Once free of the vexing blue cloth, Belac saw that he was in a bedroom that was much the same as the one above it. He did not find the development reassuring. *I need to get out of this place.* Naked and unarmed, Belac stumbled away from the crumpled curtain as booted feet stomped around on the floor above him. The door to the room was already open. Carefully, he peeked out through the open doorway.

Though the hallway on his level was clear of guards, the men above continued to make their presence audible. *It sounds like they are beginning to move away from the bedroom.* Belac glanced left and right. *They must be going for the stairs.* He stepped out into the hallway and turned right, hoping that he could find the stairs before his pursuers found him.

Above rich wooden running boards, paintings hung from white walls. Between each of the hallway's stout wooden doorframes, a small accent table held a blue and white vase filled with dead flowers. Lit by only what scant sunlight filtered through the open rooms, the hallway presented an uninviting atmosphere. Belac absently attempted to calculate how long the nillanan had imposed its dominion, but he quickly realized that he did not know how long it took for flowers to wither.

Belac glanced through open doorways as he hurried down the hallway. There was a uniformity to the chambers that made him suspect that they were guest quarters. He reminded himself that he did not know how expansive the building might be. *This could be part of a citadel or even a palace.* He worried what it would mean for the world to have a kingdom ruled by the nillanan.

Ahead, the hallway turned sharply to the left. Belac slowed as he approached the blind corner, all but convinced that there would be a curtain waiting to jump out at him. *Stupid curtains.* He froze as he heard the footsteps coming from the hallway beyond. *Curtains don't have feet.* He began backing away from the corner.

When he reached an open doorway on his left, Belac stepped into the room without looking inside. Quickly, he shut the door, barely remembering to not slam it closed. He slid the privacy bolt into place, then turned around and pressed his back against the door. Belac noticed the room's unpleasant smell before his eyes adjusted to the dim. *What is…* Belac had to stop himself from growling out loud when he realized where he was. He was hiding in a privy.

It's a conspiracy! Belac wanted to bang his head against the door in frustration. Footfalls sounded in the hallway behind him. Belac did not know how cognizant his pursuers were, but he felt certain that it was only a matter of time before someone checked the only closed door in the hallway.

Belac considered the polished wooden bench in front of him. *I am not dying in the privy!* He stepped away from the door and looked down into the opening of the garderobe. On the other side of the rounded seat, a squared shaft tunneled straight down through the building's gray stone. Faint light wavered at the bottom of the darksome shaft. *Oh, Vairug is going to love this…*

Belac reached down with both hands and grabbed the edge of the wooden toilet where its top protruded from the side. The lid swung on two hidden hinges as he lifted it up and then leaned it against the back wall. *I can't believe that I'm going to do this.* While it would be a tight fit, he thought that he could climb through the hole. The smell had become no more pleasant.

Someone attempted to open the door. Belac spun around, eyes wide and harried. Multiple feet outside cast shadows under the door. The gap became more shadows than light as men gathered in the hallway outside. *There is no choice now.* Belac turned away from the door and began climbing into the stone shaft. Something slammed into the door behind him.

With the lower half of his body in the shaft, Belac grabbed the seat of the garderobe and pulled the lid toward himself. He put his head through the hole in the seat, resting its wooden bottom on his shoulders. Then he began to scootch down into the stone shaft, lowering the lid until it closed quietly. Using his hands, his knees, and his backside, Belac began the arduous prosses of descending through the narrow shaft.

The sound of the men battering the door to the privy was thunderous in the small room. Violent echoes chased Belac down into the shaft, spurring him to crawl faster. As the stone wall grated into his flesh, he tried not to think about what he was crawling through. *There had better not be another prison at the bottom of this thing.*

Wood cracked as the door to the privy burst open. Belac braced himself in the stone shaft and gazed up into the room above. *Please don't look in the hole. Please don't look in the hole.* Scattered light played inside the privy. *I should have hidden under the bed!* After a moment of shuffled footsteps, the glow above became steady. Belac lowered his head and continued to wait silently as his racing heart slowed.

Belac considered climbing back up and trying to find some other means of escape, but he could not think of a way to sneak past so many guards. *They are not going to stop searching for me.* He took a deep breath, immediately wishing that he had not. *I can't just wait here forever.* He glanced up at the wooden seat above him. *Eventually, someone is going to need to use the privy.*

Resigned to his current plan of action, Belac resumed lowering himself deeper into the shaft. *It's easier to go down that up anyway.* He tried not to think about what was waiting for him on the bottom. Before long, he began to detect the gentle sound of flowing water. *This city must have a sewer system.* He was not convinced that being lost in a sewer would be much better than finding another prison.

When Belac reached the end of the shaft, he discovered that there was nothing but empty space between him and the water below. *I am going to have to drop down.* A slow current echoed in the stone passage, but he had no way of knowing how deep the water would be. Belac thought back to how he had been captured. *All this because I peed on the wrong bush.* He tucked his arms in and extended his legs.

Three

As Belac fell from the ceiling, he gripped his nose and covered his mouth. Then he splashed feet first into a river of diluted filth. He sank waist deep into the water before his feet slipped on the slimy stonework beneath. Scrunching his eyes tightly, he tried to shut out the water as he crashed below the surface. Though the water was far cleaner than he had expected, its liquid touch made him vomit in his mouth.

Belac cringed at the feel of the water against his scalp. *I am never going to get my hair clean after this!* He flailed his arms against the current and kicked his feet as he fought for the surface. Once his legs were under him, he pressed down with his feet. His face contorted in disgust at the feel of slime between his toes.

Despite the slimy stone bottom of the sewer, Belac was able to stop himself from being carried away by the current. Knees bent for balance, he pushed his head and shoulders out of the water. His head slammed into the underside of a stone bridge, knocking him back down into the water. Disoriented, he lost his footing and was pulled downstream. Flailing under the water, he regained his balance and then attempted to stand again. This time, he was careful to move slowly.

With his head and shoulders above water again, Belac wiped his eyes with the back of his wrists and then spat to the side. *I remember a time when things like this almost never happened to me.* Though he could see well enough, diffuse light from distant side channels was all that lit the sewer. *If the light can get in, maybe I can get out.* The city's smooth stone construction seemed far less grand, now seen from his miserable perspective. Raised ledges lined both sides of the waterway, positioned far enough apart to avoid what spilled down from above. Arched bridges connected the two sides and spanned the other channels.

Belac glanced over his shoulder, seeing that the tunnel was significantly darker behind him than it was downstream. *I guess I know which way to go.* Careful of his footing, Belac waded to the walkway on his right. The ledge was well above the waterline, but he would have been able to reach it easily by standing up straight. Instead of standing tall in the water and grabbing the ledge, Belac lowered himself deeper into the water and then jumped up as high as he could. With a splash, he shot up above the waterline. His palms slapped down on the stone ledge, allowing him to pull then push himself up.

Water dripped from Belac's naked body as he crawled up onto the walkway. He rolled over and sat on the ledge with his feet dangling over the edge. He flicked both of his wrists, slinging water off his hands with disdain. Then he untied his long, black hair and did his best to squeeze the water out before retying it in place. *I am never going to feel clean again.*

Belac climbed to his feet and began following the walkway downstream, leaving wet footprints on the smooth surface of the stone. *This place kind of reminds me of the tunnels beneath Tariel.* Belac stopped walking. *There were sneaky lizard monsters under Tariel.* He glanced backward hastily, and then began scanning the sewer around him. *What if this place has something that wants to eat me?!*

Belac decided that if there was something in the sewer that wanted to eat him, he should probably not stand there, waiting for it to find him. He hurried onward, walking at almost a run. *Why does everything want to eat me?!*

The elf was moving mostly on his toes by the time he reached the first of the side channels. Angled sharply to his right, the side channel ended a few paces away in a round cul-de-sac. Sunlight shown down through an iron grate above, bathing the space in a warmth that contradicted its dank location.

Belac frowned up at the circular grate. Despite the promising radiance, he had no way to reach the world above. *Even if I could get up there, I can't fit through those bars.* He redirected his gaze to the walkway that followed the flowing sewer. A narrow bridge arched over the waters of the side channel, providing him with a dry path forward.

After accepting that he would need to find another exit, Belac stepped onto the bridge and continued downstream. He passed five more side channels before he stopped keeping count. Though some cut to the left and others to the right, none of the short canals offered him an apparent means of escape. *There has to be a way out of here. This place is really clean for a sewer. There must be some way for people to come down here and clean it.*

As Belac followed the flowing water, he became increasingly aware of his own thirst. He glanced down at the sewer water. *That is not going to happen. I would rather die of thirst.* He began to feel like the echoing sound of the tainted water was taunting him.

Belac narrowed his eyes at the sewer water and then pointed at it. "I am not going to drink you!"

Grumbling to himself, the elf continued through the sewer. *Stupid water thinks it can trick me.* He wondered why the sewer water would want him to drink it. *Maybe there is something living in it.* He scanned the surface of the water. *Maybe they are working together.* He did not question why such a collusion would take place. Instead, he began to speculate on what variety of monster it was that wanted to eat him.

Belac's first guess was that the monster was a zombie-fish-monster. He could still see their wicked fangs in his mind. With a nervous glance at the water, he began walking closer to the wall.

Then the elf shook his head. *No. I don't think that the zombie-fish-monsters would swim in a sewer.* He considered the sewer's smooth blocks of gray stone. *Not even a clean sewer.*

His second guess was only slightly less frightening. He thought of the sneaky lizard monsters in the cistern under Tariel. *The absolutely-not-dragon-babies.* He recalled how the jaws of one of the monsters had crushed Vairug's metal hand. Belac jerked his left hand away from the water, holding it above his right shoulder protectively.

More monsters came to mind as Belac hurried onward. Suddenly, the most terrifying prospect pushed its way to the forefront of his thoughts. *What if it is something that I have never seen before?* Belac had survived every monster that he had ever faced. If what stalked him now was something new, he would not know how to handle it. He imagined a giant, floating head covered in countless, glowing red eyes. Tentacles emerged from behind it, each of the undulating arms ending in a fanged maw.

Belac shook his head to dispel the image. *Please, let it be absolutely-not-dragon-babies.* He thought that he might be able to outrun the vicious reptiles. The elf felt no safer in the sewer than he had in the building he had escaped. *I should have hidden under the bed.*

Belac's optimism improved when the sewer he followed junctioned with a larger tunnel. Square, stone pillars rose from the center of the new waterway, adding support to the ceiling above. Quarter arch walkways ringed the supports, each connected by matching stone bridges. *They must have diverted an entire river to keep the sewer flowing like this.* Light shown down through long, rectangular gratings, creating a tranquil atmosphere.

Belac looked right and then left. *Do I go to where the water comes in, or gets out?* He turned left. *It will probably be easier to follow the water out if it comes to that.* He crossed over the stone bridge that spanned the waterway he had followed thus far. *But there has to be some other way out of here.*

Ahead, something liquid spilled down into the sewer from one of the rectangular grates. Belac began running toward the grate, worried that whoever was there might leave before he could reach them.

"Hey!" Belac shouted. "Hey, you up there! I need help!"

"Hello?" a man called down from above, his voice sounding timid and confused.

'Hello?' Belac thought irritably. *I don't need a greeting. I need a ladder!* He stopped and looked up at the hole in the ceiling. "I'm trapped down here!"

The hunched figure of a man was outlined by the sun above. "You are not supposed to be down there. It is against the law."

Belac smiled and ground his teeth before replying, "Good! Then, help me get out!"

There was a moment of silence before the old man responded, "How do I know that you are not a mugger?"

Belac snarled up at the shadowy figure. "What kind of mugger traps themself in a sewer?"

The old man did not have an immediate answer.

Impatient, Belac shouted, "I am not a mugger!"

The old man was unconvinced. "You could be a mugger," he argued defensively.

Belac smiled broadly and laughed in an effort to control his growing frustration.

"Why are you naked?" the old man asked suspiciously.

Belac shook his head before answering. "It's a long story. Why don't we talk about it after you help me get out of here?"

"I don't know…" The old man's voice trailed off in a way that was not reassuring.

Belac held up a hand. "Wait!" He tilted his head to the side and pressed down his hair with one hand. He put the forefinger of his other hand behind his pointed ear and pushed it out away from his head. "See?! I'm an elf. Who ever heard of an elven mugger?"

When the old man replied, he sounded sure of himself. "There is an access to the south. I will have the entry opened for you."

Belac looked around for some means of establishing direction before realizing that it was an unlikely achievement. "Which way is south?" he called up to the man.

"The river flows under the city from the north to the south," the old man explained. "If you follow the water, it should take you south."

That is what I was going to do anyway. Belac nodded. "Thank you." He began walking downstream, eager to get out of the sewer. "I will meet you at the access."

"You shouldn't dawdle," the old man warned. "You do not want to be found by one of the sweepers."

Belac pictured the sweepers as a group of toothless old women with straw brooms. *At least they don't have fangs.* Then the real horror hit him. *What if they try to put me to work?!*

Four

Locating the sewer access proved easy enough for Belac. As soon as he saw the short passage and the stairs that led upward, he was convinced that he would have found the exit without help. *All that old man did was tell me to keep going the way I was already going.* He began to climb the stairs that would deliver him from the sewer. *That, and call me two kinds of criminal.*

When Belac reached the platform at the top of the stairs, he found an iron gate waiting for him in the shadowed space. The empty chamber beyond was open to both the left and right, allowing for fresh air and ambient sunlight to liven the gray stone interior. The gate itself, was chained.

Belac gripped the bars and pressed his forehead against the gate. "I hate prison!"

An acrid smell wafted up the stairs behind the elf. He pushed himself away from the gate and looked over his shoulder. Then he spun around and slammed his back against the iron bars. *What the death is that!* Below, a blue-green blob of translucent goo was in the process of squeezing itself into the stairwell. Slow and ponderous, the blob rolled over itself as it worked its way inside. Any sounds its movements made were washed out by the echoes of the flowing sewer behind it. As the thing filled the base of the stairwell, Belac realized that it was too large for him to get around. *I'm trapped!*

Belac spun around, grabbed the bars of the gate, and began to shake it. "Help!" he yelled. "Let me out! A giant-blue-booger is trying to eat me!"

Belac glanced back at the giant-blue-booger. Like a man rolling his shoulders, the gelatinous blob began to crawl up the stairs.

Belac shook the gate harder. "Let me out!" he yelled loud enough to hurt his throat.

The elf looked back again. The blob was steadily slogging up the stairs. Now closer, Belac saw that a dead rodent floated inside the translucent mass. Stripped of skin and fur, the small animal was being digested. The elf suddenly understood why the sewers were so clean.

Belac threw his shoulder into the gate, attempting to break through. "Help! I don't want to be a dead rat!" He slammed into the gate again. "Help!"

A woman's head popped into view on the left. Her eyes widened at the sight of the terrified elf. Quickly, she backed away and then called out, "Hurry! There is a naked man trapped in the sewer!"

Belac shouted after the woman, "And there is a giant-blue-booger that wants to eat me!" He pressed his face between the bars, attempting to see where the woman had gone.

A stout man ran into the vestibule and rushed to the sewer gate. Belac looked from the bold red stripe on the man's blue gambeson, to the cudgel hanging on his hip. *It's a watchman! Maybe he can get me out!*

Belac shook the gate frantically. "Let me out!"

"Stop shaking the gate!" the watchman ordered as he fumbled with a ring of keys.

Belac let go of the gate and turned around to face the stairs. The acrid smell had grown stronger in the air as the gelatinous blob crawled closer and closer. Naked and unarmed, Belac saw no way to fight the slow death coming for him. *If I jump and then run along the wall, I might be able to get past it.* He knew that landing on the stairs would be dangerous, but he did not see another option.

The gate swung open, and a hand gripped the back of Belac's hair. Yanked off balance as he was pulled out of the stairwell, the elf fell down on his backside. The blob crawled up onto the platform, not yet ready to surrender its meal.

Belac began pointing vigorously at the giant-blue-booger. "Shut the gate! Shut the gate!"

The watchman frowned down at the animated elf. "The sweepers won't leave the sewers."

Belac attempted to glance at the watchman, but his eyes would not leave the blue-green blob. "Shut it anyway!"

The giant-blue-booger stopped on the platform, its gelatinous body pressed against both sides of the stairwell. Then it began to roll back down the stairs. Belac let out a sigh of relief as the watchman closed the gate. *Even things without teeth want to eat me.* Movement on the elf's right finally drew his attention away from the sewer. He turned his head to find a hunched man approaching.

Belac narrowed his eyes at the old man that had directed him to the access. "You said that you would have the exit open."

The old man regarded the elf disapprovingly and replied, "No. I told you that I would have it opened." He gestured to the gate as the watchman secured the chain. "I have neither the means nor the authority to open the sewers." He crossed his arms and frowned. "I also told you to be wary of the sweepers."

Belac pursed his lips.

The watchman turned away from the gate and looked down at the elf. "There is a reason why people are restricted from entering the sewers."

Belac climbed to his feet and then brushed off his bare backside. "I was not there by choice," he said defensively. "I was escaping a nillanan."

The watchman's face went slack. "A nillanan?" he asked emotionlessly. "Right."

Belac narrowed his eyes at the watchman. "I'm serious."

The watchman nodded disbelievingly. "A nillanan dragged you into the sewers."

Belac shook his head. "No. It was a castle."

The watchman nodded again. "So, you are telling me, that there is a nillanan, living in a castle, hidden in the sewers."

"No." Belac glared at the watchman. "That is not…"

The watchman held up a hand. "I don't have time for this," he interrupted and then gave the elf a stern look. "Listen. I don't know what you have been drinking, but you should stop." He shook his head reproachfully before adding, "And put on some clothes."

As the watchman turned to leave, Belac argued, "The nillanan stole my clothes!"

The watchman waved the elf's protest away without stopping to look back.

Belac pointed angrily at the departing watchman. "Well, don't blame me when a faceless hand monster comes to eat your brain!"

The old man untucked his cream colored blouse from his gray trousers and then pulled the loose garment over his balding head. "Here," he said, holding the blouse out to the elf. "You can cover up with this until we get to my shop. Then we can find you something better to wear. I am certain that I will have something that suits you." He smiled at his own joke. "So to speak."

While Belac appreciated the offer, he detected a mercantile tone to the man's phrasing. As he accepted the blouse, Belac noted the obvious. "I don't have any way to pay you."

The old man nodded professionally. "That is not a problem. I will have a bill sent to your delegation." He smiled again. "What is important now, is seeing to your needs."

Belac tied the arms of the blouse around his waist and then turned the hanging cloth to cover his front. *Where am I?* The presence of an Elven delegation meant that the city must be in one of the human kingdoms south of the Elven forests. *I can't ask where I am, or the old man will know that I am not with the other elves.* Avoiding the delegation while still receiving aid was likely to be difficult. *I will just have to ask somebody else later.*

Once the elf had covered himself, the old man bowed and announced, "Horis Palow, at your service."

Belac was beginning to expect that the service would be expensive. "I'm Belac."

Horis tilted his head to the side as he scrutinized the elf. "Belac? The Belac?" He raised his bushy eyebrows questioningly. "Belac Melavar? The Dragon Slayer?"

Belac sighed with resignation. "Yeah. That's me." *This is going to make it harder to hide from the delegation.*

Horis reappraised the elf. It was obvious that the man was unconvinced. "The Dragon Slayer?"

Belac scowled at the old man. "What part of, 'I was captured by a nillanan,' do you people not understand?"

Horis held up his hands placatingly. "My apologies. It is simply… The Dragon Slayer?" He wiggled his shoulders and then stood taller. "It will be my honor to assist you, Sir."

He just realized that he can boast about helping The Dragon Slayer, even if I'm not me. Belac nodded tolerantly. "Lucky for you, I'm not hunting dragons right now."

"Ah." Horis smiled. "Quite."

Five

Belac stepped out from behind the privacy screen and inspected himself in the standing mirror. While the gray trousers and cream colored blouse that had been provided were of average quality, the black, knee-high boots were surprisingly nice. He preened in the mirror for a moment, and then scanned the room. The old man's bed chamber was modest in size, but well furnished. The walnut accouterments had all been recently polished and there was no dust to be found.

Belac walked over to a vanity and picked up a wooden comb. "Do you mind if I use this?" he asked, holding up the comb.

"Of course, not," Horis assured the elf. "It is important that you feel presentable."

I wonder if he plans on charging the delegation a rental fee for the comb. Belac untied his hair and began to work out the tiny knots that had formed on the ends. He had wanted to spend longer bathing, but he had also felt a pressing need to keep moving. He worried that if the nillanan did not find him, the Elven delegation would. The cold bath water had encouraged him to be quick as well.

Once his hair was combed and retied, Belac returned the comb to its place on the vanity and then turned to face the old man. "I am going to need a weapon."

"A weapon?" Horis asked with confusion.

Belac shrugged. "A sword. A knife. A stick if that is all you have."

Horis was still confounded by the request. "But, surely the streets will be safe enough for you to reach the palace unmolested."

Belac's face hardened. "It's not 'the streets' I plan on killing." The nillanan had taken something from Belac. Something intimate. Something that he could still feel missing. He was not going to let them take his sword also. "And I'm not going to the palace."

Horis's bushy eyebrows lowered with concern. "There really is a nillanan? Truly?"

Belac nodded. "There might be more than one. If the watchmen won't help me, I will just have to take care of them myself." *Those monsters are not taking anything else from me.*

Horis obviously doubted the wisdom of the elf's plan. "You are going back into the sewers?"

Belac shook his head. "No. I saw some of the castle from above. I think that I can probably find it. It was at least five stories tall. It had a hedge maze between it and the city…" He paused, attempting to recall more details. "And the guardsmen were dressed in blue with a gold star on their chests."

Horis frowned. "That sounds like House Vesper."

"Can you give me directions?" Belac asked with enthusiasm.

Horis nodded thoughtfully. "I can have my apprentice show you the way." He held up a gnarled finger. "And I can scribe a message to the Elven delegates for you. They may be able to secure the aid that the watchmen have denied you."

Belac did not like the idea of involving the delegation, but he did not see how it could be avoided. *Horis will probably send the message along with the bill.* There was no assurance that the Elven delegates would help Belac once they learned who he was. Depending on what they had been told, it was possible that they might even try to have him arrested.

"One moment," Horis declared before hustling over to a large, wooden trunk. He flipped open the lid and began to dig around inside. "I know I have it somewhere."

As the old man rummaged through the trunk, Belac tried to figure out how he was going to find his friends. *I might not know where I am yet, but I know that everyone was supposed to meet up in Harbridge.* The city that Belac had found himself in was too grand for it to not have a pond. *Wherever I am, I'm going to need permission to use the pond.* He worried that the delegation might be his only option after all.

Horis returned to the elf and presented a scabbarded dagger. "This is from a time when I was younger and more prone to flights of fancy."

Belac took hold of the leather wrapped scabbard and then drew the dagger's blade. Despite being pitted with spots of rust, the blade seemed serviceable. Belac grinned at the old man. "Put it on the bill."

Horis grinned back. "I intend to." He held up a gnarled finger again and then turned away.

Belac sheathed the dagger as the old man went to retrieve something from one of two tall armoires. Reminded of an ancient legend, Belac asked, "Are you looking for a magic horn?"

"Sadly, no," Horis replied as he closed the doors to the armoire. He walked over to the elf and held out a narrow belt.

Belac took the belt and rubbed it between his fingers, noting its thinness.

"It is my wife's," Horis explained. "It has not fit her for quite some time." He smiled sheepishly.

Belac shrugged. "It will do." He did not think that the supple leather would hold up under hard use, but he also did not think that it would need to. *I wonder how much he is going to charge for this old belt.*

Belac slipped the belt through the strap on the back of the scabbard, then buckled the belt around his waist. He positioned the dagger comfortably on his left hip, the scabbarded blade in line with his thigh. Despite its relatively diminutive size, Belac felt reassured by the presence of the weapon. *Clothes or not, I still feel naked without a sword.*

Horis gestured to the door. "Let us go find Nagle," he suggested before leading the way out of the room.

As Belac followed the old man out into the den, he was struck with the smell of spiced stew. He had already eaten a bowl of the stew while Horis donned a fresh blouse and prepared the elf's bath, but Belac considered asking for another serving before he left. The spices in the stew had tasted wonderful, and the ale that had washed it down had been considerably better than average. *There is no time. The nillanan are not going to stop looking for me while I sit around, shoving food in my face.*

Though Horis moved like an old man, he moved like one with a purpose. Exiting the den and then continuing down the stairs to the lower level of the building, Horis kept a pace that required Belac to step quickly or risk getting left behind. *I wonder if he actually believes me, or if he is just in a hurry to get paid.*

Horis walked through a small entryway at the bottom of the stairs, passing by the closer of two doors as he moved to the one on the far side of the room. "Nagle should be minding the shop."

"Who is Nagle?" Belac asked as he followed the old man.

"Nagle is my apprentice," Horis explained as he opened the door. "He can show you the way to House Vesper." He walked into the shop, leaving the door open behind him.

Belac took two steps into the shop and then froze. *No...* His eyes swept across the room. *This is not happening.* He squeezed his eyes shut. *This can't be real.* He refused to believe what he saw.

"Lord Belac?" Horis asked with concern in his voice. "Is there something wrong?"

Belac opened his eyes and stared at the old man. The old man who had helped him; the old man who had provided him with clothing so as to cover his naked form. Belac had to stop himself from growling in aggravation. *It's a conspiracy!* His azure eyes moved over the various footwear proudly displayed on hardwood counters. He wanted to set everything on fire. Then he looked back to the cobbler.

Six

Belac fumed as he followed the cobbler's apprentice through the city. *A cobbler!* Tall buildings of homogeneous design, the unknown city defied the elf's expectations of humanity. Despite the impressive architecture of the city, Belac was unable to appreciate its beauty. *I am not telling Vairug that I was given clothes by a cobbler.*

Belac growled. "Why a cobbler?!" he asked rhetorically of no one. *Why couldn't Horis be a blacksmith or a baker?!*

Nagle glanced at the elf nervously. "My dad said it was the best apprenticeship I would be able to get." He nodded a head that was too large for his skinny body, and then his hand absently swept dark hair out of his eyes. "It's not so bad. I mostly just watch the shop."

Belac understood why the apprentice thought that he had been speaking to him. *It is not his fault that Horis is a cobbler.* Belac forced himself to speak in a friendlier tone. "Do you like being a cobbler?"

Nagle shrugged his scrawny shoulders. "I like having a profession," he answered without much feeling. "But, if given a choice, I would rather have just been born rich."

Belac grinned at the young man. The elf suspected that most rich people needed to work also. Especially if they wanted to keep being rich. *Though, I would rather do rich people work than poor people work.* He realized that something about that thought seemed a little off. ...*Shouldn't it be the other way around?*

Belac considered the magnificent city of smooth stone and bright blue tiles. Such a place was a testament of not merely prosperity, but of the strength of its people's values. The city could not have been built in a single human's lifespan, and multigenerational competence was an achievement as grand as the architecture itself. *Maybe I should be careful not to judge them too quickly.*

When Belac had been led to the cobbler's shop, Horis had kept to the alleys in an effort to avoid offending any of the other denizens with the sight of the elf's posterior. The alleys alone were nicer than any human city Belac had ever seen. Now, as he trode up one of the central streets, Belac saw the finery of the people that dwelt there. Though most of the citizens were attired in varying shades of gray, blues were prevalent as well. Belac found himself wondering if the people intentionally dressed to match their city.

"Are you a proud people?" Belac asked his guide.

Nagle shook his head as he shrugged his shoulders again. "Proud of what?"

I guess that kind of answers my question. Belac held out his hands, indicating to the city around him. "Your home. Your lives. Your people." He lowered his arms and tried to think of another way to ask the question. "Do you feel a sense of loyalty to your kingdom?"

Nagle frowned. "I am not a traitor, if that is what you are asking."

Belac shook his head. "No. That's not what I meant." *Maybe the kid just doesn't understand how amazing this place is.* He thought back on his own homeland. *Was I any different?*

Once they moved beyond the trade district, the buildings became larger and more spread out. Behind barred fences of black iron, the massive structures and their expansive grounds were segregated from the populace. It was clear that the private castles were owned by people that were more than merely rich; they were wealthy. *This has to be where the nobles live.*

When they came to an empty roundabout, Nagle pointed to the right. "We need to go this way."

Belac studied the iron grate in the center of the circular intersection. He recognized its shape from his time in the sewer. *That is not necessarily one of the openings I saw. Those things are probably all over the city.* He glanced at the closest of the castles, wondering how he would know which of them was the one that he was searching for. *I hope hedge mazes are not something everyone has.*

Two watchmen passed by on the opposite side of the street. Upon seeing the red strip across each of their chests, Belac considered asking them for help. Then he remembered how the other watchman had treated him. Belac decided that the watchmen were more likely to arrest him for being a crazy person, than they were to help him infiltrate a noble's estate. *They might not even know what a nillanan is.*

As he continued on, Belac wondered if it was normal for the streets in the area to be so empty. While he knew that there would be fewer commoners loitering around, he would have expected agents, solicitors, and numerous deliveries to be flowing to and from the estates. *Could the nillanan have captured more than one of the castles?* Despite the warm midday sun, he began to feel a cold dread.

Belac pushed the feeling away. *Those things are not keeping my sword.* If he had to conquer the entire city and find a way to burn stone, then that is what he would do. He would have back what had been taken. *And I am going to kill every one of those faceless monsters that tries to stop me.*

Nagle halted at a wide, flagstone road that led to one of the castles. "This is House Vesper," he announced, gesturing to the closed gate that stood in the way. "I hope everything works out for you."

Belac considered the square horseshoe shaped castle on the other side of the gate, then he turned to his right and compared the view to what he remembered from the fifth story window of the building he had fled. *Yeah. This could be the place.*

Nagle began to walk away, but then stopped. "Don't forget to come back to us to have your boots resoled when they get worn. Master Horis says that it is bad luck to let another cobbler repair a shoe if they did not make it."

Belac grinned at the young man. "So, Horis doesn't ever take money to fix shoes made by other cobblers?"

"Of course, not." Nagle smiled shamelessly. "Master Horis would need to make that person a new pair."

Belac could not help but chuckle a little. "Of course," he allowed before turning back to the castle.

As the cobbler's apprentice walked away, Belac looked for more signs that he was at the right castle. The gate had the name 'Vesper' worked into the bars, but Belac was still not certain that it was House Vesper that the nillanan had captured. *It's not like I can just knock on the front door and ask to talk to the nillanan in charge.*

Belac glanced at the attendant's booth on the other side of the fence. The small, stone structure was empty. *There is no one to let me in.* He took a few steps closer to the gate. *But there is also no one here to keep me out.* With his head next to the bars of the gate, Belac searched the other outbuildings for movement. Though much of his view was blocked by trees and other greenery, he saw something on the right side of the estate that he thought could be a hedge maze.

Belac stepped away from the gate and looked down the street to his left and right. *No watchmen.* He rushed toward the gate and then jumped. His left foot landed on the lower part of the letter 'S' stylized into the gate. With the force of his left leg, Belac launched himself up. His midsection collided with the top of the gate, and then he swung himself over. Twisting as he fell, Belac landed facing the castle.

While his ingress had been far from silent, Belac did not think that there was anyone nearby to hear him. *I wonder if nillanan can hear.* He began walking away from the still rattling gate. *How would they? Nillanan don't have ears.* Belac found the absence of groundskeepers both reassuring and unnerving at the same time. While he was growing more convinced that he was in the right place, the silence of the castle felt wrong to him. What should have been a calm sunny day, seemed like something crafted to hide shadows.

Belac stopped and reconsidered the square horseshoe shape castle. *I don't want to go into the courtyard.* The walled in space looked like a trap. *Are they expecting me to return?* His hand touched the dagger on his hip. *This won't be much use against an army of armed guards.* He turned to the stables on his left. *Maybe I can find an axe or something.* As Belac made his way toward the stables, he toyed with the idea of killing a nillanan with a pitchfork.

Seven

Though the stables had been built with the same gray stone as the rest of the city, they had later been outfitted with wooden additions to expand their utility. *I wonder how they get all those little, blue tiles on the rooves to all be the same color.* Belac shook his head and dismissed the quandary. *I bet the humans cheat somehow.*

Belac considered the two sets of barn doors on the front side of the stables, then instead walked over to a smaller door on the left side of the building. He pushed and pulled on the door, but someone had barred it from the inside. The elf frowned at the obstinate door, then walked around to the front of the building. Without any expectation that they would open, he pushed and pulled on both sets of the large double doors. His pessimism was confirmed.

Belac glanced toward the castle anxiously, but the cold stone gave no indication that his trespass had been noticed. His attention returned to the task at hand as he rounded the corner of the stables. He found another side door waiting for him to try. *If this one doesn't open, I might have to find a way to break in.* He thought that he might be able to get in through the roof if he could pull up some of the tiles.

As he approached the side door, Belac began to detect the sour smell of death. *Maybe they dumped the dead guards inside.* He nodded to himself. *It would probably draw attention if they started dropping dead bodies down into the sewer.* He remembered the giant-blue-booger that the watchman had called a sweeper. *Maybe not.*

The door to the stables swung in easily under Belac's touch. *It's not even latched. I wonder…* An escaping waft of rot disrupted the elf's thoughts. *How many guards did they kill?* He waved a hand in front of his face as he entered, but it did not provide the relief he wanted. *I can taste it in my throat.* He turned his head and spat to the side.

With his face pinched in disgust, Belac moved forward until he reached the first set of large, double doors. Unlike the unsecured side entrance, the barn doors had been barred from the inside. Belac looked to his right and gazed down a wide aisle between two rows of horse stalls. *Why are there no horses?* The awful smell was obviously coming from the stalls. Compelled by morbid curiosity, Belac crept into the aisle.

Flies buzzed above the stall on the left, betraying what was hidden inside. Belac looked over the top of a stall door and found a dead horse rotting on the floor. Something had eaten the animal's eyes. Belac stepped back, shoving flies away from his face. *How long has this been here?* He continued down the aisle, checking the other stalls.

Of the six box stalls on the left, five sheltered a dead horse. Victims of dehydration and neglect, the noble beasts had been beneath the nillanan's attention.

The dead horses bothered Belac more than dead guards would have. Humans were responsible for their own choices; and to some extent, dying was part of a guard's job. The horses had suffered for trusting humans.

Belac checked the stables on the other side as he walked back to the barn doors. All of the box stalls were empty of anything other than straw. He turned right and continued past a tack room, wanting to see what was behind the second set of barn doors. What he found was a well-kept coach house.

Piles of hay and barrels of grain were stored along the back wall behind an unhitched carriage. On the right, tidy tools hung above a counter, and a pitchfork leaned against the wall next to a shovel.

Belac picked up the pitchfork as he considered the other tools. *I wonder if I will be the first person to kill a nillanan with a pitchfork.* He hefted the long, four-pronged fork. *Maybe I should shout, "Hay!" just before I stab it.* The more he thought about it, the less Belac wanted to try killing a nillanan with a garden tool. He set the pitchfork down and decided to go see what was in the tack room. *Is a gardening sword a thing?*

The tack room was longer than it was wide. Belac stepped through the cased doorway, then walked past the fabric halters and leather bridles that hung on the wall to his right. He stopped in front of the other assorted tack hanging next to the bridles, wondering if there was anything he could use. He glanced at the saddles racked on the back wall to his left, and then looked to the bridles. *Maybe I can build a trap or something.* He grinned as an idea came to him. *Or something.*

Belac began grabbing bridles and hanging them on his left forearm. *This is totally going to work.* Once he had collected four of the bridles, Belac left the tack room and returned to the coach house, the metal bits of the bridles clinking against each other as he walked. He slung the bridles onto the counter and then unsheathed his dagger. He dragged one of the bridles closer to himself and proceeded to saw at the leather, cutting it away from the H-shaped leverage bit.

After he had the bit removed from the first of the bridles, Belac set the metal piece to the side and repeated the process on the other three. Once the bridles had been separated into a tangle of leather straps and a pile of metal bits, he set his dagger down and took a step to his left. He reached up and unhooked a farrier's hammer that was hanging on the wall by a ring at the end of its handle. He set the hammer down on the counter and then began to arrange the four leverage bits into the shape he had in mind. He placed two of the bits on each side of the hammer, just below its iron head.

One of the leverage shanks from each of the bits ran along the side of the hammer, with the mouthpieces aligned perpendicular to the half.

Belac grabbed one of the ruined bridles and shook it loose from the others. He untangled a leather strap that still had a buckle, then tossed the rest to the side. He picked up another bridle, shook it out, and pulled free another leather strap. Once he had two straps that he thought would work, he laid them out flat on the counter. Stretching to reach another tool on the wall, he unhooked an awl hanging on his left. He began using the awl to punch eyelets in the straps, but he was not sure how much of the leather he would need. When Belac was finished, he had punched a series of holes into almost half of both straps. *Rolan is not the only person that knows how to make stuff.*

Belac tossed the awl onto the pile of ruined bridles and then used the two straps he had tooled to secure the bits onto the hammer. With the leather straps holding the leverage shanks against the haft of the hammer, he wiggled the bits on both sides until they stuck out in four different directions. Then he held up his sloppy invention, smiling at his own cleverness. *This is totally going to work.* He twisted the hammer's handle back and forth, causing the leverage bits to flop around on the sides.

Belac picked up his dagger and resheathed it. Then he snatched up the pitchfork and returned to the tack room. He leaned the pitchfork against the wall as he selected a thick coil of lead rope from among the other equipment. *That looks like the longest one.* He removed the coiled rope from its hanger and slipped it over his head and left arm, careful to keep his improvised tool from getting caught.

With the lead rope hanging across his chest and back, Belac reclaimed the pitchfork and left the tack room. *It's time to get out of this stinky place before the rot seeps into my lungs.* He felt another pang of pity for the deceased horses as he moved past their stalls and to the open side door. After peeking outside to ensure that the building had not been surrounded by guards, Belac walked out and hurried back to the flagstone road.

Belac watched the castle as he crossed to the other side of the road. He saw no signs of residency; nothing moved, and no lights flashed in the tall windows. *No cats. No dogs.* He scanned the trees. *Not even the birds want to be here.* He shrugged. *At least I won't have to worry about owls.* He imagined owls flying around, dropping stolen curtains on his head as he tried to fight the nillanan.

Belac continued to circle the castle until he reached the hedge maze on the right side. He frowned at the hedges disapprovingly. *This has got to be the laziest hedge maze ever.* Though he had not noticed from the perspective of the fifth story window, the hedges of the maze were only slightly above waist high. *How is anyone going to get lost in there?* He saw that there was more than one entrance to the maze, and that there seemed to be no goal. *Someone needs to explain to the gardener how a maze works.*

Belac's heart sank as he realized what he was looking at. *It's a maze for children.* The height of the hedges would allow small children to enjoy the maze while remaining under the watchful eye of an adult. *What would the nillanan do with children?* In his mind, Belac heard the laughter of children at play. The silence of reality had never sounded so cruel.

Eight

Belac found the lost side-sword lying in the grass where it had fallen. *Well, that kind of worked out.* He tossed the pitchfork aside and bent to pick up the sword. *I wonder if I should lie to people and tell them that I planned this.* He took hold of the sword's hilt and then straightened.

Belac gazed up the side of the castle and evaluated the distance that the blade had fallen. He did not think that he would have fared as well as the sword had, if it had been himself that had fallen. He stepped away from the castle as he considered the windows that he had used in his escape. *They just left them open.* He decided that the open windows were either an oversight, or the nillanan simply did not think that anyone would attempt to enter the castle through the fourth or fifth floors. *Stupid nillanan.*

Belac looked at the sword in his hand, realizing that he would need to set the weapon back down. He raised his right knee, balanced the blade of the side-sword across the top of his boot, and then lowered his foot to the ground. With his free hand, he slipped the coil of rope over his head, moving it to hang on his left forearm.

He transferred his makeshift grappling hook to his right hand, gripped a loose end of the rope with his left, then let the coil fall down onto the grass. He tucked the grappling hook under his left arm and then proceeded to tie the rope onto the ring at the bottom of the farrier's hammer.

With the rope secured to the end of his grappling hook, Belac took hold of the handle and then relaxed his grip, allowing the improvised tool to fall as the rope slid through his fingers. Before the grappling hook could hit the ground, Belac tightened his grip. He began to swing the hook back and forth as he built momentum. Once the hook had enough speed, he began swinging it above his head in a vertical circle that barely missed the ground in the downswing. Then he launched the hook at the fifth story window.

The grappling hook did not reach the fifth story. It did not even reach the fourth. Instead, the hook smashed into the lower portion of the closed window on the third floor. Belac immediately let go of the rope, kicked the side-sword up into his hand as he turned around, and then sprinted for the bushes. He tossed the side-sword over one of the short hedges, then dove into the maze.

Though he was able to slow his fall with his hands, Belac's chest still hit the ground with a thud. Despite the impact, he hastily low crawled further into the maze. Once hidden in the vegetation, he rolled around in the grass and pressed himself longwise against the base of a hedge. *Don't see me. Don't see me. Don't see me.*

Belac's heart pounded distractingly loud as he listened for sounds of alarm. Time stretched as he waited. *Someone had to hear that.* He crept to the edge of the hedge and poked his head out. Azure eyes wide, he searched for any indication that an army of guards was coming to kill him. There was no movement from the castle. *How did no one hear that?*

Belac crawled back behind the hedges on his hands and knees. He retrieved the side-sword and then stood up in the maze. Sword held low and body still, he waited for something to happen. Only his eyes moved.

I am starting to think that this might be a trap. He allowed himself to take a breath. *Maybe not. It's a big building. Maybe there was just no one near the window.*

As Belac began to breathe normally, he considered another possibility. *The nillanan may have taken too much of the guards' minds.* The city that Belac had found himself in was grand. It was conceivable that the soldiers of such a society might very well be too proud to submit to monsters. If the nillanan removed anything that would not serve them, they may have been forced to ruin their own guards. *It's sad, but that would definitely work in my favor.*

Belac walked out of the hedge maze and returned to the rope hanging out of the third story window of the castle. He grabbed the rope, looped it around his left hand, and backed away from the building. The rope pulled easily, then the hook caught on something in the room above. Shards of glass rained down, prompting the elf to release the rope and hop away. Though the broken pieces of glass did not hit him, he disliked the idea of it getting into his hair as he climbed up the side of the building.

Unhappy with how his plan was developing, Belac took hold of the rope again and began tugging on it in hope of freeing the hook from whatever it was caught on. More glass fell, but the hook remained fixed. Belac stopped tugging on the rope. *I guess I made the grappling hook too good.* He frowned up at the broken window. *It does not seem right that doing one thing well would ruin the rest of my plan.*

Belac shrugged and decided that he would simply need to make do. He moved closer to the building, tightening the slack on the rope as he neared. Once he was standing at the base of the castle, he created a loop in the rope and then slipped the hilt of the side-sword into it. With the blade of the sword pointed away to Belac's right, he wrapped his hand over the loop, positioning the ascending rope between his index finger and middle finger. Below the sword, he looped the rope around his left hand, then placed his left foot against the stone wall. He began to worry that what he had planned might not be safe.

With most of his weight on the hilt of the sword, Belac lifted his right foot off the ground and placed it on the wall next to his left. Both feet braced against the side of the castle below the first of its tall windows, Belac looked up and gauged how far he would need to climb. *Maybe it's a good thing that the hook did not make it all the way to the top.* Holding firmly to the rope with his left hand, he slid the hilt of the sword up above his head. He tightened his right hand on the loop that was wound around the hilt, then walked up the wall as he pulled himself up the rope.

Belac repositioned his left hand and then gazed upward again. *This is going to take a while.* He knew that he could make the climb faster if he abandoned the sword, but he did not want to enter the castle with only a rusted dagger for protection. *I could tie the sword to the end of the rope.* He looked down. Though he could have safely dropped to the ground, he decided to continue on as he was.

Belac climbed again, this time hopping as he pulled himself up. *That is a lot faster.* Attempting to establish a rhythm, he made an effort to climb at a quicker rate. When his boots landed on the panes of the first-floor window, they gave out under his feet. As the window split open freely, Belac swung into the castle. Panicked by the sudden disruption, the elf floundered on the rope. His legs got tangled on the curtain hanging inside, and then the rope above went slack.

The blade of the side-sword pierced the thick curtain, tearing the cloth as Belac tumbled into the building. He banged the right side of his forehead on the window seal and then crashed onto the floor. Surging to his feet, he began jerking on the sword's hilt in a clumsy attempt to untangle the blade. As he fought with the uncooperative cloth, the curtain rod bounced off its hooks and struck the elf in the head. *Sneaky owls!*

Once both Belac and the side-sword were free of the curtain, he spun around and faced the room. Holding the sword out in front of himself defensively, he appraised his surroundings with hunted eyes. He was in a stately meeting room, standing next to a long table that was surrounded by wooden chairs with padded backs. He was not alone.

Two men sat next to each other on the opposite side of the table from the windows. One young, and the other advanced in age, they were both dressed in noble attire. With their palms on the table and their backs straight, they stared away at nothing. Neither of the men moved.

Belac considered the older man's crisp blue vest and fluffy white blouse that was covered in a pattern of tiny peacock feathers. *That could be Lord Vesper.*

The elf frowned on one side of his face. *Though, I guess he is not the lord of anything anymore.* Belac's attention moved to the younger man. *That has to be his son.* Though the younger man's blouse was plain, his navy-blue vest was filigreed with gold thread.

Belac moved his sword to the side and leaned forward slightly. "Are either of you just pretending?" he asked in a hushed voice.

Neither of the men responded.

Belac lowered the sword. "Okay. You two just stay here and keep being lords." *While I sneak around and loot your castle.*

Nine

One of Belac's azure eyes peeked out through the gap of a cracked open door. *Even if this is a trap, no one is going to expect me to sneak in from here.* On the other side of an empty hallway, a wall of thick curtains held back the sun. A warm glow shone around the edges of the blue cloth, providing the elf with plenty of light to see. Though the hallway was absent of guards, Belac was not entirely convinced that the curtains were not going to jump off the windows and attack him.

The door opened smoothly on well oiled hinges. Leaning his head out into the hallway, Belac checked left and then right. Still, he saw no threats other than the curtains. Down the hallway to his left, a stairwell waited on the other side of a cased opening. The hallway was more than twice as long to the right, ending in a sharp turn. *Maybe I should see what's down here before I move up to the next level.*

Belac stepped out of the meeting room and onto a plush carpet that ran down the center of the hallway. He glanced down at the rich brown running carpet decorated with beige scrollwork. *This should help keep my footsteps quiet.* He recalled the pounding of the guards' feet as they had chased him through the floors above. *But I will need to be extra careful when I move to the upper floors.*

Maintaining a safe distance from the curtains, Belac began following the carpet away from the stairs. The doors on the right side of the hallway hung open, allowing him to peer inside as he passed. He saw that the rooms were professional spaces, affirming that rich people did indeed need to work. Though the offices were finely appointed, the décor offered little in the way of personality.

While Belac was glad that the offices were empty, he knew that the guards had to be somewhere. He glanced back over his left shoulder. *I wonder if the guards are hiding behind the curtains.* When he reached the corner of the hallway, Belac found the guards. They were not hiding behind the curtains.

Belac hopped backward away from the corner. On the other side, after a short corridor, the building opened up into a spacious foyer that reached up to the topmost level of the castle. Though Belac could not see the entirety of the foyer from the hallway, he had been given a clear enough view of the guards standing in formation. He pressed himself against the wall and peeked around the corner. He could only see two rows of twelve guards, but he suspected that there were more standing behind the ones in view. *I'm glad that I didn't try the front door.*

Belac backed away from the corner and the unwelcoming men dressed in blue gambesons. *What are they doing there? They can't think that I would actually try to come in through the front door.* He turned around and began hurrying toward the other end of the hallway. *Whatever the reason, if all the guards are gathering in that big entry room, then they won't be looking for me on the upper floors.*

When Belac reached the end of the hallway, he slowed. The rectangular stairwell was empty and unlit, but it was not visibility that concerned him. *Squeaky stairs could get me caught.* He moved into the stairwell and put his left hand on the banister. Above, the staircase wrapped around left to the second floor. A platform in each corner of the stairwell connected two shorter sets of stairs to a longer set in the center. Belac craned his neck to look up at the balcony behind him. He found nothing but shadows.

Belac looked back to the stairs. He placed a foot on the first step, positioning it at the base of the banister. Slowly, he transferred his weight. No sound came from the stairs. *I need to be super sneaky.* Keeping his feet close to the banister, Belac began to creep up the stairs cautiously. Though it became apparent that the staircase had been built too solidly for the stairs to shift under his weight, the elf restrained himself from racing up. *Super sneaky.* As he slowly made his way up the stairs, Belac listened for sounds from above, but he could hear nothing in the castle. *This place is really quiet when the guards are not stomping around in it.*

The upper entrance to the stairwell was offset from the lower, aligning it with a centered hallway on the second floor. Open doorways lined both sides of the hallway, allowing light to filter in. Despite the known presence of monsters and men, the castle had an abandoned feel to it that was beginning to make Belac's skin crawl. As he stepped out of the shadowed stairwell and into the dimly lit hallway, he wondered what the castle had been like before the nillanan. He imagined happy children running through the halls as dutiful maids gave chase. *I think I hate nillanan more than dragons.*

The second floor of the wing was a continuation of offices and storage rooms. *The stairs must be set up to keep business away from the living quarters.* Belac worried that he would not be able to sneak into the other parts of the castle. *I might need a new plan.* He increased his pace, wanting to see what was around the corner on the other end of the hallway. He glanced into the open rooms as he passed by, but the action was mostly perfunctory.

Belac almost tripped over his own feet as he stumbled to a halt. A lone woman stood in an office to the elf's left. Dark of hair and slim in figure, the woman wore nothing but a baldric strapped between her breast and a harness belted around her waist and thighs. She stood motionlessly, staring at nothing, and silent as death. *My plans are awesome!*

Belac hurried into the room, barely remembering to check for other occupants. His starmetal sword was strapped to the woman's back, and his sephen daggers to her thighs. He set the side-sword he carried down on a nearby desk as he moved to retrieve his stolen weapons. He felt a little conflicted about the nude woman. While he did not like the idea of a woman being used to represent him, he had to admit that he would greatly prefer removing his equipment from a female model.

Belac could not help but appreciate the woman's form as he removed the harness from around her hips. There was nothing to distinguish her from being a servant or the lady of the house. Though less striking than the women that had been present in the other nillanan's subterranean lair, the woman before him would not have escaped Belac's notice even had she been clothed. He paused and considered her vacant eyes. *The nillanan ruined the most beautiful thing about her.*

Belac turned his head away. It suddenly hurt to look at the woman. He watched the door as he buckled the harness around his waist and thighs. He almost wanted a nillanan to walk into the room. *It might be worth dying if I can kill another one of those things first.*

With the daggers in place on his thighs, Belac turned back to the woman. He slipped his baldric up over her head, and then slung the starmetal sword onto his back. The woman's face made him want to cry.

"I'm sorry I can't help you," Belac said softly.

As the elf turned to leave, two men in blue suits entered the room. When they saw Belac, the two men tilted their heads up toward the ceiling and began screaming. *Not good!* Belac rushed forward, grabbing the side-sword in an underhanded grip as he ran toward the door. He thrust his right hand out, stiff-arming one of the men out of the way. The man on the right stumbled backward into the wall, but the second one grabbed Belac, one hand on the elf's left arm and the other on the blade of the side-sword.

The sharpened steel cut into the man's hand as Belac attempted to jerk his arm free. Blood smeared the blade, but the man would not relent. Belac reached across with his right hand and drew the rusted dagger hanging on his left hip. He stabbed the man in the chest three times before the man's hold lost its strength. No sooner was Belac's left arm free, than his right was grabbed from behind.

Belac spun to his right, bringing the bloodied sword up in an underhanded slash that hacked into the side of the assailing man's neck. The blade pushed against bone as its edge slid over the man's spine. The man lost his grip as he collapsed backward, blood pumping from his neck.

The struggle had brought Belac back around to face the nude woman. She was charging at him with her arms held wide. Belac's sword was already in position, the hilt held up to his right shoulder. He leaned in toward the woman, bracing himself as she ran into the tip of his sword. The blade punched through the woman's breastbone and heart, then slid to the side of her spine before exiting her back. When the sword's hilt slammed into her chest, the woman's arms swung forward and slapped the elf feebly.

Belac looked away as the woman slipped from his sword. Then he forced himself to look down at where she lay bloody on the floor. "I'm sorry," he breathed out.

Boots on stairs echoed through the hallway. *They're coming.* A small army of armed guards was not something that Belac thought he could overcome on his own. *I have to get out of here.* With the starmetal sword, he could prove his identity. He could enlist the aid of the city and return. Then he could exterminate the nillanan.

Ten

Still held underhanded, the side-sword swung on Belac's left as he ran down the hallway. A glance over his right shoulder showed him the first of his pursuers rounding the corner. *I just have to get to the window downstairs.* He thought that if he could reach the meeting room, the only thing standing between him and freedom would be a diabolical curtain. He did not consider what would happen when the guards followed him outside.

As Belac entered the stairwell, he was tackled to the floor by a young man wearing a filigreed vest. On his back with the man's shoulder pressed into his midsection, Belac stabbed his rusted dagger into the man's neck twice and then kneed him. As the two rolled to Belac's left side, he saw the young man's father bearing down on them.

Belac braced himself with his left forearm and kicked out sideways with his right foot. The heel of his boot connected with the older man's hip, causing the man to spin as he fell to the floor on Belac's right. Belac rolled toward the older man, stabbing down at him with the tip of the side-sword. The blade sank into the man's back easily but was stopped by a rib on the inside of his chest. Belac stabbed the older man twice more and then scrambled to his feet. The guards were almost to the stairwell.

Belac stumbled to the stairway and then leapt down the top flight of stairs. He landed on the corner platform, bounced off the wall, and then stumbled toward the next flight. Below, guards were rushing up toward him. *I'm trapped!* Belac quickstepped a third of the way down the middle flight of stairs, then stopped. He threw his rusted dagger at the oncoming guards, grabbed the banister, and then vaulted over the side. He continued to turn in the air as he fell until he landed on the ground floor, facing the guards clustered at the entrance to the stairwell.

Shuffling forward, Belac slung his side-sword up above his right shoulder and transferred it to his right hand. His left hand shot out toward the guards for balance, and then he swung the sword over his head in a savage slash that tore through a man's torso where shoulder met neck. Pressing forward, Belac swept his sword to the right, the blade cutting into another guard's neck.

A guard grabbed the elf's left arm. Belac turned toward the guard and slammed the pommel of his sword into the man's forehead. Bone crushed, and the man fell away. Stepping back with his right foot, Belac whipped his sword over his head, swinging it across to his right. The last hand of the sword's blade caught a guard under his cheekbone and ripped into his face.

Belac's left hand swung up and over his head, directing his momentum as he turned around. Using the strength of his entire body, Belac brought his sword over to follow his left hand. The blade arced down, cleaving through another guard's chest. Then a body slammed into the elf from above, driving him to the floor.

Belac twisted under the oppressive weight, shifting onto his back. He pulled his right arm away from the guard as far as he could, then thrust his sword into the side of the man's chest. Hands grabbed Belac's right arm. More pinned down his legs. As his grip was peeled away from his sword, Belac reached for the sephen dagger on his left thigh. The elf's arm was captured before he could touch the dagger's hilt.

Belac thrashed against the guards, attempting to get one of their hands close enough for him to bite it. When he could not reach their hands, he began lunging for their throats. *You people are not feeding me to a nillanan!* The dead guard was pulled from atop Belac, only to be replaced by still more hands to hold the elf captive.

Belac could feel his strength faltering. He continued to struggle as his ability to move became more and more constrained. Bodies filled the bottom of the stairwell until the guards from the upper level were forced to wait, standing on the stairs. There were dozens of men, all silently coordinated. Deft hands confiscated Belac's sephen daggers and then his starmetal sword, leaving the empty scabbards in place. Belac fought for the blades as they were taken from him. However, none of the voiceless guards struck the elf. Through numbers alone, they assured their dominance. *There are too many of them!*

Belac yelled wordlessly in frustration.

The guards seemed not to notice.

Panting, Belac glared at the guards holding him down. *I need to wait for one of them to make a mistake.* He reminded himself that the preservation of strength was not surrender. *Not everything that Ecard said was wrong.* Once more, the elf found himself in a situation in which his greatest advantage was that his enemies did not wish to kill him.

Belac decided to find out if any of the guards were capable of speech. "Oh, hey. I'm... I'm sorry. Am I trespassing?" His eyes searched the guards for awareness. "This is totally my mistake. Complete misunderstanding. How about you just let me go, and I will be on my way?"

None of the guards answered.

Belac turned his head to the left, speaking directly to the man holding his shoulder. "I won't even report this assault to the watchmen."

The guards did not respond.

Belac turned his head to the right and raised his eyebrows at the man holding his other shoulder. "Come on. I sound nice, right?"

There was no response.

Belac shook his head as he searched the other guards. "What if I promise to not come back?" *At least, not without an army of people with pitchforks.*

As one, the men holding Belac lifted him off the floor. *I don't think that they are going to let me go.* His body held horizontally, the elf tilted his head back and attempted to look into the hallway. Blue gambesons blocked his view. *The worst part about this is that I crawled through the privy for nothing.* The guards clogging the stairwell began moving into the hallway, making room for Belac to be carried out behind them.

Belac raised his head up as he was carried from the stairwell. He looked to the guards transporting him. "Hey. You don't need to carry me." He gestured to his right with his head. "You can just set me down, and I'll walk."

The guards did not seem to hear the elf.

"Really," Belac insisted. "You can put me down anywhere." Then he corrected himself. "Well, not anywhere anywhere. Anywhere not prison." *I hate prison.*

As the guards carried Belac past the meeting room, he caught a glimpse of the torn curtain inside. Suddenly, he was overcome with a suspicion that the curtain had somehow found a way to tell the nillanan's servants where to look for him. *Sneaky curtains.* He accepted that his revenge would need to wait.

After being carried through the hallway and into the foyer, Belac was dropped onto the floor. Though his fall was short, the thick carpet that ran down the center of the room was not enough to stop the elf from landing on his tailbone painfully. *Are they really letting me go!* Despite the pain in his backside, Belac sat up. *I can't believe that worked!*

The guards behind him parted to the side of the carpet, creating a path away from the castle's front doors. Belac sighed. *I don't think that they are letting me go.* He rolled onto his hands and knees, and then moved into a kneeling position with his left foot forward.

The foyer was a remarkable display of architectural design. After a broad central stairway, symmetrical flights of stairs connected tiered platforms that would allow access to the various floors of the castle. Though the complex arrangement of staircases was a work of art, Belac's attention was focused on the black robed figure that stood afore them.

The faceless nillanan regarded Belac silently, giving away none of its thoughts or motivations. One of the guards on the elf's left presented the starmetal sword to the nillanan. With the milky white blade resting on his hands, the guard held the hilt out toward his master. On the other side of the divide, two guards each held out one of the elf's sephen daggers in a similar fashion.

The nillanan ignored the weapons, and continued to study the kneeling elf.

Belac stood. Staring into the monster's flesh covered eye sockets, he pointed and spoke with all the authority he could muster. "I want to talk to the nillanan in charge!" *There is no way this works.*

The nillanan rotated its palms, exposing their toothless mouths to the elf. "You are confused," the nillanan's harsh voice spoke in the elf's mind.

Belac was confused. *Why am I here?*

"You do not understand what is happening," the nillanan silently spoke. "You are confused."

Belac staggered, suddenly dizzy. *What… Where….*

"You should not resist," the nillanan's voice grated in the elf's mind. "There is nothing to fear."

The silent words angered Belac. *Fear?! What do you know of fear?* He embraced the memory of the emerald flame. *I will show you fear!* The flames burned the elf's mind. He did not care.

The world sharpened in Belac's vision. *My mind is my own.* The nillanan stumbled back, no longer confident in its superiority. *You are not getting away!* Belac took a deep breath and then roared, imagining a spray of emerald fire.

In the psychic space of their joined minds, virulent green flames poured from the elf's mouth in a torrent that blasted into the unprepared nillanan.

Tears ran down Belac's cheeks as imaginary flames enveloped the nillanan. *You will burn!* The nillanan fell to its knees and held its hands up in impotent defense. Its arms writhed as it attempted to ward off the imagined flames.

As soon as his breath ran out, Belac rushed forward. He grabbed the hilt of the starmetal sword still held out by a mindless guard, and slashed violently at the nillanan. The milky white blade sliced through the nillanan's neck and left arm, severing both its head and arm from its body. Belac stumbled sideways onto the stairs as his momentum drove him past the decapitated monster.

Laid out on the steps, Belac turned to look down at the thing that he had slain. *My mind is my own. But now, the fear is yours.* He let go of the emerald flame.

Eleven

Blood dripped from the butchered curtain that Belac was using as a sack. The dark maroon droplets left a trail on the flagstones that led back to the castle of House Vesper. The guards inside had died immediately after the nillanan, leaving Belac seated alone on the magnificent staircase like it was a throne in the halls of Death.

Too much of the men's minds had been taken from them. Without the will of the nillanan to rule them, the guards had simply stopped breathing. Belac had felt no thrill of victory as he stood and walked over the bodies of the fallen guards. Pressing into the silence of the dead castle, Belac had then began calling out to anyone who might be able to hear him. He had searched every floor, but found no one still drawing breath. Unless the building contained a hidden storage room or secret dungeon, there had been no children there for him to find. He was not comforted by their absence.

Belac stopped at the estate's black iron gate. *I wonder what the watchmen will do if they see me climbing over this thing. I'm covered in blood, and I'm carrying a bloody sack. I don't think that they will offer me a medal.*

He glanced at the gate's attendant's booth. *Maybe there is a key in there.* He shook his head. *I don't feel like searching for something else that is probably not there.* He swung the lumpy sack back, and then lobbed it up over the gate. The sack landed on the other side with a wet thud.

Belac ran forward, leapt, and put his left foot in the 'S' of the gate's iron letters. He grabbed the top of the gate as his waist slammed into it, and then he swung his legs over. As he attempted to vault over the gate, the empty scabbard on his left hip got caught in the bars. Instead of landing deftly on the other side, Belac found himself hanging sideways by the belt around his waist. *Please, don't let this be how the watchmen catch me.*

With his right hand gripping one of the gate's vertical bars for balance, Belac tried to dislodge the scabbard with his left. The supple leather belt snapped, dropping Belac on one side of the gate, and the scabbard on the other. The elf landed on his feet and stumbled away from the gate. Then he tripped over the bloody sack and fell backward onto the flagstones. *Graceful! I'm an elf. I am supposed to be graceful!*

Belac sat up and glared at the gate. "Fine! Keep the stupid thing!" *I am not crawling back over that gate to get an empty scabbard.*

Belac got to his feet, snatching up the sack as he stood. *I didn't need that old scabbard anyway.* He wondered how much the cobbler would bill the Elven delegation for the rusted dagger. It was possible that they would not pay the man anything. Belac did not know how expenses were handled by the delegation. For all he knew, it might very well be the crown that paid for the dagger.

As Belac stepped off the flagstones and began walking up the city street, he questioned what else he might not know. The list grew rather quickly. *I need to talk to whoever is in charge of this city. If they can't help me, then maybe I can use them to make the delegation help me.* His plan was a bit stifled by the fact that he did not know who was in charge of the city. King or council, each would present their own difficulties.

Ahead, two men stood next to an iron grate in the center of a roundabout. Though both were younger than the watchmen that Belac had seen earlier, the red stripe across each of their chest marked them clearly. The men seemed less concerned with the safety of the nobles, and more with whatever it was they were speaking about. One of the men gesticulated as he spoke, while the other stood with his arms crossed. They did not appear to be discussing the many dangers of their city. *I bet that they can tell me where I need to go.*

Belac walked up to the two watchmen and stopped. Neither of the men seem to notice him.

"I'm telling you, it was Charly," the gesticulating watchman said to his partner. "He hates Michels."

The other watchman shook his head. "It wasn't him."

The more animated watchman held out his hands. "What makes you so sure?"

Arms still crossed, the other watchman replied, "Charly has been sleeping with Hariet. If she found out, she would cut that man's…" The watchman noticed that he and his partner were no longer alone. He uncrossed his arms and motioned to the elf.

Belac waited for both of the men to look at him before asking, "Which way to the palace?" *A city this size has to have a palace.*

Both of the watchmen stared at the elf as if they were uncertain that he was real.

Weapons strapped over his blood-soaked clothes, Belac stared back unapologetically. "Which way?" he asked again.

The more animated watchman pointed uncertainly to the northwest.

Belac nodded a curt thanks and then marched off in the direction indicated.

The other watchman noticed the elf's bulging sack. "What is that there?"

"Hey, you," the animated watchman began and then raised his voice. "Wait there!"

Belac ignored the command and continued walking away. He was in no mood to argue with another watchman.

The watchmen let Belac go. Evidently, they decided that if the elf needed to be arrested, there would be plenty of guards at the palace who could do it. With an Elven delegation present in the city, the arrest of an elf might prove detrimental to the men's careers. Neither of the young watchmen had any desire to trade gossiping amidst gardens and castles for an assignment that could get them murdered in a darkened alleyway.

Belac returned to the artisans' district. However, instead of turning south toward the old cobbler's shop, he continued to follow the early evening sun. Though there were fewer people in the streets, all of them moved out of Belac's path. *These people are acting like they have never seen an elf before.* A trail of murmurs drifted along behind him as he carried the bloody sack through the district.

When a second pair of watchmen saw the disturbing elf, they responded with more alacrity than the first. The watchman on the left held up a hand as he and his partner approached. "Stop there," the watchman ordered. Despite the authority in his voice, the man could not have been much older than the last two watchmen.

Belac accepted that the city watch was not going to allow him to pass unmolested. Even if he were able to convince the two watchmen attempting to stop him now, there would certainly be more on the way to the palace. *Maybe this is a problem that can fix itself.*

Belac halted. "Excellent," he said approvingly. "I found you." He pointed past the men with his entire hand. "You two need to escort me to the palace."

The watchman on the left furrowed his brow distrustfully. "Says who?"

Belac shook his head. "I didn't get a name." He tried to think of a vague description that would sound specific. "Older man," he held a hand up to his own jaw, "had a beard."

The watchman on the right ventured a guess. "Sergeant Reagan?"

Not wanting to give the men too much time to think, Belac waved his hand forward. "Let's go," he ordered impatiently.

The two watchmen turned to look at each other, the motion creating a momentum that encouraged them to keep turning until they were facing the direction that Belac wanted to go. Though their steps were hesitant at first, they quickly became more sure. *And now, I look official.*

As Belac followed the watchmen, he took the opportunity to appraise the city. Collectively, the shops and small businesses were as impressive as the homes of the nobles. Despite their smaller size and tightly packed arrangement, the buildings had been constructed with the same materials and mastery of craftsmanship as the private castles. He decided that the exaggerated edging on the buildings' corners and entries was just enough to prevent the gray stone from seeming stark.

Belac and his escort passed by several pairs of watchmen as he was led toward the palace, but none did more than stare. When the palace came into view, Belac was stunned by its size. *That thing is bigger than all of Gofell!* He was amazed that something so large could be hidden behind the three and four-story buildings that it dwarfed. Twice as tall as even the largest of the nobles' castles, the palace was a monument unto itself.

The less authoritative of the two escorts glanced over his shoulder and asked, "Do you mind if I ask what is in the bag?"

Belac hefted the lumpy sack before answering, "It's a delivery."

"For the king?" the inquisitive man asked.

Now, I know there is a king. Belac nodded. "It is important that he gets it soon." *Before somebody tries to take it away from me.*

"It uhm…" The watchman glanced back again. "It must be important."

Belac nodded. "I will be sure to tell him that you kept me safe," he said in a tone that he thought was both reassuring and dismissive.

Pleased by the promise, the watchman slapped his partner's arm. "Did you hear that, Preston?"

"Enough, Hanze," Preston snapped irritably. "The elf would not need an escort without reason. Shut your mouth, and do your job."

Yes, please.

Twelve

While the walk to the palace was not exactly quiet, Hanze kept his questions to himself. Preston, the other of Belac's two escorts, gave no indication that he was interested in conversation. *I don't want to talk to him anyway.* Belac did not think that the authoritative watchman was very nice. Also, dialogue would only make it more difficult for Belac to maintain his own authoritative facade.

It took longer to reach the palace than Belac had originally anticipated. Along the way, he alternated between carrying the bloody sack in his left and right hand. By the time he reached the hardscaped public square in front of the palace, he found himself regretting his decision to bring the sack. *I am committed now. I think my escorts would probably notice if I dropped my 'important delivery' in the street and then just kept walking.*

The palace itself was a mammoth structure of gray stone and bright blue tiles. *That thing has to be at least twice as tall as any of the smaller castles. That makes it what? Ten, twelve stories high? And that is not counting attics and anything built underground.* Though the multi-teared design of the palace's rooves made it difficult for Belac to determine how many floors the building might have, the esthetics were not lost on him.

Scattered groups of petitioners, courtesans, and soldiers moved about the square, each cadre intent on their own personalized endeavors. Despite the elf's gruesome state, none of the drifting groups seemed to take notice. As Belac crossed the square, he wondered how such oblivious people could maintain wealth and power. *How prosperous does a nation need to be for ignorance to become a virtue?* He shook his head and marched on toward the wide, gentle steps that would take him and his escorts to the palace doors.

The steps irritated Belac. *These stairs are made wrong.* The top of each step was deep enough to necessitate a walk to the next, and the distance did not match the elf's natural gait. *Stupid humans. Either make your stairs right, or just put in a ramp!* His disgruntlement did not prevent him from acknowledging that the visual effect was actually rather artful. *Still... They could have just painted stairs on a ramp. Then, I wouldn't have to trip the whole way up.*

After the relatively short climb up the stairs, Belac stepped into the shade of the palace's stone portico. To each side of the open doors ahead, stood an armored guard bearing a short-handled pike with a rounded guard under its long spike. Belac thought that the doorway was too large for two men alone to halt a determined force, and that the doors would be too heavy for them to close quickly. *The guards are just for show. No one here really expects to be attacked.*

Clad in steel plate and holding their awl pikes grounded, the ornamental guards gave no sign that they even registered the elf's presence. As Belac approached the entrance, he appraised the guards' flat-topped, full-faced helmets and their long battle skirts edged in white fur. *Those guys have got to be miserable in that stuff.* He did not think that the guards would be able to fight for very long before heat exhausted them.

The motionless nature of the palace guards concerned Belac. What appeared to be discipline, might actually be enslavement to the nillanan. *If the nillanan have infiltrated the palace, I am going to have bigger problems than just a couple of guards.*

Hiding his reticence behind a stoic face, Belac followed his escorts into the palace. The guards remained motionless at their posts. *Maybe they just figured out how to sleep standing up.*

The interior of the palace was warm wood over a cold stone floor. Six tall pillars held up a vaulted ceiling three stories high. Though the pillars gleamed with the luster of polished wood, Belac thought that there must be stone cores underneath. Carved into the palace's dark stained wood, leafy vines crawled along the walls. Belac narrowed his eyes at the first pillar on his left, disliking the carvings' resemblance to Vaquian iconography. *If I see one thorn, I am setting this place on fire.*

Without so much as glancing at the passageways to the left and right, the two watchmen escorting Belac marched forward between the central pillars and began making their way toward a larger corridor. Five men in stately attire crossed from one side of the foyer to the other, bickering quietly as they passed by. Belac's attention tracked the five men as he followed his escorts through the otherwise empty foyer. *That is what scheming looks like.* The men moved into one of the side passages shortly before Belac stepped into the central corridor.

The men blocked from his view, Belac redirected his gaze into the corridor. Ahead, at the end of the corridor, a palace guard waited on each side of a set of closed double doors. *It looks like they are supposed to keep people out.* Though the palace guards ahead were as motionless as the ones outside, the closed doors and walled space made them seem far less welcoming. Belac hoped that his escort would be able to convince the guards that his arrival was official. However, he worried that it might be difficult to seem sufficiently officious while covered in dried blood. *Maybe I should tilt my head back and look down my nose. Self-important people do that all the time.*

One of the palace guards took a step forward, planted his awl pike and declared, "None shall pass," in a haunting voice that echoed in his helmet.

Hanze laughed.

Preston did not. "Stuff it, Danny. You are supposed to be serious." With his head, he indicated to the elf behind himself. "We are escorting one of the delegates."

Danny chuckled inside his helmet. "I am at least half serious." He did not sound fazed by the elf's presence. "They are still holding court in there."

Preston would not be deterred. "We are under orders from Sergeant Reagan."

No, you're not.

From his place next to the closed doors, the other guard said, "Maybe you are finally going to get promoted."

Probably not.

Danny shrugged his steel clad shoulders and then took a step to the side. "If you want to go in, that's on you. But, you know how the king can be." He pointed his free hand at the elf. "You can leave your weapons out here with us."

"No," Belac replied in a tone that brooked no argument. "If I cannot enter armed, I am not welcome. If I am not welcome, I will leave." He decided to make the threat more overt. "If I leave, I will not return."

Danny turned to the other palace guard, unsure how to handle the nonviolent threat.

The other guard held up a hand, indicating that he had no insight to offer.

Preston attempted to intervene. "This is a special case," he insisted. "You have to let us in."

Hanze leaned forward and spoke under his breath. "He is just a skinny elf. What do you think he is going to do?"

Belac narrowed his eyes at the back of the watchman's head.

"Yeah, okay. Fine," Danny said, waving them on. "But the Watch can take the heat. I am not getting reassigned over this."

The other guard reached for the door closest to himself. "It's your funerals." He pulled open the door.

"...will not grow..." a man's voice carried into the corridor before stopping abruptly.

Belac turned sideways and stepped between his two escorts. "You can all wait here." *I don't see how bringing more armed men into the courtroom would be in my favor if the king decides to kill me.*

Before any of the four men could argue, Belac strode into the courtroom. The circular chamber was even larger than the foyer. High above, a dome ceiling of blue and white glass lit the interior. *How does that not fall down?*

To the elf's left and right, ostentatiously dressed nobles congregated on either side of a roped walkway. Quiet anticipation had spread through those gathered. On a raised dais ahead, a barrel-chested man clothed in gray velvet sat on a silvered throne.

The king of this unknown city looked exactly how Belac thought a human patriarch should look. Much of the man's rounded features were hidden behind his long, wavy, black hair and his neatly trimmed beard. However, his posture was that of a man expecting to be seen. Seated alone in his place of elevation, the king shared his dais with none. *That is not a friendly looking man.*

Though the king said nothing, hushed voices followed Belac as he walked down the aisle. Covered in darkly dried blood and armed with a sword, the elf knew it was only a matter of time before the palace guards responded to his intrusion. While blood no longer dripped from the sack he carried, it glistened wetly still. *I need to explain myself before everyone's confusion wears off.* He kept his stride confident, and his gaze focused on the king. *This may not have been my best idea ever.*

As Belac stepped away from the gathered nobles, two palace guards moved forward to intercept him. Belac halted, realizing that he would be allowed to get no closer to the king. The two guards halted as well, each with their awl pike held at the ready.

The king continued to say nothing.

Belac raised his voice above the hum of the crowd. "You have a problem," he announced as he began untying the bloody sack.

Still, the king said nothing.

"Nillanan have invaded your city," Belac stated loudly and then shook out the contents of the sack.

Two severed heads and four hands fell onto the courtroom's stone floor. One of the heads rolled toward the dais before rocking to a stop. Though faceless in the strictest sense, the shape under its scar-textured skin belied the humanoid skull. Three of the hands landed palms up, displaying toothless mouths that gaped open slackly.

The nobles who could see the presentation gasped in dismay. Many backed away in horror while others moved forward to view the macabre scene. Speculative chatter rose in the crowd.

With his eyes locked on the king, Belac said, "You're welcome."

The king studied the gruesome evidence for a moment and then met the elf's eyes. Drawing in his air of command, the king pointed at the elf before bellowing, "Somebody get that elf a drink!"

Thirteen

Though the king's private pool offered little in the way of actual privacy, Belac had decided that it was by far one of his most favorite places in all the world. It was not the finely sculpted stone or the open balcony that he appreciated, but the very servants that denied the king and him privacy. There, they could relax in the heated water while anything that they wanted was brought to them. The elf had mostly wanted wine.

King Rodric Everan, sovereign of the Kingdom of Lindell, spoke with a theatrical voice that was confident to the point of sounding boisterous. "Right!" He laughed. "But what I don't understand, is why you did not simply use the curtains all the way down."

Belac turned to his left and looked at where the king sat in the water on the other side of the corner they shared. He closed one eye to better scrutinize the king. "What?"

Rodric gestured vaguely with a heavy goblet and explained, "The castle almost certainly has curtains on every floor. Why did you not simply repeat the process of lowering yourself with the use of the curtains? Surely it would have been a way down that was both safer and faster than going through the sewer."

"I..." *I did not think of that.* Belac pointed his empty goblet at the king. "There was kind of a lot happening all at once, Roger."

Rodric laughed.

Belac gestured dismissively with his goblet. "Besides, I think the curtains were working for the nillanan."

Rodric slammed his goblet down by the side of the pool and roared with mirth.

Belac found himself laughing with the king. It was hard for him not to. The king's laugh had a lack of restraint that made it infectious.

Rodric pointed a finger at the elf. "I will tell you what. I will gift you the castle, and you can deal with the traitorous curtains however you see fit."

Belac's eyebrows attempted to rise off of his forehead. "You want to give me a castle?!" His ensuing smile showed off every tooth that he had. "Are you making me a lord?"

"No," Rodric shook his head. "No, Belac. I would not do that to you," he said as if sparing the elf a punitive sentence.

Belac held up a hand. "Okay. I'll take it." *Because… It's a castle. Who doesn't want a castle?* He pointed a finger at the king. "But, won't the other nobles get upset if you start just giving away their castles?"

"I do not give one whit if I upset those milksops," Rodric proclaimed as he took up his goblet. He drained the contents and then shook the empty goblet at the elf. "You know what? Scratch that. I hope I do upset them." He pointed away with the goblet. "The first one of them that complains, I am going to order to go out and hunt a nillanan for me." He smiled at the idea. "I hope it's that twit Nasher."

Belac glanced at the servants attending the swim room. *Something tells me that Nasher will know to keep his mouth shut.* It suddenly occurred to Belac that the king might be using the gossipy servants to manipulate the nobles. He reconsidered the hairy man sharing the pool with him. *This guy is really smart for a human.*

Rodric gestured for a servant to refill his goblet. "The two nillanan heads that you brought me, I am having mounted. All that remains is for me to decide where I want them displayed."

Belac furrowed his brow. "Why is it, 'one nillanan' and 'two nillanan?' It's 'one human' and 'two humans.' Why is there no 'S?' Shouldn't it be, 'one nillanan' and 'two nillanans?" Belac was only reasonably sure that his question made sense.

Rodric shrugged. "I have never thought about it. It is 'one sheep,' 'two sheep."

Belac nodded and pointed at the king. "It should be sheeps."

Rodric took a drink from his goblet before replying diplomatically, "I am sure that the Dwarves had reasons for constructing the language as they did."

"Why don't humans just make their own language?" Belac asked as he set his goblet down and waved a servant to fill it. "Maybe you could get a wizard to make it for you."

Rodric tipped his goblet slightly, acknowledging the elf's suggestion. "We, humans, are accustomed to speaking Dwarven. It has become our language now as much as it is theirs. Besides, I do not know any out-of-work wizards to employ."

"Serath is a wizard," Belac thought to remind the king. "I bet he could help you find someone to make the language." He frowned. "Or maybe not. Do you think wizards have meetings?" He looked up as he considered. "I bet they have meetings."

"You say, Serath is a wizard?" Rodric asked speculatively. "That... That would certainly make sense."

Belac redirected his attention to the king. "You said that you know Serath."

"I do," Rodric agreed. "I was simply not aware that he is a wizard." He shrugged. "Though, he is a man of many secrets." He waved the matter aside. "Fret not. You will be reunited soon enough. I will have word sent to the Temple of the Ancient. They can use the ponds to relay your message to Harbridge." He smiled. "Maybe I should have some more wizardly looking robes made for him."

Belac scoffed. "Unless they are black, I don't think he would wear them." He began drinking from his freshly filled goblet, and then pointed at the king insistently as a thought came to him. "But maybe we could trick him into wearing a fancy cape!"

"Do wizards wear capes?" Rodric asked skeptically.

Belac shrugged. "Why wouldn't they?" He began gesticulating with excitement as another idea came to him. "What if we just start sowing patches onto his big coat when he is not paying attention?!"

Rodric laughed.

Belac pointed at the king. "The first one needs to have a pink bunny on it."

"You are going to get yourself turned into a frog," Rodric said, laughing.

Belac nodded and pointed at the king approvingly. "We also need one with a frog."

"Belac, my friend," Rodric said loudly, his voice both commanding and concerned, "this is a truly awful idea." He leaned toward the elf. "But, I dare say, I should like to see it done!"

Belac had found that his plans worked better when he had more than one. "Maybe we should try the cape first."

Rodric held up a finger. "Or a hat!"

"A hat?" Belac had a hard time picturing the wizard wearing a hat.

Rodric nodded. "I am certain that I have seen a portrait of a wizard wearing a hat." He gestured dismissively. "Somewhere." He looked away as he attempted to recall the image. "It was tall and pointed, with an excessively wide brim." He returned his attention to the elf. "It was a silly looking thing, really."

Belac drank from his goblet. *I don't think that Serath is going to wear a hat like that.* He held the goblet up as an idea came to him. "I know who needs a hat!" He pointed at the king with the edge of the goblet. "Rolan." He furrowed his brow. "Do you know Rolan?"

"I cannot say that I do," Rodric admitted. "Is he another wizard?"

Belac considered some of the things he had seen the dwarf do. The glow of soulstones filled his mind. "Almost."

Rodric waved for more wine. "Then, he should have a hat."

Belac nodded in agreement. "He is kind of short. A hat would make him look bigger."

Rodric set his goblet down so that it could be filled. "I suggest that you refrain from explaining your reasoning when you present him with the hat. That is, if you wish to see him wear it."

Belac shrugged. "I don't know if he would wear it anyway." *If Rolan wanted a hat, he would probably have one.*

Rodric reclaimed his goblet and took a drink from it before replying, "Still, it is best not to insult a man with a gift."

"How is a hat an insult?" Belac asked, confused. "Is it because I said, he was short?" He leaned in and nodded confidingly. "Rolan knows that he's short."

Rodric lost no confidence for being challenged. "As that may be, my Elven friend, your reasoning implies a deficiency that need be corrected." He tapped the tip of his own nose. "Insult."

"That..." Belac trailed off as he worked through the logic. *I... I think I may have just figured out why a lot of people don't like me.*

Fourteen

Two elven men draped in long, silk vestments hurried through the palace hallway. As their amethyst eyes searched the shadows, the glossy black strands of their hair splayed over their slim shoulders. Farther down the hallway, an elegant woman in a voluminous, powder blue dress stood to the side, regarding the elves curiously.

"I know that he went this way, Vaserie," one of the elves said to the other in Elven. "There is no other way that he could have gone."

Vaserie swept his long, black hair off of his left shoulder as he turned toward the other elf. "No, Alamain," he disagreed in Elven. "You believe that he went this way. Just as you believed that he went the way that you believed, the last time that you believed that you knew he could go no other way. And the time before that. And the time before that. And so on." He swept the hair off of his other shoulder as he looked away. "You will need to forgive me if I no longer have faith in your beliefs."

Alamain scowled at his compatriot and then gestured to the woman ahead. "We should ask the human if she has seen him," he suggested in Elven.

"Is that because you believe humans to be universally wise and observant?" Vaserie asked snippily in Elven.

Alamain glanced irritably at the other elf before replying in Elven, "It requires no great wit to see an aberrant elf running through the king's palace."

"Is that the belief that has led you to believe that you know which way he has gone?" Vaserie asked, the Elven language straining the insult.

Alamain said nothing more as they approached the woman, then he smiled broadly and addressed her with refined politeness. "My greetings, fair lady. Would you by chance have happened to see Belac Melavar? He is of elven heritage," he indicated to his left ear, "such as myself."

Blushing, the woman replied, "The Dragon Slayer?" She nodded. "He is very handsome."

Vaserie closed his eyes and muttered in Elven, "Simple minded human."

Alamain fought to maintain his false smile. Ignoring the other elf, he acknowledged, "It seems as though he has so been called." He held his hand out with his palm up, and gestured to the woman as if offering her something. "Do you know where he has gone?"

"I…" the woman shook her head as if unsure how to answer. "When?" she asked.

"No great wit indeed," Vaserie said in Elven before walking away.

Alamain turned his head toward the other elf. "Shut up, Vaserie!" he snapped in Elven. Turning back to the woman, he returned to speaking Dwarven. "Thank you for your time. It was very much appreciated." He almost sounded sincere.

Alamain hurried off after the other elf, his steps swift and determined. He caught up to Vaserie, and then continued down the hallway with him until they decided to explore different directions; Alamain going left, and Vaserie right.

Once the Elven delegates were out of view, the woman said, "They are gone."

Belac's wine bottle clunked on the wooden floorboards as he climbed out from under the hem of the woman's dress. He untangled his sword from her petticoat and then stood. With his free hand, he brushed off his newly tailored, gray trousers, and fluffed out his crisp white blouse. Then, holding his bottle of wine out for balance, he leaned over and kissed the woman on her cheek. "Lovely."

The woman rolled her amber eyes.

Belac hopped back and then spun on one foot before walking away with a bounce in his step. Headed in the opposite direction as the other elves, he began making his way back to the king's parlor. Recently, Belac had spent his days cycling between enjoying the king's hospitality and hiding from the Elven delegation. He had come to believe that each activity was dependent on the other. *If those stuffy elves catch me, there is no way that they will let me keep having fun.*

The king's parlor was a large room connected to a theater by a series of more modestly sized chambers. Belac liked the parlor more than even the swim room. He could still have anything he wanted, but if he drank too much and passed out, he would not risk drowning while seated on the parlor's padded leather furniture the way he had in the heated water. Such an occurrence had only happened twice in the pool.

In that moment, what Belac wanted was to watch another play. More than merely entertaining, the plays had become somewhat of a project for the elf. He had thought it strange that they made men act out the parts of women, when there were so many beautiful women in the palace. He had needed to beg Rodric to allow women to play the roles of women. So far, all the women's performances had been abysmal. However, Belac had insisted that the women would improve if given the chance. Rodric had continued to allow their participation, though it was largely because he found their blundering on stage to be amusing.

Once the women had improved enough to prove his point, Belac's plan was to replace all the male actors with women. *Who wants to watch a bunch of men sing and dance anyway?* Belac did not understand how such a wise king had allowed his entertainment to become so backward. *Helping to design the new costumes should be fun too.*

Belac halted in front of two palace guards that were standing in the hallway next to the doors to the king's parlor. He crossed his arms and made a show of inspecting the posted guards. "What's the password?" Belac asked suspiciously.

The flat-topped helmet of the guard on the left shook side to side. "That is not how passwords work."

Belac nodded as if in deep contemplation before replying, "I think you forgot the password." He uncrossed his arms and shook a finger at the guard. "You did, didn't you."

The metal helmet lowered slightly as the man inside shook his head again. "There is no password, Belac."

Belac nodded and then shook his finger at the guard again. "Then, how am I supposed to know if it is safe to go inside?"

"It's safe," the guard replied, deadpan.

"And I would believe that," Belac said as he crossed his arms again. "If you knew the password."

The guards helmet tilted up toward the ceiling. "That is not how passwords work, Belac."

Belac threw his arms out wide. "How would you know?!" He leaned forward. "You don't even know what the password is!"

The guard on the right broke out in laughter, the sound echoing in his helmet.

Belac stepped closer to the guard on the right and then gestured to the other. "This guy." He shook his head. "He doesn't even know the password." He held out his bottle of wine in camaraderie.

The guard on the right turned toward his partner.

"Don't," the other guard said.

The guard on the right turned to the elf and shrugged. "Can't"

Belac shrugged in return and then took a drink from the bottle. "Fine." He gestured to the doors. "I guess I will just have to risk my safety inside." He rolled his shoulders bravely. "For the king."

"Right," said the guard on the left, deadpan again. "For the king."

The guards opened the doors and Belac stepped into the lavishness that was the king's personal reprieve. *Anyone that does not like humans has never been in a place like this.* Belac could not fathom how the Elves ever got their delegates to return home.

"Hey, Roger!" Belac called out happily as he entered the parlor.

A dark-haired woman in a gown of spiraling blue and white strips turned toward the elf's bombastic entrance. Tall and thin, the woman had a severe beauty that was at odds with her surroundings. She studied the elf openly before issuing a wicked grin. "My, you are pretty," she said as if eyeing a meal.

Belac preened. With a smile, he tilted his head back and replied, "I like you too."

Rodric's commanding voice carried from the other side of the room. "She is married, Belac."

Belac hopped back like he had almost stepped on a snake. *It's a trap!*

The woman spun toward the king and glared. "Why must you ruin everything?!"

Rodric walked closer, the cup of his goblet resting in the palm of his hand. "I am the king," he replied reasonably. "Evidently, it is my highest duty to ruin everyone else's fun."

"Not mine," Belac objected without thinking.

Rodric held his goblet up in salute. "Quite right."

The woman made a sound of irate frustration and then began marching toward the doors behind Belac, causing him to stumble out of her way as she stormed out of the room. *I like her a lot less now.*

Belac looked to the king. "Aren't married women supposed to wear a shawl or something?" *Or at least act like they're married.*

Rodric gestured vaguely with his free hand. "Some other kingdoms use bits of cloth. In Lindell, married women wear earrings to declare their unions."

Belac thought back over the last few days, realizing that he had made more than one mistake. *This is not my fault!*

Rodric's gray velvets shimmered as he took a seat in an oversized armchair. "I am convinced that a jeweler invented the custom."

Belac pointed his thumb toward the doors. "But she wasn't wearing anything on her ears."

Rodric nodded. "Women will often remove them." He frowned. "Some women have more virtuous reasons than others."

Belac took a drink of wine and then pointed the neck of his bottle at the king. "You should make married people tattoo an X on their forehead or something."

Rodric laughed at the suggestion. "I will be sure to relay your proposal at the next convening of the high council."

Fifteen

Belac's bare feet were silent as he walked through the palace hallways. Clothed in nothing but gray swim shorts, he knew that he must look odd traipsing around the palace with his starmetal sword strapped to his naked back. He was not overly concerned with his appearance. While he was willing to risk leaving his sephen daggers in his quarters, the starmetal sword was simply too important to leave unattended. No amount of assurance had been able to convince him otherwise.

Belac walked into the king's swim room, disappointed to find only two servants waiting for him. He would need to send at least one of them to fetch wine. He had wanted to try having music brought into the swim room, but sending both servants on errands would leave no one there for him to talk to. *I guess some sacrifices must be made.*

"Hello, gentlemen," Belac said as he walked over to the edge of the pool. He set down an almost empty bottle of wine and then turned to the two men dressed in gray suits.

As both of the servants bowed, the younger of the two replied, "Hello, Master Belac."

Belac like being called 'Master' even less than he did 'Lord.' *Maybe I should make up a new title. I could use an Elven word. That way, I could make people call me whatever I want.* He decided that he could think of something later. *I need to prioritize.*

Belac walked over to the two servants and then crossed his arms. "Which one of you is the spy?" he asked authoritatively.

Both of the men glanced at each other. Neither of them had any idea how to answer the question.

Belac narrowed his eyes. "Maybe… It's both of you!" he declared dramatically.

The men began shaking their heads emphatically, the younger man on the verge of panic.

Belac laughed. "I'm just playing with you." He pointed toward the men without indicating to either of them. "I need one of you to go get wine. And the other to go get a harp and someone that knows how to make it work."

"A harp?" the older servant asked as if worried that he had misunderstood.

Belac nodded. "One of those big musicy things with the strings." He mimed playing a harp with both hands.

"Of course, Master Belac," the older servant replied before grabbing the younger's arm and pulling him away.

Belac considered the men as they all but fled the room. *It's possible that one of them might actually be a spy.* He shrugged. *At least now, they will think that I am on to them.*

Once the servants had exited the swim room, Belac walked over to a large, iron strongbox. He reached up to his chest and took hold of the key that hung there by a leather thong. He slipped the thong over his head and then inserted the key into the lock hanging from a latch on the front side of the strongbox. He disengaged the lock with a twist, then removed it from the box. Using both hands, he lifted the hinged lid and leaned it against the stone wall. He had been told that he did not need to lock the strongbox every time that he left the swim room, but he worried that if he did not, something hazardous might be waiting for him inside when he returned.

Belac removed his scabbarded sword and placed it into the empty box. *Maybe I should keep a snake or something in the box.* He closed the heavy lid and then relocked it. *That way, if somebody breaks in, they get bit.* He frowned as he slipped the key's thong back over his head. *I just need to figure out how to not get bit myself.*

Belac walked over to the pool, stepped down into the heated water, and took a seat. *I wonder if my castle has a pool.* He let himself relax in the water. *I guess I don't really need a pool. I can probably get by with just an extra big bathtub.* He grabbed his bottle of wine and finished off its contents. *How big can they make bathtubs?* He imagined a copper bathtub approximately half the size of the pool he was in. *That would probably work.*

The younger servant walked into the swim room pushing a wine cart with a collection of goblets rattling around on top. Belac held up his empty wine bottle, glad for the man's return. The servant positioned the cart against the wall, and then began preparing a goblet for the elf. *I wonder if the castle comes with new servants.* Belac suspected that his castle would probably come unstaffed.

That's fine. I can go get my own wine. An idea came to him. *Or, I could get a dog!* He envisioned a large hound with a harness that held multiple bottles of wine against the beast's sides. *It could bring me wine, and it would bite anyone else that tried to take it!*

The servant brought over a goblet filled with wine. "Here you are, Master Belac," he said as he presented the drink. "This is one of the reds that the king favors."

Nodding his thanks, Belac traded his empty bottle for the goblet. He leaned in toward the servant and asked conspiratorially, "Do you think the other guy is the spy?"

The servant's eyes widened. "I... He..." he stammered, shaking his head in denial.

Belac nodded. "Don't worry." He shook his head. "I won't tell him that you told me."

The servant backed away hurriedly, retreating to the wine cart.

Belac took a drink of the wine and then set the goblet down. *I wonder how long I will need to wait for the harp to get here.* He imagined a beautiful woman in a sheer gown strumming a harp that was larger than she was. Then the woman lunged at Belac and stabbed him with a knife.

"Aaaah!" Belac yelled as he splashed away from the edge of the pool.

To cover his response to the imaginary attack, Belac swam to the far side of the pool before returning to his goblet. *Living in a palace is dangerous.* He narrowed his eyes and scanned the swim room. *There are spies everywhere.*

The door to the swim room opened and a palace guard stepped inside. He looked around, and then marched back into the hallway. A moment later, King Rodric walked into the room wearing swim shorts that matched the elf's.

Belac's arms splashed out of the water as he raised them. "Roger!" *Now, I have someone to talk to that is not a spy!*

Rodric held up a magnum bottle that was encased in a pewter shell. "Look at what I found."

"Hey, that looks fancy," Belac acknowledged. Intrigued, he leaned forward and asked, "What is it?"

Rodric spread his arms wide. "It is a mystery, my friend." He smiled broadly. "But I bet we can drink it."

Belac nodded happily.

Rodric walked over to the wine cart and handed the fancy bottle to the servant. "Bring the bottle with my goblet."

The servant took the bottle as if accepting a sacred artifact. "Yes, Your Majesty."

Rodric then climbed down into the pool and sat in a corner with his arms resting on the sides. "Just between you and me, Belac. Some days, I wish a plague would take the noble houses."

You mean, between you and me and that spy over there. Belac narrowed his eyes at the servant.

Rodric gazed out to the failing light beyond the balcony. "Every one of them has more than they could ever need, and yet, all of them want more. Always more."

"You need to pit them against each other," Belac replied without thinking.

"Oh?" Rodric asked as if preparing himself for a joke. "Why do you say that?"

Belac shrugged. "If you don't trick the nobles into stealing from each other, they are just going to steal from you and your people instead."

Rodric was quiet for a moment before decreeing, "You, my friend, deserve a fancy drink." He turned toward the wine cart. "Where are we with that bottle?"

The servant turned around and bowed his head. "I am sorry, Your Majesty. The muselet was difficult to remove. I am about to pull the cork now."

Rodric nodded, waving his hand dismissively. He turned toward the elf and inquired, "Has your delegation caught you yet?"

"Nope." Belac shook his head and then pointed at the king. "And don't say, 'yet."

Rodric chuckled. "They are different than you are."

Though Belac now knew why, he could not tell the king. *I may not get my fancy drink if I tell him, it is because my father is a giant-evil-lizard-with-wings.*

The servant brought Rodric the opened bottle and a filled goblet. The king took both of the items, but then set the bottle aside. He sniffed at the goblet.

"Interesting," Rodric assessed, moving the goblet away from his face. "It is strong, whatever it is." He dared a drink. "Oh. This is rather nice." He waved the elf closer as he reached for the bottle. "You should try some of this."

Belac snatched up his own goblet and downed the rest of the wine. Then he waded over to the king and held out the empty goblet. Thick golden liquid poured from the ornate bottle as Rodric filled the elf's cup. *It almost looks too thick to drink.*

His goblet full, Belac took a sniff of the golden liquid it held. *Oh. Yeah. That's strong.* He took a sip and then exclaimed, "Wow! It's like honey that can get you drunk!" The drink was accompanied with a warm buzzing sensation that he found rather pleasant.

Rodric held the bottle out for his own inspection. "I will need to ascertain the…"

The door to the swim room banged open as two servants stumbled through the doorway carrying a cumbersomely large harp. Behind them, an elderly man in a gray vest entered the room, followed by the second of the pool's attendants. The attendant carried with him a simple stool with a padded seat.

Rodric turned toward the commotion. "What's this?!" he demanded irritably.

Belac held up a slender finger. "It's music," he answered, unfazed by the irritated tone. The king's irritability was nothing compared to a dwarf's.

Rodric settled back into the corner of the pool. "Well… The swim room will make for interesting acoustics." He took a drink from his goblet before asking, "But why a harp?"

Belac shrugged. "It was the first thing that came to mind." *And, I want to watch the pretty woman that is going to play it.*

Once the harp had been set up, two of the unknown servants left the room and the elderly man sat down on the stool behind the harp. The man tipped the harp back into his shoulder and began running his fingers over the strings. While the sound was pleasant enough, Belac felt like he had been tricked.

Rodric closed his eyes as he listened to the music reverberate through the swim room. He took a drink from his goblet, then pronounced, "This is undoubtably one of your better ideas."

Belac narrowed his eyes at the old man playing the harp. *My idea had a woman in it.*

The door suddenly banged open again and then a dark figure stormed into the room. The harpist stopped playing, leaving an echo of music that faded away.

Belac shot to his feet in the water. "Serath!" he called out happily.

"Ut-oh," Rodric muttered as he moved to the side of the pool that was farthest from the wizard.

Serath swept out his arms angrily. "This?! This is where you have been?!"

Belac looked around the swim room, confused. "I haven't been in the pool the whole time."

Serath's green eyes pierced the room. "Where is the sword?"

Belac pointed to the strongbox. "It's right over there."

Serath strode over to the strongbox, ripped the lock off with one gloved hand, and threw the lid open with the other. He took a deep breath as he stared down into the box. Turning around to face the pool, he held his hands out low. "Why are you here?"

Belac was confused again. "I'm waiting for you."

Serath closed his eyes, took another deep breath, then opened his eyes and asked, "But why here?"

"In the swim room?" Belac was no less confused.

"In Lindell," Serath clarified with forced patience. "If not for tales of your… escapades, there is no telling how long it might have taken for me to find you."

Though Belac liked the idea of his 'escapades' becoming legendary, he still did not understand the problem. He pointed with his thumb. "Roger sent messages to the Temple of the Ancient. He said, they could use the ponds to get them to you."

Serath glared at the king.

Belac followed the wizard's stare.

Rodric looked from the wizard to the elf, then held up his hands. "Okay. So, don't be cross with me."

"You didn't send the messages?!" Belac yelled accusingly.

Rodric shrugged uncomfortably. "I had every intention of doing so." He gestured away vaguely. "Eventually."

Belac splashed water at the king angrily. "I am supposed to be killing a dragon!"

Rodric frowned at the elf. "No one kills a dragon." He waved toward the wizard. "Let him find someone else to get roasted alive."

Serath's rich voice drew the king's attention. "This is a serious affair, Rodric."

Rodric's shoulders slumped. "You don't understand, Serath," he complained, drawing out the words. "It is sooooo boring here." He gestured to the elf. "Belac is fun."

Serath continued to glare at the king for a moment and then firmly stated, "I want the Royal Guard for the raid on the dragon."

"What? No. Absolutely not." Rodric shook his head. "Do you have any idea how many people want to kill me?"

Serath's face was unyielding. "I can think of at least one."

Sixteen

Belac wrapped the last strap of his black leather harness around the inside of his thigh and then buckled it in front, securing the strap over his gray velvet trousers. With his sephen daggers now belted to the sides of his thighs, he stood from the stool in his changing room and faced a tall, standing mirror. Though the tooling on his black leather fencing vest was too intricate to be easily seen, the fluffy white sleeves of his blouse would not go unnoticed. *I look dashing!* He spun in front of the mirror so that it might get a full view of him.

Serath's rich voice carried through the elf's opulent suite. "Belac. It is time for us to depart."

Belac snatched up his scabbarded, starmetal sword and slung it onto his back. "I'm ready," he said as he stepped out of the changing room and into the dayroom. "But we are going to need to get some people to carry my bags." He gestured to the twelve canvas bags of luggage piled next to the suites entrance. Each of the gray bags had been detailed with silver thread.

Serath looked at the bulging luggage, then back to the elf. "No." He shook his head. "We are not bringing an entourage. Anything you cannot carry yourself, will need to be left behind."

Belac gazed wistfully at his bags. "But… My stuff."

Serath ran a gloved hand over the neatly trimmed beard that framed his mouth. "Everything you require will be provided," he assured the elf patiently. "Even now, you have new equipment waiting for you in Aldenon."

"Aldenon?!" Belac met the wizard's eyes with sudden interest. *Aldenon is fun!*

Serath studied the elf for a moment and then changed the subject. "You need to tell me what happened with the nillanan."

Belac shrugged. "I killed them."

Serath nodded. "How?"

"I used a memory." Though Belac could feel the memory, he did not shy away. "A memory of fire that burned all the world around me." Belac began to hear phantom screams. "When the nillanan touched my mind, I could touch theirs." He could see the raging flames. "They used confusion." His face hardened. "I used fire."

Serath nodded thoughtfully. "A memory…" He shook his head and then grinned. "It seems as though you will be known as the slayer of more than merely dragons."

Belac laughed. "Merely dragons." *I haven't even fought a dragon yet.* He smiled at the wizard. "Maybe I should start calling myself The Nillanan Slayer."

Serath shook his head. "You will face the dragon soon enough. It would be better to not confuse people with an ever-changing title."

Belac grinned slyly. "Is that why you didn't tell people that you're a wizard?"

"No," Serath answered before proceeding to expound. "To some, the word 'wizard' is a description. To others, a title." He put a gloved hand to his chest. "I have not earned the title."

"But, you are a wizard," Belac asserted.

Serath nodded in admission. "In so far as the word would mean to you."

It's the other wizards. Belac nodded to himself. *The 'official' wizards might take issue with Serath claiming to be one of them.* He pointed at his scrawny friend. "Are you going to get into trouble?"

Serath grinned and raised an eyebrow, pleased by what the elf had been able to piece together. "Time will tell. There are very few wizards left in the world."

Belac nodded. *Wizards are humans. And humans don't live all that long.* "Maybe they will let you join their team."

"I find that rather unlikely," Serath replied with a smile. "Besides, there would be costs associated that I would prefer to avoid."

Belac recalled the wizard's words. *"Everything has a cost."* He nodded. "It is probably just as well. You already have a team." *I should come up with a name for our team.*

"Speaking of which," Serath indicated to the exit, "we should get back to the others."

Belac looked to his pile of luggage. *I guess I can come back for most of this.* He walked over to the pile and began rearranging the bags. "Just give me a moment. I know they put it here somewhere."

Serath dropped his arm and stared blankly at the elf.

Belac pulled out a bag that was roughly half the size of the others. He used its cloth handles to move it away from the pile, then slipped its long strap over his shoulder. "I can carry this one."

Serath nodded noncommittally and then walked out of the room, his long legs whisking him away quickly.

Belac hurried after the wizard, not wanting to be left behind. "Hey, Serath."

"Yes, Belac."

"Why Aldenon?"

"Because there, we will find The Tears of the Dead."

Belac smiled despite the ominous appellation. "We are going to finish the sword?"

"We are indeed." There was no doubt in Serath's statement.

"Uhm… Is the sword going to throw beams of light, or maybe fly around and fight all by itself?"

"No."

"…Are you sure?"

"Yes."

Belac was not enthused. "I am going to have to actually fight the dragon myself, aren't I."

Serath's smile was in his voice. "Yes, Belac. But not, by yourself."

The route that Serath chose to leave the palace by was efficient and uneventful. Along the way, Belac realized that the wizard knew the palace's corridors better than he did himself.

Though the night had crept into the palace, many people still walked its halls. However, no one that Belac passed by was an Elven delegate nor an angry husband. For which, the elf was grateful. Outside the palace, the rising moon lit the capital city of Lindell. The blue tiles of the rooves shone brightly above the shadows like a calming blanket of light. Though few people still walked the streets, the glow of the lanterns that were carried by the city watch could be seen floating in the distance. *This is a place I could call home.*

As Belac followed the wizard across the public square, he tried to focus on where the wizard was taking him, as opposed to what he was leaving behind. He was marginally successful. *My friends are waiting for me.* As much as he liked Rodric, Belac did not think that the king would stand with him against the monsters of the world. It was one thing to issue orders from behind stone walls, and another to pick up a weapon and face the threat without.

Belac thought of a giantess wearing nothing but the blood of her enemies as she wielded her hammer against them. "Do you think that Breana will be alright?"

Serath continued down the street for a moment before answering, "No."

Belac wanted a different answer. "I know that she is stuck in a rock right now, but maybe Rolan can find some way to get her out."

Serath shook his head. "What Rolan did to her was wrong. Even if," he looked at the elf, "and I cannot overemphasize the 'if.'" He returned his gaze forward. "If, her will survived intact, she is now in limbo."

"Limbo?" Belac asked. "What's that?"

"Imagine experiencing nothing," Serath instructed. "Forever."

Belac frowned. "That does not seem too bad."

"Then, your imagination is wanting," Serath replied coldly.

Belac felt like maybe he should have accepted the 'no.' *Rolan thinks that she is strong enough.* "Rolan said that you think giants are better than everyone else."

Serath glanced at the elf and raised an eyebrow.

Belac could not remember exactly what the dwarf had said. "He said, that is why they run around naked."

Serath shook his head. "That is not my position. However, common biases being what they are, I can understand how someone could misunderstand."

Belac pointed a finger at the wizard. "You did not answer the question." *He is being all wizardy.* "What is your position?"

Serath shrugged. "I do not believe that superiority exists as an absolute. If anything, I was likely attempting to explain how a trait, which might otherwise be perceived as an inferiority, can often incite a compensation which results in a greater advantage."

I am too drunk for this. Though he could not remember what the dwarf had said verbatim, Belac could remember that at least the words had made sense. "Do wizards have to read a book or something to learn how to speak in riddles?"

Serath smiled at the elf. "Perhaps it is simply an unavoidable consequence of being correct."

Seventeen

Belac gazed out between the bronze bars of the ornate gate that provided rear entry to the Temple of the Ancient. Within the protective walls of stone that encircled the temple grounds, moonlight bathed the pale marble. The swirling sapphire streaks in the stone glittered in the night, granting the temple a magical sheen. Despite approaching from the rear, Belac thought that the temple looked exactly like the ones in Tariel and Harbridge. While the sapphire marble seemed less out of place in Lendell, the temples wide stretching buttresses and bronze metalwork set it apart from the rest of the city.

A silent man in a white, hooded robe opened the gate from the inside, pulling the bronze bars inward. Another hooded figure stood just beyond the gate, an arm stretched out toward the temple in polite invitation.

The men's somber demeanor made Belac worry that it might be rude to break the silence. So, he smiled and gave the men a friendly wave as he followed Serath past them.

Neither of the men waved back.

Belac whispered to the wizard, "They are not very friendly here, are they?"

Serath grinned at the elf fondly. "It has been arranged for us to receive minimal interference."

Belac's eyebrows rose. "Roger must be trying to help us make up for lost time."

Serath frowned. "He has cost us more than he can repay." He shook his head. "I would have expected better of the man."

"I like him," Belac said in defense of his friend. "He is my favorite king so far. No question about it."

Serath grinned ruefully, chuckled, and then sighed. "Well, that must be worth something."

"How about, you not turn him into a frog?" Belac suggested.

Serath raised an eyebrow as he reached for the handle of a large bronze door on the side of the temple. "A frog?" he asked as he pulled the door open silently, revealing a glowing chamber inside.

Belac glanced at the shining walls of the narrow chamber and then looked at the wizard. "He does not want to be a frog,"

Serath shook his head. "Fine. I agree to not turn Rodric into a frog." He motioned for the elf to enter the temple.

Belac held up a finger. "Or a rabbit."

Serath nodded tiredly. "Or a rabbit," he agreed. Then he held his hand out toward the chamber again.

Belac smiled, pleased by the concession. He walked into the glowing chamber and stopped in the center. Above reflective walls of uninterrupted glass, a pure white ceiling radiated a pale, homogeneous light. Ahead, another bronze door waited to be opened. *There is no handle.* When Belac turned to inform the wizard that there was no way forward, the open door closed, seemingly of its own accord.

Serath grinned reassuringly. "It will take a moment for them to cycle the doors."

Though Belac disliked the confinement, he trusted that the wizard had not led him into a trap. He turned to the wall on his right and began inspecting his own reflection. *I'm so pretty.* He turned his head to the side, admiring the curve of his pointed ear. *Whoever thought to make an entire wall out of a mirror was a genius.* He turned away from his image as the second door swung open.

Belac narrowed his eyes at the door that had seemed to open on its own. "How do they know who's in here?"

"They can see through the glass walls," Serath explained.

Belac's attention snapped back to the reflective wall. He pointed his finger threateningly at whoever might be on the other side. He then narrowed his eyes at his own reflection as it stood there pointing at him.

"Belac," Serath said, drawing the elf's attention. He gestured to the open doorway. "There will be mirrors in Aldenon."

Belac glanced at the mirror again through the corner of his eye. "Well, I hope the next one doesn't spy on me." He walked out of the chamber and into a corridor of sapphire marble and bronze inlay.

Floor to ceiling half-columns decorated both sides of the corridor between more doors of solid bronze that were nestled in shallow alcoves. Belac gazed up at the strange luminaires that hung from the ceiling. Small, white crystals suspended by silvery wire inside bronze rings, the luminaires threw rays of light that varied in intensity. *It feels like I'm walking through an ocean of light.*

Belac glanced at the wizard. "Are those soulstones?"

The bronze door had shut behind Serath. "Nothing so vulgar," he replied. "Think of them as tiny windows into a world that is brighter than your own."

Belac stopped under one of the luminaires and stared up at the crystal suspended within. "Are there people inside?" He wondered if someone was staring back at him.

Serath halted next to the elf. "You should not look too closely."

Belac recognized the wizard's tone. *That is the same way that he sounded just before his magic almost made me deaf.* He looked away from the crystal and turned to the wizard. "What happens if I do?" Belac asked with honest curiosity.

"You could go blind." Serath gazed up at the luminaire. "You could go mad." He returned his attention to the elf. "You could realize how dark this world truly is."

None of that sounded very pleasant to Belac. "That kind of seems like a dangerous way to make light."

Serath smiled. "Perhaps that danger is their true purpose," he suggested, then resumed walking down the corridor.

Belac glanced up at the luminaires and then quickly lowered his head back down. He cupped both hands and used them to shade his eyes from the mesmerizing lights.

Magic traps are the worst kind of traps. They're sneaky, they don't make any sense, and I can't clever myself out of them. Keeping his eyes fixed on the sapphire marble floor, he hurried after the wizard. *Magic is cheating.*

Serath halted again, this time next to a bronze door on the left side of the corridor. He took hold of the handle and pulled, opening the door on its impossibly quiet hinges. He chuckled at seeing the elf's improvised brim. "This way, Belac," he offered helpfully as he held the door open.

Belac quickstepped through the doorway and into a long stairwell. Though the stairwell was filled with the same irregular lighting as the corridor, he did not look up to confirm the luminaires. *Sneaky magic traps are not gonna trick me.* He began walking down the steps, glad that he could at least look where he was placing his feet. *There might be more traps on the stairs.*

As Belac descended the stairs, a thought came to him. *Why are we going down?* He was immediately proud of the thought. *I am getting good at this paying attention thing.* He wondered what else he might have noticed recently without actually noticing that he had noticed it. *I bet I noticed all kinds of things.* He attempted to recall an example. *I guess I need to start working on my memory next.*

At the bottom of the stairwell, a straight-walled corridor led off into the distance before coming to a dead end. The ceiling was low enough that Belac could have reached up and touched it with his hands. Silvery wire netting ran along the corners where the walls and ceiling met. Spaced at regular intervals in the netting, white crystals illuminated the corridor.

Belac covered his eyes more. "This is starting to look a lot like a trap." He tried to not sound overly suspicious.

Serath's grin was in his voice. "While the temple implements traps aplenty, none of them are for you, Belac."

Choosing to trust the wizard, Belac continued walking toward the dead end. "What about the sneaky crystals that want to make me crazy?"

"Typically, one is not forewarned of a trap," Serath replied with good humor.

Belac risked a glance back at the wizard. "Typically,' means, 'not always."

Serath smiled broadly. "Belac, that is an almost wizardly observation."

Eighteen

Belac attempted to study the wall at the end of the corridor without looking at any of the crystals that illuminated his way. *Maybe it's a secret door. Secret doors are a thing.*

Serath spoke from behind the elf. "Stop here for a moment."

Belac halted. "Is it safe for me to try to open the secret door?" He gestured to the dead end ahead. *I kind of want to see if I can get it open by myself.*

"I would not recommend it," Serath said with a grin.

A deep, brassy woosh of sound rolled through the corridor, and then the dead end was gone. In place of a solid wall of sapphire marble was a distorted continuation of the corridor. *That's... That's the pond!*

Belac looked up at the stone ceiling. "We are under the courtyard."

"We are indeed," Serath replied agreeably. He gestured to the pond. "And Aldenon awaits."

Belac walked forward and into the wall of distortion. Once again, he found it odd that he felt nothing as he passed through the pond. *It seems like it should at least be cold or something.* The world sharpened on the other side. *They should really put up a welcome sign or something to let people know that they are in the right place.* He continued on toward a set of stairs that mirrored the ones on the previous side of the pond.

Belac considered the arch that encased the pond above. *It must be a ring.* He reasoned that the underground corridors existed to allow select travelers improved discretion and safety. *I wonder if Roger needed to pay extra for this.* He did not know if governments could command the temples. If the temples acted independently of their respective cities, then it meant that the Temples of the Ancient controlled practically all trade between the kingdoms. With a sudden rush of insight, Belac realized how much power that would give the temples.

Another deep woosh issued from the corridor behind Belac, the sound oddly reversed. He stopped and looked back, finding a dead end in the direction that he had come from. His eyes drifted up to the white crystals that lit the corridor. He quickly covered his eyes with both hands, remembering what could happen to him if he looked at the lights for too long. *Sneaky lights are not going to trick me!* He cupped his hands and kept his head down as he turned back to the stairs.

"While I applaud your caution," Serath said grinning, "a modicum of self-discipline is all that is required."

Belac thought that it would be safer to just keep his eyes protected. "I will try self-discipline once I'm away from the sneaky crystals that want to make me crazy."

Serath offered no further advice on the matter, allowing the elf his eccentricity.

When Belac reached the stairs and began his ascent, he asked, "How do you know that we are in Aldenon?"

Following the elf up the stairs, Serath replied, "At this point, we have only faith." He seemed to find his answer amusing. "Perhaps that is why they call these 'temples."

Belac glanced up toward the top of the stairwell. "Then, that means that they could have sent us to an island covered in snakes and giant spiders."

Serath laughed. "I doubt that they would see any advantage in such an action."

Belac was not convinced. "What if it is part of a super sneaky plan to get the sword?"

"Administration of the ponds requires an immense amount of trust," Serath explained. "Such a betrayal would have dire ramifications."

Belac stepped onto the landing at the top of the stairwell. As he walked toward the bronze door that would access the ground floor, he argued, "Only if everyone found out. If the guys in white robes think they're smart, they might believe that they can keep the betrayal a secret." *And everyone thinks they're smart.* "If no one finds out, then they can get away with it."

Serath shook his head as the elf opened the door. "No betrayal can be kept secret. Someone will know. Others will discover it. And a price will be paid." He gave the elf a meaningful look. "Everything has a cost," he concluded and then stepped through the doorway.

Belac followed the wizard into a corridor that matched the one he had entered through in the other temple. "Right," he said, conceding the wizard's point. "But what if the priests are not as smart as you?"

Serath's steps slowed. He turned to look back at the elf. "That is a clever argument," he acknowledged before quickening his pace.

Belac smiled, pleased with himself. "Hey, Serath."

"Yes, Belac."

"Did I just win a debate with a wizard?"

"No."

"What? Yes, I did!"

"You may have," Serath corrected the elf. "But then, you asked me to make the determination, thereby granting me the authority to do so. Therefore, you lose."

Belac narrowed his eyes at the back of the wizard's black coat. "That's cheating."

Serath held up a gloved finger. "Wizard."

Belac kicked nonexistent dirt at the wizard, the movement causing him to stumble over his own feet as he walked. After regaining his balance, he lowered his head and kept his focus on the floor.

If not for the variation in the sapphire marbling, Belac would have questioned if they were still in the same temple as before. *I hope we are on an island with spiders and snakes. Then, I can dance in a circle around that wizard and laugh at him. …After he uses magic to kill all the spiders and snakes.*

Pale, homogeneous light poured into the corridor as Serath opened the bronze door to the admission chamber. Belac walked inside while the wizard held the door open for him.

It was not until the door closed behind him, that Belac finally lowered his hands. *At least I escaped the sneaky crystals that want to make me crazy.* He checked his reflection on the left wall and then remembered that someone was watching from the other side. He narrowed his eyes at the window before turning away.

Frowning at the wizard, Belac declared, "I won." *And you know it!*

Serath smiled. "Did you?"

Belac pointed at the wizard hastily. "Yes!" He hopped up and down jubilantly. "It works both ways! You asked! I win!"

Serath chuckled, taking no offence at having his own argument used against him. "How about we allow the truth to break the tie?" He gestured to the exit as the bronze door opened outward.

Belac spun around toward the exit, suddenly unsure how he was going to survive an island of snakes and giant spiders. *Maybe I should just let the wizard win.* Serath walked past the elf and out into the night. Belac waited for a moment, listening for the wizard's impending screams. The elf frowned at the silence. *Maybe he is not scared of spiders and snakes.*

Belac pitched his voice to carry. "Hey, Serath."

"Yes, Belac."

"Are wizards scared of spiders and snakes?"

"I suspect that would vary from wizard to wizard."

Belac frowned at the non-answer. "Are you scared of spiders and snakes?"

Serath's smile was in his voice. "Not particularly. No."

Belac did not like that answer any better. "Uhm… Are there any spiders and snakes out there?"

"I would be surprised if there were not."

I think I might hate wizards. Belac squared his shoulders and then walked out into the night. Though the sky was cloudy, he could recognize Grayden Tower in the distance. *Aldenon.*

Belac turned to the smiling wizard. "I let you win."

Serath's smile broadened. "Then, my victory is even more complete."

Belac narrowed his eyes at the wizard.

Serath waved for the elf to follow. "Come. The others will be glad to see that you are well."

Belac followed the wizard toward two men in white robes that were standing next to the rear gate. *I don't think that he was talking about those guys. He must mean Rolan and Vairug.* "Do they know that you found me?"

"Not as of yet," Serath replied. "I have not spoken with them recently. I cannot even be certain that they are here. When I left, they were in a state of disagreement. Despite Rolan's insistence that they should wait for me to locate you, Vairug wants to avenge you." He shook his head. "If Vairug had actually had anyone to blame, I do not think that there would have been any reasoning with him."

"They think, I'm dead?" Belac found the idea a little insulting.

Serath glanced at the elf. "They think that you melted."

"What?!" Belac began patting his own chest to make sure that he was still solid. "Why would they think that?"

"Because, they saw you melt," Serath explained. "I was worried that you may have been decorporealized. However, I now suspect that what happened to you was mostly an illusion."

Belac did not like the sound of any of that. "Mostly? How does a person 'mostly' not melt?"

Serath halted and turned toward the elf as one of the robed men moved to open the gate. "I do not think that you melted." He tilted his head slightly. "However, it was not an illusion that brought you from Harbridge to Lindell."

Belac remembered how the world had melted around him. *Magic is cheating.* "Do you think it was a wizard?"

Serath nodded. "I think it must have been." He sighed. "Time is against us, Belac. We need to stay ahead of our adversaries."

Belac nodded seriously in return, but then grinned. "Maybe my 'legendary escapades' in Lindell will confuse anyone that is looking for us."

Serath raised an eyebrow.

Belac's grin became a smile. "I am awesome at distractions."

Nineteen

Though Belac had always liked Aldenon, it was a crude place when compared to Lindell. The sprawling buildings were constructed of rough-hewn rock with an almost complete absence of city planning. The shops and homes were intermingled, and only the wealthiest of citizens had access to grassy spaces and parks. While the care given to each home varied, most seemed forgotten by the people who dwelt in them. The wooden shingles and matching trim of the common structures had an aged appearance that spoke more of neglect than of inveteration.

In the darkened sky above, clouds were aglow with the light of the moon behind them. Below, the shadows of the night painted the city with gloom. Belac furrowed his brow at the sky. The obfuscating clouds made it difficult for him to be certain, but he thought that the moon was in the wrong place. *How does that even happen? More magic?*

Without slowing his step, Belac turned to the wizard that walked beside him. "I think there is something wrong with the moon."

Serath raised an eyebrow and gazed upward. "Oh?"

Belac nodded. "I am pretty sure that it should be higher than it is."

Serath grinned. "There is nothing wrong with the moon. We are simply farther west than we were."

"What?" That did not make any sense to Belac. "Why would that matter? It's the same moon."

Serath nodded. "Yes." He paused for a moment as he briefly contemplated how best to explain. "But now, we are farther from where it rises."

Belac had never considered how his position would alter the relative orientation of the moon. He leaned toward the wizard while looking up at the sky. "Yeah, okay. I guess that makes sense." He stumbled, the act of leaning while walking too complicated for him in his current state.

Serath caught Belac's upper arm, stabilizing the elf until he could regain his balance.

Belac grinned sheepishly at the wizard. "It's that honey-booze."

"Honey booze?" Serath asked with an arched eyebrow.

Belac nodded. "Roger found a fancy bottle of honey that gets you drunk."

Serath frowned. "Rodric gave you…" He shook his head. "How much did you drink?"

Belac gave the wizard a queer look. "I don't understand the question." *I have had kind of a lot to drink lately.*

Serath closed his eyes, took a deep breath, and then opened his eyes again before elucidating. "How much of the 'honey-booze' did you drink?"

Belac shrugged animatedly, "However much fits in a goblet. Twice." *It would have been more, but I thought it would be rude to take the bottle with me.*

Serath took another deep breath. "I do not have what you need." He shook his head. "I need to run errands anyway. Let's get you to the smithy. Rolan and Vairug can watch after you while I see to our concerns."

Belac did not feel like he needed much of anything. "Why a smithy?" He raised his arm above his head and pointed down at the scabbarded sword on his back. "The sword is fine."

"You have been missing for over a week," Serath explained. "Rolan and Vairug needed a place to stay while I searched for you."

That almost made sense to Belac. "But why a smithy? Why not just stay at an inn?"

Serath scanned his surroundings before answering, "Aldenon borders The Divide. There are those here who have encountered the Orcs. They were not friendly encounters. Due to Vairug's condition, I thought that it would be prudent to obtain more private accommodations. Rolan chose a smithy."

Belac wondered what the dwarf was constructing. *He would not choose a smithy for the décor.* The elf imagined a giant, mechanical goat that could breathe fire. Then he shook his head. *No. How would he get up there to ride it.*

From the shadows of an alleyway ahead, three men stepped into the street and began walking towards Belac and Serath. Though the night was cool, Belac distrusted the men's hooded cloaks.

Serath gently veered to the right side of the street, moving himself and Belac out of the men's path. The men continued on, course unaltered, until they were only a few paces away. Then the men spread out, one moving to block Belac and the wizard's way.

Serath came to a stop and then crossed his arms. "You are making a mistake," he told the man standing in his way.

Belac nodded his head agreeably as he took a place behind and to the left of the wizard.

The man in the middle spoke as if he had not heard the wizard. "It is nice to see such finely dressed men out and about, this late at night."

Serath turned toward the speaker.

The speaker threw back his cloak and brandished a long knife. "How about, you let us carry that bag for you?" His words were not a question.

Belac looked at the wizard. "Does he not see all the sharp, pointy things I have strapped to me?"

The men to the left and right threw back their cloaks, revealing that they too bore weapons. The man on the right held a rusted axe; the one on the left, a spiked cudgel.

The man in the middle pointed his knife at the elf. "We will carry your weapons too."

Serath's rich voice issued with calm command, "Leave. While you still can."

Belac was not certain that they should let the men leave. *They will just find someone else to mug.* He stepped over to the man in the middle, leaned forward, and squinted in an obvious attempt to see inside the man's hood. *That's a big mustache.*

The man gestured with his knife, the movements more confused than threatening. "Are you..."

Belac reached inside the hood and grabbed one side of the man's droopy mustache. "How does this thing not fall off?"

The man's head followed the elf's tug. "Stop it!" the man slurred, his knife forgotten.

Belac let go of the man's mustache. He pointed a finger close to the man's face and asked, "What do you use to make that thing stick to your lip like that?"

The man swatted at the elf's finger with his free hand. "Get away from me!"

Belac lowered his arm. "Do you want to be a frog, or a rabbit?"

"What's wrong with you?" the man asked angrily.

Belac shrugged. "Thieves are trying to rob me?"

The man remembered his knife. He held the weapon out in front of himself. "I don't think you understand how this is going to go."

Belac leaned back as if confused by the statement. "Sure, I do." He glanced over his shoulder and pointed a thumb at the wizard. "That wizard over there is going to turn you into something small enough for me to step on."

The man lowered his knife in complete bewilderment. "You want me to believe that he's a wizard?" He gestured toward the wizard with his free hand. "He is just some rich fop that thinks he can buy himself a good time."

Belac laughed. Stumbling with mirth, he turned around to look at the wizard. *I think I might fall over!*

Serath was not amused.

Belac took a step backward toward the man in the middle, bringing his right shoulder close. Glancing over his shoulder at the man, Belac asked, "Do you want to see a magic trick?"

The man's answer was a confused grimace.

Belac held up his left hand. His palm was bright in the moonlight as he wiggled his fingers. Smiling, he turned to look at the man's confounded face.

Gazing up at the elf's hand, the man said, "I don't get it."

I am awesome at distractions. The tip of Belac's sephen dagger slid up under the man's chin and into his skull, the movement steady and controlled. The man dropped his knife and began twitching before finally crumpling to the ground. Belac casually turned away from the man's body and flicked his dagger, splattering the cobblestone street with blood. The city was silent around him.

Facing the wizard, Belac indicated with his dagger to his left and right. "I am allowed to kill these guys, right?"

The other two muggers dropped their weapons and ran, each headed in a different direction.

Belac chuckled merrily. He pointed a finger to his left. "Is it too late to turn that one into a rabbit?" *I think I might kind of like to have a pet rabbit.*

Twenty

Rolan had bought more than just a smithy. Belac could not even see the actual smithy. The building that abutted the street was a two-story structure with a storefront on the bottom and a family sized apartment above. Two short chains hung from the side of the storefront, but the smithy's nameplate had been removed. In a recess on the left side of the ground floor, a wide gate made of wooden planks closed off entry to a passage that ran under the upper story. A tailor's shop on the left side of the building and a girdler's leatherworking shop on the right denied side access to what lay behind the smithy's storefront.

Belac was less interested in the abandoned looking enterprise than he was in the blood that had stained the fluffy sleeve of his blouse. He held his arm out in front of himself as he followed the wizard. "I keep getting blood on my clothes," Belac complained and then dropped his arm. "I think I might just start wearing red."

With a grin, Serath raised an eyebrow at the elf. "The color would clash with your eyes," he warned in a gently teasing tone.

Belac's arm shot back up. "Does the blood clash?" He began studying the stains worriedly.

Serath stepped into the recess under the smith's living spaces. He reached up into the right corner and took hold of a thin cord dangling from a small hole in the ceiling. He tugged on the cord twice, ringing a bell inside the apartment above.

Belac drew a sephen dagger from its sheath on his left thigh. Bringing his right arm close to the side of his head, he held the dagger out in front of himself and attempted to use the blade's shiny surface as a mirror. *Why didn't anyone ever tell me that blood clashes with my eyes?*

The bottom of the gate dragged loudly over the cobblestones as Serath pushed it inward. "I suspect that there will be better lighting inside," he said, gesturing to the gap he had created.

Belac sheathed his dagger. "Is there a race of people that have blue blood?" he inquired as he walked into the passage. "I mean, when it's on the outside."

Serath followed the elf into the passage and then pushed the gate shut. "There are a few such races." He arched an eyebrow at the elf. "Why do you ask?"

Belac shrugged. "Maybe I should go live with them." He held up a finger. "After I kill the dragon."

"Why would you…" Serath stopped as he comprehended the elf's reasoning.

Belac nodded. "That way, I wouldn't need to worry about getting blood on me." He frowned. "Not unless it was mine." *And I should probably be worried about that anyway.*

Serath sighed and began walking away from the elf.

Belac hurried after the wizard. "Hey. Is there something I can eat or drink that will make me bleed blue? When I get cut, I mean. Not, just for no reason."

"Not that I am aware of," Serath replied dismissively.

Beyond the shadowed passageway, a dark and silent smithy waited on the other side of a cobblestone yard. Serath turned right, leading Belac to a covered porch on the backside of the main building. Afore the porch was a single step that looked to be a more recent addition.

One of Serath's long legs stretched easily over the step as he placed his foot directly on the porch. "Be careful not to use the step," he advised as he moved onto the porch. "Doing so will trigger an alarm."

Belac almost fell over backward as he followed the wizard up onto the porch. "Why didn't we just use the front door?"

"Rolan has it nailed shut and barred from the inside," Serath explained as he reached up and took hold of another thin cord that was hanging out of a small hole in the side of the building. Another bell rang as he tugged on the cord.

While Belac was not likely to ever describe the dwarf as 'friendly,' he thought that nailing the front door shut was a little excessive. "What if we need to get out and we can't use the back door?"

Serath's answer carried with it a lack of concern. "The barred windows in the workshop open outward."

A meaty fist pounded twice on the inside of the door.

I don't think that is how knocking works. Belac smiled, thinking that he should ask for the password.

Before the elf could speak, Serath answered the knock, "It's Serath."

Belac narrowed his eyes at the wizard. *That's a bad password.*

A series of bolts slid open inside the building, then the door swung inward, revealing an empty store. A single lamp sat on the counter, its flickering flame illuminating a room of bare shelves. *That looks a lot like a trap.* Belac decided to let the wizard go inside first.

Sensing the elf's hesitation, Serath walked into the store. "Don't close the door yet. I am not alone."

There must be someone behind the door. Since nothing had exploded or shot out at the wizard, Belac followed him inside. "This is a terrible welcoming," he muttered as he walked through the doorway. "I'm not saying I expected a party… But, come on." *There is not even any music.* He stepped away from the door. *Maybe I should have asked Roger if I could take that big harp with me.*

Serath nodded to the person behind the door. "No one else should be coming."

A scruffy dwarf in a splotchy gray uniform shut the door and began resetting the bolts. *That's a lot of locks.* There were two bolts on each side of the door and another two on the bottom that slid down into the floor. Once Rolan had secured the door, he turned around and crossed his arms. "Vairug," he called out. "He's not dead."

Belac smiled happily at seeing another one of his friends alive and well.

Rolan uncrossed his arms. "You're not dead, are you?" He reached out with two fingers extended and poked the elf in the gut.

Belac let out an "Oof," as the jab bent him over.

Rolan leaned away from the elf's breath. "Are you drunk?"

Belac rolled his shoulders as he straightened his back. "Not as much as I would like."

Rolan frowned and then looked to the wizard. "Where did you find him? In a brothel?"

Serath gave a faint shake of his head. "Your guess is not far off. He was the guest of King Rodric in Lindell."

Rolan scratched his stubbly beard. "I don't know much about him. Dwarves are not allowed to operate in Lindell."

Though Belac had spent most of his time in the palace, he did not recall encountering any dwarves in the city. "Why not?"

Rolan shrugged. "They think that our longevity gives us an unfair advantage."

Gray arms wrapped around the elf's shoulders from behind. Belac's joints popped as the heavily muscled arms lifted him off his feet. He squirmed in the orc's embrace, but was unable to free himself. *This is it. This is how I die.*

Vairug set the elf back down and then pushed him away. "I'm glad that you're not dead."

Stumbling, Belac turned around to face the orc. "Then, why are you trying to crush me to death?"

Dressed like a buccaneer, Vairug had taken time to put on his silvery, mechanical hand, but not his crimson sash. Belac thought the orc looked odd without it. *He's lucky that red doesn't clash with his eyes.*

Vairug ignored the accusation, instead asserting, "You melted."

Belac shook his head. "No. It just looked that way. We were magiced. The world went all wonky for me, and the next thing I knew, a nillanan was trying to eat my brain."

Rolan's features grew angry. "A nillanan?"

Belac nodded. "There were two of them."

Vairug looked to the wizard. "You saved him from the nillanan?"

Serath shook his head. "By all accounts, Belac escaped unaided, fought and killed an army of trained men, slew both of the nillanan, and then claimed their castle as his own."

Vairug's tusks jutted from his open-mouthed smile. He punched the elf in the arm affectionately.

Ow. Belac rubbed his arm. "It did not all happen in that order." He tilted his head back in a failed attempt to seem nonchalant. "But, who doesn't want a castle?"

Rolan responded by asking the wizard, "And they just let him keep the castle?"

Serath nodded and then sighed. "Evidently, Belac presented the king with the nillanan's severed heads."

Rolan put a hand to his forehead.

Vairug, however, looked like he was about to start hopping up and down with pleasure.

Belac grinned. "I brought him their hands too."

Rolan lowered his hand. "Why?" he asked as if he expected the answer to be imbecilic.

Belac thought that he understood the dwarf's confusion. "One of the heads was in pretty bad shape. I wanted him to believe that there were two of them."

Vairug had never looked so happy.

Rolan shook his head slowly. "The world made more sense when we thought that you melted."

Twenty-One

Belac did not enjoy climbing the stairs. He was tired, and his head hurt. He had wanted to spend more time catching up with his friends. However, fatigue had washed over him suddenly, flushing away all the color from the world. *Maybe I should just sleep right here on the stairs.* While the aged wood of the staircase looked not at all comfortable to rest on, Belac cared less and less with each step. *It wouldn't even be the first time that I have passed out on a set of stairs.*

"I think I am going to just sleep here," Belac decided.

Serath was mildly amused. "I am fairly certain that you would find the cot more comfortable."

Belac was not sure that the climb was worth it. "Do I get my own room?"

Serath grinned on the left side of his face. "If you can make it up the stairs."

Belac gazed up at the five steps left for him to climb. They seemed a grueling distance to travel. *Sleeping on the steps would kind of be like asking to get stepped on.* He recalled Vairug's warning to not let Serath step on him. Belac looked at the wizard suspiciously. *How far back did he plan this?*

Serath smiled.

"Fine," Belac said petulantly. "I will go to my room."

Serath waited patiently, holding aloft a candle that lit the elf's way. Candlelight flickered in the stairwell, the movement reminding the elf that he was standing still. Belac did not like the idea of a candle telling him what to do, but he resumed his climb none the less. *Stupid, bossy candle. It doesn't even have to climb the steps. It just gets carried!*

Serath walked up to the second floor with the elf, and then led him to a door that faced the stairs. "Fortunately, Rolan reserved the first room for you." He pushed the door open, allowing the candle to dimly light the interior.

Belac narrowed his eyes at the candle. *It is too late for you to try and be friendly now. I don't care how helpful you are.* He looked away from the candle and into his new quarters.

The room that had been set aside for Belac seemed cramped despite having no furnishings other than a cot and an old crate that had been turned upside down. *I want to go back to the palace.* A rough spun blanket had been nailed to the wall on his right, covering up what he assumed was a window that would look down on the smithy.

Serath stepped into the sparce room and set the candlestick down on the wooden crate. He gestured to an unbleached canvas duffle bag in the corner. "You will find a change of clothes in the bag."

Belac walked into the cramped space and dropped his smaller bag next to the one in the corner. "I will change in the morning." He removed the starmetal sword as he stepped over to the cot. "Is there any chance of getting a bath?" He set the scabbarded sword down on a folded quilt laid at the foot of the cot, and then began unbuckling the leather harness from his thighs.

Serath shook his head. "Not tonight, nor in the morning. However, I do suspect that one can be arranged for you tomorrow evening."

Once the harness was unbuckled, Belac dropped it on the floor next to the cot. He considered removing his fencing vest, but decided that he could just sleep in it. "Then, can I just sleep until tomorrow evening?" He sat down on the edge of the cot.

Serath grinned like a man with a secret. "I believe that you would regret doing so."

Belac began removing his boots. "How bad is this hangover going to be?"

"I will have something for you in the morning," Serath assured the elf. "Just try to rest as comfortably as you can."

Belac picked up the starmetal sword and set it on the floor behind the cot. "You know… There is this thing. That I could keep with me. That would be way more comfortable to sleep on…" He laid out on the cot and covered himself up with the quilt.

Serath chuckled. "You are not getting a flying carpet, Belac." He waved a gloved hand, and the candle blew out.

Belac closed his eyes. *I am not giving up.* He imagined sleeping on a flying carpet while a magical sword flew around and fought his enemies for him.

Serath's rich voice pulled the elf out of his dreams. "I hope you slept well."

I haven't slept at all. Belac realized that his head felt like it was being squeezed in a vise. *Was I asleep?* His throat was raw, and his spine felt like shattered glass. "I'm dying," he croaked.

"I would prefer that you did not," Serath replied with a grin. "It would disrupt a great deal of my plans."

Belac opened one eye to look at the wizard. "I hate your face."

Gray dawn shone from the edges of the blanket nailed to the wall, the morning light casting the wizard in a villainous glow. In the palm of a gloved hand, he clutched the base of a wooden tankard. *I bet that is for me.*

Belac pointed at the tankard feebly. "Is that going to cure me?"

Serath held the tankard out, offering it to the elf. "Only if you drink it."

Groaning as he struggled against his suffering, Belac sat up and put his feet on the floor. He immediately lifted his bare feet off the cold floorboards. The motion made him feel like he had broken his own back. With a foot, he dragged one of his boots in front of himself so that he could rest his feet on its shaft.

The leather upper of the boot was cold also, but he was too exhausted to pick his feet back up again.

As the elf took the tankard, Serath warned, "This will taste rather unpleasant. Try not to spit it out."

I don't care what it tastes like, as long as it makes me feel like I'm not dying. Belac looked down at the dull brown liquid in the tankard. *At least there is not an eyeball or something floating in it.* He lifted the tankard to his mouth and took a gulp of the wizard's medicine. *Ugh!* Belac almost vomited into the tankard. The brown liquid had the consistency of milk and tasted like rancid bacon.

Belac held the tankard out as far away from himself as he could with his left hand, while bringing his right hand up to protect his face from it. "No." *I'll just die.*

Serath seemed unsurprised by the elf's reaction. "I did warn you."

Belac glared at the wizard. "You can't make something taste this bad on accident!"

In lieu of arguing with the accusation, Serath grinned.

Belac pointed at the tankard. "These things get worse every time you make one!"

Serath continued to grin.

Belac narrowed his eyes.

Serath gestured to the tankard. "You should drink it."

Belac recognized the wizard's tone of, 'I am not going to make you do it, but you will wish that I had.' He looked at the tankard. *Maybe if I just chug it fast.* His stomach gave a heave. *That honey-booze was not worth all this.* Like jumping into a frigid lake, he brought the tankard to his mouth and gulped the contents as quickly as he could. Then he threw the empty tankard away from himself and covered his face with the backs of his hands. *Why?* He fought not to vomit. *Why is it so bad?!*

When Belac finally lowered his hands, he saw that the backs were wet with tears. *Never again.*

Serath held out his hand, a disc shaped pebble resting on his gloved palm. Even in the dim lighting, the tiny stone's off-white color contrasted brightly with the wizard's black glove. "This will help."

Belac leaned away distrustfully. "What is it?"

Serath kept his hand held out. "It is simply a pastille."

Belac did not know what that was. "What do you want me to do with it?"

Serath exhaled at the elf's delay. "It is meant to be placed in your mouth, but not to be chewed or swallowed." He moved his hand closer to the elf. "You will need to forgo breakfast this morning. This should help."

Belac reached out and took the tiny stone between his thumb and forefinger. "Will it make me not hungry?"

Serath shook his head. "That is not its purpose."

Belac brought the pastille up to his nose and sniffed at it. *It smells kind of minty.* He looked up at the wizard. "Then, why do you want me to put it in my mouth?"

Serath crossed his arms, shrugged, and then shook his head as he answered, "So that no one else is forced to smell that foul concoction you just drank."

Twenty-Two

Belac finished tying his hair before bending over his cot and picking up the starmetal sword. He slung the scabbarded sword over his head, then ran a thumb under the leather strap as he positioned the baldric across his new fencing vest. He had chosen to wear the new vest that Rolan had provided. While the new vest was not as decorative as the one that had been crafted for him in Lindell, the elf found its design more comfortable.

With the vest, Belac had also donned a fresh set of clean clothes. He had replaced his blood stained blouse with a creamy gray one that he had pulled from his new duffle bag. As he had not liked the way that the creamy gray garment looked with his gray velvet trousers, he had deemed it necessary to change his trousers as well. His only other options had been two identical pairs of trousers tailored from a coarse, black fabric. All and all, he thought that his ensemble would suffice for Aldenon.

Belac reached down to his cot and picked up a gray, wide-brimmed hat with a long, white plume sticking out of its hatband. He had done his best to straighten the brim, but the left and right sides refused to lay down flat. *The distinctive bends might actually make this work better.*

He ran his slender fingers along the white feather, appreciating the flair it gave to the hat. *This is such a good idea.* He turned around and began humming the tune of 'How Many Fish in the Barrel' as he walked out of the room.

Belac's gaze swept across the landing that wrapped around the stairwell, but the closed doors he saw offered him little information. Leaving the door to his own room open behind him, Belac descended the stairs to the ground floor. At the bottom of the stairwell, he turned into the main hallway. Another right turn would lead him past a small office and to the empty storefront. He turned left. *I can check the office if I don't find Rolan in the workshop.*

Belac knocked on the door to the workshop before opening it. Not because it was polite, but because he did not want Rolan to shoot him with something. However, Belac was too excited about his gift to wait for a response. He pushed the door open and stepped inside with a grand flourish, holding the hat up high.

"I have a gift!" Belac announced proudly.

No one else was in the workshop.

Frowning, the elf lowered his arm. *Serath said that Rolan would be in here.* Unlike the empty storefront, the workshop was well equipped. Cabinets, bins, and racks of tools lined the walls around two workbenches in the center of the room. A full-length platform had been built between the workbenches, presumably to help the dwarf make use of them. Belac noticed that no tools had been left out on the workbenches. *Maybe Rolan is in his office.*

Rolan walked into the workshop via an open hatch in the floor that was hidden from Belac's view. Belac stepped farther into the room and turned to his right, wondering what else he might have missed. *I'm counting that as a secret door.*

Carrying a leatherbound trunk in front of himself, Rolan walked toward the workbenches. "Good. You're here. I thought I was going to have to go look for you." He set the trunk down on the platform.

Belac remembered the hat. He raised his arm up high, holding the hat aloft. "I have a gift!" he announced again.

Rolan shrugged one shoulder. "Someone got you a fancy hat?" he asked without showing much interest in the answer.

Belac lowered his arm. "No. Well, yes. But it is not actually for me." He took a step closer to the dwarf and held out the hat. "I have a gift for you."

Rolan shook his head. "I don't want it."

Belac dropped his arm again. *Does he know that I am giving him the hat because I think he's short?* "It will look good on you."

Rolan crossed his arms. "Not if I don't wear it."

Belac held the hat out. "Just try it on."

Rolan made no movement to take the hat.

Belac shook the hat enticingly. "Come on." He grinned. "You know that I am just going to pester you until you do."

Rolan growled. "Fine." He snatched the hat out of the elf's hand. "If it will make you leave me alone." He placed the hat on top of his head and then held out his arms. "There. Are you happy."

Smiling, Belac nodded his head. "You should keep it." He liked how the hat made the dwarf look roguish.

Rolan removed the hat and tossed it onto the workbench to the elf's right. "I don't need a hat. If I did, I would not want one that big."

Belac shrugged. "Maybe you will change your mind."

Ignoring the comment, Rolan turned around and knelt down in front of the mysterious trunk that he had carried up from the basement. As he began unbuckling the leather straps that held the trunk closed, he said, "Take off the sword." With his chin, he indicated to the workbench on his left. "You can just set it up there."

As he removed the starmetal sword from his back, Belac asked, "What are you going to do to it?"

"I am not going to do anything to it," Rolan replied and then flipped open the lid of the trunk. "That's the wizard's job."

Belac set the sword down on the workbench. "Then, why do I need to take it off?" *Maybe he needs to measure me for something.* He imagined a collapsible set of mechanical wings that he could strap onto his back.

Rolan stood from the trunk, a scabbarded sword with a tangle of straps in his hands. "It is in the way." He held up the new sword. "We need to fit this to you."

Belac knew what blade the scabbard hid. While he was disappointed that he would not get to fly, a sephen sword was not something that he could complain about. "You made my dwarf-sword!"

Black leather and polished steel, the scabbard of the sword had a small, indented ring above its chape, and another below its locket. The sword's minimalistic cross-guard sat flush with the sides of the scabbard, presenting no opportunity for it to snag. *That is not going to do much more than prevent my hands from sliding up onto the blade during combat.* Rigged leather had been molded to the long hilt, further aiding in the blade's control. A simple, unobtrusive pommel of rounded steel capped the sword's end.

Rolan nodded. "Luckily, I was able to get my hands on some real Dwarven steel." He began shaking out the black leather straps.

Belac pointed to the dangling straps. "Those seem a little more complicated than they need to be."

Rolan laughed. "Wait until you see the rest of this thing." He stepped up onto the platform and pushed the starmetal sword aside to make room for the dwarf-sword.

Belac did not know if he wanted his sword to be complicated. *I just kind of want my swords to be sharp and pointy.* He decided to withhold judgement until he had seen if the dwarf had found a way to make the sword fly around and fight all by itself.

Rolan set his arms down on the workbench and angled the flat side of the scabbard toward the elf. "Do you see this ring here?" He tapped the small ring indented in the scabbard just below the metal collar around its mouth.

Belac leaned closer, noticing a recessed track between the ring and the locket. "Is that some kind of lock?" He thought of the thumb snap on the scabbard of his starmetal sword.

There was reserved pride in Rolan's reply. "It is more than just that." He put his left thumb inside the ring and slid it toward the locket. With a click, the scabbard popped open along the top edge like a clamshell.

"Awesome!" Belac exclaimed. He looked closer, noticing that the tip of the sephen blade was still enclosed in the chape. He pointed to the shining steel enclosure. "Is that to keep the sword from falling out when I open it?"

Rolan nodded. "That. And it helps to align the blade with the scabbard's mechanism." Holding the scabbard in place with his left hand, he reached his right hand over and gripped the sword's hilt. As he lifted the hilt like a lever, a V-shaped track rose with the blade before stopping at the top of the back side of the scabbard. Once the blade had cleared the track, Rolan pulled the tip of the sword out of the chape.

Though he found the device fascinating, Belac worried that it might not prove practical. "That is going to take a lot of practice."

Rolan did not disagree. "I think it will be worth it. Just be extra careful when you put it back in." He slid the tip of the sword into the chape. The interior shape of the enclosure aligned the blade with the track as the sword slid inside. Rolan then pressed down on the hilt, seating the blade into the track. As the sword pushed the track down into the scabbard, the two sides clamped shut over the blade.

Belac held out both hands, wanting to play with his new toy. "Gimme, gimme."

Twenty-Three

"Hold still," Rolan ordered irritably as he adjusted a leather strap that ran over the elf's right shoulder and across his chest.

Belac did his best to stand still. "I am just trying to see how it works." He glanced down at a metal ring in the baldric's main strap that was held flat against the center of his chest.

Rolan did not seem to find the excuse adequate. "It's a strap, Belac. It's not that complicated. You can fiddle with it later."

With the main strap of the baldric now holding the dwarf-sword against Belac's back, Rolan reached under the elf's right arm and took hold of a second leather strap. Sliding the leather through his fingers, Rolan flattened the strap against the elf's ribs and brought it up to the ring in the baldric's main strap. He squeezed a spring-loaded fastener at the end of the stay and then clipped it to the ring.

Belac looked down as the dwarf began tightening the stay. "You really don't want me to lose this thing."

Rolan frowned at the rhetorical accusation. "It is only one extra strap. It won't take that long for you to get use to buckling it, and it will help make sure that the scabbard stays in place." He took a step back and crossed his arms. "That will make the sword safer and easier to use. With a little practice, you can be faster in the fight. And in a fight, speed can often mean survival."

Belac grinned. "You don't want me to die," he said playfully.

"Of course, I don't want you to die, you stupid elf," Rolan replied gruffly. He uncrossed his arms long enough to motion for the elf to back away from him. "Go ahead and try it out."

Belac took hold of his new baldric and tugged on it, testing its retention. Then he let go of the leather strap and proceeded to hop up and down while turning left and right. While the sword jostled around on his back, it stayed in place better than any other sword he had ever worn. When Belac was finished hopping around, he turned to the dwarf and held out his arms. "I think it works."

"I meant, the sword," Rolan clarified. "See how it draws."

Belac smirked. "I can't see it. It's on my back."

Rolan gave the elf a stonefaced stare.

Belac's smirk became a smile. "Okay, fine." He reached up and gripped the hilt of his sword just behind his right shoulder. The release ring was easy enough for him to find with his thumb, but he worried that he might have a problem if he were wearing gloves. *I may need to spend more time training with gloves on.* When the scabbard clicked open, he pushed up on the hilt, raising it above his head. Then he simply rotated his shoulder, drawing the sword to his right side. "That feels a lot more natural that I expected it to," he admitted to the dwarf.

Rolan grinned smugly.

Belac brought the sword up in front of himself, the flat of the blade turned inward. *It's perfect.* He ran his left thumb over the cross-guard. *This looks like something made for a dagger.* He lowered his left arm and pointed the sword away from himself, gazing over the length of the sephen blade. The abbreviated cross-guard would allow him greater mobility and reduce the chance of it being inadvertently caught on something; however, he would not be able to rely on it to protect his hand from an opponent's blade.

"The balance is fantastic," Belac remarked with a nod to the dwarf. He moved the sword in a cross pattern, then spun around and swept the blade through the air.

Rolan was too pleased with himself to sound gruff. "Alright. You can play with it later," he chastised. "Let's see if you can sheath it without stabbing yourself."

Belac grinned at the dwarf. "I am not playing with it. I'm practicing."

Rolan nodded his head. "Right. Then, go ahead and practice putting it away."

Belac raised the sword above his head with the tip pointed downward behind his back. "Is there a trick to getting it in that little metal cup?" He looked over the top of his left shoulder and arched his back so that he could see down into the scabbard.

"Practice," Rolan answered dryly.

Though the movement was awkward, Belac was able to slide the tip of the sword into the chape. The enclosure aligned the blade with the track, allowing him to easily complete the process of sheathing the sword. *Yeah. I am going to have to work on that.* Once he had the blade locked into the sheath, Belac pulled on the hilt, wanting to see if the sword could be drawn more conventionally. The blade lifted the scabbard up with it.

Rolan shook his head. "That is not going to work. The scabbard clamps down on the blade."

Belac let go of the sword. *This has got to be the most complicated scabbard ever made.* "What keeps dirt and stuff from getting into all the little, moving parts when the scabbard is open?"

"Nothing," Rolan replied without much concern. "But you can just reach back with your left hand and close the scabbard without the blade in it. The track will stay raised inside, so don't try to slide the sword back in like you would a normal scabbard."

Belac reached up with his right hand, gripped the sword's hilt, actuated the release on the scabbard, pushed up on the hilt, and unsheathed the blade. *I think I could get really quick at that.* With the sword held low and to his right, he reached back with his left hand and squeezed the scabbard closed.

Belac frowned. "I like that it will keep all the complicated bits protected, but now I have to juggle my sword to get it back in the scabbard." He was beginning to think that the mechanical scabbard was not worth the hassle of using it.

Rolan shook his head. "There is another release ring on the other side. Just reach back with your left hand. You should be able to find it with your fingers."

Belac did as he was instructed, recalling that he had seen the location of the ring earlier. The scabbard popped back open as he slid the ring with his middle finger. Though he still needed to look over his shoulder, he found it less difficult to sheath the sword that it had been the first time. *I can probably get used to this.*

Rolan had more advice. "One thing you will need to watch out for, is your hair. It is not going to hurt anything if you accidentally cut some of it off, but if it gets caught in the scabbard, you are going to be in for a surprise."

Belac's left hand shot up to the back of his head. *Did I cut my hair?!*

Rolan chuckled at the elf's reaction. "I could always braid it for you."

Belac thought of the long braid that the orc had once had. *That almost got Vairug killed.* Belac shook his head. "No. I don't think that would help."

"Are you sure?" Rolan teased. "I could braid it into one big spiral on the top of your head."

Belac disliked the imagery. *Maybe if it was braided into rows…*

Rolan was not finished with his teasing. "Or, I could put it in a double bun like I did for Breana." His mirth died at the mention of the giantess's name.

Belac was suddenly unsure about what he should say. "Do you think that she's okay?"

Rolan nodded. "She will be safe in the stone until I can find a way to get her out."

Belac was careful with his words. "Serath says, she is in limbo."

Rolan nodded again. "She would rather be in limbo than dead."

Belac did not want to ask his next question. "Why are you so sure?"

Rolan frowned at the elf. "Because Breana is not stupid."

If I needed to choose someone to save me, it would be Rolan. "You will figure it out," Belac assured the dwarf. "And that means, I can't braid my hair. When she gets back, I don't want Breana to be mad at me for stealing her hairstyle." He tried not to imagine himself with two braided buns on top of his head.

Rolan shrugged the matter aside. "You still need to think about doing something with your hair."

I am not cutting my hair. Belac realized that his hair was not his only problem. "What about the starmetal sword?" He pointed to his own back. "I don't think that this thing is going to work right with another sword bouncing around on top of it."

Rolan nodded. "You're right. You are going to have to start wearing the starmetal sword on your hip." He knelt down and reached into the leather trunk. "I already have a belt for you." He pulled out a black leather belt that had been laced through a matching frog. "Go ahead and put this on like you would a normal belt," he said, holding the belt out to the elf.

Belac grinned speculatively as he took the belt. "Is it not a normal belt?"

Rolan stood and then stepped down from his platform. "Nope." He walked past the elf and to one of the workshop's cabinets. "If you squeeze the top and bottom at the same time, the buckle splits in half." He pulled out a drawer and grabbed a hooked tool without needing to look for it. Closing the drawer as he turned around, he reiterated, "But you adjust it pretty much the same as you would any other belt. The main difference is that the strap doubles back on itself instead of continuing across."

Belac studied the three raised rings on the three overlapping discs that formed the shape of the polished steel belt buckle. Only now that he knew what he was looking for, could he make out the two individual pieces that he would need to squeeze to release the internal mechanism. *This is a really nice belt.* Holding the belt at the frog, he swung the buckle around his waist.

"Did you make this yourself?" Belac asked as the dwarf walked back to the workbenches.

Rolan stepped up onto the platform that joined the workbenches before answering, "Not by myself." He turned to his left and grabbed the starmetal sword. "I had the parts commissioned to save time." He gestured vaguely with his hooked tool. "There are some artisans in Aldenon that are not half bad. One of them is even a dwarf."

Belac looked up from adjusting his sword belt. "Did you do the same thing with my nifty scabbard?"

Rolan nodded. "That thing has a lot of small parts. I did not think that I would have time to fabricate them all myself." Using the hooked tool, he began cutting through the laces on the inside of the starmetal sword's baldric. "It was faster to just draw everything up, and then have a handful of professionals follow the designs." He shrugged. "They used the materials I gave them, and I was able to correct their mistakes during assembly. All and all, I think it worked out pretty well."

Aldenon craftsmanship did not inspire Belac's confidence. He imagined pulling the release on his scabbard and having tiny cogs and bolts pour out of it. *Maybe I should get a leather sheath. It would be no trouble to carry it in one of my bags, and I would have a spare in case this fancy scabbard falls apart.* He pushed down on his belt's frog to make sure that the new belt was properly fitted.

Rolan ripped off one of the leather cuffs that secured the starmetal sword's scabbard to its baldric. "Using Dwarven steel should make a tangible difference. It is more difficult to work with, but it's also more consistent than the stuff that humans make." He ripped off the second cuff, freeing the scabbard.

Belac did not think that he would be able to distinguish one type of steel from another. He ran his thumb over the ringed discs of his new belt buckle. *I am just glad that the colors all match. Otherwise, I would need to make sure that everything I wore was the same type of steel.*

Starmetal sword in hand, Rolan stepped down from his platform. "Stick out your hip."

Belac turned to his right, presenting the dwarf easier access to the frog on his left hip. Rolan slid the sword's scabbard through the frog and then wiggled it into position.

As the dwarf tightened the first of two small straps that would keep the scabbard secured, Belac interrupted, "Hey, Rolan." He waited for the dwarf to look at him. "Do you think that blood clashes with my eyes?"

Twenty-Four

Belac held up a grimy, brown cloak. "I don't want to wear this."

Rolan shrugged. "Do it anyway."

Belac looked around the workshop as if searching for something that might explain what, in his mind, was an unreasonable argument.

Rolan exhaled gruffly. "Belac, you are carrying some of the most valuable objects in the world."

Belac lowered the cloak, causing the bottom half to pile on the floor next to his feet. "How much do you think they are worth?" he asked without considering the dwarf's point.

"That is exactly what everyone from here to Lost House is going to ask," Rolan replied with frustration.

Belac held up a slender finger in interjection. "You know? That's a bad name for a temple. It's not just depressing; it sounds like they don't know how to find the place."

"It is where they house the dead and care for lost souls. The name makes sense," Rolan contended. "What would you want them to call it? 'Big-fancy-gray-building?"

Belac shrugged, not wanting to challenge the proposed name change.

Rolan frowned at the elf. "Put on the cloak."

Belac held up the grimy cloak again. "This thing is going to look worse on me than dried blood."

Rolan crossed his arms. "That is kind of the point, Belac."

"Fine," Belac accepted petulantly. "But everyone is going to think that you are walking around with a vagabond."

"Oh no," Rolan replied with absolutely no sincerity. "Whatever will I do?"

Belac tried to think of a consequence that would persuade the dwarf to reconsider. "No one wants to do business with a vagabond."

Rolan shook his head. "That is not true. Especially in Aldenon. But even if it were, I wouldn't care. I don't do much business here. At least, not directly."

"Why not?" Belac inquired, willing to follow a topic that did not require him to put on the grimy cloak.

Rolan shrugged. "There is too much crime here. It's just not worth the hassle."

Belac held up a hand, indicating to the building around them. "You bought a smithy."

Rolan nodded. "And it's a hassle." He looked at the cloak significantly.

Belac pursed his lips. "It is not illegal to want to look nice."

"You know what else is nice?" Rolan asked and answered, "Not getting shot or stabbed on our way to the temple." He gestured to the elf. "You are going to need to cover those ears up anyway. Serath can get you into the temple, but the priests are going to have a fit if they realize that you're an elf."

Belac slung the cloak around his shoulders and then closed its clasp. "There. Are you happy?" The hood of the cloak was voluminous enough to accommodate the hilt of the dwarf-sword, but attempting to draw the blade from its complicated scabbard would undoubtably result in damage to the cloth.

"Great," Rolan replied. "Now, let's go."

Belac was not ready to leave. "Uhm… Let me go say goodbye to Vairug first."

Rolan scowled at the elf.

"I'll be quick," Belac promised while backing up toward the exit. "I will meet you at the back door." He turned away and hurried out of the workshop.

Belac shut the door, hoping that it would stop Rolan from yelling at him. *I can do this quick.* As the elf made his way to the stairs, he gathered his cloak into the crook of his right arm. Then, with his left hand on the starmetal sword's hilt, he raced up the staircase. After using the bedpan in his room, Belac continued to the first doorway across from the banister. He knocked on the frame of the open door, not wanting to surprise Vairug.

Though the blanket that covered the window was red, the orc's bedroom was much the same as Belac's, the most notable difference being a small desk in place of the elf's overturned crate. Vairug's size made the room seem even more cramped. *I bet he's tired of needing to hide here.*

Seated on a stool in front of the desk, Vairug looked up from the book that he had been reading. "Is there a problem?"

Belac shook his head. "I am just letting you know that we are leaving." He pointed to the book on the orc's desk. "What are you reading?" *And don't say, 'A book.'*

Vairug's eyebrows rose slightly at the elf's interest. "A human history. It is a recounting of a plains war." He looked down at the book and frowned. "It is not very well written."

Belac thought of the libraries in his homeland. "It is a shame I can't take you to Naravere. They have libraries filled with songs, and poems, and stories about things that never happened."

"Then, they do not have libraries in Naravere," Vairug replied disapprovingly.

Belac laughed. "Why? Because the stories are fictional?"

Vairug did not seem to think that the question deserved a response.

Belac pointed at the book on the desk. "A human wrote that." He grinned at the orc. "How many humans have you met that were honest?" *They can't even be honest with themselves.*

Vairug looked down at the book with sudden distrust.

Belac backed out of the doorway, leaving the orc to reevaluate the history. *That was kind of mean.* Belac shrugged as he walked around the banister. *It is probably better for him to be skeptical anyway.* He began descending the stairs unhurriedly, no longer feeling the need to outpace Rolan. *Maybe I should get Vairug another book.* Belac smiled as the idea began to take shape. *Maybe one filled with stories for children.* He thought that the orc's indignant responses would be worth whatever the book cost.

The staircase creaked behind Belac. He halted and turned sharply, finding Vairug following him down.

Vairug waved the elf onward. "I will need to bolt the door when you leave."

Belac continued down the steps. "I wish you could go with us."

"That is a waste of a wish," Vairug replied. "Why not simply wish the dragon dead?"

Belac looked over his shoulder and narrowed his eyes. *I am getting you a book.* He turned to his right when he reached the hallway, heading toward the storefront. On the other side of the open doorway, Rolan was waiting impatiently with his arms crossed.

Rolan uncrossed his arms and began unbolting the back door. "Pull the hood up over your head," he called out into the hallway.

Belac did as he was bid, positioning the hilt of his dwarf-sword under the hood with him. Though it created a noticeable bulge, the sword would be less conspicuous under the brown cloth. As Belac walked into the storefront, he asked, "Are you not bringing your pack?"

"It would just draw attention that we don't need," Rolan replied as he opened the back door. "I am coming right back after I take you to the temple." He nodded to the orc. "Vairug can protect my stuff while I am gone."

Vairug smiled. "Maybe I should reorganize the workshop while you are away."

Rolan chuckled. "That would worry me if I were not just about done with it." He stepped out onto the porch. "Just watch out for traps."

Vairug took hold of the back door. "You would not put traps in the workshop." He sounded sure of his assertion.

Rolan turned around and grinned at the orc. "Really? You don't think that a dwarf would trap his tools?"

Vairug frowned, suddenly unsure. He looked to the elf.

Belac shrugged. "Just wait until after I leave."

Twenty-Five

Though clouds still covered the city, the rays of the midmorning sun pierced through to the people that walked its streets. The citizens moved with resignation, unmotivated by their daily tasks. *I remember Aldenon being more fun than this.* Belac searched the faces of the men and women around him as he followed Rolan. *Why are these people so dirty?* The elf's gaze drifted up to the walls of the bordering buildings. Even the stacked stones seemed filthy to him.

The air smelled faintly of the sea, a gentle reminder of the southern ports. *Why don't these people just go bathe in the ocean?* Belac imagined the entire population of the city standing in lines along the shore, each person waiting for their turn to bathe. *Yeah, okay. Maybe that wouldn't work.* He looked up into the clouded sky. *Maybe everyone is just waiting for it to rain.*

Belac returned his attention to the dwarf walking in front of him. *This is as good of a time as any.* Belac opened his cloak and pulled out a wide-brimmed hat with a white feather sticking out of its hatband. Moving as sneakily as he could, Belac reached out and placed the hat on top of Rolan's head. *He can't just set it down out here.*

Rolan grabbed the brim of the hat and slung it up into the air without saying anything.

Belac leapt up, snatched the hat out of the air, and then tucked it back under his cloak as he landed. "Come on, Rolan. It's a really nice hat."

"Then, you wear it," Rolan replied without looking back.

I don't want to wear it. Belac's face twisted in thought. He snapped his fingers and pointed at the dwarf. "I have to wear this hood."

Rolan did not argue.

Belac considered placing the hat back on Rolan's head, but decided to bide his time instead. *Dwarves are stubborn.* Belac was not ready to give up on the hat, but he knew that patience would be every bit as important as persistence. *There is no need to rush.*

As Belac followed the dwarf onto a bridge that spanned a wide canal, he saw that traffic was noticeably more sparce on the other side. Heavy timber held up by stone, the bridge felt solid beneath him. Though the city bridge was of superior construction, Belac was reminded of the bridges outside of Gofell. *I hope all those people stay safe. What they went through was horrible.* In his mind, he saw red lights in darkness.

"Hey, Rolan," Belac said as he moved forward to walk beside the dwarf. "There is something I wanted to ask you about."

Rolan glanced at the elf. "Are you waiting for permission?"

Belac grinned briefly, unable to hold his amusement. "It's about what happened in Gofell."

Rolan shrugged. "What of it?"

"The Vaquian magic," Belac clarified, "that awful stuff that the exiles were using. It was always red. An evil, blood red."

Rolan waited for the elf to continue.

Belac did not know how to ask his question. "When you put Breana in the soulstone. The light was red."

Rolan nodded in understanding. "It is not the same thing," he asserted. "The only reason that the light was red is because the stone was red. If the stone had been blue, the light would have been blue." He grinned at the elf slyly. "Or green, if it was green."

Belac smiled at the jab. "I was hoping it was something like that."

Rolan did not allow the elf relief. "But it does not matter. If blood magic could accomplish what I wanted, I would use it. Magic is a tool. I will not forgo a tool just because someone else used it for evil."

Belac did not believe that magic was only a tool. He could also not imagine the evil he had witnessed in the Vaquian stronghold being used for anything good. "How much magic do you know?"

"None, really," Rolan admitted without reservation. "Dwarves can't use magic."

The dwarf's answer did not match up with what Belac had seen. "I watched you trap a woman's soul in a rock, Rolan."

Rolan nodded. "I can make the soulstones work. But that is not the same thing as using magic."

Belac frowned on one side of his mouth. "It kind of seems like it is."

Rolan shrugged. "Well, it's not. I can usually figure out how to make magical 'things' work, but the power is not coming from me."

"The subjects own soul powers the soulstone," Belac concluded, understanding intuitively.

Rolan nodded. "Serath does not agree with me, but I think that magic is just too nonsensical for dwarves to be able to use it." He gestured at nothing in particular. "But there are a lot of devises that can use magic." He glanced at the elf and then nodded to himself. "That is how I met Serath. He needed help organizing an expedition to hunt down an artifact. It turned out that I was pretty good at it."

Belac had not considered that the wizard and the dwarf could be business partners. "What was it?"

Rolan grinned at the memory. "It was a dancing figurine."

Belac wondered why the wizard had gone through all the trouble to acquire such a thing. "What did you do with it?"

"We sold it," Rolan replied merrily. "We both liked watching it dance, but expeditions are expensive."

Belac found himself nodding involuntarily. "A wizard and a clever dwarf could track down a lot of artifacts." *And make a lot of money.*

Rolan did not disagree with the assessment. "Finding credible leads is usually the most difficult part."

"Usually?" Belac asked.

Rolan nodded. "Sometimes, things explode."

Belac suspected that there would be quite a few dangers in such an enterprise. He smiled. "Maybe someday, a couple of friends will set off on an expedition to find the starmetal sword."

Rolan's face became contemplative.

Belac's smile broadened. "I wonder what's going to blow up."

Rolan chuckled, but continued to explore his own thoughts.

Belac allowed the dwarf to ruminate silently as they continued on to Lost House. *Maybe I can go on an expedition with them after I kill the dragon.* He liked the idea. *I am going to need money if I want to staff my castle.* He realized that he might have another problem. *What if Vairug gives me a castle in Enevic? I can't just move my staff back and forth every time I want to stay in the other castle.* He frowned. *I am going to need more money.* He wondered how much people would be willing to pay for dragon's teeth.

The architecture of Lost House set it apart from the rest of the city despite being constructed of the same stacked stones. High walls and domed rooves, the temple had been built to endure harsh weathers as well as the ravages of time. Tall, narrow windows of red glass striped the walls in wide intervals, providing character without ostentation. Outside of an arched passageway in the front of the building, a dark figure waited with his back against the wall and his arms crossed. *I am starting to think that he just sleeps like that.*

Rolan strode up to the wizard and then indicated to the elf. "I got him here. Now, it's your turn."

Serath's smile twisted his neatly trimmed beard. "I will endeavor to not lose him."

Belac frowned at his friends. "I am right here."

Rolan nodded. "That is what I just said."

With his arms still crossed, Serath poked out a gloved finger. "I can confirm that."

Belac narrowed his eyes at the wizard.

Rolan clapped the elf on the back. "Don't die," he advised and then turned around to leave.

Turning quickly, Belac reached out and placed the gray hat on the dwarf's head.

Rolan removed the hat and kept walking.

Belac grinned. *Elves can be stubborn too.*

Twenty-Six

The interior design of Lost House did not align with Belac's expectations. The raised ceilings were not domed, and the walls were not rough stone. Warm, polished wood of a cherry hue formed the inside of the stalwart exterior, reshaping the space within. *At least the floor is honest.* The stone floor had been left bare, presumably to account for high foot traffic. Iron wrought chandeliers hung from the ceiling on chains, their fluttering candlelight adding a welcoming warmth to the temple despite the absence of other furnishings.

Belac looked up at the lit candles. "Are these lights going to try to make me crazy?"

"That would be unlikely," Serath replied. "I do not believe that Lost House employs magical defenses." He looked at the elf. "However, we will receive considerably less resistance if you can remain silent while we are in the temple."

Belac frowned. *I think, that wizard just told me to shut up.* He scanned the round chamber again, finding nothing new of interest. The spacious room appeared to exist for no other purpose than to serve as a nexus for multiple corridors. *There sure is a lot of waiting involved in dragon slaying.* He turned and looked down over the top of a waist-high wall of mortared stones that ringed the center of the room.

The floor on the other side was noticeably recessed. *What do they do with this?* If not for a chained off opening in the wall, he would have thought that it was an empty fountain.

A man robed in layers of gray cloth walked into the chamber, looking over his shoulder as if worried that he might be followed. His unkept mop of long, dark hair whisked to the sides as his head swiveled back to the wizard. Below eye sockets darkened with soot, a patchy beard evidenced the priest's youth.

Too harried to bother with pleasantries, the priest indicated to his left and loudly whispered, "We need to hurry. If anyone finds out..." He left the consequence unsaid.

Serath followed the priest into the indicated corridor, silently complying with the man's plea. Belac trailed after. Though the priest inspired no confidence in the elf, Belac had faith that Serath would use magic to smite the man if he betrayed them. *I wonder what Serath promised this priest.* Belac imagined the priest laughing hysterically as he flew away on a magic carpet. The elf narrowed his eyes at the wizard's back.

After a corridor that was longer than Belac thought it really needed to be, an ironbound door denied further progression. A ring of jawless skulls decorated the center of the door. *I'm guessing that means, 'Keep out.'* The door shared none of the welcoming feeling of the previous areas.

The priest wasted no time. Reaching out, he began pressing on the skulls in a seemingly random pattern. Mechanisms within the door responded audibly with each press. *This is why we needed to wait for a priest.* With a final press, the door swung inward, revealing a stone chamber with another short, circular wall in the middle of the room. An iron wheel, styled to resemble chains, ornamented the far wall. *I can't imagine anything good happening in a room like this.*

The priest hurried into the chamber. He hustled around the circular wall and took hold of the iron wheel. Dull, mechanical clunks sounded from within the walls as he spun the wheel to the left. With the faintest sound of grating stone, the floor inside the center of the circular wall began to slide away.

Belac stepped over to the short wall and stared down into a growing blackness. An iron staircase spiraled around a cylindrical shaft, descending into an abyss that seemed to swallow the light. *I don't want to go down there.* He looked at the wizard. *You are going to make me go down there, aren't you?* Belac turned to the open doorway. *How mad would Serath be if I just left?*

Once the stairwell was fully opened, the priest rushed over to the opening in the circular wall and unhooked the chain that closed it off. He dropped the end of the chain on the floor as he turned to the wizard. "You need to be quick. Go down the stairs and then follow the main tunnel all the way down to the bottom. Do not go into any of the side passages. It would be easy to get lost among the crypts. You need to hurry." His daubed face suddenly looked not only worried, but confused. "You said, you would bring your own light."

Serath raised his arms and passed the palms of his gloved hands over each other; right over left, left over right. When his left hand uncovered his right, a small orb of clear light was floating above his palm. "And so, I have." He lifted his hand like he was launching a raptor, and the orb of light floated out over the stairwell.

The priest gazed at the orb as it hovered over the stairwell, the whites of his eyes bright against the soot darkening his eye sockets. "That's…" He began backing toward the door. "You need to hurry," he restated and then fled the chamber.

Belac pointed to the exit. "I don't think that he liked your magic ball of light."

Serath walked around to the stairwell's entrance. "The man has many concerns." He stepped down onto the iron staircase.

Belac looked down into the open stairwell. The magical light did little to make the descent seem more safe to him. *Why is there no railing?* "Do these people have some kind of problem with banisters?"

Serath's floating light began to descend as it followed him down into the darkness. "They believe that no one should feel safe when visiting the dead."

Belac realized that he would need to stay close to the wizard if he wanted to make use of the magical light. He moved to the opening and stepped down into the stairwell. "Okay. But why not just paint scary pictures on the walls or something?" *Then, they could add banisters so that I don't fall off.*

Continuing down at a steady pace, Serath replied, "Perhaps the somber atmosphere has more than one purpose."

Despite the hollow sound that his boots made on the metal steps, Belac thought that the staircase felt unexpectedly well built. *Maybe if I just stay close to the wall, I won't die.* "Hey, Serath."

"Yes, Belac."

"Do you know what would make this a lot safer?"

Serath's grin was in his voice. "You are not getting a flying carpet, Belac."

After a moment, Belac asked, "What about a bedsheet?"

"You can have a bedsheet."

"A flying bedsheet?"

"No."

"Then, why would I want one?!" Belac's gesticulations caused him to stumble. He skipped the next step, regained his balance, and then moved closer to the wall as he continued down.

"Sometimes, the dead are covered with veils that could be called bedsheets," Serath suggested with amusement.

"Oh, that's funny," Belac responded with a distinct lack of amusement. *Stupid wizard thinks he's funny.*

When Serath reached the bottom of the stairwell, the ball of light followed him through a cased opening and into a stone passageway that sloped downward. Belac followed with the light, noticing that false bevels had been carved into the gray stone. Though the passageway had been cut into the bedrock under the city, additional time and effort had been taken to smooth and shape the surfaces to resemble block construction. *Why would they bother decorating a place that stores dead bodies?*

Beyond the reach of the light, darkness awaited their approach.

Twenty-Seven

"How far down does this go?" Belac asked and then pointed at the wizard's back. "And don't say, 'To the bottom."

Without slowing his pace, Serath looked over his shoulder. "What metron would you prefer?"

"What?" Belac did not understand the question.

Serath grinned and returned his attention to the tunnel ahead. "This passageway will take us under the city's cemeteries. Fallen rain seeps into the soil above, filtering through the decaying dead. The water is then funneled by the natural bedrock into a place known as The Tears of the Dead." He gestured forward. "This, goes down to The Tears of the Dead."

Belac shook his head in agitation. "Why can't our quest ever take us to places with names like, 'The Land of Happy Thoughts?"

Serath had no sympathy for the elf. "You recently sojourned in a king's palace."

Belac was determined to be malcontent. "That was after a nillanan tried to eat my brain!"

Serath held up a gloved hand. "Then, what marvels might you find, after visiting a place such as this?" His tone was only slightly sarcastic.

Belac found this line of thinking intriguing. *If things don't work like that, they should.* He realized that the concept was a cynical attempt to find Balance. *Uhm... That might be heresy.* He rarely contemplated about Balance anymore. To him, there seemed little place for it in human cultures. *Maybe what I really want, is Balance without having to work for it.* He shook his head. *Forget Balance. I just want the good stuff.*

Belac quickstepped forward to walk beside the wizard. Serath moved a step to his right, making room for them to walk abreast comfortably. The wizard's magical orb floated along above them, lighting their way unobtrusively. Belac thought that the orb seemed somehow playful, almost as if it were happy to be of help.

Belac inquired, "Why do humans worship death?"

Serath spared the elf a glance. "Not all of them do."

Belac nodded impatiently. "Yeah, okay, sure. Then, why do these humans worship death?"

"We are closer to it," Serath explained. "Humans," he clarified. "You would be hard pressed to find one of us that has not lost a parent, sibling, or friend. The majority of children do not live to see adulthood. And those that do, soon feel themselves edging ever closer to the inevitable. Elves have lifespans that can surpass entire civilizations. Humans do not. When a people live their lives surrounded by death, constantly reminded that their turn will come, faith can become morbid."

Belac could not help but feel pity for the humans. "Wouldn't it be better if they worshiped life? The less of something there is, the more valuable it becomes."

Serath grinned at the elf fondly. "There are many humans who do. However, yours is a materialistic perspective. Those who worship death, weigh temperance verses intemperance."

"Death lasts longer," Belac voiced in comprehension.

The outline of another cased opening came into view as they approached the end of the passageway. Larger than the various side passages that they had forwent on their way down, the opening almost filled the main passageway.

Belac slowed his pace, allowing the wizard to move ahead of him. *You and your little ball of light can go into the creepy, dark room first.*

Belac peered into a side passage on his left as shadows reclaimed the crypts recessed into the walls. *Maybe I should ask for my own ball of light.* He thought back on all the crypts that they had passed by on their way deeper into the catacombs. Countless dead waiting in darkness, their silence suddenly felt like a threat. Belac was less than a step behind the wizard as they walked through the opening at the end of the passageway.

Serath glanced over his shoulder, frowning at the elf's proximity. He stepped to the side and held out a gloved hand. "Behold, The Tears of the Dead."

Belac took in the circular pool dominating the center of the chamber. Water dripped from stalactites above, the droplets sending ripples across the pool's silvery surface. "Where does the water go?"

Serath smiled. "To the bottom."

Belac narrowed his eyes at the wizard. "Die in a fire."

Serath ran a hand over the trimmed beard that framed his mouth, wiping away his smile and leaving behind a grin. He laughed quietly to himself and then gestured to the pool again. "The blade of starmetal sword needs to be completely submerged in The Tears of the Dead. I suggest that you make every attempt to not fall in."

Belac walked over to the side of the pool and looked down into the silvery water. *It doesn't look like a trap…* He narrowed his eyes at the pool. *Which would make it a good trap.* "Is there anything in it?"

"Water," Serath replied with good humor.

Belac turned his head to scowl at the wizard. At seeing the magical light twinkling in the man's green eyes, Belac relented. *It makes sense that he would be in a good mood. We have gone through a lot to get here.* He began removing his cloak. *Far too much to be chased away by a pool of water.* He tossed the cloak aside and then stared down into The Tears of the Dead. *I really hope that this thing does not try to eat me.*

Serath's rich voice filled the chamber. "As simple as it may seem, this task will be the object of speculation for ages to come. Future scholars will devote their lives to unveiling this moment. They will question whether or not it was truly your hand that sanctified the blade. And ask themselves, how such a thing could be possible."

Not if this pool eats me. Belac's right hand reached across to the sword on his hip. The thumb snap came free with a dull pop, and then he drew the blade. He brought the hilt up and studied the stylized dragon claws that pinched at the milky white blade. *It might be my hand on the sword, but there would be no sword without my friends. They deserve to be remembered too.* He knelt down next to the pool's edge. *Especially, if this pool eats me.*

Belac lowered the starmetal sword into The Tears of the Dead. Nothing happened. He stared down past the metallic sheen of the water's surface. *I really kind of expected something to happen here.* "Did I do it wrong?" he asked the wizard without looking away from the sword.

"You need only submerge the blade in the water," Serath assured the elf. "However… Please, don't drop it."

Belac swished the blade around in the water just to be sure. Then he pulled the sword from the pool. Still, nothing happened. He stood and faced the wizard. "I don't see why we needed to come all the way down here just to get the sword wet."

Serath beckoned the elf closer. "We are here for more than that." He reached into the bag that he wore under his coat. "The Tears of the Dead are meant to purify the blade in preparation for what we do next."

Belac walked over to the wizard. "And what are we doing next?" He frowned. "I am not going to dance around naked."

Serath's handsome face contorted in perplexion. "Why in the world would you…" He shook his head, dismissing the notion. "Just set the sword down on the ground." He pulled a brass cylinder out of his bag and then lowered himself onto the stone floor, sitting down on his ankles.

Belac plopped down cross-legged and placed the starmetal sword on the ground between himself and the wizard. "Are you going to sing to it?"

Serath raised an eyebrow. "You have some peculiar expectations," he said before returning his attention to the brass device in his hands.

Belac craned his neck forward, affecting a better view of the strange object. Tiny symbols had been worked into a series of cylindrical bands that made up the body of the device. "Can you read those?"

Serath began rotating the bands in sequence. "They are the characters of a forgotten language."

Belac frowned suspiciously. "If they are forgotten, then how do you know what they are?"

Serath grinned. "Have you never remembered a thing that you had previously forgotten." The device clicked as he aligned the last symbol.

I need to stop trying to argue with wizards. The device separated in the middle between two of the bands as Serath pulled from both ends. A copper capped vial of dark red liquid protruded from the half of the device held in the wizard's left hand. He set the other half down on the floor next to him and then pulled the vial out of the device with his free hand.

"Is that blood?" Belac asked. *That looks like blood.*

Serath set the second half of the device down. "Yes, Belac. This is blood. Blood, and power."

Belac did not understand. "Power?"

"The power to forge legend," Serath replied oracularly. Holding the vial vertically in his right hand, he began unscrewing its copper cap with the gloved fingers of his right.

He said that he needed my blood to make the sword work. "Is that my blood?" Belac asked incredulously. "How did you get my blood?" *Did he steal it while I was sleeping?*

Serath removed the copper cap from the vial. "It is your blood." He met the elf's eyes. "However, it was not taken from you."

Then how… "The dragon!" Belac exclaimed.

Serath nodded solemnly. "It will be The Danorin's own blood that enchants the sword."

Belac's mind flashed on a dragon breathing fire into the night sky just before attacking his ship. "How did you get a dragon's blood?"

"I have spent much of my life searching for objects of power." Serath held up the vial as if in salute. "This, is one such object."

This quest began before I was part of it.

Serath reached out with the vial and began slowly pouring its thick contents onto the arcane symbol that had been stamped into the base of the starmetal blade. When the blood touched the symbol, blue fire erupted from both sides of the blade and scattered across the stone floor. Belac rolled backward, hastily moving away from the magical conversion. Serath continued the controlled pour, the blood becoming blue fire as if filtered through the starmetal blade.

With the vial emptied, Serath replaced its copper cap. He picked up the half of the brass device on his left and reinserted the vial. Then he picked up the other half of the device and resealed the vial before slipping the unified cylinder into his bag.

Belac crept closer on his hands and knees, curious how the magical sword may have been altered. His eyes still refused to focus on the symbol that marked the blade. "Is it safe?"

Serath smiled darkly. "Not for the creature you will slay." He held both hands out toward the sword, inviting the elf to take it.

Belac reached down to claim the sword. When his hand touched the hilt, the milky white blade became alive with cerulean light. The elf recoiled, jerking his hand away so fast that he fell onto his backside. "What in death was that?!"

Serath chuckled triumphantly. "That, was an enchanted sword responding to the blood of the dragon."

Belac leaned to his right and repositioned the empty scabbard belted to his left hip. Then he shifted forward into a kneeling position. Staring down at the sword, he asked, "It's not going to explode or anything, is it?"

"Not unless I have made a serious miscalculation," Serath replied with a smile.

Belac's eyes moved up to measure the wizard. "And it won't eat my soul, or sap my luck?"

Serath shook his head. "I would say that it is still a normal sword, but it no longer is. It will glow when you touch it. And it will burn the dragon."

Belac's hand wrapped around the hilt of the starmetal sword. Cerulean light filled the space between him and the wizard, casting their faces in surreal shading. Belac stood, holding the sword out before himself. *It's finally complete.* He thrust the glowing blade up into the air above him. "I am The Dragon Slayer!"

Twenty-Eight

Belac swept the magical sword side to side in front of himself, marveling at the visual trail of its glowing blade. "I feel like this thing should hum or something."

Standing safely behind the elf, Serath was less impressed by the display. "It is not a toy, Belac."

That doesn't mean that I can't play with it. Belac flourished the blade and then returned it to the scabbard on his hip. As the starmetal blade slid into its scabbard, the sword's cerulean light faded from the subterranean chamber. It was not until Belac released the hilt, that the glow leaking from the scabbard's mouth finally went dark.

Belac turned around, intending to ask Serath if they should take some of The Tears of the Dead with them. Behind the wizard, two lanky humanoids silently entered the room. Belac's eyes widened at the sight of the emaciated figures. Wrapped completely from head to toe in strips of cloth, the silent intruders could only be one thing. *Mummies!* In both of their closed fists, long bladed katars had been wrapped in place.

Belac pointed hastily. "Sneaky-knife-mummies!"

Serath spun to face the sneaky-knife-mummies. The one on the left leaned forward, wheeling its right blade back and up to slash downward.

Serath stepped forward and caught the mummy's cloth wrapped wrist with his left hand. His right hand reached down, grabbing the mummy's left forearm before it could recover. Then, with brutal efficiency, he swept the mummy's left katar up between them and severed its right arm at the elbow. He released the mummy's left arm, while keeping a firm grip on its severed right. Holding the severed arm like a hilt, Serath slashed the katar across horizontally and chopped through the mummy's neck. Stepping back on his right foot to redirect his force, Serath whipped the severed arm out in a backhanded throw. The katar flew tip first into the bandage wrapped face of the second mummy with enough impact to knock it off its feet.

Even as the two mummies fell, three more ambled into the chamber. Belac unsheathed his dwarf-sword and rushed forward. Leaping, he placed his left hand on the wizard's right shoulder and vaulted toward the first of the mummies. The sephen blade pierced the center of the mummy's withered chest as Belac collided with it. The tip of the sword clinked on the stone floor, and then the mummy's torso shot down the blade and slammed onto the ground.

Jerking the remainder of the blade free as he leapt away, Belac slashed upward and to his right. The sephen edge sliced into the ribs of the next mummy and out where its opposite shoulder met its neck. As the mummy on his right fell away in two pieces, the one on the floor began to rise. The third mummy lurched forward, slashing directly at Belac. There was no time for the overextended elf to recover from his previous swing.

Cerulean light shone out as Belac's left hand raised the hilt of the starmetal sword. The mummy's katar clashed with the exposed length of the glowing blade, hammering the sword's scabbard against Belac's hip. As the katar rebounded, Belac plunged the starmetal sword back into its scabbard, quelling the cerulean light. Right foot stepping forward, he slashed downward with his dwarf-sword. The sephen blade cut through the top of the mummy's head and then its right shoulder, dropping the mummy to the floor.

The first of the three mummies was already on its knees and moving to strike. *I need to hit it in the head.* Belac's dwarf-sword traveled up and then back down in an angled, backhanded slash that sliced through the mummy's bandaged skull. As the mummy fell, a katar clanked on the stone by Belac's feet. Belac moved his foot away and stared down at the single arm still attached to the second mummy's head by its right shoulder and part of its chest. The arm's movement was limited.

Belac pointed his sword at the cleaved mummy. "Did you know that there was going to be sneaky-knife-mummies?!" he asked the wizard accusingly.

Serath walked forward and kicked the flailing arm aside. "This is worse than that." He closed his eyes and held a gloved hand out toward the entrance.

Belac shook his head and pointed at the wizard. "You are supposed to reassure me." *That has to be at least half of a wizard's job.*

Serath opened his eyes and dropped his hand. "Then, I assure you that this is worse than mummies." He began striding toward the entrance.

Though the cleaved mummy had stopped flailing, Belac did not want to be left alone in an underground chamber with it. "I don't think that you know how reassurance works," he called after the wizard.

Serath strode out of the chamber, trailed by his floating ball of light.

Dwarf-sword still in hand, Belac chased after the wizard. "What's worse than being trapped underground with a bunch of sneaky-knife-mummies? Wait… Are zombie-gorilla-wolf-monsters a thing?"

Serath shook his head. "The mummies are nothing more than undead vessels. They require an animus to function."

Belac thought it was more important to know how to make them not function. "I need to hit them in the head, right?"

Serath nodded. "Anything that sufficiently damages the cranium or separates it from the body."

Belac glanced at the wizard. "Do mummies have brains?" He had not thought to check.

Serath nodded again. "Yes. Though, they are withered things, only metaphysically significant."

Farther up the passageway, three sneaky-knife-mummies broke into the wizard's light. Moving with lurching motions, the mummies seemed to have forgotten how to use their own bodies. To Belac, the silence of the profane corpses made their unnatural movements all the more revulsive. Aided by the downward slope, the mummies would soon be close enough to carve flesh.

Belac hurried forward to walk on the wizard's right side. "Do you want one of my swords?"

Serath shook his head. "The starmetal sword should be reserved for the dragon."

Belac drew the sephen dagger on his left thigh and offered it to the wizard.

Serath held up a gloved palm in rejection. "I should keep my hands free."

Behind the three oncoming mummies, two more lurched into the light. There was no time for further discussion. Belac moved ahead, wanting to give himself space to both dodge and swing his sword. *Maybe Serath can help me with magic if I keep the sneaky-knife-mummies away from him.* He flipped his dagger into an underhanded grip. *At least sneaky-knife-mummies won't try to eat me.*

Belac swung his sword low as he moved to the left of the first sneaky-knife-mummy, his blade slicing through its bandaged knee. While he knew that the mummy would not bleed out, the maneuver was quick, and it positioned him for his next attack. Mindful not to clip the wall, Belac lashed out with a backhanded swing, cutting through another mummy's neck. Before the corpse could fall, Belac put his left shoulder against it and rammed it into the mummy now positioned on the other side.

Dry ribs cracked as they collided with the stone wall. Leaning away, Belac stabbed with his dagger horizontally. The short sephen blade pierced the pinned mummy's skull and then pulled free in a silvery flash. Spinning right, the elf swept his sword toward the last two mummies.

On the ground behind him, balanced on forearm and knee, the first mummy slashed at the back of Belac's leg. Rusted steel cut through the air as Serath pulled the mummy away by its single remaining foot. Then a black boot stomped down on the back of the mummy's head.

While the mummy on Belac's left was completely out of range, the other was not. The dwarf-sword's blade cut through the mummy's right arm and part of its chest, then clanged against the wall. The one-armed mummy slung its katar up at the elf's face. Belac ducked down and to his left, bringing the hilt of his sword in tight. As soon as the katar passed by, he thrust upward, driving the tip of his sword into the mummy's skull.

The last mummy lurched forward, bringing its katar downward in a backhanded slash. Belac parried the katar with his dagger and then drove the narrow blade into the mummy's head. Spinning around to face the downward slope as he pulled his dagger free, the elf searched for the one-legged mummy. *I still need to finish that first one.*

Belac pointed his sword at the one-legged mummy lying lifeless at the wizard's feet. "I get half credit for that one."

Ignoring the comment, Serath walked around the elf. "We need to keep moving. There will be more."

Twenty-Nine

Belac slid his sephen dagger into its sheath and then hurried after the wizard, wanting to stay with the floating ball of light as much as the man. "How many of these things do we have to fight?"

Serath did not slow his pace. "There will always be five," he replied before amending, "At least until we stop this madness."

Belac frowned thoughtfully. "Why always five?"

Serath's frown was one of displeasure. "Because every time we destroy one of the vessels, the nillanan will awaken another."

Belac blinked. "A nillanan is controlling the sneaky-knife-mummies?"

Serath shook his head. "There are at least six of them." Despite the quick pace up the sloping passageway, his voice remained unwavering. "Possessing one of the vessels requires a nillanan's full attention. It leaves their corporeal selves vulnerable, and they would not risk relying on mere slaves to protect them. Ergo, there will be at least six nillanan in the temple above."

Belac's eyes searched the passageway ahead, straining to see into the darkness beyond the wizard's magical light. *Six?!* "They must reeeeealy want me dead. Why do the nillanan hate me so much?" *It can't be just because I have a face.*

"You have been directly involved with the deaths of three of their number," Serath reasoned. "The nillanan are the fractured mind of a dead god. They do not reproduce as other creatures do. Every one of them lost is an affront that harms them all."

Belac did not think that was very fair. "They keep abducting me!"

"That does not appear to be their intent this time," Serath remarked calmly.

They want me dead. Belac pointed back toward The Tears of the Dead. "What's to stop them from waking up one of the mummies in the crypts behind us?"

"Nothing," Serath replied. "However, the farther away a vessel is, the more difficult it becomes for the nillanan to possess it. The guardians are housed closest to the entrance. They are also armed."

Belac nodded. "Maybe we should keep a lookout behind us, just in case."

Serath nodded in return. "That is well advised."

Belac quickened his pace, moving ahead of the wizard. As Belac's shadow merged with the darkness beyond, his eyes searched for movement. *New plan.* When he saw the movement that he had been searching for, he slowed, allowing the light to grow in front of him. Three sneaky-knife-mummies ambled into view, one slightly ahead of the other two.

Belac dashed forward toward the first of the sneaky-knife-mummies. He fainted left, then right; each faint bringing him closer to the mummy. With a quick thrust, Belac jabbed the tip of his sephen sword into the mummy's cloth covered face. As the mummy collapsed lifelessly to the ground, Belac began to slowly back away, moving closer to the wall on his right. *Let them think I'm scared.*

The next two sneaky-knife-mummies split apart from each other, each moving around the fallen corpse. Belac waited for the mummy on his right to lurch forward and swipe downward with a katar. He dodged left and then thrust his sword into the mummy's skull, purging the life from the undead guardian.

Again, Belac began to slowly back away, his left hand held out and his sword ready to thrust.

Behind the third sneaky-knife-mummy, the last two ambled into the light. Belac ducked then dodged as the third mummy slashed at him with each of its long bladed katars.

Serath had stopped moving forward. "What are you doing?" He sounded rather impatient for a wizard.

Belac did not register the wizard's tone. "They telegraph their attacks." *They put their whole body behind every swing.*

As the mummy slashed down again with its left katar, Belac reversed direction. He stepped across with his left foot, ducking as he spun right. As he came back up, his blade swept out in a backhanded slash that cut through the side of the mummy's head. Before the blade could strike the wall, Belac recovered from the attack, pulling the sword back into a charged position. Left hand held out in front of himself again, he slowly backed away from the fallen mummy.

Belac realized that he was too close to the wizard. "We need to back up," he said without looking away from the last two sneaky-knife-mummies.

Serath's voice moved away as he inquired, "Why are we retreating?" He sounded more put-upon than concerned.

Belac kept his eyes on the sneaky-knife-mummies. "If the nillanan are just going to get a new body every time that I kill one of these things, then I want to space them out."

"That is a commendable stratagem," Serath acknowledged. "However, we are almost at the entrance. It would be better to hasten forward."

Belac frowned. *It feels like that wizard goes out of his way to ruin my plans.* He rushed forward toward the sneaky-knife-mummy on the left. The mummy lurched at him, slashing downward with its right katar. Belac's dwarf-sword intercepted the katar, directing it safely downward as he pointed the tip of his sephen blade at the mummy's head.

Belac's left hand grabbed the mummy's right shoulder, and then he thrust his sword up into the bandages under the mummy's jaw. Pulling his blade free, he shoved the lifeless corpse at the last sneaky-knife-mummy. The twice dead guardian slammed into the oncoming mummy's legs, toppling it forward. Belac stepped in with his right foot, bringing his sword across in a wide swing that chopped off the top half of the mummy's head. Dry bones fell at the elf's feet.

After a quick scan of the vanquished undead, Belac resumed walking up the sloped passageway. *My plan totally would have worked.* True to the wizard's words, the entrance soon came into view.

Belac turned around and began walking backward. "Why are the sneaky-knife-mummies not on us yet?"

"It takes time for them to be risen," Serath explained as he dug into the bag he carried under his long, black coat. "The nillanan will also need to reach farther into the catacombs each time."

Belac glanced left and right as he passed the last of the crypts before the entrance. He saw movement in the shadows. *It looks like they are going to get behind us after all.*

Serath pulled a sinched pouch out of his bag and began loosening its drawstring.

Still walking backward, Belac pointed at the pouch. "What's that?"

"It's magic," Serath replied enigmatically. When he finally had the top of the pouch open, he said, "Hold there." He began pouring purple sand from the pouch into the cupped palm of his left hand.

Belac halted outside the entrance to the stairwell, his body turning to track the wizard as he walked past him. "What are you doing?" *This is not the best place to stand and fight.*

Serath stepped into the stairwell. "Turn away and shield your eyes," he ordered and then threw the handful of sand into the air.

Belac watched as glittering purple filled the stairwell, the arcane sands falling upward instead of down. *It's beautiful.*

As Serath turned around, he saw that the elf was watching. He yelled, "Shield your…"

Belac's world became white and then something slammed into the back of his head. He could not feel his body. He was floating in an endless white, no longer a member of the present. Then he felt the screams. Horrific wails of torment and death, the screams were steeped in terror. The silence that followed was more frightening still. Alone in whiteness, Belac wondered who would hear his screams.

Thirty

Sound slammed into the white void of Belac's existence. He followed the sound, eager for anything other than the nothingness around him.

A rich voice spoke into the whiteness. "Belac." Then sound slammed once more.

My head hurts. Belac considered withdrawing back into the white. Then a gloved hand slapped him across the face.

Serath's voice was calm but insistent. "Belac, you need to wake up."

I don't think that he is going to stop hitting me. Belac's eyes cracked open. The brightness of the world stabbed into his skull. He clinched his eyelids shut. "It's too bright," he moaned.

Serath somehow dimmed the light before asking, "What about now?"

Belac opened his eyes again. The floating ball of light had been moved into the stairwell. He looked at the wizard. "I didn't shield my eyes."

Serath grinned. "I noticed."

"I hate your face," Belac replied. He consoled himself with an image of the wizard; aged and hunched over, the man clumsily tripped over his own long beard of wispy, white hair. *Let's see how handsome you are when you get old, Human.*

Serath seemed unoffended. "You need to get up. We cannot stay here." He put a hand under the elf's arm and helped him to stand.

As Belac struggled with his equilibrium, he said, "I need my sword."

Serath bent and picked up the dwarf-sword, then stepped behind the elf. "Unlock your scabbard."

It must have closed when I fell on my back. Belac reached back with his left hand and actuated the scabbard's lower release ring. The scabbard clicked open, exposing its innerworkings to the wizard. Belac then covered his eyes with the palms of his hands and attempted to will his headache away. *If the wizard says to plug your ears, plug your ears. If the wizard says to shield your eyes, shield your eyes.* Belac took a deep breath. *If he tells me to stand on one foot, I am going to do it.*

Serath slipped the tip of the dwarf-sword into its scabbard and then locked the blade into place. "Rolan never ceases to impress me." He walked around the elf and into the stairwell.

Belac dropped his hands and opened his eyes. The light was slowly fading from the passageway. *I should have asked for my own ball of light.* He stumbled his way into the stairwell and began to climb the stairs. *I guess I could use the starmetal sword for light if I needed to.*

As Serath's magical ball of light levitated up the stairwell, the gray stone walls became black. To Belac, climbing up into a burned world felt more ominous than had descending into the darkness of the catacombs. All that dwelt in the catacombs was meant to be dead; the world above was one of life.

Belac suddenly remembered what had been waiting for them in that brighter world. "The nillanan!"

"They are now but ash and memory," Serath assured the elf. "At least, the ones that occupied the chamber above."

The final spiral of the stairs at the uppermost portion of the stairwell had been warped out of shape. Twisted and bent, the hanging edges of the metal steps looked to have been caught in a vortex.

Serath put his back against the wall and continued to climb upward using the more supported side of the steps. Belac mimicked the wizard, appreciating the slower pace while disliking the reason for it.

Belac's gaze drifted past the twisted steps and into the darkness of the abyss below. *Why am I so dizzy?* He felt the darkness begin to swallow him.

Serath's gloved hand shot out and grabbed the elf's arm. He pulled the elf back against the wall and then placed his hand on the elf's chest, holding him upright. "Can you make this climb?" he asked calmly.

Belac nodded, immediately regretting the action. *I think my headache is getting worse.* "I am just a little dizzy."

Serath took his hand off the elf's chest and then gripped the baldric of the dwarf-sword. "We cannot rest here. Try to focus on one step at a time. I will help you keep your balance."

Belac attempted to swallow though his mouth was dry. *Why can't I remember how to swallow?* He resumed his climb, relying on the wizard for support as they slowly made their way to the surface. Only when the elf stepped from metal to stone, did Serath finally release him.

Even after seeing the twisted stairs, the devastation above surprised Belac. No chandelier hung from the blackened ceiling. Horizontal gouges had been torn into the stone walls and half of the entrance had been ripped away. The metal wheel that operated the stairwell had slogged off its mechanism and fallen to the stone floor among piles of scattered ash. *I am really glad that Serath did not try to use this kind of magic down in the catacombs.*

Belac tried not to breathe in floating ash as he followed the wizard out of the chamber. Past blackened rubble, dead men lay sprawled on the floor of the corridor. Outfitted with heavy scimitars and chainmail vest over thin gambesons, the men had come prepared for battle. *They don't have any visible wounds. They must have been slaves of the nillanan, and died when their masters did.*

With a wave of his hand, Serath dispelled his magical ball of light. The corridor darkened around the dead. Candlelight waited in the chamber beyond. To Belac, the light seemed like a promise of freedom. Suddenly, the light began to pull away from him. *It wants to leave me here.* The world spun as Belac crashed to the floor, his fall softened by the corpse of a dead slave.

As a pair of hands pulled Belac up into a seated position, he mumbled, "I think there is something wrong with this floor."

Serath's gloved fingers took hold of the elf's chin. "Look at me, Belac."

Though it required effort, Belac was able to focus on the wizard's green eyes. "This is worse than the honey-booze."

Serath nodded. "I will get you something to help with that. But first, we must leave this place. We cannot stay here." He gestured toward the blackened chamber. "This will escalate. Delay has become a dangerous thing."

Belac remembered to not nod. "I can walk." *...If I can get up.*

Serath helped Belac to his feet and then stood by while the elf regained his balance. Once Serath was reasonably sure that Belac was not going to fall back over, the wizard continued on toward the light. Belac, for his part, focused on the complicated task of repeatedly putting one foot in front of the other. He felt like the chore would have been simpler, had the dead people not been in his way. *It seems kind of inconsiderate that they just died in the middle of the walkway like this.*

In the chamber beyond the corridor, priests joined the ranks of the dead. Men in gray robes and soot darkened eye sockets had been piled inside the short, circular wall in the center of the room. The priests' slaughter had been a bloody thing.

As Belac stumbled toward the gruesome heap of dead men, he asked, "How are we going to explain this?" He stopped and looked on the priests with pity.

Serath turned around and walked back to the elf. "We are not." He took hold of the elf's upper arm and began leading him away. "At least, not now. We cannot allow ourselves to be detained."

Belac agreed. "I hate prison."

Serath guided the elf through the temple and out into the warmth of day. Belac shut his eyes tight to block out the painful light that pierced the clouds above. Trusting in the wizard's guidance, he continued to put one foot in front of the other. Despite the city's smells, the air outside felt fresh in Belac's lungs. Still, as they left the temple behind, Belac was forced to rely more and more on the wizard for support.

Serath led the elf into a building that smelled of spiced fish and sour ale. "I am in need of a private booth."

Belac opened his eyes. *Who is he talking to?* The old tavern he found himself in was dimly lit and free of patrons. *I could use a drink.*

A potbellied man with thinning hair gestured to the room. "The whole place is private right now."

Serath's voice took on an edge. "I am in need of a private booth," he repeated.

The man nodded quickly. "Yes, my lord. I apologize for the impertinence."

As the man turned away, Belac closed his eyes again. He had decided that the old tavern was simply not worth the effort of looking at it.

Thirty-One

A feminine hand slapped Belac across the face. Though it was a familiar experience, he did not understand why it had happened on this particular occasion. "I didn't mean it," he mumbled to whoever it was that he may have offended.

A woman with a loose accent replied, "I have told you three times now, you are not allowed to sleep."

Belac opened his eyes. He did not know who the woman sitting across the table from him was, but he hoped that he had not married her while he was drunk. "You're not the boss of me."

Young and thin, the woman wore a cream-colored apron over her mauve dress. "I am until that man gets back."

What she said made no sense to Belac. "Who are you?"

The woman's homely face became ugly as she frowned. "You can't remember my name?"

I can't even remember where I am. Belac decided that he was just going to go to sleep.

The woman leaned over the table and slapped the elf across the face. "You can't sleep."

Dizzy, Belac struggled to focus on the tyrannical woman.

The woman pointed at the elf and said, "You are not getting me in trouble. I'm supposed to keep you here, and I'm supposed to keep you awake."

That is just mean. Belac did not think that he liked the woman very much. "Who are you?" he asked again, not remembering that he had asked before.

A faded red curtain to Belac's left was suddenly drawn open. He had not realized that one of the walls of his cozy booth had been made out of cloth. He reached over to his right and poked the wall, wondering if it was solid. The wall was obviously constructed of dry lumber.

Serath spoke from the opened curtain. "You can go now. Thank you."

The woman hurriedly left the booth, not bothering to bid the elf farewell.

Belac turned toward the wizard. "You just saved me from Slaparella." That had not been the woman's name.

Serath set a wooden tumbler down on the table. "Here. Drink this."

I could use a drink. Belac wrapped a hand around the tumbler and slid it closer. *As long as I don't get so drunk that I wake up married.* He looked up at the wizard. "I don't want to get married."

Serath shook his head. "I am not proposing." He gestured to the tumbler. "Drink."

Belac lifted the tumbler to his mouth and began to drink thirstily. The world dimmed and he became so dizzy that he lost his balance despite being seated.

Serath put one hand on the elf's shoulder to steady him, while the other took away the tumbler. "It will pass."

Belac felt like he was falling into a bottomless pit. Then the world brightened as his eyes dilated. He could feel every hair on his body standing on end. *Wow!* He gazed over at the wizard. "Did you just drug me?"

Serath tilted his head to the side and shrugged slightly in admission. "There is medicine in the ale." He let go of the elf's shoulder and then set the tumbler on the table. "You need to drink it."

Belac looked down at the tumbler. "Is it going to do that every time?"

"The effects should become increasingly more mild," Serath assured the elf.

Belac frowned. *At least the first time was fun.* He picked the tumbler up and took another drink. Though the medicine made his head feel like it was buzzing, he felt in no risk of falling out of his seat. *This is nice. It's not worth almost getting killed by an exploding cloud of magic dust. But, it's nice.* He finished off the drink and then pointed at the empty tumbler. "Is it okay to eat after this one?"

Serath nodded. "Yes. But that will need to wait until later."

Belac gazed down into his empty tumbler wistfully. "Can I get another drink?" *I think I deserve another drink.*

Serath reached down, took the tumbler, and set it on the table. "No. We need to leave."

"Yeah, okay," Belac muttered as he stood. *At least I'm not dizzy anymore.* He turned toward the wizard. "What's the plan?"

Serath shook his head. "This is not the proper place to discuss it."

Belac followed the wizard out into a narrow corridor that reminded him of a ship's alleyway. *He must be worried about spies.* Belac grinned as an idea came to him. "Don't worry. The king's cousin said that he would pay us even if we failed."

Serath looked over his shoulder at the elf as they passed by the open booths on their right. "What are you talking about?"

Belac winked overtly and then whispered, "I am trying to trick the spies." He raised his voice. "It's the captain's wife that we need to worry about." He winked again.

Serath shook his head dismissively as he led the elf out into the main room of the tavern. Other than the balding bartender, the only other people present were a young man and woman sitting together at a table in the far corner of the room. *They must be the spies.* Belac deliberately kept his gaze away from the couple.

The bartender held his arms out wide. "Is there anything else that I can do for you?" he asked with a voice that sounded sincere.

Belac narrowed his eyes at the balding man. *That is exactly what a spy would sound like.*

If Serath thought that the man was a spy, he did an excellent job of not showing it. "Not at the moment," he replied. "But I will keep you in mind."

That's right. Let them know that you are watching them too. As he followed Serath out of the tavern, Belac kept an eye on the suspiciously helpful bartender. Outside, clouds had covered the city as if jealously guarding it from the light of the sun. Few people still walked the streets, and those who did, were in an obvious rush to avoid the expected rain.

Serath too, moved with a sense of purpose. While the impending rain may have had something to do with the wizard's haste, Belac doubted that the weather was their biggest problem. *He thinks that something else is coming for us.* Belac kept pace with the wizard, intent on doing what he could to help identify the dangers lurking around them. *I don't want to get wet, but it might be worth it if the rain helps me pick out the spies. It is kind of hard to hide in the middle of an empty street.* He scanned the faces of the people he passed. None of them gave any indication that they were trained operatives. *Aldenon must have really good spies.*

Light drops of rain began to fall, spurring the denizens on. Belac looked up as thunder rolled in the distance. It occurred to him that the coming storm would soon feed The Tears of the Dead. *We left the magic pool of water unguarded. What happens if someone pees in it or something?* Belac's hair was matted from the sprinkling rain by the time he and Serath arrived at the smithy. After pulling the first bell cord, Serath pushed the gate open and stepped into the passageway under the rooms above. He moved to the side and waited for the elf to follow him inside before closing the gate.

Now sheltered from the rain, Belac halted and asked, "How far can the nillanan send their zombies?" He was concerned that the rain would loosen the soil. "There are a lot of dead people in Aldenon."

Turning to face the elf, Serath replied, "I cannot provide you with a meaningful measurement." He shrugged. "However, I doubt their next offensive will come in the form of the undead. In order for a nillanan to possess a vessel, the corpse must be properly prepared. The nillanan at the temple were destroyed. It is unlikely that they would risk more of their number to collect tools that have proven to be insufficient."

"They can only possess mummies?" Belac asked to be sure that he understood.

Serath nodded. "It was they who taught the humans to embalm."

Belac did not like the idea of the nillanan having an influence on human culture. "Why has no one hunted the nillanan down?" he asked angrily. *Those things are worse than dragons.* "They need to be..." he paused as he searched for the appropriate word. "Eradicated." He nodded with forceful approval. "The nillanan are in need of eradication."

Serath gave no indication that he disagreed. "There have been many who have attempted to do so. Your sentiment is not an uncommon one. It is why the nillanan rely on secrecy and seclusion." He motioned for the elf to follow him as he began walking through the passageway. "However, I urge you to keep in mind, that as vile as they may be, there are entities of far greater evil than the nillanan."

Belac frowned. "Then, we should kill those too."

As Serath stepped out into the gentle rain, he turned his head and smiled affectionately at the elf. "It is a marvel to witness how quickly your ambitions grow."

Staring at the wizard, Belac realized something. "You are not getting wet." He pointed at the wizard. "Why are you not getting rained on?"

Serath's smile broadened. "Because, I do not want to."

Thirty-Two

As Belac walked through the back door of the smithy, he congratulated himself for remembering to not use the trapped step. *I bet they put that trap there, just so they could get mad at me when I step on it.* He smiled to himself. *Now, they did all that work for nothing.*

As Vairug closed the back door and began securing its locks, an angry dwarf stormed into the storefront holding a hat.

Rolan held the wide brimmed hat up and demanded, "How did you do this?"

Belac's smile showed his teeth. "You are going to need to be more specific."

Rolan shook the hat. "I threw this in the canal!"

Belac had expected the dwarf to throw his hat somewhere. "That is a good way to get your hat wet," he replied as if attempting to be helpful.

Rolan glared at the elf. "How did you get back here before me?" He looked at the wizard suspiciously.

"I didn't," Belac answered honestly.

Rolan pointed at the hat. "Then, how is this not in the canal?"

Belac's azure eyes glittered happily. "Maybe it's a magic hat."

Rolan tilted the left side of his forehead forward aggressively in thought.

Vairug laughed as he asked, "You gave him a magic hat?" He had to fight to control his laughter. "And he cannot throw it away?" He lost the fight.

Rolan slammed the hat down on the counter, then drew a knife and stabbed it. Leaving the knife stuck in the countertop, he grabbed the hat's brim and yanked it free, slicing the back half of the hat in half. He took hold of the cut ends and finished ripping the hat in half. Then he threw the two pieces of the hat onto the floor and declared, "I do not. Want. A hat."

Belac crossed his arms. "Well, that's just rude." It was difficult for him to not smile.

Rolan turned around and marched out of the room.

Vairug slapped the elf's shoulder with the back of his gray hand. "I do not think that Rolan likes his hat." He laughed silently.

Belac bent down and picked up both pieces of the hat. "That's okay. The hat doesn't mind."

Serath raised an eyebrow at the elf.

Belac grinned at the wizard. "Did you want a hat?"

Serath returned the grin. "I believe that I can make do without one." He shook his head and then gestured to the elf and orc. "You two need to go pack your bags and bring them down here. I will speak with Rolan."

Vairug did not seem surprised by the instructions. "When do we leave?"

Serath reached out and removed the dwarf's knife from the countertop. "Immediately. Or rather, as soon as we are able. Aldenon is no longer hospitable."

Vairug looked over at the elf as if he suspected that the development was his fault. "What happened?"

Belac shrugged. "Nillanan, magic, a bunch of dead people. It was a whole thing."

Serath walked past the orc. "Gather your things quickly if you do not want them left behind." Before stepping into the hallway, he stopped and looked back. "And Belac… Don't play with the sword. Save its light for the dragon." Without waiting for a reply, he left the room.

Belac looked at the orc. "It glows now."

Vairug held up a gray hand to halt the elf. "You can show me later. I own too little to leave any of it behind." He began walking toward the hallway.

Belac followed Vairug out into the hallway, at first confused as to why the orc was not more interested in seeing a glowing sword. Then he remembered that Vairug thought swords were stupid. *We will see how stupid he thinks my sword is after he watches me chop a dragon's head off with it.* Belac imagined himself standing with one foot on a dragon's severed head, his glowing sword held high, while Vairug looked on, slack jawed.

After climbing the stairs up to the second floor, Belac went into his room and prepared his bags for travel. He stacked his two bags next to his door and then walked around the banister, a wide brimmed hat in his hand. Belac's fingers ran over the hat's long, white feather as he made his way into Rolan's bedroom. *I wonder if it's possible to make a person so frustrated that their head actually explodes.*

The dwarf's bedroom was even more sparce than Belac's. Other than a cot with a wrinkled blanket on it, the only thing in the room was Rolan's rucksack sitting neatly in the corner. Belac set the hat on top of the rucksack and then hurried out of the room. As he stepped out into the walkway, he heard someone coming up the stairs. *Ut-oh.* Quickly, he ducked into Vairug's room and hid with his back pressed against the wall.

Vairug, seated on the edge of his cot with an open duffle bag on the floor in front of him, regarded the elf curiously.

Belac held one finger up to his lips and waved his other hand vigorously.

Rolan walked past the doorway, grumbling to himself as he headed to his bedroom.

Vairug looked at the elf and made a poor attempt at raising one eyebrow.

Belac held up a finger, indicating that the orc should wait.

In his room, Rolan said, "No…" his disbelief carrying through the walkway.

Belac covered his mouth with both hands to stop himself from laughing.

Vairug tilted his head in curiosity.

Rolan marched past the doorway with his rucksack slung over one shoulder, and a gray hat crumpled in his fist.

Vairug's eyes widened at the sight of the hat. He pointed toward the doorway with one of the fingers of his mechanical hand. "Did the hat heal itself?" he whispered to the elf.

Belac held up his hands and shook them, indicating that the orc should not yet speak.

Vairug gasped. "You gave him a cursed hat!" he accused in a hushed voice.

Belac covered his eyes with the palms of his hands and laughed.

Vairug shook his head but smiled. "You are not going to think it is funny when he makes you eat that hat."

Leaning forward and twisting at the hips, Belac peeked out through the doorway. Once he was certain that there were no angry dwarves waiting for him, Belac stepped out into the walkway and peered down over the banister. *I have to remember that Rolan is sneaky too.* He turned away from the empty stairwell and spoke through the doorway. "Are you trying to get me caught?"

Vairug frowned. "You cannot evade Rolan forever."

"I don't need to evade him forever," Belac replied as he moved into the room. "Besides, if I evade him forever, I won't get to watch his head explode."

Vairug's back straightened. "You gave him a hat that will make his head explode?!"

Belac held up his hands and began shaking his head. "The hat will not hurt him," he enunciated clearly as he attempted to pacify the orc.

Vairug pointed a gray finger at the elf. "You just said that his head was going to explode!"

"Keep your voice down!" Belac admonished in a hushed voice. "That is just something people say. It means that somebody is angry or frustrated," he gestured to the orc inclusively, "or over excited."

Vairug crossed his arms.

Belac shrugged. "Blame the Dwarven language."

Vairug said something in Orcish.

Belac narrowed his eyes at the orc. "I don't know what you are saying," he replied in Elven.

Vairug's face suddenly took on a look of concern. He sniffed the air. "I smell smoke."

Belac turned and sniffed at the air, but he did not smell anything out of the ordinary. *Vairug's sense of smell is better than mine.* He looked back to the orc. "Maybe they are cooking me something to eat." *Someone would probably have yelled by now if the fire were uncontrolled.* "You stay here and finish packing. I will go check downstairs. If we are about to die, I will let you know."

Vairug gave a nod and then began hurriedly stuffing books into his duffle bag. "Go quickly."

Belac backed out of the doorway and then headed for the stairs. Though he did not think that the building was on fire, he moved expediently all the same. *I hope it's food.* He wondered if there would be any sweets to go with his meal. Halfway down the stairs, he began to detect the smell of smoke. *That does not smell very tasty, whatever it is.*

When Belac got to the hallway at the bottom of the stairs, he turned left. Following the smell of smoke, he walked into the workshop and found Rolan standing over a metal bin. A small fire burned in the bin, its smoke rising up to the ceiling. *Yeah. That is not food.*

Arms crossed, Rolan stared at the elf through the thin smoke. "I do not want. A hat."

Belac pointed at the burning hat. "I am not eating that."

Thirty-Three

Belac slipped the strap of his duffle bag over his head and then positioned the bag low on his back, with the strap riding on his left shoulder. *I am not going to be able to draw my dwarf-sword with this bag pressing down on the scabbard.* Once again, he questioned if the mechanical sword was worth the complications that accompanied it. *I don't have any other options right now. Sephen blades are sharp. I can't just stuff the naked edge in my bag.* He picked up his smaller bag and slipped its strap over his head. Then he began shifting the bag back and forth, trying to get its strap to lay comfortably behind him and the bag resting in front of his right hip. *I need to sit down with Rolan and invent a better way to carry things.* He wondered if the dwarf could create a mechanical carpet that flew.

Once his bags were situated, Belac walked into his bedroom and retrieved a gray cloak that he had left draped over the side of his cot. He slung the cloak over his shoulders, then fastened its silvery buckle. While the waxed canvas of the gray cloak would not disguise his wealth as well as the ratty one that Rolan had provided, Belac had left the other cloak in a dark catacomb with the dismembered bodies of unalived undead. He was not going back for it.

After collecting his belongings, Belac hurried down the stairs, grinning the entire way. *This whole place still smells like burning hat.* He found his friends waiting for him in the storefront. None of them seemed particularly well pleased with the lingering smell of burned felt.

Vairug flipped the hood of his white cloak up over his head, signaling that he was ready to depart.

Rolan was not wearing a cloak. He was also not wearing a hat. "…The plan 'B,' to make plan 'A' work," he said, finishing a joke.

Serath chuckled as he pulled open the back door. "I do not believe that roosters grow quite that large." He stepped out onto the porch and extended an arm low, his palm facing down.

Belac followed the wizard out onto the porch, trusting that Serath would warn him if something were about to explode. The dreary weather had persisted, its sprinkling rain coating the city in a wet sheen that glistened dully. Belac drew up the hood of his cloak, hiding more from the climate than the attentions of other pedestrians. *I feel like I am forgetting something.* He turned around, wondering what he could have forgotten.

Vairug halted in the doorway. "You are in the way."

With a frown, Belac turned and began walking toward the edge of the porch. *Usually, when I forget something, I don't feel like I have forgotten it. That is how I forget it. So… If I feel like I am forgetting something, then maybe I am probably not…* He shook his head. *That does not make sense.* As his foot came down on the porch's single stair, a click sounded from within the wooden step. A cacophony of metal pans being banged together erupted inside the building.

Belac froze in place. *Who can I blame this on?*

"You are still in the way," Vairug said impatiently over the noise.

Belac moved away from the porch. He waited until the alarm stopped before turning around to face his friends. None of them seemed surprised that he had set off the alarm. Serath walked off the porch, joining Vairug as Rolan locked the back door. The wizard did not use the step.

Belac narrowed his eyes at the orc. "Who won the bet?"

Vairug shrugged, not bothering to dissemble. "Rolan."

Belac sighed. "At least you didn't think that I would step on the trap."

Vairug shook his head. "I bet that you would step on it the first time."

Belac narrowed his eyes at the orc again. "Die in a fire."

Vairug's tusk jutted from his grin. He waved for the elf to follow him and then began walking toward the passageway that led to the street.

Belac followed, half-worried that he was being led into another trap. "Did you step on it?"

Vairug shook his head. "No. But I stayed inside the whole time. This is a dangerous place for me to be." He pulled the side gate into the passageway. "I will be glad to finally leave this city. It seems a poor example of what humans can achieve."

Belac nodded in agreement. "Aldenon is not much fun when you're sober."

Serath walked through the open gate. "There will be time enough for celebration later."

I don't need a celebration to get drunk. Belac followed the wizard through the gate. "Are you promising me a celebration?" He stopped next to the wizard and smiled with anticipation.

Rolan stepped past the elf, moving to stand on the wizard's right. "I can pretty much guarantee that there will be a celebration."

Belac turned his smile on the dwarf. "Are you saying, you can guarantee that we are going to win?"

Rolan was unaffected by the smile. "No. But if we lose, all the people that want us dead are definitely going to celebrate."

That was not a guarantee that Belac liked. He pointed at the dwarf. "You are not allowed to plan my celebrations."

The gate scraped as Vairug pulled it closed. "If no one celebrates your death, you did not live properly." He clapped the elf on the shoulder.

Rolan pointed his hand at the orc. "Keep your hands hidden."

Vairug nodded, accepting the reprimand without protest.

Serath began walking away, expecting the others to follow as he took the lead. Rolan and Vairug did indeed follow the wizard, walking side by side as they marched into the gloomy weather. Belac trailed behind, a mischievous smile growing on his face. He waited until their small procession turned onto a different street, and then he pulled a wide brimmed hat out from under his cloak. Struggling not to laugh, Belac crept closer to the dwarf. *You cannot escape the magic hat!* He set the hat down on top of Rolan's head and then shuffled to the right, putting Vairug between Rolan and himself. The elf wheezed with insuppressible laughter.

Vairug regarded the laughing elf curiously.

The attention made Belac's laughter more difficult to contain. He held his right hand up in front of his face and pointed to his left, not trusting himself to speak.

When Vairug and Belac looked left, they both saw that Rolan had stopped walking. They halted, turning around to better view the dwarf. Belac knew what Rolan was thinking. The magic hat was not going to leave him alone. It was raining, albeit lightly. The hat would keep the rain from falling on his head or running down his collar. He could use the hat now and throw it away later, just as easily as he could throw it away right then.

Having stopped farther down the street, Serath called out, "Why have you stopped?" He chuckled at seeing the hat. "It looks better than a barrel, Rolan."

Rolan looked like a dwarf that wanted to kill a hat.

Belac had to lean on Vairug's arm for support as he laughed through his nose.

Vairug was polite enough to laugh silently.

Rolan began walking, saying nothing as he resumed his trek through the unpleasant weather.

Vairug matched pace with the dwarf, leaving Belac to laugh alone. Stumbling forward, Belac followed his friends. Serath waited until the group had caught up, before continuing to lead them onward. *Someone needs to make a song about a magic hat.*

After his mirth had died down, Belac began scanning his surroundings. He found both the gloom and the glistening stone buildings to be rather uninteresting. However, he did think that the long feather sticking out of Rolan's hat was amusing. Belac watched the white plume bounce up and down as the dwarf marched along stoically. *I wonder how long it will be before Rolan asks Serath for help countering the magic of the hat.*

When they reached the Temple of The Ancient, Belac saw that the pond was already active. A series of horse drawn carts were being pulled out of the distorted field under the crystal arch. Belac watched through the bars of the back gate as two men in white robes moved to open it. He considered the glowing magenta runes of the pond's arch, wondering if hidden runes glowed underground.

Once the gate was open, Belac and his friends filed into the temple grounds. As they walked toward the temple, Belac asked, "Are we going through the same way as before?" *I will need to warn Vairug about the sneaky lights that want to make him crazy.*

Still in the lead, Serath shook his head. "No. Not on this occasion. This time, we will be passing through directly."

Despite being in the rear where none of his friends could see him, Belac pointed. "The pond was already open when we got here."

Rolan glanced back at the elf. "Did you figure that one out on your own?"

Belac frowned at the dwarf. "What would we have done if we had not gotten here before it closed?"

Serath turned his head and raised an eyebrow. "You are paying attention," he said in a congratulatory tone.

Belac did not feel complemented. "Enough to notice that you did not answer the question."

Serath grinned and then nodded toward the pond. "If we had arrived after the pond's closing, we would have needed to either convince the attendants to reestablish the connection, or wait until its next scheduled opening."

Belac did not like how the wizard had so plainly stated such an obvious answer. "You could have warned us that we might miss the pond being open." *I would have brushed my hair faster.*

Serath seemed genuinely confused by the elf's accusatory statement. "I did tell you that we needed to hurry."

Belac sighed. *Maybe wizards just know so much, that they don't know what needs to be explained.* "You're right. You told us to hurry, and you got us here on time." *I am not sure why I am so irritated.* He forced himself to grin. "Do you know what would..."

"No," Serath interrupted the elf. "You are not getting a magic carpet."

Belac's grin suddenly felt more honest. *I'm hungry, the weather is miserable, and a lot of things want to kill me. But at least I have my friends.* "What about flying boots?" he asked playfully.

Rolan seemed to support the idea. "I think you should get him some of those," he told the wizard.

Serath frowned at the dwarf. "He would kill himself with them," he argued disapprovingly.

Rolan gave a nod. "I know."

Belac smiled. "Die in a fire."

As they approached the backside of the pond, Belac wondered what the other travelers thought of his strange group. *The bag under Vairug's cloak makes him look like a hunchback.*

Remembering that he too was carrying a bag under his cloak, Belac glanced over his own shoulder. *I hope I don't look like a hunchbacked orc.*

Serath led the group through the back of the pond without ceremony. The world on the other side was both brighter and colder. *I did not think to ask where we were going.* Belac gazed up over the walls surrounding the temple grounds. He recognized the blocky architecture immediately. *We're in Lindell!* Belac felt like he had come home.

Rolan stopped, turned around, grabbed the brim of his hat, and then slung it off of his head. Spinning, the hat flew through the pond and landed on the wet stone in Aldenon. He squared himself with the hat, crossed his arms, and stared.

Halting with the others, Serath complained, "This is a waste of time, Rolan."

Rolan did not budge. "I'm waiting."

Belac laughed reservedly. He did not mind waiting. *Totally worth it.*

Vairug frowned at the elf. "This is your fault."

Still laughing, Belac nodded his agreement.

Stubbornly, Rolan waited for the pond to close. Then he nodded his head aggressively before turning left and walking away.

Struggling to suppress his laughter, Belac hustled after Rolan and set a wide brimmed hat on the dwarf's head.

Thirty-Four

Rolan's head did not, in fact, explode. Nor did he murder Belac for gifting him a magic hat. Rolan did not even force the elf to eat the hat. However, he did begin to plot his revenge. Belac could feel him doing it.

Rolan had removed the hat, crushing it in one of his square fists. Hat held as if it might try to escape, he silently followed the wizard through the streets of Lindell. Belac attempted to remain silent as well, but he was not very good at it while laughing.

Vairug nudged the elf and nodded toward the dwarf ahead. "Are you worried that Rolan will kill you in your sleep?"

Belac frowned at the orc. "Rolan is not going to kill me in my sleep."

"I believe you are correct," Vairug agreed before qualifying, "I think that he would want you to be awake for it."

Belac narrowed his eyes at the orc.

Vairug grinned inside his hood.

Belac looked away from the orc. *Rolan is not going to kill me.* He considered the dwarf's disgruntled posture. *Uhm…* "Hey, Rolan." Belac did not wait for a response. "If you kill me, the hat turns into a giant spider." *A magic hat might do that.*

Rolan gave no reply.

The group arrived at the king's palace without discovering if Rolan's hat would turn into a giant spider. As they ascended toward the front doors, Belac found it vexing that no one else seemed to care that the steps had been made wrong. *I should ask Roger if there is a secret entrance that I can use. I hate these steps.*

The two guards standing outside the doors to the palace made no move to impede Serath as he led his group past them. Though Belac could not see the guard's faces inside their helmets, he waved as he walked between them. Neither of the two guards moved from their posts, nor gave any indication that they had noticed him. *They probably just don't recognize me with my hood pulled up.* Belac had not met all of the palace guards, but he liked all of the ones that he had. More than once, he had needed their help to elude the Elven delegates.

Inside the palace's grand hall, a gathering of advocates milled about on the left, while others traveled through the spacious room. Finely dressed men and women, they passed by each other without comment as they moved intently from one corridor to another. *It seems kind of busy in here.*

Serath moved the group off to the right side and then stopped. He waited for the other three to gather in close before saying, "It would be best if you were to wait here while I arrange for accommodations. The guardsmen have been made aware of Lord Vairdoe's condition, but many of the people here would find him alarming."

Vairug nodded inside his hood. "I will keep my hood up and my head down."

Belac disliked that the orc needed to hide who he was. *Vairug is a better person than any of these stupid humans.* "Why don't we just announce him?"

Serath nodded. "We may need to. However, I would prefer to avoid the attention that such an action would attract. Our circumstances are not as secure as they might seem. Discretion and expedience will be necessary if we are to succeed in our quest."

Belac frowned, but nodded his consent.

Serath smiled reassuringly. "Take heart, Belac. We will succeed." Then he turned and strode away, his strides quick and determined.

Belac was still not happy that Vairug needed to hide who he was. *Well, at least I don't have to hide. They like me here.* The elf unbuckled his cloak and removed it. He dropped it onto the stone floor and then set his luggage down on top of it. *I hope Serath brings back someone to carry my bags for me.*

Belac began stretching his back. "Just you wait, Vairug. This place is great. Once we explain to everyone who Lord Vairdoe is, you can run around and have fun with me."

Rolan interjected disagreeably, "We are not here on holiday."

Belac's brow contorted. "If you think that you have to wait for a holiday to have fun, then it's no wonder why you're always so grumpy."

Vairug spoke, choosing his words carefully. "Is it not likely, that there are people here who would be familiar with Enevician nobility?"

Belac reconsidered his plans to have fun. *Someone here might suspect that a rowdy orc stumbling around drunk is not actually a well-bred lord of Enevic.* "Maybe we should just have drinks brought to our rooms." He nodded at the idea. "I bet that we can even get a harp."

Vairug's hood shook side to side. "I don't know what a harp is."

"It's a big musical instrument," Belac explained, holding his hands out in approximation.

Vairug seemed to find the prospect of music appealing. "Do you play well?"

"Me?" Belac asked. *Probably not.* "I know that you strum the strings to make noise." He mimed playing a harp.

"That cannot be how it is done." Vairug said reprovingly.

Belac shrugged. "We can just keep drinking until it sounds good."

Vairug chuckled amiably.

Out of the corner of his eye, Belac saw an elf in silk vestments walk out of a corridor and into the grand hall. *I should have kept my cloak on!* Belac spun around, facing away from the other elf. *Don't see me. Don't see me. Don't see me.*

Rolan looked at Belac's face, then to the Elven delegate, then back to Belac, then down to the hat he held crushed in his own grip, then back up to Belac. Rolan grinned villainously.

Belac glared at the dwarf. *Don't you do it, Rolan!*

Rolan took a step to the side. Raising his voice, he called out in Elven, "Greetings, Noble Elf."

When the delegate turned to see who had addressed him, Rolan asked, "Have you met my friend Belac Melavar?" He gestured. "He's The Dragon Slayer." Under his voice he grumbled in Dwarven, "He likes magic hats."

Fists clinched, Belac bared his teeth at Rolan. *Stupid dwarf!*

Keeping his head turned away, Vairug laughed silently.

Belac turned to face the Elven delegate. Holding his hands out to his sides invitingly, Belac offered the fakest smile he could muster. "Cousin!" he said in Elven as if pleased to see the delegate.

Vaserie swept his long, shimmering black hair off of his shoulder and then pointed at the other elf. "We have been looking for you," he proclaimed in Elven.

Belac dropped his arms. "Really?" he asked in Elven.

Vaserie stopped a pace away. "We have questions for you," he asserted in Elven.

Belac raised his hands, each with a finger pointed at the delegate. "And I would love to answer those questions," he lied in Elven. Leaning to the side, he waved to someone behind the delegate.

Vaserie turned around, but was unable to determine whom Belac had been waving to. Perplexed, Vaserie turned back to the other elf, only to find that Belac was already half-way to the nearest corridor.

Arms and legs pumping, Belac fled like an orphan who had just stolen sweets. *Let's see if you can catch me while wearing that stupid dress!*

Thirty-Five

After losing Vaserie in the interconnected hallways of the palace, Belac had sought refuge in the king's parlor. Though King Rodric had not been present, Belac had been content to wait. He had not even asked the guards to provide a password.

Belac was laid out on a sofa, enjoying chocolates and wine. He had needed to twist his sword belt and move the starmetal blade in front of himself to get comfortable, but coming up with the solution had made him feel good about himself. When the king finally walked into the room, Belac raised his bottle of wine up high and shouted, "Roger!"

Rodric smiled at the elf fondly. "If I had known that you would only be gone for but a single day, I may not have been so worried."

Belac hopped off the sofa and hugged the king. "You're my favorite human."

Rodric hugged the elf back, unconcerned that the open bottle of wine might stain his gray velvets. "And you, Belac, are by far, my favorite elf."

Belac released the king and then stumbled back a step. "They almost caught me!"

Rodric frowned with amused befuddlement. "The elves?" he guessed.

Belac responded with an exaggerated nod. He leaned forward and confided, "I was worried that I might have to crawl through the privy again."

Rodric chuckled. "I will see about having escape passages commissioned for you."

Belac nodded happily. "That's a good idea." He pointed with his free hand. "You could use them too."

Smiling behind his beard, Rodric walked over to the bar and began to fix himself a drink. "When I was a child, I use to enjoy searching the palace for secret doors."

Belac imagined a bearded little boy holding up a lit candlestick as he checked behind a painting for a hidden passage. "Did you find any?"

"Of course," Rodric replied proudly.

Belac adjusted his sword belt and then plopped down on the sofa. "Did you ever burn your beard?"

"What?" Rodric turned around, a silver goblet in his hand.

Belac pointed to the king's goblet. "Don't you have people to fill that for you?"

Rodric looked at his goblet as if just reminded of its purpose. He took a drink and then began walking toward the closest of seven empty armchairs. "I thought it best if we spoke privately."

Belac nodded. "Spies," he said, believing that he completely understood the king's concerns. *Why else would anyone take a job like that?* Belac wondered if he could catch spies by simply walking around and asking people if they wanted to be a servant. *Maybe I could build a booth. With a sign. And a little trap door…* He took a pull from his bottle of wine. *I could just sit there and let the spies come to me. Then I could drop them down into a pit.*

As Rodric took a seat, Belac began to contemplate the various horrors that he could have waiting at the bottom of his pit. *Spikes, snakes… Zombies! But where am I going to get zombies from?* He swished the wine inside his bottle. *Maybe I could put something in the pit that kills the spies and then turns them into zombies.*

Rodric took a sip from his goblet and then said, "Serath."

Why would I want to put Serath in the pit? I don't think that he would even let me. Belac looked at the king, not comprehending why he had brought up the wizard. *He might be talking about something else.* Belac thought back on their earlier conversation. *I told Roger that he was my favorite human. And Serath is also a human.* Belac nodded, thinking that he now understood. "I like Serath," he told the king. "But he's a wizard. He doesn't count." *I think that wizards should probably get their own category.*

Rodric gave the elf a confused look and then waved his words away. "He is going to get you killed."

"Serath?" Belac did not want to get killed.

Rodric nodded. "The man's plan is madness. If he were one of my generals, I would have him discharged summarily."

Belac raised an eyebrow at the king. "You know that wizards are sneaky, right?"

"I know that they cannot be trusted," Rodric replied with conviction. He took a drink before continuing, "I think he means to feed you to the dragon."

That's crazy talk. "I am not food," Belac stated brusquely. "Besides, Serath would not have gone through all the trouble of making me a magic sword, if he were just going to feed me to a dragon."

Rodric was unconvinced by the argument. "It is nothing more than a sharpened piece of metal."

Belac shook his head and sat up. "Not anymore." He set his bottle of wine on the floor and then stood up. "It's a magic-dragon-killing-sword now." He straightened his sword belt and thumbed the snap on the scabbard. Cerulean light spilled into the parlor as he drew the starmetal blade.

"By my father's eyes," Rodric exclaimed softly. He set his goblet on the end table next to him and leaned forward. "That is a magic sword in truth."

Belac held the glowing sword up above his head vertically. *With this sword, I will free the world.*

Rodric held out his hands. "May I?"

Belac lowered the sword. "Sure." He sheathed the blade, squeezed the quick release on his sword belt while maintaining his hold on the scabbard, and then tossed the sword to the king.

Surprised by the abruptness of the action, Rodric almost dropped the sword as he fumbled to catch it. He took a deep breath and then asked, "Are you not concerned that you might break it?"

Belac shrugged. "If it breaks from getting tossed across the room, I don't think that it would hold up very well against a dragon."

Rodric tilted his head in acknowledgment of the point. He took hold of the sword's hilt and drew the blade halfway from its scabbard. He frowned at the milky white blade. "Why is it no longer glowing?"

"It only works for me," Belac explained as he picked up his bottle of wine.

Rodric looked up from the blade. "Why?"

Belac grinned. "Because, I'm The Dragon Slayer."

Rodric returned the exposed blade to its scabbard, and then secured the leather thumb snap. "You believe that this can kill a dragon?" he asked honestly.

Belac nodded. "As long as I am the one who wields it."

Rodric set the sword down on his lap and sat back with a sigh. "And there are people who believe that kings have choices," he muttered to himself.

"Cheer up." Belac took a drink of wine. "Serath says that I get a celebration once the dragon is dead."

Rodric laughed. "Belac, if you kill that dragon, I will give you your own holiday."

Belac's eyebrows shot up. "Belac-Day!"

Rodric shook his head as he continued to laugh. "I am certain that we can devise a better name for it."

Not likely. Belac reached forward to a side table and took a small chocolate from a long, white plate. "Maybe we can set tiny paper dragons on fire or something." He popped the chocolate into his mouth.

Rodric nodded agreeably. "We could call it, "Slayer's Rest."

Belac swallowed the chocolate while shaking his head. "I don't want a holiday where everyone just rests the whole time." *Then, I would just have to do everything myself.*

Rodric shrugged and reached for his goblet. "We will think of something."

I did think of something. Belac-Day. Belac ate another chocolate instead of arguing.

Rodric took hold of the starmetal sword and stood. "I will do what I can to aid you, Belac." He held out the scabbarded sword.

Belac set his wine bottle down on the table and then rose to his feet. "You already gave me a castle," he mused as he took back his sword.

Rodric picked up his goblet and used it to salute. "And if all you faced were the rain, that might be enough."

Thirty-Six

Belac stumbled drunkenly through one of the palace's dimly lit corridors. *I am not lost.* He was lost. *Is this the third hallway… or the fourth?* He had passed six other corridors while searching for his turn. *How does anybody find their way around here?* Belac had never been in the area of the palace that he now found himself. Secluded and previously unoccupied, the wing of guest suites that his friends were quartered in had not been selected for ease of access.

I should help Roger come up with a new system. Belac stopped and fingered his chin. *Maybe we could train animals to lead people around. Something small and fuzzy.* He frowned. *No. Animals would not know where people wanted to go.* He imagined a foreign dignitary getting lost because a cat wanted to chase a mouse. *Maybe we could hire some of those little people. What are they called?*

Belac snapped his fingers and said out loud, "Scamps!"

He nodded to himself. *They're not fuzzy, but they are small enough to stay out of the way when they are not leading people around.* He smiled excitedly as another idea came to him. *We could let them ride the cats!*

He could see it in his mind; tiny little people riding on the backs of saddled house cats as they led fancifully dressed humans through the palace. *We would need to find some way for them to open doors…* He began to design an overly complicated pully system in his mind. It would not have worked.

Belac turned around, accepting that he would need to retrace his steps and recount the corridors. *I know that I know how to count to five.* A man dressed in the gray uniform of a palace servant was walking toward him. While Belac could have asked for directions, he instead held two fingers up, pointed to his own eyes, and then pointed at the oncoming man. *I see you.*

Typical of a well-trained servant, the man gave no indication that he was offended. He lowered his head slightly and continued about his business. When he was one pace away from the elf, the man raised a dagger over his head and then stabbed downward as he lunged forward.

Caught completely off guard by the attack, Belac raised his left arm up in alarm. The man's forearm slammed into the elf's, and then the inside edge of the dagger cut into Belac's arm.

"Assassin!" Belac cried out as he held back the blade.

The assassin put his left hand on top of his right and pushed the dagger down into Belac's upper chest. Belac stumbled and fell backward in his struggle to keep the blade from plunging deeper. Steel bit into the bone of Belac's forearm as the assassin followed him to the floor. The tip of the assassin's dagger sank deeper into Belac's chest.

Belac's right hand clinched the hilt of the dagger strapped to his thigh and drew the sephen blade. The assassin's left hand shot out and grabbed the elf's right wrist, pressing the sephen dagger to the floor. With his knees straddled atop the elf, the assassin brought his own dagger up and then back down. The assassin's blade stabbed through Belac's triceps and down into his chest. Only the daggers hilt catching on the elf's upper arm bone stopped the blade from sinking deeper.

As the assassin raised his dagger again, Belac twisted in, pressing his left shoulder against the man's chest. The assassin's dagger stabbed into Belac's shoulder blade, the steel tip catching on bone. Belac twisted in tighter, moving his head down to his captured wrist. In desperation and rage, he bit the assassin's thumb.

The last segment of the man's thumb tore free in Belac's mouth as the assassin jerked his hand back. The sephen dagger surged upward, its blade punching between the assassin's ribs and into his heart. Belac stabbed the assassin three more times and then spat the severed joint at the man's face. With a snarl, Belac pushed the assassin off to the left. Leaving his sephen dagger in the assassin's chest, Belac rolled to his right. He wanted to call out for help, but he could not catch his breath. *Is this happening because I wanted to listen to music in the pool?*

Using his right arm, Belac pushed himself up onto the carpeted hardwood floor. *He could have just quit.* The elf sat back on his ankles. *If the man didn't want to do chores or go fetch things, he shouldn't have been a servant.* Belac took hold of his left hand with his right, pulling it against his body. *I would have just quit.* He coughed blood and then wheezed as he struggled to breathe. *I hope the other servants don't try to turn this guy into some kind of servant folk-hero.*

Though Belac's breath was slow and labored, he could feel his heart beating raggedly in his chest. Blood continued to seep into his clothing and drip from his elbow. *I could really use one of those cat-mounted scamps right about now.* He coughed blood again, the heaves bringing pain to his numbing wounds. *I can't just sit here and die.* He leaned forward. *Well, I guess I could. But that seems like a bad plan.* He shifted his weight and planted his right foot on the floor. *I am not going to let some guy kill me, just because he hates music.*

The world turned black as Belac stood. Luckly, the elf had a considerable amount of experience with staying on his feet while dizzy. He waited for his vision to return, and then he turned around. Another man dressed as a servant was standing a throws distance down the corridor. The man stood motionless, as if unsure how to react.

Belac glanced down at the dead assassin. "I can totally explain this," he said weakly. *I hope the new guy likes music.*

The world spun around Belac. He did not feel his face hit the floor. He did not feel anything.

Thirty-Seven

Air rushed into Belac's lungs. Like fire, he felt his wounded flesh knit back together. Light flooded his eyes, the world too bright to see. A stout hand held his chest down against something soft. The world dimmed as a painted ceiling came into focus; tiny, red leaves on a field of white. Slowly, his breathing normalized.

Rolan removed his hand from the elf's chest. "You almost ended up in a soulstone," he claimed annoyedly.

Vairug's voice came from the other side of the bed. "We would have used a green one."

Belac closed his eyes. "Die in a fire."

Rolan poked at the elf's bare chest where his wounds had once been, and then he lifted the elf's healed arm up for examination. "You let yourself get carved up pretty bad."

Belac recognized the affect that had brought him back from the brink. "You used a full-strength potion on me."

Rolan dropped the elf's arm. "The choice was to either let you die, or risk killing you with the potion. You're welcome."

Belac opened one eye and aimed it at the dwarf. "Healing potions can kill me?" *It does not seem like it should work like that.*

Rolan nodded. "That's one of the reasons why I dilute them."

You need more reasons than, not killing me? Belac opened his other eye. "What are the other reasons?"

Rolan shrugged. "They're expensive. They're rare." He shrugged again. "And they can kill you."

Belac closed his eyes. *It is starting to seem like everything wants to kill me.*

Rolan continued, "Speaking of which. Where is that squarish, leather pouch that I gave you?"

Belac knew what pouch the dwarf was referring to. "It's in my bag." He remembered the pouch being empty.

Rolan spoke from across the room. "Vairug?"

"I will get it," Vairug assented to the implied request.

As Rolan walked out of the room, he said, "I will be right back."

Belac breathed deeply and attempted to relax. *The worst part, is that I'm not even drunk anymore.*

Vairug began to laugh. What started as little more than a chuckle was soon full bellied laughter that could undoubtably be heard from outside the room.

Belac opened his eyes and sat up on his elbows. *Did Rolan sneak something into my bag?*

Rolan walked back into the room. "What are you laughing at?" he asked as he moved closer.

Crouched on the floor to the right of the door, Vairug held up Belac's smaller bag. The top flap had been opened and pulled back, revealing a stack of gray hats, the sides of their wide brims bent up to allow them to fit in the bag. There was a leather tube sitting on top of the hats that Belac knew was filled with long, white feathers. *Wrong bag.* Rolan looked from the hats, to the elf. Rolan was not laughing.

Belac smiled weakly. "Uhm… What? How did those get in there?"

Vairug dropped the smaller bag on the floor and reached for the duffle. "Do you think that we will find more hats?" He laughed as he began opening the duffle bag.

Belac forced his smile bigger.

Rolan held up a wooden block with three vials protruding from it. "These are for the assault on the dragon. They are full strength. So don't use them unless you are sure that you need to."

Belac frowned. *You just said that those things can kill me…* "How will I be sure?"

Rolan shrugged. "If your face gets burned off or something."

Belac's eyes went wide. *Not my face!* "Why didn't you give me those things sooner?"

Rolan shook his head dismissively. "Some people get addicted to them." He pointed a finger at his head and whirled it. "They can also make a person go wrong in the head."

How many of those things have I drank?! Belac narrowed his eyes at the dwarf. "That seems like something you should really tell people."

Rolan shrugged. "I am telling you now." He gestured to the elf. "Would you rather be dead?"

Belac puckered his lips. *No.*

Vairug twisted at the hips and held out a squarish, black leather pouch with a steel, tuck lock clasp. Rolan took the pouch and then walked over to the foot of the bed as Vairug began stuffing things back into Belac's duffle bag. Rolan set the wooden block down on the bed, freeing his hand to depress the lock on the clasp of the pouch and open its rigid top. He picked up the wooden block, slipped it into the open pouch, then closed the lid over the vials inside.

After securing the clasp, Rolan walked over to a chair and set the pouch down on the padded seat. "The pouch will fit on your sword belt."

Belac saw that both of his swords had been lain on the floor next to the chair. His right hand went to his thigh. "Where is my dagger?"

Vairug stood. "It is in the other room." He began moving toward the door. "I will get it for you."

Belac gave a sigh of relief and then reclined back on the bed. His left hand touched the dagger on his left thigh, assuring him that it was there. *Maybe I should tie cords to them or something so that I don't lose them.* He imagined himself spinning like a top as his daggers windmilled from the cords tied to his belt. *I think that would just make me dizzy.*

Belac felt someone remove his right boot. He opened his eyes and tilted his head up. The boot clomped onto the floor, and then Rolan reached for the elf's other.

"Thanks, Rolan," Belac said with genuine gratitude.

Rolan shrugged the sentiment away. "I did not save your life, just to let your feet rot."

Belac dropped his head back down onto the bed. *That would be kind of a mean thing to do.* "Is it too late to save that assassin's life and then let his feet rot?"

Rolan chuckled. "It is too late to save his life, but I bet his feet still rot."

Belac wiggled his toes. "Does anybody know why he tried to kill me?"

"It was probably because someone hired him to do it," Rolan speculated dryly. "There are a lot of people that want us dead."

Belac still did not understand why anyone would want to stop him from slaying a dragon. "Maybe it was a jealous husband."

Rolan's frown was in his voice. "If that is what you are worried about, then maybe you deserved to get stabbed a bit."

Belac rocked his head side to side on the bed. "Not my fault."

"Right," Rolan replied sarcastically. "The women drugged you and tied you up."

"They tricked me!" Belac argued in his own defense.

Rolan harrumphed.

"They did!" Belac insisted.

Rolan did not bother arguing.

Thirty-Eight

A night in a soft bed and a morning in a warm bath left Belac feeling more relaxed than he had felt before getting stabbed. His bottle of breakfast wine may very well have also had something to do with his current state of relaxation. *I think lounging in the parlor might be worth getting stabbed every once and a while.* Though Belac could have had food and drink brought to his room, he knew that the fare would be superior in the King's parlor. *I wonder if Roger will let me just start sleeping in here. No one is going to try to stab me to death in the parlor.*

Belac slid his feet off the sofa and set them on the floor. He considered a long serving table that was positioned against the wall to his right. *If I sleep under that table, I won't even be in the way.* His thoughts were derailed by the pastries laid out on the table. *It would be kind of rude to not eat some of those.* He stood and adjusted his sword belt. *I would not want Roger to think that I'm ungrateful.*

Wine bottle in hand, Belac walked over to the serving table. While he appreciated the variety of pastries on offer, the quantity made him question if the king was expecting more guests. *More people means, more spies and assassins.* Belac selected a tiny cake and popped it into his mouth. *Oh, this is good.* It tasted of cherry and sugar. He picked up another tiny cake and then turned to face the king.

Seated comfortably in one of the oversized armchairs, Rodric's head was leaned back, his eyes closed.

Belac pointed with one of the fingers wrapped around the neck of his wine bottle. "You still haven't apologized."

Rodric's eyes did not open. "I am sure that I must have at some point in my life."

Belac took a drink from his bottle, disliking that the sweetness of the pastry had made his wine taste bitter. "I mean, for letting one of your servants stab me." He pointed at the king again. "He stabbed me a lot."

Rodric shook his head without lifting it. "That was not one of my servants."

"He looked like one of them to me," Belac retorted and then popped the second tiny cake into his mouth.

"Obviously, that was intended." Rodric opened his eyes and sat up. "It is not terribly difficult to find gray cloth in this city, Belac."

Belac frowned. *That's a good point.* "Yeah, okay. I guess I forgive you."

Rodric chuckled and leaned his head back again. "There is an investigation underway. Anyone that was involved will be interrogated and then executed."

Belac could not help but notice that the king spoke of execution with the same tone that he used when ordering lunch. *You probably don't get to be king without killing a few people.* Belac turned back to the table. *Besides, people need to be killed, and food needs to be ordered. Getting all emotional about it is not going to make either chore more palatable.* He set his bottle of wine down so that he could use both hands to pick up a large pastry that was covered with walnuts and cinnamon.

As Belac took a bite of the pastry, a knock came from the doors behind him. He turned, chewing the delicious pastry as he wondered who had come to join them. *There is plenty of food to share.* He swallowed and then frowned. *As long as it's not another assassin.*

Rodric swiveled his head to look at the doors. "What is it?" he asked, though his words sounded an order.

One of the doors cracked open and a palace guard leaned into the room. "Your Majesty, the Elven delegates are here to see you."

Belac tossed his unfinished pastry on the table, grabbed his bottle of wine, and ran. Vaulting over the sofa in his mad rush to escape, he sprinted for a side door that would lead him into the theater.

Rodric was laughing too hard to reply to his guardsman.

Once in the theater, Belac turned right and hurried to the doors that would open into the hallway. He pushed one of the doors open a fraction and whispered, "Psst. Hey."

One of the two palace guards that stood outside the doors replied, "Belac?"

"Keep your voice down!" Belac hissed. "And don't say my name." He knew the guard. *Auster probably won't turn me in.*

Amused, Auster asked, "What are you doing?"

"Quiet!" Belac insisted again. "Let me know when those snooty elves leave the hallway."

The second guard asked, "And why would we want to do that now?"

Ut-oh. Belac grimaced. "Uh… Hi, Bannam." *Don't ask him how his sister is doing. Don't ask him how his sister is doing.*

"Hello, Belac," Bannam replied and then elevated his voice. "My good friend, Belac."

Belac covered his eyes with one hand. *This is not fair.*

In a disingenuously helpful tone, Auster suggested, "We could ask the delegates, when they plan on leaving."

Bannam matched the other guard's tone. "Maybe if we let them know that Belac is waiting for them to leave, they might be willing to change their plans."

I didn't know that she was your sister!

Auster laughed. "I bet that they would even thank us."

Belac dropped his hand and threatened, "If you turn me in, I am telling Lord Vorwell about your loaded dice!"

Suddenly serious, Auster replied, "Hey, that's not funny, Belac."

Belac pushed the door open farther and leaned his head out. "Neither is…" There were no elves in the hallway.

Auster's laughter echoed in his helmet. "You should see his face!"

Belac narrowed his eyes at the guard. *Everyone should see my face. It's beautiful.*

Bannam tapped the side of his own helmet with a gauntleted finger. "You know… It's not too late to go tell them." He only sounded half-joking.

Belac shoved the door open and stepped out of the theater. "That's what you think." He turned around to face the guards. "I would be gone before you got back."

Bennam shrugged. "One of us could hold you here."

Belac bounced side to side playfully. "Have you ever tried to catch an elf?"

Bannam laughed despite himself. "Go. Get out of here."

Auster pointed. "But you can leave that bottle of wine if you want."

Belac pulled his bottle back and away from the guard protectively. *You are not getting my wine, Human.*

Bannam laughed again. "Let him go," he said charitably.

Belac began backing away from the guards. "Tell Tiffany I said, Hi." He turned and ran.

Belac did not stop running until after he had rounded the corner of an intersecting corridor. Laughing, he took a drink of wine. *Maybe I should give Bannam a hat.* Wine shot out of Belac's nose at the thought of a wide brimmed hat sitting on top of the palace guard's helmet. *I could bring what's left of my bag of hats, and use Bannam's head like a ring toss!*

Thirty-Nine

Belac was still laughing when he reached the secluded suite that he and his friends had been provided. However, his idea to use Bannam's head for a ring toss had evolved into a game that included every guard in the palace. Belac felt certain that the ones who participated involuntarily would prove to be the most fun. *I just need my bag of hats.* A new element of the game spontaneously developed. *And a wheelbarrow!* Eager to begin organizing his game, Belac opened the door to the suite and stepped into the sitting room that served as a lobby for the bedrooms.

Rolan walked out of the elf's bedroom. "Where have you been?" he asked irritably.

What was he doing in my room? Belac pointed at the dwarf. "Did you burn my hats?"

Rolan came to a halt and crossed his arms. "Are you drunk?"

Belac raised an eyebrow. "What does that have to do with my hats?" He stopped in front of the dwarf and pointed at him with one of the fingers holding his bottle of wine. "Are you drunk?"

Rolan snatched the bottle out of the elf's hand. "You almost bled to death just last night!"

Belac held out his empty hands. "And now, I'm trying to replace the blood." He laughed.

Rolan clenched a fist and bared his teeth. "Our goal is not, to get the dragon drunk when it eats you!"

Belac swiped at the air dismissively. "I'll be sober when we fight the dragon." *Probably.*

Rolan nodded. "Alright then. I'll make you a deal." He held up the bottle of wine. "You can have this back, if you promise, that from now on, you won't drink any alcohol on the day that we plan on slaying the dragon."

Belac knew that he could easily go and get another bottle of wine. The problem was that he would need to go get it. *I kind of just want to drink that one.* "Fine. I promise." He held out his hand.

Rolan slapped the bottle into the elf's hand. "Good." He crossed his arms again. "Because today, is the day we slay the dragon."

Belac shook his head. "No, it's not."

Rolan nodded his head affirmatively in contention. "Yes, it is."

Belac tried to think of a better argument. *Uhm…* "No, it's not."

Rolan pointed his hand at the elf's left hip. "We have the sword. It's time to put it to work."

Belac had not stopped shaking his head. *I'm not ready.* He forced his head to stop. *I have an idea.* "Yeah. So… We have the sword. And that's great. But now… Now, we need to go on the quest for dragon-proof armor." He nodded his head. "It can be a whole thing. Maybe this time we will need to find a talking lama or something."

Rolan shook his head.

Belac held up a finger to forestall the dwarf's response. "It doesn't have to be a lama."

"Belac…" Rolan began before he was cut off by the elf.

"It could be a racoon," Belac interrupted. *It has got to be hard to find a talking racoon.* For some reason, he expected the racoon to be rude.

Rolan pressed on. "There is no such thing as dragon-proof armor. Even if you had a full salamander suit, the dragon's fire is so hot that it would cook you inside. Just breathing the air could burn your lungs."

This was not making Belac want to fight a dragon. "But... Magic."

Rolan shook his head. "Even if we found something, the dragon would just swallow you whole. You do not want to die that way."

"I don't' want to die any way!" Belac protested.

Rolan nodded. "And that's why we need to kill the dragon quick. At this point, there are too many people that know what we are up to. Killing that dragon is the only thing that is going to make our enemies back off."

"How does that work?" Belac demanded. "Killing their dragon is not going to make them want to kill us any less!"

Rolan shrugged and gave a nod. "Revenge will be a problem. But most people won't work if they're not getting paid. Whatever it is that they expect to get from the dragon, they are not going to get it if the thing is dead. Besides, stopping us seems to be their primary motivation right now. Once we kill the dragon, that motivation goes away. No one is going to try to stop us from killing a dragon that is already dead."

Belac wanted to argue more. *I thought I would have more time.* "Do you really think that we can do this?"

Rolan pointed his hand at the elf's wine bottle. "If you can stop trying to drink yourself stupid."

Belac looked at the bottle of wine. *I guess it's time to get serious...* "How do dwarves get sober?"

Rolan laughed. "Mostly, they don't. But don't worry. There is still time. I'll ask Serath to give you something to sober you up, and then we can get you something to eat. Besides, it's early. You can't be too drunk."

Belac raised an eyebrow at the assessment.

Rolan clapped the elf on the shoulder. "You'll be fine." He turned around. "Let's get you suited up," he said as he walked away.

Belac's eyes brightened. "I get new clothes!"

"Something like that," Rolan replied without looking back.

Belac stepped over to an end table, set his bottle of wine down, and then hurried after the dwarf. "Is it flying boots?!"

Rolan walked into the elf's bedroom without answering.

I am going to get to fly again! For a moment, Belac forgot about the dragon he was meant to face. *I would rather have a carpet. Or a chair. Or anything other than boots, really. But I'll take boots if it means that I get to fly.*

When Belac walked into his bedroom, he found what looked like a pile of snakes on the bed. He jumped back through the doorway, stumbled to the side, and hid behind the wall. "That is not flying boots!"

"You're right," Rolan agreed from within the bedroom. "There is a pair of boots though."

Belac peeked around the edge of the doorframe. "Why are there snakes on my boots?"

"What are you..." Rolan's original question ended when he saw the elf's head sticking out into the doorway. "Would you get in here?" he asked irritably as he waved the elf into the room.

Belac could see that the pile of scales on the bed was not writhing. *I don't think that is snakes.* He stepped into the bedroom. The glossy black scales remained motionless. *Those look like clothes.*

Belac pointed at the scaly garments. "Is that a salamander suit?"

Rolan nodded grumpily. "For all the good it will do."

Belac grinned. "You said that there was no such thing as dragon-proof armor."

"And I was right," Rolan insisted. "There is no such thing as dragon-proof armor. So, don't climb into the dragon's mouth." He gestured to the crumpled salamander suit. "This thing is just to help you not get caught on fire."

Belac walked over to the bed and picked up a glass jar that was sitting next to the pile of scaly black leather. "What's this?" He tilted the jar sideways, but the yellowy substance inside did not move.

"You have to wear your weapons over the suit," Rolan explained. "If you rub that stuff into your leather straps and your scabbards, it should keep them from getting burned up." He pointed his hand at the elf's right hip. "Don't forget to do the pouch also."

Belac thought he had a better idea. "I might just have one of the serving girls come in here and smear this stuff all over me."

Rolan shook his head. "Don't waste it." He nodded toward the bed. "The suit will keep the flames off you."

Belac set the jar down on the bed and picked up part of the salamander suit. He shook it out, discovering that it was a jacket. "This thing sure has a lot of buckles on it."

Rolan nodded. "That is just how they are made. The buckles allow for a more universal fit."

Belac lowered the jacket. "You didn't make it?"

Rolan shook his head. "I don't like working with that stuff. There is something about it that makes the bones in my hands itch."

Belac reconsidered the jacket. "That does not make me want to put this on."

Rolan had no sympathy for the elf. "Would you rather burn to death, or itch a little?"

Belac did not realize that the question had been rhetorical. "How much am I going to itch?"

Forty

Belac did not think that the salamander suit itched. *Rolan is just a crazy person.* The leather's black scales shimmered as the elf preened in the mirror. The boots, over-pants, long gloves, and hooded jacket were held tight to his slim form by a series of straps and buckles. The hood was his favorite part of the suit. Not only would it protect his hair from fire, it would keep the long strands from getting caught in his mechanical scabbard.

After applying the yellowy grease to his equipment, Belac had moved his potion pouch to the belt of the harness that secured his daggers. The pouch hung a little loose on his hip, but he wanted to be able to remove his sword belt without it taking the pouch with it. The longer he carried the starmetal sword on his side, the more certain he became that he did not want it there. He liked the sword, but when the time came that he needed to run, he wanted to be able to do it unincumbered. He expected that there would be running involved when facing a dragon.

"I don't look very heroic…" Belac muttered to himself. *Maybe I should go see what Vairug thinks.*

Belac left the bedroom without having any actual plan as to what he would do if Vairug disapproved of the salamander suit's appearance.

As Belac walked through the sitting room, he gazed at the open bottle of wine that he had left on the end table. He was hungry and thirsty, and he knew that the wine would ease his worries. *I have work to do. It is not just me that suffers if I make a mistake.* He knocked on Vairug's door and then waited for an answer. *I wonder if Vairug knows that we are supposed to kill the dragon today.*

"Come in." Despite the words, Vairug did not sound particularly welcoming.

Belac ignored the orc's tone. He opened the door, expecting to find his friend reading a book. Instead, he found Vairug standing afore the foot of the bed, attempting to adjust a long sleeve of black scales over his silvery mechanical hand. Though the scales covering the orc's left shoulder and upper back were a vibrant red, he wore a salamander suit that matched Belac's. *Vairug must be too big for an unblemished hide to fit him.*

Belac walked into the room. "If you try to tuck it in like that, it is just going to pull loose." He took hold of the orc's wrist and began readjusting the sleeve. "Why don't you just put a glove over this?"

Vairug held up his other hand, displaying the scaly glove that covered it. "This one barely fits my real hand."

Belac grinned as he tightened the last strap on the orc's salamander sleeve. "We could stuff an empty glove with cloth and then swap it with your metal hand."

"Only if you want me to slap you with it," Vairug countered.

Finished with the adjustment, Belac released the orc's wrist. "Well, you're grumpy today."

Vairug frowned. "I dislike this plan. It seems foolhardy."

Belac shrugged. "A wizard and a crazy dwarf made it. Maybe they thought that if it made more sense, it wouldn't work."

Vairug shook his head. "You are as crazy as they are."

Belac held his hands out to his sides. "Do you have a better plan?" *Because, I kind of hope you do.*

"Goats," Vairug replied forcefully.

Belac raised an eyebrow. "Does that mean something different in Orcish?"

Vairug shook his head. "We use goats." He held up a gloved finger. "First, we feed them something that will poison the dragon. Then we set them loose in the city." He rotated his hand, turning his palm up. "We let the dragon eat the goats." He held up his finger again. "Once the dragon is suffering from the poison, we go in and finish it off." He made a fist.

Belac found himself nodding along with the orc's plan. "I like this plan." He held up a finger of his own. "As long as we leave out the poison and the goats when we tell people the story."

Vairug shrugged. "You can tell people whatever you want."

Belac grinned. "It's not like the dragon will be around to contradict us." *I am going to need a good story.* "Maybe I could say that I jumped on the dragon's back and flew it into a building."

Vairug saw a problem. "If the crash killed the dragon, how would you survive?"

Belac held up his hands. "I could say that I jumped off at the last moment."

Vairug shook his head. "You would still die."

Belac clapped his hands together excitedly and then pointed at the orc. "And that is why Serath needs to get me a flying carpet!"

Vairug frowned. "You are complicating my plan."

Belac was undeterred. "Do you want it to work?" He did not wait for an answer. "Of course, you do." He held up a finger. "We are also going to need a wheelbarrow."

From out in the sitting room, Rolan called, "Vairug. I have something for you."

Vairug stepped around Belac and then walked out of the room as if grateful for the excuse.

Belac turned, tracking the orc as he walked around him. "Do you think he has the wheelbarrow?"

Vairug did not answer.

Belac followed the orc out of the bedroom. In the sitting room, he discovered that Rolan had not brought a wheelbarrow into the palace. However, what the dwarf had brought was just as big.

Belac stepped to Vairug's side and considered the tall tower shield of dull gray metal that had been laid out on the sofa. Stood up on its edge sideways, the shield's face had been leaned against the cushions, exposing the handles and straps on its back.

On the right side of the shield, at what Belac assumed was its top, a hexagonal recess had been set into the center. *I am glad I don't have to carry that thing.*

Rolan gestured negligently toward the shield. "This is Sulvendar's Sheild." He looked at the orc. "Serath wants me to make sure that you know, you are not allowed to keep it."

Vairug nodded solemnly. "I understand."

Belac looked from the shield to the dwarf. Rolan too was outfitted in a solid black salamander suit, his belted pouches and knives holding the dark leather tight to his stocky form. *I wonder how long it took him to grease all those leather straps.*

Rolan raised his right fist, holding up a hexagonal medallion hanging from a chain. Both the medallion and its chain were obviously made from the same dull metal as the shield. "This is the key." On the surface of the medallion, three line segments converged in the center of a raised hexagon, creating the illusion of a cube inside a cube.

Belac pointed to the hexagonal recess in the back of the shield. "I'm guessing, it goes there."

Vairug stepped closer to the shield to better study its workings. "Why does a shield need a key?"

Rolan lowered the medallion. "When you fit the key into that socket, the shield projects a magic barrier." He pointed his hand at the orc. "Don't use the magic when you are in a building. Or if anyone is standing to the left or right of the shield." He shrugged. "At least, not if it's someone you like."

Vairug glanced at the dwarf. "Is the magical barrier hazardous to touch?"

Rolan shook his head. "Not so far as I know. But anything that is in the way when the barrier gets deployed is going to get moved out of the way. Hard."

Vairug reappraised the shield. "Can it be used as a weapon?"

Rolan scratched his stubbled cheek. "Maybe. But once you deploy the barrier, the shield won't move. Plus, the magic does not always work if you try to use it again too soon."

Vairug gave the dwarf a skeptical look. "Its function is unreliable?"

Rolan held his arms out to his sides. "It's old."

Vairug frowned.

Belac grinned at the orc. "Are you going to let him talk about your shield like that?"

Forty-One

Vairug's hooded cloak rippled in the breeze, the white fabric held down by the carry strap of his tower shield. Rays of sunlight reflected off the geometric patterns worked into the shield's surface. Standing tall, the orc held a leaf bladed spear with its butt planted on sapphire marble and its tip aimed at the midday sky. From within the folds of his hood, he gazed out at the dormant arch of the pond. Stoic and resolute, Vairug showed no fear of the impending assault on the dragon.

How come I don't look that heroic? Belac turned away from the orc and studied the men standing in formation on the other side of the arch. Five rows of twenty, the men of the Royal Guard each wore a suit of the ornamental armor that set them apart in the palace. They stood with their feet wide and their awl pikes held at their sides, each of the shinning spikes aligned perfectly in the formation. *Even the humans look more heroic than I do.* Belac did not see how flat toped helmets and fur edged skirts were going to help the men fight a dragon. *Maybe the fancy armor is meant to distract the dragon so that I can stab it.* He tongued one of his teeth. *If that was not the plan, it is now.*

After drinking a bitter tonic while eating a quick lunch that Belac had thought was far too small, Rolan had led Vairug and the elf through the city and to the Temple of The Ancient.

Once there, Rolan had left Belac and Vairug outside with the soldiers while he went into the temple to find Serath. Belac was tempted to lay down on the ground and relax while he waited. *I never would have expected dragon slaying to have this much waiting involved.* He looked down at the bronze inlayed marble that made up the temple grounds. *That does not look very comfortable.* Belac wondered if he could convince someone to bring him a chair.

Vairug growled irritably. "Why would we need to bring priests?"

Belac turned around and followed Vairug's gaze toward the temple. Serath, Rolan, and another member of the Royal Guard had exited the gothic temple. Behind them, four men in hooded, white robes trailed closely.

"They must want to retake the temple in Enevic," Belac told the orc. "I bet that there are more of them traveling through below." He gestured to the pond. "I don't know how to make that thing work. It is probably a good idea to have people on the other side that can operate it." He frowned. "Though, I guess we could just wait until they open it up for us again on this side."

Vairug nodded. "Serath may not wish to risk waiting."

Belac's eyes moved toward the wizard, but were drawn instead to the gilded staff that Serath carried. A golden snake spiraled up the black core of the staff, giving it a twisted shape. At the top of the staff, the serpent's head held a glittering orb in its open mouth. As Serath moved closer, Belac saw that the orb appeared to be a transparent enclosure containing a piece of the night sky captured inside. *That's new…*

Belac took a moment to consider Rolan. *What new magical stuff is he bringing?* The dwarf carried nothing that Belac had not seen before. Though Rolan had traded his rucksack for a salamander hide satchel, he had done so before leaving the palace. Even the oblong, wooden box strapped to his left arm had been present when they left. Belac had found the device mildly interesting, but it had not seemed magical. He had assessed the T-shaped handle sticking out on one side of the box and the rectangular opening on the other, recognizing the work as Rolan's.

Belac did not know what the small, round disc on the top of the box would do, but he assumed that it would activate an overly complicated mechanism and reveal a weapon inside. When asked about the device, Rolan had replied dismissively.

Oddly enough, Belac found what the armored man carried to be more intriguing. Contrasted with the grandeur of the temple and the regalia of the Royal Guard, the rough-spun haversack seemed out of place to Belac. *That looks like something a farmer would stuff with grain.* There were no pack animals prepped for the assault, and he did not think that a dragon was likely to eat oats.

As Serath, Rolan, and the armored man approached Belac and Vairug, the priest diverged and continued on toward the arch of the pond. Though no order had been given, the priests behavior appeared coordinated to Belac. *They know what the plan is.* He reconsidered. *Or, at least they know their part in it.*

When Serath reached the elf and orc, he stopped and gestured to the armored man that accompanied him. "This is Captain Harshaw. He commands the detachment of the Royal Guard that will be assisting us." Serath grinned. "He knows who you two are."

Captain Harshaw bowed slightly from the waist. "It will be an honor."

Belac gave a nod to the captain. "I appreciate the help." He almost made a joke about having a ballad written for each of the men who died, but he decided that it would be in poor taste. "There are no soldiers I would rather have with me, than the noble guardians of Lindell." While the statement was untrue, he thought that it sounded good.

Harshaw bowed again.

Belac pointed a finger at the wizard's obviously magical staff. "That's a fancy stick."

Serath smiled. "It will serve as a lure."

Belac raised an eyebrow. "You want the dragon to focus on you?" *That's fine with me, but it might not go so well for you.*

Serath shook his head. "The nature of the staff is not something that will attract the dragon."

Belac frowned with confusion.

Rolan explained in an offhanded fashion. "It is for the ghosts."

"Ghosts?!" Belac exclaimed.

Vairug asked, "When did this become about ghosts?!"

Belac pointed at the orc and nodded his head vigorously.

Rolan shrugged. "A lot of people died in Enevic. Some of them became ghosts. Now, they are wondering around, protecting the place."

Serath offered a slightly different scenario. "It has been hypothesized that the ghosts linger so as to warn people away from the danger of the dragon."

Rolan shrugged again. "It amounts to the same thing."

Vairug no longer looked like an orc without fear. "How are we to fight ghosts?"

Belac pointed at the orc insistently.

Serath raised his staff off the ground. "This will draw the apparitions away." He lowered the staff, causing it to clink on the sapphire marble. "I will take the Royal Guard through the pond and then lead them west." He reached into the black bag he carried under his arm and pulled out a wood framed sandglass. "Wait until the sands fall. Then travel through the pond and head north." He handed the sandglass to the dwarf. "Rolan knows the way."

Belac was suddenly angry. "You want to feed the soldiers to ghosts?" He pointed at the wizard aggressively. "Humans are not food!"

Serath's ensuing smile held both pride and affection for the elf. "The soldiers will be in no great danger." He indicated to the captain of the Royal Guard. "Each of the men will be given an enchanted talisman. It will provide them with protection and allow them to disrupt the apparitions."

Captain Harshaw opened the sack he carried and then held it out for inspection. Silver gleamed within. Belac reached into the sack and took one of the talismans. Inside a solid ring of silver, copper wire had been strung into a five-pointed star. *Maybe I should keep one of these.*

Belac held up the talisman and looked at the wizard. "Can I…?"

Serath nodded. "We have more than we need."

Vairug dropped his spear, stepped forward, and took one of the talismans for himself.

Belac grinned at the orc. *How can he be more scared of ghosts than dragons?* Belac opened his potion pouch and forced the talisman in between the wooden block and the rigid leather. As he closed the pouch, something occurred to him. His eyes snapped to the wizard. "You're not coming with us." *He can't lead the ghosts away and still be there when we face the dragon.*

Serath smiled reassuringly. "You will triumph without me." There was no doubt in his words.

Maybe. But I bet it would be a lot easier if I had a wizard with me. Belac thought about the arcane sands that the wizard had employed in the catacombs. "Can I at least take some of that purple dust with me?" *I will remember to shield my eyes.*

Serath seemed to know what the elf was asking for. "Having such a thing would serve no purpose. You would be unable to activate it. And even if you could, it would not harm the dragon." He gestured to the sword on the elf's hip. "You take with you the magic you will need."

I am going to die. In his mind, Belac recalled the dragon breathing fire into the night sky, its dark blue scales glistening in the fire's radiance. *How am I supposed to kill that thing with just a sword?*

Serath placed a hand on the elf's shoulder. "You will succeed, Belac. Though the task before you is great, you need only accept that you are greater."

Belac shook his head. "I am not greater than a dragon." *Because… It's a dragon.*

Serath found the statement amusing. "Maybe not yet." He removed his hand. "But still, you will succeed."

Belac thought back on how his day had begun. When he had awoken, safe in a luxurious bed and surrounded by opulence, the morning had enticed him with the promise of self-indulgence. There had been no call to responsibility nor any perception of imminent danger. He now felt as though he had been tricked. *I should have hidden under the bed.*

Forty-Two

The sands of time fell faster than Belac would have liked. He stared at the sandglass, dreading the fall of the final grain. He thought it odd that such a small thing would decide when he was going to die. *I wonder if I could just flip it over when no one is looking.* Seated cross-legged with the sandglass in front of him, Belac slowly turned his head side to side as he investigated who might be watching.

Rolan and Vairug stood off to the side, gazing into the pond. Though only a distorted view of another Temple of The Ancient could be seen, Enevic waited on the other side. Two priests stood on each side of the magical portal next to one side of the glowing arch.

No one would see the elf if he flipped the sandglass. *I can't do that to Serath.* Belac sighed. *Besides, putting off what needs to be done, won't make it not need to be done.*

Rolan glanced down at the sandglass. "It is almost time to go." He reached into his salamander satchel and pulled out a diminutive water bladder. He removed the stopper with his teeth and then took a drink. After two gulps, he lowered the bladder. "Here. Drink some of this." He held out the bladder, its stopper dangling from a cord.

Belac put his right hand on the ground and stretched out with his left to take the bladder. "What's in it?" *It seems like a bad idea to try to fight a dragon drunk.*

Rolan shrugged dismissively. "Water mostly."

Belac narrowed his eyes at the dwarf. "Rum is mostly water." He held up the bladder. "What is the not-mostly part?"

Rolan exhaled tolerantly. "I added something to help with endurance." He waved his hand as if brushing the elf's concern away. "It's mild."

Belac sniffed at the bladder's mouth and then took a drink. Though it tasted like water as he drank it, the mixture left a faint sweetness behind. "I kind of like it." He held the bladder up for the orc.

Vairug tilted his head back slightly. "My fortitude is not in need of aid."

Rolan took the bladder. "Sure." He held the bladder out to the orc. "But drink it anyway."

Scowling, Vairug accepted the bladder. He then made a show of rubbing the bladder's mouth around the insides of his lips before drinking the contents.

Rolan chuckled. "What do I care? Your spit doesn't work anymore."

Vairug glared at the dwarf.

Rolan laughed. "It's not my fault you're broken."

Vairug threw the bladder at the dwarf.

Treated water spurted out of the bladder's mouth as it smashed into Rolan. He caught the bladder and then held it up. "You can thank me later." He replaced the stopper.

Smiling at the exchange, Belac glanced down at the sandglass. Every grain of sand had fallen. His smile died. *It is time to learn the truth. Am I a fool that is about to feed myself to a dragon? Or am I The Dragon Slayer?* Belac stood and straightened his sword belt. "Let's go kill a dragon."

Rolan dropped the bladder on the ground next to the sandglass. "I am just coming along to watch you do it."

Vairug unclasped his cloak and then tugged it out from under the carry strap of his shield. "If this shield's purpose is to give you a place to hide, Rolan, we could have brought a smaller one." He tossed his cloak aside and grinned at the dwarf.

Rolan frowned at the orc.

Vairug laughed silently as he bent down to pick up his spear.

Belac took a deep breath and then marched into the pond. The cool air of Enevic enveloped the elf's face, tightening his skin and reminding him that he was no longer in the vaunted city of Lindell. He pulled up the hood of his salamander jacket. *All those people from Cavasca are in for a surprise when they get here.*

Belac turned and gazed over the temple walls at the burned rooves of a dead city. He wondered how much of the blackened buildings could be salvaged. *It will be even colder when the Cavascans get here. They will need homes that can keep them warm.* Frozen mountains in the distance stood like a warning of the weather to come.

Rolan stepped through the pond, his head shaking side to side.

Vairug followed immediately after. "My plan was better," he insisted.

Rolan threw up his hands. "Well, I don't see any goats."

Vairug pointed his spear at the dwarf. "That is because the wizard is impatient."

Rolan began shaking his head again. "I don't know of anything that can poison a dragon, Vairug. There might not even be anything."

Vairug slammed the butt of his spear down on the sapphire marble of the temple grounds. "I know that there is a weed called 'dragon's bane."

Rolan dropped his head and sighed. "Yes." He looked up at the orc. "But if I call a donut 'orc's bane,' that does not mean that it will kill you if you eat it."

Belac turned toward the dwarf. "Do you have a donut?"

Vairug frowned at the elf. "You would eat something called 'orc's bane?"

Belac shrugged. "I'm not an orc."

Rolan began walking around to the other side of the pond. "We can eat later."

Belac followed the dwarf. "Okay. But you owe me a donut."

Walking beside the elf, Vairug muttered, "I hope he calls it 'elf's bane."

The main gate to the temple had been left open. Beyond it, the true ruin of the city could be seen. Though most of the buildings still stood, portions of them had been toppled. Charred wreckage lined the streets in testimony to the cruelty of flame. There was no mirth waiting in the city; no peace, save that which was promised in death.

The silence of the city was complete as the three friends left the temple behind. It did not stop Belac from imagining the screams of the past. He saw that the stone surrounding the buildings' doorways had been melted. He imagined terrified people fleeing for shelter, only to have fire breathed into their homes. *This was not about food or nourishment.* Belac could feel the evil of what had been done. *This was an extermination.* His left hand gripped the hilt of his starmetal sword. *I will kill you, Father.*

Vairug spoke into the silence. "I hear no sounds of battle."

Rolan nodded. "It's Serath's job to draw the ghost's west." He gestured to his left. "They might already be outside of the city by now."

Vairug cleared his throat. "You don't… You don't think that they might have left some of them behind, do you?"

Rolan turned his head and grinned at the orc. "They might have. A city this size would have to have a lot of ghosts." His gray eyes twinkled mischievously. "I wonder if they'll be mad that you have been pretending to be their lord."

Vairug glared at the dwarf. "They will not know, if you don't tell them!" He began looking around, obviously worried that they may have been overheard.

Rolan chuckled. "Maybe. Maybe not. They're ghosts. Sometimes, ghosts just know things."

Vairug glowered. "This is not funny, Rolan." His dark eyes darted side to side as he searched for ghosts. "Ghosts attack not just the body, but the soul."

Rolan did not seem terribly concerned. "You should have thought of that before you made them mad."

Vairug stopped walking. "How is this my fault?!"

Rolan continued on. "Maybe we should ask one of the ghosts."

Vairug glanced left and right, and then hurried to catch up.

Belac found none of the banter amusing. As he marched through the dead city, all he could taste was blood and ash. He knew that people had once been happy there. He knew that men and women had toiled for their families, and that children had played in the streets. He knew that joy, and love, and aspiration had once animated the city of Enevic. He could see it all in his mind. And he knew that the dragon had burned it all.

There would always be pain and strife in the world. However, the malevolent force that was The Danorin was not something Belac could tolerate. He hated that such a thing could exist. He hated that it was his father. *I will avenge these people.* He imagined the dragon in crisp detail. *And I will burn what is left of your corpse.*

Forty-Three

The buildings that surrounded the public square were a crumbled arrangement of ruin and rubble. Burned stone and charred wood had been pushed to the sides to make room for the monstrous thing that slept there. Laid out in the center of the flagstone square, leathery wings tucked tight to its sides, it slumbered with feline languidness. Its deeply saturated blue scales glimmered in the afternoon light as it breathed slowly in and out. A creature made for the darkness of night, it seemed content to sleep surrounded by the shadows of ruin.

That dragon is bigger than some of the buildings we passed by getting here. Belac looked to his friends, checking their resolve. Vairug's face was hard, his eyes staring out at the dragon intently. There was a determination in his orcish features that spoke of a commitment to violence. Rolan, however, looked like he could have been out for a stroll in the park. Calm and collected, the dwarf's eyes swept over the ruins in search of movement. Belac's attention moved back to the dragon. *I should kill this thing before it wakes up.*

Belac's left hand gripped the scabbard of his starmetal sword, while his right squeezed the buckle of his sword belt. The buckle separated, freeing the belt from his waist. His right hand moved over to the hilt of the sword. *I hope this doesn't wake it up.*

Eyes locked on the dragon, Belac thumbed the scabbard's safety strap and then drew the starmetal sword. Cerulean light pressed back the shadows as the glowing blade left its scabbard.

Belac crouched down and quietly set the empty scabbard on the ground. *I can come back for this after I don't die.* He slowly straightened, continuing to watch the dragon for any indication that his presence had been detected. *Just keep sleeping, you evil piece of filth.* Carefully, Belac began skulking toward the dragon. *Just keep sleeping.*

Belac could feel the emptiness of the city around him. He could feel the emptiness of death. *Humans bring laughter and joy to the world.* His azure eyes bore into the dragon. *And you burned them.* His grip tightened on the hilt of his sword. *Now, it's your turn to burn.* In his mind, he heard Serath speak of the starmetal sword. *"And it will burn the dragon."*

Halfway to the dragon, Belac held out his left hand, signaling for his friends to halt. He could hear neither of them behind him, but he thought it best to minimize the risk of waking the dragon. *We are here to kill this thing, not fight it.* With slow, stealthy steps, he continued on. As he approached the sleeping dragon, its true size became more apparent.

Despite being laid out in the open square, the dragon's ridged spine was higher than a giant was tall. Even with the jaw of its angular head resting on the flagstones, the dragon's massive eyes were level with those of the elf.

The dragon's eyes opened.

Belac froze. He stared into a single, deep blue eye as its vertical pupil focused on him. All of Belac's righteous anger bled from him in an instant as it was replaced with fear. He slowly raised his left hand, palm facing the dragon. "Hi, Dad," he said weakly and then waved his hand from the wrist.

Though hardened scales covered the dragon's head, its face more closely resembled that of a wolf than of a reptile. Its scaly lips pealed back in a snarl, revealing rows of black fangs. An angry wolf.

The air vibrated as the dragon growled. It raised its head and leaned to its left. The dragon's right hand swept out, its taloned fingertips raking the air as it swatted at the elf. Belac dropped to the ground and rolled as the claws passed over him. Coming to his feet, he knew that indecision would kill him as surely as the dragon's wrath. *I have to strike now.* He rushed forward, his glowing sword held ready to thrust.

Off-balance from its attack, the dragon dropped onto its right shoulder. Belac leapt, placed his left hand on the dragon's scaly shoulder, and then drove his sword into the side of its long neck. Blue fire erupted from the wound, lighting the snarl on Belac's face. *Die!* The dragon roared in anger and pain. But it did not die. It shifted its weight to its left side and lashed out with the back of its right arm, throwing the elf away. Belac held tight to his sword, the glowing blade a blur as he spun through the air.

Landing on the flagstones shoulder first, Belac rolled to his feet and faced the dragon. Dark blood leaked from the wound in the side of its neck. *Now, I know you bleed.*

A leaf bladed spear flew overhead and struck the dragon's snout. The sharpened steel bounced off harmlessly, only stoking the dragon's ire. The dragon rose to all fours, causing the air to shudder as it drew in breath. *Dragons breathe fire.* Belac charged, sprinting directly toward the dragon.

Fire spewed onto the flagstones as Belac ran underneath the dragon. Crimson flames flowed past his ankles as the dragon's breath spread out. Heat bit into the flesh of his ankles and calves despite the protection of his salamander suit. Screaming, Belac thrust his cerulean blade up into the dragon's exposed chest. Blue fire erupted from the wound, and dark blood spilled down onto Belac's face. He cared no more about the blood on his face than he did about the burns on his legs. In that moment, he wanted to burn the dragon's heart more than he wanted to survive.

The scaly fingers of the dragon's left hand wrapped around Belac and then jerked him backward. The elf's hand slipped from the bloody hilt of his sword as the starmetal blade caught on the dragon's ribs. Then Belac was soaring through the air, his arms and legs flailing for balance. His left hand hit the ground, and then his face hit the back of his hand. After tumbling awkwardly over the flagstones, he came to a stop on his back with his feet pointed at the dragon.

Belac stared up at the monster towering above him. The dragon glared down with rage. Blue fire still sprayed from the dragon's chest. Supporting its weight on its left hand, the dragon reached under itself with its right and took hold of the hilt of the starmetal sword. It yanked the sword out of its chest and then held the baneful weapon out in front of itself. The blade burned with blue flames.

Eyes still glaring down at the helpless elf, the dragon shifted its grip on the sword, and then snapped the flaming blade with its thumb. The top portion of the blade flew to the dragon's left as smaller pieces flashed into the air. *No…* With open contempt, the dragon tossed the broken sword to its right. The cerulean light was no more. *I am going to die.*

The air shuddered as the dragon drew breath. *I was a fool to think that I could do this.* Vairug stepped in front of the elf and planted his shield on the ground. His right hand pressed the key to Sulvendar's Sheild into its socket. Hexagonal plates of golden light crystalized into existence above and to the sides of the shield, creating a wall between them and the dragon. Fire slammed into the wall, the crimson flames fanning across its golden surface.

Belac remembered that he was not alone. *My friends could die too.* He sat up and searched for Rolan. The dwarf was behind him and to his left. *He's not dead. We could still all escape.*

Rolan pulled a rectangular metal box out of his salamander satchel and rocked one end into the opening on the side of the contraption on his left arm. He rotated his left forearm and grabbed the T-shaped handled on the other side of the device. Then he yanked his arms apart, pulling a captured cord out of the wooden box. A high-pitched spinning noise issued from the box and continued to hum persistently. When he let go of the T-shaped handle, the cord retracted back into the wooden box, pulling the handle back into place.

As soon as the flames stopped, Rolan ran to the left of the shield. Once past the golden barrier, he extended his left arm and pointed his fist at the dragon. With his right hand, he reached across and repeatedly slapped the round disc protruding from the top of the humming box. Small wooden missiles shot out of the front of the box, flying over the dwarf's fist and toward the raging dragon. Light exploded when the missiles collided with their target. Yellow, purple, red, blue; each explosion staggered the dragon. *That crazy dwarf is shooting soulstones!*

Black smoke fumed from the dragon's right wing. Dark blood glistened on the broken bones and ravaged flesh. Rolan slowed as he analyzed the damage his weapon had inflicted. He gripped the metal box and rocked it out of the wooden launcher. Then he dropped the metal box to the side and reached into his salamander satchel for another.

Fire sprayed wildly as the dragon swept its head toward the dwarf. Instead of reloading his launcher, Rolan sprinted into one of the ruined buildings. Irate, the dragon breathed in and then blasted a torrent of flame into the doorway of the building. Stone melted as crimson fire chased the dwarf inside.

How can I help without the sword? Belac looked to Vairug, only to find that the orc was no longer there. The key to Sulvendar's Shield was still socketed, but its chain hung loose. Belac scrambled to his feet, searching for the orc with worry. *Vairug would not flee.*

From far to the right, Vairug was racing toward the dragon. In his mechanical hand, he held the top half of the starmetal blade in an underhanded grip. The blade was glowing cerulean blue. He came up behind the dragon's left arm and drove the blade into the back of the dragon's elbow. He pressed his right hand against his mechanical left and dragged the starmetal blade through blue flames.

The dragon collapsed onto its chest with a roar of surprised pain. Its left wing swept forward and smashed into Vairug, sending the orc flying across the square. Though Vairug was able to keep hold of the starmetal blade, he landed without grace. The dragon pulled its left arm back and pushed itself up with its right. Vairug attempted to rise, but fell back down to his hands and knees. The air shuddered as the dragon drew in breath. *He can't get away.*

Belac ran from the safety of the magic barrier. He dove through the air and crashed into Vairug, rolling him out of the way as dragon's fire scorched the ground. Searing heat flashed against Belac's back as he and Vairug rolled away. Once they came to a stop, Belac rolled off the orc and stared up at the dragon.

Azure eyes wide, Belac had no idea what to do next. With lunging motions, the dragon limped closer, its monstrous fangs bared. In growing terror, Belac began scooting away from the dragon. His right hand came down on a broken piece of metal. He glanced down at the cerulean light shining from between his gloved fingers. The air shuddered as the dragon breathed in. Belac picked up the starmetal shard and threw it at the dragon in an act of pure desperation. The cerulean light blinked out and then flared to life inside the dragon's mouth.

The dragon's head snapped back, its fiery breath shooting up into the sky. Fire swept through the air as the dragon thrashed its head side to side. It slammed its head down on the flagstones and then began clawing at its own face. Its roars became sounds of unbearable anguish. Its pain echoed in the square as the dragon's talons dug bloody chunks from the side of its skull. Its claws curled into fists, and it let out a wail of unadulterated misery.

There was no fight left in the dragon. It was dying, and the dragon knew that there was nothing it could do to stop it from happening. It wailed again as it grieved its own passing.

Belac could not look away from the display of torment. And he could not shut out the sounds of despair. The awful scene he witnessed tore at his soul. Despite the dragon's malicious nature, Belac thought that no being should suffer so. The elf was struck with a sudden feeling of guilt. He knew that he had helped to create that moment. And it was a moment of agony and sorrow.

It needed to be done.

Forty-Four

Trancedly, Belac stared at the lifeless body of the monster that he had come to kill. Black smoke and the smell of sulfur rose from the dragon's nostrils. *I'm The Dragon Slayer.* Belac's title had always felt like a lie. *I did it. I had help. But I'm the one who killed it.*

Rolan approached from the elf's left. "Are either of you dead?"

Vairug answered with a strained voice. "I think my leg is broken."

Belac turned his head to look at the orc. A jagged bone protruded from Vairug's lower leg. Sticky blood glistened on the salamander scales of his pants. *Yeah. I think it's safe to call that broken.*

Rolan walked past the orc. "Let me reset it, and then you can take one of your potions." He halted in front of the elf. "Here. This is yours." He held out the hilted portion of the broken starmetal sword. What was left of the blade glowed cerulean blue.

Belac looked at the glowing blade with consternation. *It shouldn't be doing that.* He had seen the blade not wake for Rodric. *The sword is only supposed to work for me…* He remembered that the top half of the broken blade had been glowing in Vairug's metal hand. *No, that is not how the sword works…*

Belac's mind flashed back to a moment when understanding had passed between Rolan and Vairug. Standing under stalactites that to Belac had felt like fangs, the black abyss beside them could have been the throat of the world. Rolan had just broken a man's arm for reaching into his rucksack. The man had then fallen to his death. As Rolan lamented the lost opportunity for interrogation, Vairug had mentioned the man's smell. *Rolan had noticed his eyes.*

Belac looked past the broken sword and into Rolan's stony gray eyes. *Gray eyes are just a shade of blue.* Belac recalled a vision of Vairug at sea. Gazing out into the infinite, the orc's dark eyes had appeared blue. *Black, is also a shade of blue.* In his mind, Belac heard Serath's voice. *"A dragon can be whatever it wants to be."* The elf's mind reeled. *If a dragon can be an elf, why not a dwarf, or even an orc?*

Belac felt like he was falling. "But that means…" *You're my brothers.*

Rolan nodded impatiently. "That's what it means." He moved the broken sword closer to the elf. "Now, take your sword. I need to help Vairug."

Belac reached out and accepted what was left of his sword. "Why didn't you tell me?"

Rolan knelt down next to the injured orc. "At first, we just wanted to see how long it would take you to figure it out." He shrugged. "Then, we thought it was funny that you hadn't." He pulled out a knife and began cutting open the orc's pantleg.

Vairug added, "Then, Serath convinced us that we should keep it a secret." He frowned. "I dislike how easily I was persuaded."

Rolan shook his head. "I have told you, Vairug. He did not use magic on you." He set his knife down and took hold of the orc's ankle.

"You would not know," Vairug argued and then growled when the dwarf tugged on his ankle.

Rolan picked up his knife and finished cutting off the lower half of the orc's pantleg. "Go ahead and take a potion." He sheathed his knife and then moved over to the orc's left side.

Vairug opened the potion pouch on his hip and pulled out one of the glass vials it carried. He yanked the stopper with his teeth, spat it out, and then downed the potion. His spine arched back, and his head hit the flagstones. The empty vial shattered in his grip as his arms and legs spasmed. *I am glad that I don't have to drink one of those things.*

Rolan picked up the broken blade of the starmetal sword. Cerulean light was summoned by his touch. He wrapped the blade in the salamander hide that he had cut from Vairug's pantleg, then he tucked the wrap into his salamander satchel.

Belac looked at the broken starmetal sword that he held in his own hand. *This is not really a sword anymore.* Little more than a hand's length of blade remained. *Now it's just a fancy knife.*

Lying on his back, Vairug said, "That was worse than the broken leg."

Rolan chuckled. "You say that, but I don't think that you would have enjoyed walking back with one of your legs snapped in half." He gazed south. "We still need to get back to the temple." He looked down at the orc. "And you are too big to carry."

Vairug sat up. "I would spend no more time here than I must."

Belac winced in pain as he stood, his salamander suit rubbing against the burned skin on his back side. He took a step toward the dead dragon and stared down at it. The monstrous body had begun to collapse in on itself. Black smoke rose from the lumpy mass of blue-black sludge that had once been the dragon's head. "Aw-man..."

"What's wrong?" Vairug asked as he got to his feet.

Belac gestured angrily at the melting dragon. "I wanted to sell its teeth!"

Rolan shook his head. "There is no time for that anyway. This city is still not safe."

Belac turned toward the dwarf. "What?" He gestured to the decaying corpse again. "The dragon is dead." *Melting has got to mean dead.*

Rolan nodded. "It's dead." He held up a hand. "But so are the ghosts."

Oh! Right. The ghosts. Belac nodded. Then something terrifying occurred to him. *No…* "We don't have to fight a ghost-dragon, do we?!"

Vairug took an involuntary step away from the dragon.

Belac flipped his glowing knife into an underhanded grip and raised his arms into a fighting stance. His azure eyes scanned the ruins around him.

Vairug began easing toward Sulvendar's Sheild and its magical barrier.

Rolan pinched the bridge of his nose. "There is no ghost-dragon."

Belac glanced at the dwarf. "How do you know?"

Rolan sighed and then turned toward the orc. "Vairug, grab the shield and let's get out of here."

Vairug hustled over to the shield. He slipped his mechanical hand through the shield's enarmes and then used his other hand to pull the shields hexagonal key from its socket. The golden barrier fell to pieces, the hexagonal plates scattering on the flagstones before fading from existence.

Belac continued to scan the ruined buildings encircling the square. *I wonder if this starmetal knife will work on The Danorin's ghost.* He was more than willing to leave the glowing blade untested.

Rolan was not through issuing orders. "Belac, get your scabbard. Then start thinking up a better story about how you killed the dragon than: You, screaming like a little girl and throwing your broken sword at it."

Belac narrowed his eyes at the dwarf. "I did not scream like a little girl."

Rolan nodded. "That's a good start. But you are going to need to come up with more than that."

Belac marched over to the edge of the square. *I can't believe that stupid dwarf is my brother.* He winced again at the stinging in his back side as he bent to retrieve his empty scabbard. *I need to do something about these burns.* He knew an easy way to fix the problem. However, 'easy' did not necessarily mean 'pleasant.' *The pain is getting worse. And I still have work to do.*

After sheathing his starmetal knife in its overlong scabbard and snapping the retention strap, Belac slung the sword belt around his waist and secured the buckle with a click. It felt like fiery claws were raking at his lower back. He slipped open his potion pouch and pulled out one of the glass vials inside. *Maybe if I only drink half…*

Rolan spoke from behind the elf. "You don't need that."

Belac turned around. "I have burns on my back and legs. It hurts like crazy and my muscles are starting to get stiff."

Rolan frowned. "You are supposed to tell me stuff like that."

Belac shrugged, causing pain to flare in his upper back. "I am telling you." He narrowed his eyes at the dwarf. "Besides, there is kind of a lot going on. What with the ghosts… the ghost-dragon… and oh... You two being my brothers!"

Rolan shook his head. "There is no ghost-dragon."

Vairug halted next to the dwarf. "I told them we should tell you," he informed the elf.

Rolan shot the orc a frown and then pointed his hand at the ground. "At least sit down before you drink it."

Belac pursed his lips. "I just told you that my backside hurts."

Rolan was unsympathetic. "A little discomfort is better than bashing your skull open on the flagstones."

Belac felt fluid seep from the burns on his back as he lowered himself to the ground. "Will it still work if I only drink half?"

Rolan shook his head with exasperation. "Just drink the whole thing."

Belac narrowed his eyes at the dwarf. "You said that it could make me crazy."

Rolan covered his eyes with his left hand. "Belac, you are already crazy." He dragged his hand down over his stubbled face. "Drink it, or don't."

Belac wondered if his brothers would be nicer to him if he had actually turned into a gorilla-wolf-monster. *They would probably just make fun of the way I smelled.* He pulled the potion's stopper with his teeth, spat it out, and then grimaced as he laid out flat. *This is going to hurt.* He poured the potion into his mouth and then quickly tossed the empty vial aside. As soon as he swallowed, his body began to spasm. *Yeah, it hurts!*

Grinning, Vairug asked. "Did I look that silly?"

Rolan scoffed. "No. Your twitchy kicks were fearsome," he replied sarcastically.

Vairug ignored the sarcasm. "Of course, they were."

Once the potion had done its work, Belac sat up. "I say, we make Rolan drink one of his potions, just to make things fair."

Rolan crossed his arms. "That's a bad plan."

Vairug's tusk jutted from his grin. "You can have one of mine."

Rolan frowned at the orc.

Belac got to his feet and then rolled his shoulders. *Good. I don't have time to be injured.* "We're not done yet."

Rolan nodded. "You're right. We need to get back to the temple. Then we're done."

Belac shook his head. "That is not what I mean." He pointed west. "We can't just leave the humans to fight alone."

Rolan was unmoved. "Sure, we can. Besides, Serath is with them. They will be fine."

Vairug asked, "You want to fight ghosts?" He sounded concerned.

Belac did not want to fight ghosts. He wanted to return to Lindell and get drunk enough to make mistakes. But something pulled at him. The Royal Guard had come to fight for him. He could not flee while they fought. "We have talismans too." His right hand touched the side of his potion pouch.

Rolan shook his head. "We can't help them." He uncrossed his arms and gestured to the orc. "We need to get Vairug back to the temple before any of the soldiers see him."

"Why?" Belac asked but then immediately realized the answer. "It's because of Lord Vairdoe." *Everyone thinks that he will turn back into a human when the dragon dies.*

Rolan nodded. "The priest will stay silent, but the soldiers will talk. It doesn't matter who tells them not to."

Belac was not ready to concede. "I already came up with an answer for this." He pointed to the orc. "Lord Vairdoe didn't kill the dragon. I did." He held his hands out to his sides. "So, the curse doesn't get lifted."

Rolan shook his head. "Lord Vairdoe died fighting the dragon."

"What?!" Belac glanced at the orc. *He doesn't look like a ghost.*

Rolan held out a hand, his gloved palm facing upward. "Serath wants the royal succession to be clean. Alive, Lord Vairdoe is a problem. Dead, he's a hero."

Vairug voiced his support for the narrative. "It's for the best, Belac."

Belac wanted to argue more, but he knew that the men of the Royal Guard might be dying already. "You two don't need me to find your way back to the temple." *We can argue about this later.* "I am going to go save as many of the humans as I can." He began backing away in preparation for his run.

Rolan shook his head. "You don't even know where you're going."

Belac pointed. "I know that's west. I will just head that way until I get to the city wall, and then I'll look for the gate."

Vairug disapproved of the elf's plan. "You should come with us."

Belac could still feel himself being pulled west. "Maybe. But what if the world needs a hero?" He turned around and ran into the ruins of the city, leaving his brothers to find their own way.

Forty-Five

Though finding a gate in the city wall proved easier than Belac had expected, he soon realized that he had chosen the wrong one. For many roads led to Enevic, and not all of them used a singular gate. *Why did they bother building such a ginormous wall if they were just going to put a bunch of holes in it?* Running south over rolling hills of dead grass, the elf feared that he would arrive too late to help. He found himself wondering how many men would die because he could not run faster. *If I get there exhausted, I won't be able to fight.*

Belac halted at the crest of a hill, seeing the gleam of steel in a shallow valley ahead. *That must be them!* Blueish white shadows flittered among the gleams, the amorphous shapes floating high in the valley. Angled sunlight made the apparitions difficult to make out, but Belac knew that what he saw were ghosts. *This talisman had better work.* He decided that if the talisman failed to protect him, his ghost was going straight for Serath.

With his left hand holding the scabbard of his starmetal blade, Belac ran toward the battle. At each rise in the terrain, he was given a clearer glimpse of the clash between the living and the dead. That there were no screams of panic, spoke to the bravery of the Royal Guard. Even from afar, Belac could feel the wrongness of what the men fought.

When Belac reached the final rise, he stopped and gazed down into the fray. He allowed himself a moment to catch his breath as he appraised the ghastly conflict. The valley of undead was wider than he had anticipated. Serving as the roadbed for a stretching highway, the open space seemed an uncalculated location to defend. Ghosts swam in the valley, their blueish white forms in numbers beyond counting. And there, in the middle of a sea of undead, Serath stood with the Royal Guard.

Bad plan, Wizard. The stars contained within Serath's staff shone brightly, their light sparkling on the backs of the soldiers that had surrounded the wizard protectively. Serath's eyes were closed, his forehead pressed against the vertical shaft of his magical staff. Inside the soldiers' double ring formation, fallen men lay motionless at their commander's feet.

Captain Harshaw's voice called out with command, "Trade! Now!"

The inner ring of soldiers expanded as the outer ring contracted, resulting in a trading of position. The men now on the outside began thrusting their awl pikes at the ghost with a vigor that the other men had lacked. Without shields, the soldiers' only defense was the quick thrusts of their nimble pikes. Though most of the ghosts circled out of range, those closest attacked at any perceived opportunity.

The fresh ring of soldiers proved too agile for the ghosts that attacked. Each time that one of the men's long spikes pierced a ghostly form, the apparition was ripped apart as if blown away by an invisible gale. However, the men lying motionless in the center of the defensive rings were evidence of the unrelenting peril. *Even trained soldiers can't fight forever. As they tire, they will lose men. As they lose men, their defense will falter. Then their gradual loss will become sudden.*

From the edge of Belac's peripheral, a ghost floated in into view and then stopped. A spectral skeleton draped in rags of mist, the ghost studied him with baleful curiosity. *Not good.* Like a ripple, other ghosts turned to face the elf. Belac puckered his lips. *I really should have made a plan before I got here.* The ghosts rushed up the hill.

Belac's left hand swept the thumb snap on his scabbard as his right hand grabbed his belt buckle. He squeezed the buckle, drawing his starmetal knife in an underhanded grip as the scabbard fell away. Cerulean light brightened the hilltop as his right hand reached up to the hilt of his sephen sword. His thumb actuated the scabbard's release, and then he drew the silvery blade.

One of the soldiers called out, "North rise!"

Another yelled, "Up on the hill!"

Belac had no time to watch the other soldiers respond to the calls. He brought his dwarf-sword up in an angled backslash that tore through a charging ghost. Spinning, he raked the air with his starmetal knife. A blur of cerulean light sliced through another ghost. Belac's heart pounded in his chest, fear threatening to wear him out faster than exertion. *I can't let them touch me.* If he fell, there would be no soldiers to pull him away from the ghosts.

Floating nightmares swarmed the hill, their skeletal hands reaching for the elf. *I think I've gotten too good at distractions!* Belac slashed and spun, his blades a whirling pattern of postmortem banishment. A trail of cerulean light danced between him and the ghosts as he moved along the top of the hill. His heart pounded in his chest like a drum keeping cadence. So, Belac swung his blades to the rhythm of the elven drum.

As the elf fought for his life, a deep, otherworldly voice rang out. "uooM Dah!" Then an invisible wave pulsed from the wizard's staff, the unseen force blasting through the ghosts in an expanding ring that swept the valley.

Belac continued to dance on the hilltop, his blades tearing through the ghosts that had escaped the blast. It was not until after his sephen sword slashed through the final ghost, that he allowed his feet to stop. Breathing labored breaths, he lowered his arms to his sides. He stood alone on the hill, his back to the Royal Guard.

Elated cheers erupted from behind the elf. *Yeah, yeah, yeah. The wizard killed everything with magic.* Belac grudgingly admitted that Serath deserved the applause. *All I did was almost get myself killed.* The winded elf attempted to focus on breathing in life.

A chant broke out among the cheers. "Mel-la-var! Mel-la-var!"

What? Belac turned around.

The men in gleaming armor thrust their awl pikes into the air with each syllable. "Mel-la-var! Mel-la-var!"

Belac spread his arms, his blades held out to his sides. *Yeah, okay. You can cheer for me if you want to.*

The chant was drowned out by wild cheering.

Belac smiled despite his fatigue. *I bet none of these guys will try to turn me over to the Elven delegates now.* He lowered his arms and began walking down the hill. *I wonder if any of them know where I can get a wheelbarrow.*

The soldiers' lines parted to allow Serath to pass. He moved forward to meet the elf. "You are not supposed to be here."

Belac nodded agreeably. "I would have got here sooner if I had a flying carpet."

Serath's disapproval was overcome by amusement. Chuckling, he shook his head.

Belac held up his glowing cerulean blade. "The sword got broken."

Serath raised an eyebrow. "And you want me to trust you with a flying carpet?"

Forty-Six

After reestablishing order among the Royal Guard, Captain Harshaw began marching his men back to the Temple of The Ancient. Though none of the soldiers had died, eleven were still unconscious and needed to be carried by their comrades. Serath had seemed confident that the downed men would recover. However, he had offered no estimate as to how long their recovery might take. As the soldiers transported the comatose men into the dead city of Enevic, the jubilance of victory faded away. They marched on, reminded that no one who had lived in the ruined city would ever recover.

Belac gazed upon the burned buildings, questioning if hope would be enough to overcome the devastation that surrounded him. He tried to picture what the city would look like once repairs were effected. It was difficult for him to imagine a people ever being happy there again. One thing that did become clear to him, was that if the humans of Cavasca did not claim the capital soon, something else would take residence. There were simply too many monsters in the world for them to all be expected to leave the city uninhabited.

As the soldiers filed into the temple grounds, Serath broke away, his long legs carrying him toward the priests that had waited next to the pond's arch. The pond had remained active, silently attended by the men in hooded, white robes.

Not so fast, Wizard. Belac followed after Serath, wanting to speak to him away from the soldiers. Though Belac knew that Rolan and Vairug were avoiding exhibition, the elf felt their absence keenly. *You need to tell me where my brothers are.*

When Serath reached the priests, he leaned in and began speaking with them quietly. Belac had no qualms about interrupting. *I am not going through that portal until I know which side of it my brothers are on.* He walked up to the wizard and tapped him on the shoulder.

Serath turned around and raised an eyebrow.

Belac gave the priests a distrusting look. "Rolan?" he asked the wizard, intentionally omitting the orc's name.

Serath nodded with understanding. "They are well." He gestured to the pond. "They should be waiting for us inside the temple in Lindell."

Belac's shoulders released tension that he had not known was there. "I… I bet they are worried about me."

Serath grinned broadly. "Then, we should not keep them waiting." He turned and strode through the pond.

Belac followed through a step behind, warmth welcoming him back to Lindell. *The world seems brighter here.* He trailed Serath around the arch and toward the temple. It quickly became apparent that instead of using the main doors, Serath was leading him to the side entry. Belac nodded to himself. *The temple's security should help keep Vairug hidden.* He frowned. *Though, I still don't think that we need to hide him.*

As they approached the side entrance, Belac narrowed his eyes at the wizard. "You should have told me."

Serath smiled at the reprimand. "You are going to need to be more specific," he replied, quoting Rolan.

Belac did not find the wizard funny. "I know what they are." *I know that they're my brothers.*

"Ah," Serath said in an accepting tone.

"Ah?!" Belac asked in a considerably less accepting one.

Serath reigned in his amusement. "I needed more than merely the dragon slain, Belac. I needed a legend." He glanced at the elf. "And you needed a purpose."

Belac narrowed his eyes again. "That does not explain why you didn't tell me who they were."

Serath nodded agreeably before asking, "If you had known that another could wield the sword, would you have accepted the responsibility? Would you have stood before the dragon, if you had known that someone else could take your place?" He allowed for a quiet pause before continuing, "Even if that someone was your brother?"

Belac looked down, honestly unsure of the answer.

When they reached the bronze security door on the side of the temple, Serath stopped and regarded the elf affectionately. "Feeling shame for what we once were, can signify an opportunity to become more than we may have otherwise been." He placed a gloved hand on the elf's shoulder. "You, Belac. Are now The Dragon Slayer." He squeezed the elf's shoulder and then let his hand fall away.

Belac felt more emotions than he knew how to process. He lapsed into silence as he followed the wizard into the temple. *Would I have let Vairug stand in my place? Could I have been brave if there had been another choice?* There was no preening as Belac waited for the doors to cycle in the mirrored chamber. His mind continued to question. *What choice would I make now?* In a daze, he followed the wizard through the corridors of the temple. He cared nothing for the beauty of the sapphire marble, nor the hazard of the lights that wanted to make him crazy.

Serath opened a bronze door, revealing an intimately sized sitting room. Both Rolan and Vairug waited inside. As soon as Belac saw his brothers, he knew the answer to his questions. *Whatever I would have done before, I would be brave for them now.*

Vairug rose from a chair of wrought bronze. Dark eyes bright, he offered a tusked smile. "I am glad that you're not dead."

Rolan stayed in his chair. "How do you know that he's not a ghost?"

Vairug frowned at the dwarf. "He is not a ghost." He glanced at the elf nervously. "Right?"

Belac rushed forward and hugged the orc.

Vairug embraced his brother, and then pushed the elf away. "Are you crying?"

Belac wiped the tears from his eyes. "No."

Vairug scoffed. "It makes you look like a woman."

Belac scowled at the orc.

Vairug nodded. "That's better."

Rolan stood from his chair. "Right. So, Belac..." He walked closer. "We need to leave."

Belac shook his head, prepared to resume his argument.

Rolan held up a hand. "Vairug needs to get back to his people."

We are his people. Belac opened his mouth to speak, but was preempted by the orc.

"I have a clan, Belac. Family. Children." Vairug swallowed. "This was a thing that needed to be done." He held up his mechanical hand. "And a debt that needed to be paid." He lowered the hand. "But now, it is time for me to go home."

It had not occurred to Belac that the orc might have children, nor that he might have responsibilities that would call him back to the Orcish lands. Belac sighed. "Can we at least wait until after my celebration?" *I kind of feel like I earned it.*

Rolan took a deep breath and then released it slowly. "Belac. You can't go with us."

"What?!" Belac's eyebrows scrunched up. "Why not?"

"You're an elf," Rolan explained. "Every orc there will try to kill you on sight." He shook his head. "We are going there for a reunion, not a war."

Belac's entire body slumped. "But..." He could think of no argument.

Rolan accepted the elf's unvoiced acquiescence. "There is a man named Sam Brocovich. He is going to be getting in touch with you in Lindell. Do what he tells you."

Belac looked up. "Why? What does he want?"

Rolan gestured vaguely. "He is going to help you set up a trading company. We can use my connections and your friendship with the king. I am betting that there will be a lot of people that want to be able to say that they trade with The Dragon Slayer."

Belac frowned. "I don't know how to be a trader."

Rolan shrugged. "We don't need you to. We just need your name."

Belac narrowed his eyes at the dwarf. "So, I have to stay and sign contracts, while you get to go off and have fun?"

Rolan nodded. "Pretty much."

Vairug attempted to console the elf. "I will tell my clan of your bravery. For as long as the Orc's roam free, your deeds will live on in our stories." He smiled. "Especially, your epic contest… with a chair."

Forty-Seven

Belac glared randomly at the guards and attendants that had gathered in the grand hall of the king's palace in Lindell. He did not know who was responsible for his current ensemble, but he felt like someone needed to be blamed for it. Servants bustled about the hall quickly, not wanting to disappoint the king on so momentous a day. Belac wondered if the servants might have had anything to do with his plight. *Maybe they are trying to punish me for killing that assassin.*

Serath's trim beard was contorted by a smile. "You look fine, Belac."

Belac held his arms out to his sides and glared down at his formal raiment. Light glimmered from the silver flowers that had been embroidered all over the pristine white of the clothing. "I look like a sofa!" The snowy white tassels dangling from his garish epaulets were the parts that he hated most. *Only a human could design something this stupid.*

Serath chuckled and then shook his head. "You look like The Hero of Lindell."

Belac dropped his arms. "I am not wearing the hat." The tall, short brimmed hat with a fluffy, white plume was simply too ridiculous for him to put on his head.

Serath nodded in allowance. "I believe that would be acceptable."

Belac narrowed his eyes at the wizard. *Did they make that stupid hat just to trick me into agreeing to wear the rest of this outfit?* The long, white ribbon that held back the elf's hair was the only part of the attire that did not offend him.

Serath gestured, indicating to the massive doors behind the elf. "They are announcing you now."

Belac turned around. He had not been paying attention to the booming voices on the other side of the closed doors. *I was starting to think that Roger was going to go on about the prosperity of his kingdom all day.*

A muffled voice carried through the doors. "...ensuring a future free of the dragon's wrath!"

The capital of Lindell erupted in cheer as the palace doors opened. Sunshine poured over Belac, blinding him as the people's joy assaulted him. *How is this a reward?* He ran a thumb under the baldric of his dwarf-sword, repositioning the scabbard as his eyes adjusted to the radiance of the world outside. Though the belts that held his weapons in place were black, he thought that there were enough of them to not look out of place strapped over the white of his raiment.

As Belac stepped into the light, tiny bells in place of spurs jingled from the heels of his white boots. Though Belac could not hear the bells over the cheering of the crowd, he knew that the annoying things were there. *These boots are stupid!* Brass horns greeted the hero of Lindell as he walked out of the palace.

A white podium had been erected to the right of the wide stairway. On it, King Rodric stood with a collection of lesser lords. Belac narrowed his eyes at the king's gray velvets and silver crown. *Why doesn't he have to wear something stupid?*

King Rodric smiled at the elf and then bellowed, "Behold! The Dragon Slayer!" His commanding voice issued loudly from copper tubs of water that had been distributed throughout the city.

Belac winced as the people of Lindell cried out in excitement. *This is what I get for giving a wizard a new idea.* He began to descend the stairway, grumbling to himself about the irregular steps.

In the public square below, a tightly packed crowd was split by two columns of the Royal Guard. Backs to the crowd, the shining soldiers faced inward, their awl pikes angled in salute. In the center of the space created, a white horse awaited the elf.

Belac kept his left hand on the hilt of his starmetal knife as he descended the stairs. *I wonder if I should show the broken blade to everyone. It does still glow.* He considered the adoring crowd. *No. They would just yell at me again.* Back straight, he stepped out into the square.

The soldiers pulled their awl pikes upright as Belac passed by them. When he stopped to mount the horse, the pikes ahead continued to realign. After swinging up into the saddle, Belac looked down at the silver spike that had been secured to the horse's head like a horn. *They even made my horse wear something stupid.*

Belac ran a hand down the side of the horse's neck. "I know how you feel, Buddy." He squeezed gently with his legs, letting the horse know that it was time to go.

The horse began to prance forward playfully as if happy for its part in the parade. *Traitor.*

The Royal Guard turned as one and began to escort Belac away from the palace. Cheering onlookers bounced up and down as Belac rode from the square. *Celebrations should have less yelling, more booze, and a lot fewer men.*

As he moved through streets lined with applause, Belac saw that young boys raised wooden swords in his honor. The toy swords meant more to the elf than the awl pikes that had saluted him in the square. *Maybe this is not so bad.*

Belac's azure eyes widened with alarm as horror gripped his heart. *Oh no…* The reality of his role began to sink in. *I'm the hero.* In his mind, he heard Serath's voice. *"You cannot save the world merely once."* He remembered Rolan explaining that anyone saved would likely need to be saved again. *The next time something bad happens, these people are going to look to me.* It was only a matter of time before the humans asked him to risk his life for them again.

Belac's gaze settled on a little girl that was riding on her father's shoulders. The rays of the sun stuck her auburn hair, casting it a golden glow. Squealing with glee, she showed off the gaps in her tiny teeth. *Okay. I'll do it.* His left hand moved to the scabbard strapped to his back. The sephen blade inside was his only sword that he had yet to lose or break. *I better keep this close. It's my last sword.*

Epilogue

Frigid air gathered under leathery wings as its currents held the dragon aloft. A lonely wasteland of mountainous rock waited in the world below. The dragon's body gleamed blackish blue as clear sunlight played along its scaly hide. The flight was a thing of peace for the dragon. So high above the world, the dragon felt as if consequence could not reach it.

The dragon banked, aligning itself with a secluded fortress below. Maintaining its relaxed speed, the dragon descended from the heavens. A moment before it struck the rampart, the dragon brought its back legs forward and beat its massive wings. As its taloned feet touched down on the stone of the rampart, the dragon shrank in size, morphing into a slender man garbed in flowing robes of royal blue cloth. Silver etchings graced the drapery, the arcane designs more complex than the minds of lesser men. Strong hands pulled back the wizard's long, black hair, causing the strands to shimmer as they slid over his shoulders. Though obviously human, the features that framed the man's cobalt eyes could have been described as elven.

The dark thing that awaited him was one of the most dangerous beings that he had ever encountered. Few men possessed the knowledge required to truly comprehend the threat that the creature posed to the world. How reality could tolerate such a strain remained a mystery to the wizard. Grinning, he approached without fear.

Clad in immaculate black, the dark thing was leaning against a parapet with his arms crossed. "You need to stop flying around like that," he calmly chastised. "The Danorin is supposed to be dead."

Danorin nodded in acknowledgement. "You are correct." He sighed. "But I will miss being a dragon."

Serath shrugged. "It is only temporary. We can find a way to resurrect you later." He smiled. "Maybe you can even come back as the hero."

Danorin thought that such a narrative would be difficult to construct. The world still believed that he was responsible for the tragedy that had befallen Enevic. Though neither he nor Serath could be certain of the plague's origin, they both knew its orchestrator. It had been necessary for Serath to burn the dead in order to prevent the disease from spreading. Blaming the event on the 'evil dragon' had been the logical sequentiality.

Serath uncrossed his arms and pointed a gloved finger at the wizard. "That fake dragon was impressive."

Danorin waved a hand dismissively. "A mere simulacrum. It required only a trivial amount of my blood for it to be convincing. I found your ghosts to be far more interesting."

Serath laughed. "Glamoured fairies armed with sleep dust." He shook his head as he recalled the details. "They thought it was fun."

Danorin frowned disapprovingly. "I do not understand why you deal with the Fay. They pervert conditions."

Serath nodded. "There have been disagreements."

Danorin arched an eyebrow. "I take it, you handled them in the same fashion as you have been handling my fellow wizards?"

"They are not your fellows," Serath replied unapologetically. "They should have known better than to get involved."

Danorin agreed. The cult that the other wizards had chosen to support was an abomination. That they had helped to raise a kraken from the Depths, appalled him still. The hypocrisy of such an act made it difficult for him to feel sympathy for the vanquished wizards.

Danorin stepped over to the parapet and gazed out at the snow covered mountains. "I have warned them all, more than once." He glanced at the dark thing that looked like a man. "It seems that wizards do not listen to other wizards any more attentively than they do sorcerers."

Serath crossed his arms again. "I do not need them to listen. I need them to stay out of my way." His rich voice was colder than the mountains. "Their only choice is how that comes about."

Danorin nodded, still in agreement with the sorcerer. There were few wizards left in the world. He found it disappointing that they continued to make the same mistakes that had led to the downfall of their order. In his mind, wizards were meant to be wise.

Danorin saw wisdom in the sorcerer's plan. "Are you sure that you chose the right one?"

Serath's voice took on a tone of prideful affection. "I knew that he was the one the moment I saw him with the slavers. He was young for an elf; naive. He did not understand what they were, nor that they were using him. To Belac, they were just people." Passion began to creep into his words. "And he embraced them. He embraced Humanity with an openness that he had never offered the Elves." He nodded to himself. "That is when I knew." He glanced over at the wizard. "I am only glad that I was able to burn those people to ash before he realized what they were."

Danorin smiled at the sorcerer. "You like him."

Serath frowned. "Of course, I like him. I like most of your children." He grinned slyly. "Though, some more than others."

Danorin arched an eyebrow. "Do you not feel guilty for lying to them?"

Serath shook his head. "I did not lie to them. I promised to forge a weapon. Belac is my weapon."

Danorin suspected that the elf would feel differently. "Do you think he is ready for what is to come?"

"No." Serath shook his head and then turned his upper body toward the wizard. "But there is still time. Nations break if they are moved too quickly."

Danorin turned and considered the man who spoke of moving nations like pieces of a game. The sorcerer was a thing that should not have been possible. Danorin understood why the other wizards hated the sorcerer. And he knew that neither of them would ever be forgiven. He allowed himself to feel the darkness of the man. The wrongness of it made him think that the wizards might be right to hate them.

Danorin's cobalt eyes bore into the sorcerer. "Why do you insist on touching the Forbidden?"

Serath met the wizard's eyes. The green faded from Serath's irises, leaving behind a blue that was deeper than the sea. "Because, Father, I am not to be forbidden." Green flashed into Serath's eyes as the emerald flame returned.

Danorin felt both pride and worry in a way that only a parent could understand. The control that Serath had displayed was not something that a human should have been capable of. The success of a defiant child could often teach the wrong lessons. As much as Danorin worried about his son, he too feared for the fate of the world. Reality bent for the sorcerer. But the world could only bend so far.

As he took in the sorcerer's unyielding visage, pride overcame Danorin's worry. He laughed softly. "I wish I knew what your mother was."

Serath's reply was darkly playful. "Perhaps she was a dragon."

Final

I understand that you may have some unanswered questions. Don't worry, Belac will return in the next book. In the meantime, I recommend that you reread the prologues and epilogues; knowing now, that the 'dark thing' was always the same thing. And his flames were always green.

www.ingramcontent.com/pod-product-compliance
Lightning Source LLC
Chambersburg PA
CBHW020602310726
48979CB00008B/1317/J

* 9 7 8 1 9 5 7 3 2 4 1 9 7 *